Praise for Irene Ca...

'Tough . . . gutsy . . . brimming with emotion . . . a cracking yarn — all that a good North East saga should be'

Sunderland Echo

'In the best-selling tradition of Catherine Cookson'

Middlesbrough Evening Gazette

'Catherine Cookson-readalike . . . a delight'

Colchester Evening Gazette

'This novel has the clear ring of authenticity . . . the depth of the setting gives it its richness'

Northern Echo

'Cookson fans will lap up this enthralling turn-of-the-century saga'

Hartlepool Mail

'Sheer descriptive talent shines through here . . . gritty . . . powerful stuff'

Dorset Evening Echo

Also by Irene Carr

Mary's Child
Chrissie's Children
Lovers Meeting
Love Child
Katy's Men
Emily

About the author

Irene Carr was born and brought up on the river in Monkwearmouth, Sunderland, in the 1930s. Her father and brother worked in shipyards in the North East and her mother was a Sunderland barmaid. She has written six previous novels: *Mary's Child*, *Chrissie's Children*, *Lovers Meeting*, *Love Child*, *Katy's Men* and *Emily*.

Fancy Woman

Irene Carr

CORONET BOOKS
Hodder & Stoughton

Copyright © 2002 by Irene Carr

First published in Great Britain in 2002
by Hodder and Stoughton
A division of Hodder Headline

A Coronet Paperback

5 7 9 10 8 6 4

A CIP catalogue record for this title
is available from the British Library

ISBN 0 340 82034 9

Printed and bound in Great Britain by
Mackays of Chatham PLC, Chatham, Kent

Hodder and Stoughton
A division of Hodder Headline
338 Euston Road
London NW1 3BH

FANCY WOMAN

Prologue

Let people think what they liked! Laura Stanfield was twenty-three, looking younger and feeling older. She packed the old valise she had brought back from the war ready to travel home. Her heart was broken but her clothes were bright and stylish – a camel-coloured wool suit with mid-calf length skirt which showed off her legs in silk stockings, shoes with pointed toes and louis heels – they had cost most of her savings and were chosen defiantly. *Let people think what they liked.*

A honking taxi-cab carried her to King's Cross station. With the ending of the war it was crowded with demobilised servicemen that Saturday morning, a restless sea of khaki and blue, loitering or hurrying. Laura worked her way through them, suitcase in one hand, khaki valise in the other, conscious of heads turning to watch her pass by, admiring. She ignored them, her mind elsewhere.

The train for the north was filled with the men as it pulled out. Laura could not see a vacant seat but a corporal in the Lincolnshires gave up his to her and moved out of the compartment to stand in the corridor. 'You sit easy, lass. I'm only going as far as Grantham.' He swung her suitcase up on to the luggage rack, then her valise, and said, surprised, 'That's heavier than it looks.'

'Yes. Thank you.' Laura did not offer an explanation for the weight but smiled as the other men moved up to make room for her by the window. She was used to their looks, too, hungry yet shy, that she had seen on other men coming back from the front. She relaxed against the cushions, breathing easier now.

At York they stopped alongside an ambulance train taking wounded men to a hospital in Scotland. They peered out of the windows from where they lay on their bunks. Laura waved and they waved back at this slim girl with chestnut hair and wide smile. She thought that it was bravado on both sides. She had little to smile about and in her way was also grievously wounded.

Laura was travelling north against her will, in answer to the letter from Aunt Cath, a muddled, scrawled plea from an old, sick and tired woman, so different from the exuberant Cath Finley who had cared for Laura as a girl. The scratched and shaky characters had merged together in a list of random thoughts and gossip, but started and ended with a call for help: 'Your Uncle George is dead, drowned in the trench down at the sawmill. I can't manage on my own any longer. I feel there's evil at work here. Can you come up and help me?'

Laura recalled the trench, filled with salt water, in which her uncle had seasoned wood. She had thought as she read the letter that she had to help Cath. She had a job in London that would be kept open for her or – better – she could find another. She still did not want to go home, guessing at the reception she would face, and she never wanted to see Nick Corrigan again, with his cold, disapproving eyes. But she would make the journey for her aunt's sake. And it was only for a week or two, until Cath was again able to cope.

She changed from the main line to the local train at Durham. It trundled slowly through the countryside with its green fields and black pitheads, the little stations she remembered. Was it only five years she had been away? It seemed more like a lifetime.

The fog streamed past the windows of the train as darkness fell and it ran into Sunderland Central station. Laura stepped down into the echoing, glass-roofed cavern, crowded with passengers alighting from the train which smelled of coal smoke and hot metal. For a moment, recalling the wounded in the train at York, she fancied she could scent the ambulance odours of petrol and disinfectant mixed with the cordite smoke from the guns. Then she told herself that was in the past and so was her perceived sinning. Doubtless none of the people around her had even heard of her, let alone would recognise and denounce her. Laura thought, Get on with it! She started forward, eyes searching hopefully for Aunt Cath. Steam rose like mist from the engines to join the funnel smoke and blurred the outlines of the crowd. But then a tall, broad-shouldered figure loomed out of the murk and her heart checked then thumped furiously. Nick Corrigan! Good God! Was the man to haunt her for the rest of her days?

He stopped in front of her and she saw the startled expression flick across his features but then it left him stone-faced. He was in uniform, navy blue with the two wavy stripes of a lieutenant in the Royal Naval Volunteer Reserve, and a faded but colourful block of decorations on his left breast. The uniform was neat and clean but well-worn. He challenged, deep-voiced, almost a growl, 'What do you want here?' Surprise jerked the question out of him.

Laura thought she could read the rest in his face: Haven't you caused enough trouble?

She flinched, could not help it, and that angered her more than his words had done. She threw back his challenge: 'It's no business of yours. My home is here.' But was it? Was it *anywhere*? 'Will you let me pass, please.' That was not a question and she did not wait for an answer but brushed by him and walked on. She could feel his eyes on her back, following her, she was certain. She told herself that it was just bad luck, *her* luck, that she should meet Nick Corrigan at all, let alone this soon. He had no right to judge her and she didn't care what he

4

FANCY WOMAN

thought. Still, she wondered, should she have set him straight? But how would she convince him? How prove him wrong? When, in a way, he was right? It would have turned into an argument and there would be no budging him, with his mind made up. And she could not deny adultery.

Laura felt lonely now. Where was Cath?

She searched the platform with her eyes as she walked towards the steps, then as she climbed them to the concourse with the suitcase and valise dragging at her arms, but she could not see Catherine Finley. Laura had written to her, telling her which train she would be taking and its time of arrival. Now she decided the old woman might be ill or had just forgotten.

She came out of the station and into the High Street with the cab rank, some motor taxis, some horse-drawn. The electric trams ground and clanged past, materialising out of the fog and disappearing into it. This was not the yellow 'pea-soup' of London but grey North Sea fog. The gas lamps showed as blurred spheres of light in the gloom. She was aware of passers-by taking a second look at this fashionably dressed and poised girl. Then the voice skirled shrilly above the buzz of the swirling crowds and the din of traffic: '*Fancy woman!* You're no better than a whore! You should be ashamed to show yourself around here! Tarted up to the nines like that!' The woman's drink-bloated face was suffused with anger and she shook her ham-like fist at Laura. This was her stepmother, Doris Grimshaw, in a black coat shiny with age, her hat pinned

5

drunkenly on one side. Her speech was slurred but her words only too clear as she shrieked, 'You practically murdered your poor father!'

Laura would not answer her, either. She could have replied that her stepfather had been a bigot and a hypocrite but she knew there would be no reasoning with this one, either. She stared resolutely into Doris's face with the defiance she had shown all her life, and walked past the glaring, fuming woman to climb on to the platform of a tram. Doris's imprecations followed her: 'Harlot! Fancy woman! Where's your fancy man now?' That hurt and Laura winced as she took her seat and the tram rolled away. She saw the conductor was eyeing her from the corner of his eye and passengers were staring, curious, then averting their eyes when she met their gaze, embarrassed for her. When she had decided to come home she had told herself that this was a big town and she would be able to hide herself here. Now she was not so sure. She would not seek out the Nick Corrigans or those who thought like Doris, but nor would she hide from them. It was as well she would not be staying for long.

Laura stepped down from the tram by the ropery. Girls were streaming out of the factory at the end of a shift, tired but calling to each other with broad humour. Laura thought that she might have been one of them – and maybe happier. Happier than she was now, anyway. But she still managed to laugh at the shouted jokes.

She walked down Church Street with the mist wreathing in from the North Sea, but with Dundas Street and its shops in sight she turned left into Whickham Street. The suitcase and the valise grew heavier with every stride. The fog fell damp and chill on her face and made a yellow halo round each street lamp. She was heading for Cath's house but came first to the timber yard. She had played here as a child but now at night it was a lonely place. There were few houses, some little workshops that buzzed with activity during the day but now were closed, dark and silent. A high wall surrounded the timber yard, setting it in isolation. Cath had talked of the presence of evil. Laura had thought that might be the phantasm of a much-loved old woman wandering in her mind. But now it was easy to believe.

A motor car, a Standard coupé, its brasswork gleaming in the lamplight, stood by the kerb but it was empty of driver or passengers. Laura halted because someone was in the yard. She set down her luggage for a moment to rest her arms. The big double gates — with the legend in peeling paint: 'Geo. Finley. Joiner and Timber Merchant' — were shut, but she could see through the narrow gap between them to the big shed that was the sawmill. It was a black, sharp-edged silhouette in the night but a light glowed inside. Who was in there? Uncle George was dead. So . . . ?

Laura turned as she heard hurrying footsteps. The man was just an outline at first with the light from a street lamp behind him. As he came closer she could hear him panting from his haste and saw it was Joe Gibson. He was no longer the skinny, shy youth of five years ago when he had courted Laura's friend, Adeline Seaton. Laura thought, Addy was good for him. He was still thin in the face but there was a sturdiness about him now that he had lacked in adolescence.

Laura said, 'Hello, Joe.'

He had stopped short a yard away and she could see his shock. She knew that was because she was the last person he expected to see. He said it: 'Laura! I didn't think to see you!' Then shock gave way to relief – but tinged with embarrassment? He explained, 'A neighbour of ours saw lights in here and I came down because I thought it might be a burglar. I'm glad it was you.'

Laura guessed at the reason for that embarrassment. People did not forget a reputation like hers and she would have been talked about, if only because Addy would feel bound to defend her. But she said, 'I didn't put on the light; I've just got here. And why did this chap tell you?'

Now Joe was concerned. He fumbled in the pocket of his jacket and there was light enough for Laura to see that he wore a good suit, shirt and tie; so Joe had got on in the drawing office. He pulled out a bunch of keys. 'Addy and me moved in next door to Cath and George over a year ago. Addy wrote to tell you at the time but I suppose you didn't get the letter.'

'No.' Laura had been in Palestine then.

Joe explained, 'We'd been helping Cath a bit, especially when George had his accident and drowned, and we were at the reading of the wills because George and Cath had left us a bequest. So the solicitor asked me to keep an eye on the place. But you'll want these now.' He held out the keys to Laura.

She was bewildered for a moment but then took in the import of his words: 'George *and* Cath? You mean they're *both* dead?'

Joe nodded solemnly. 'Cath went ten days after George; it was her heart. We think it was the shock of losing him the way she did that killed her. The solicitor sent you a telegram but it was returned.'

Because Laura had given up her bed-sit and her job when she received Cath's letter, and went to board with her friend, Eva, for the week while she worked her notice. At the bed-sit she had left Cath's address for forwarding any mail. There had seemed no point in giving Eva's address for just one week. Laura said vaguely, numb from shock, 'I'd moved.'

Joe was still holding out the keys. He said gently, 'You'll need these. I told you we were at the reading of the wills. They left the house, the timber yard and the sawmill to you.'

Laura took this in but slowly and only in simple terms, that she, too, had received a bequest. It might just as easily have been Cath's old kitchen table for all the significance it had . . .

She remembered the light and took the keys.

Joe offered, 'I'll come in with you.'

'Thanks, Joe.'

Laura found the key which fitted the lock on the little door set into one of the big gates. It swung open and she

9

stepped in over the sill and walked up the cobbled yard, its surface gleaming damply from the fog in the darkness. Joe followed at her heels. On her left was the hut where Uncle George used to do his office work while he had fed the young Laura with humbugs. To her right, in a big, open barn, was stacked the timber in various dimensions and kinds. Ahead were the double doors of the sawmill and one was ajar, the light slicing out of it.

Laura cautiously sidled in through the gap, eyes searching for the intruder. The gas lamp hanging from the roof shed yellow light that glinted on the steam engine. It squatted at the back of the shed, shining black iron and brass, the source of power for the lathe and saws. But nearer it shone down on the huge circular saw and the man standing by, examining it. He looked round as Laura entered and she saw the expressions of surprise and disbelief slip across his fleshy face then a gloating grin took their place. He jeered, 'Well, I'll be damned! What a turn-up. It's the fancy woman come back. And dressed to kill as always. What the hell are you doing here?'

This was Seth Bullock, burly and lecherous, with his oiled hair and oily smirk. Laura let the suitcase and valise fall to the floor. She remembered Seth only too well. He had worked for her uncle in the timber yard, a bully when he could be, ingratiating when he could not. Now his eyes roamed over her, insolently, greedily. She knew what he was thinking and it brought the blood to her face. His grin widened, knowing.

Laura forced herself to face his stare, returning it with

contempt. She ignored the jibes – for the time being – and only asked, 'What are you doing here? How did you get in?'

Seth stepped away from the saw to lean comfortably on one hand set on a bench by his side. He answered laconically, 'I jumped over the wall. There's a place where it's so broken down you could just about walk in. The whole place is a wreck, run down, but I'll put it to rights.'

Laura looked around the shed. There was no denying that it was untidy. Sawdust covered the floor and the tools on the bench – a handsaw, hammer and mallet among them. A spider had spun its web on the circular saw. To one side was the black, gaping hole of the trench, still partly uncovered, in which George Finley had drowned. She averted her eyes from that and moved to the bench, picked up the mallet and traced her slim finger through the dust on it. Then she looked up at Seth, now only a yard away. '*You* will put it to rights?'

'That's the ticket. I've bought the place.' Seth licked thick lips and it was as if he had laid hands on her body.

He had frightened her, long ago when she was a young girl, but now she was a woman who had survived the horrors of war. Laura answered him, her anger mounting but still under control: 'No, you haven't. You're a liar. This place is mine.'

Joe Gibson put in, 'That's right. I was at the reading o' the wills. And the solicitor told me today he'd had an offer for the sawmill but he couldn't take it.'

Seth sneered, 'Oh, aye, he told me he couldn't do owt

until he'd found the fancy bit here.' His gaze switched back to Laura: 'But it looks like you smelled money and came running. You always followed the scent of it, ran off with it, and you'll get it now. Old George did precious little business for the past year. Nobody else will want the place but I'll put up the money, the only offer you'll get. It's as good as mine so you might as well give me them keys.' He held out his hand for them.

Laura dropped them on the bench and Seth grinned triumphantly as he reached out to take them – and Laura slammed the mallet down on his outstretched fingers. He squealed with pain and doubled over his bruised hand, clasping it tenderly to his chest. His face contorted in agony and he moaned, 'You bloody bitch!' Then he winced and retreated as Laura lifted the mallet again.

She followed him, warning, 'You keep a civil tongue in your head or you'll get more of the same!'

Seth whined, 'I'll fetch the pollis to you!'

'What? Because a lass defended her property against a thug like you? He'd laugh at you and he wouldn't be the only one.'

Seth snarled but knew she was right.

Laura pursued him. 'You can get out of here and stay out. I'm the owner and I'm not selling.'

Seth shouldered out through the doors of the sawmill and Laura herded him down to the little door in the outside gate, through it and out into the street. There she halted and watched as he started the motor car, swinging the handle until the engine fired then climbing into the driving seat. The car pulled away, but as it did so Seth leaned out to shout at her, 'I'll get my own back on you for this! By the time I've finished you'll beg me to take the bloody yard and you'll wish you'd never come back!'

Laura was already wishing that. She watched the car accelerate and putter away up the road towards Dundas Street.

Joe Gibson said worriedly, 'You'll have to watch out for yourself. Seth has a bad name. People that have crossed him have been hurt. There's never any proof that he was behind it, but there's been coincidences.'

First the Corrigan man then Doris and now Seth. Laura said wearily, 'I'll remember. Thanks, Joe.'

She turned out the lights and locked up the yard. Joe picked up the suitcase and she carried her valise and they set off for the house. Reaction was setting in now and she could feel her hands beginning to shake. She told herself, not for the first time in her life by a long way, that she had been a fool. Seth had set out to annoy her and she had lost her temper. Now she had made an enemy and rashly declared she would not sell the timber yard, nailed her colours to the mast. She remembered wryly that the man who first nailed the colours to the mast was a local hero; there was a public house named after him: Jack Crawford.

But Seth would have been an enemy anyway and she had come north prepared to brave the reception she would get from the likes of Doris Grimshaw and Nick Corrigan, because she wanted to help Cath Finley, to whom she owed so much. Now her aunt was dead and Laura admitted to herself that part of her reason for coming north was because she needed the old woman. She had come hoping for comfort and peace but had found hostility and threats. It would be easy to turn her back on all this and run away.

Laura turned the last corner, Joe at her side. They had almost reached the cottage, a bungalow one in a terraced row, each with a bay window and a front door with a polished brass knocker. A street singer was crossing from side to side of the cobbled street, his voice a wavering baritone, the medals he had won in the war gleaming on his chest. Doors opened here and there and a copper or two dropped into his cap. Laura saw Adeline Gibson contribute. *Addy!*

She stood at the door of her house, smiling, not plump now but slim in her flowered apron. Just the sight of her, rosy-cheeked and happy, lifted Laura's spirits. Addy held a baby in her arms while two little girls and a boy clustered round her skirts. Laura thought vaguely that she had known about the two little girls, but who was the boy?

Joe was pressing another key into her hand, that for Cath's house, and he whispered, 'I was going to tell you . . .' Laura knew that meant he had been putting it off. Afraid of hurting or upsetting her? But he was going on now: 'Tommy Taylor's mother worked for Cath. Her man went off to the war before they were married or Tommy was born. He was killed and she was left on her own with the bairn on the way. Cath took her on as a live-in maid but it was really to give her a home.' Joe paused a second then added, 'In her will, when Cath left the yard to you, she said she hoped you'd care for the boy. He has nobody else. First his mam died three or four months back, then George and Cath, and she was like his grannie. He's taken it very badly.'

The boy could not hear him but stared at Laura uncertainly. His hand twisted and twisted again in Addy's skirt.

Laura thought, He has nobody but *me*! God help him! She took two quick paces forward and swept him up into her arms, hugged his thin body and kissed him. She had sinned in the eyes of men, though she would always contest the charge, and she had paid, buried her child in the cold ground as she had buried her hopes and dreams. At least she could care for this one, though it meant there was now no question of running away.

The singer was far up the street now but his voice still came to her faintly. Laura recognised the old song: 'After the Ball'. There was a time she had sung and danced to that. Dear God! The years that had gone . . .

BOOK I

Chapter One

'*Af — ter the ball!*' Five-year-old Laura Stanfield piped the song in her squeaky falsetto as she waltzed alone around the kitchen, her hair hanging down her back like spun silk. She was still grubby from playing in the street and there were dirty handprints on her once white pinny. It swirled around her skinny legs in their black stockings. Her skin showed white through the heel of one of them and there was a darn in the other. There was little room for dancing. The kitchen was also the living-room and the table and four upright chairs, the two old armchairs almost filled it. A little over a square yard of space was surrounded by the furniture and the fireplace, and in that space she spun and reversed on flying feet. Her face was thin but alight with happiness. Laura danced out of the joy of living — and for the penny her stepfather might throw her.

The kitchen was a cheerful place with the gas lamp hissing, the range gleaming with black lead, the polished brass fire-irons of poker, shovel and tongs sparking light. Kitty Grimshaw, Laura's mother, had made this cosy home that the little girl loved. She sat in one of the sagging armchairs while Albert Grimshaw slouched in the other. His presence in the room was like a black cloud hanging over a summer day of sunshine. He was a middling-sized man with mutton-chop whiskers and a drooping moustache. Kitty had married him after her first husband, Bob Stanfield, was killed in a shipyard accident. She had taken Albert because she believed her daughter needed a father — and lived to regret it, bitterly.

'Watch me dance, Da!' Laura shrilled. Albert's eyes, beady but glazed, followed her. His wife watched Laura fondly but with a wary eye on Albert, gauging his mood. That should be jovial because this was Saturday, the night every week when Albert came staggering home drunk. Besides, the whole country was celebrating a victory in the war in South Africa. Mafeking, besieged by the Boers, had been relieved and there were processions and dancing in the streets. But Kitty could never be sure what went on in Albert's mind. The other six days of the week he was a Bible-punching abstainer, at home or in the chapel, when he regarded dancing as a sin and its practitioners children of the devil. And only minutes earlier he had berated her: 'That bairn's been running the streets black as a bloody sweep! Look at her!' But Laura had contrived to look remorseful, always with thought of that penny in mind, and he had gradually grumbled into silence.

So Kitty watched him.

But all was well. Albert's thin lips parted in a smile. 'Aye, you're worth a penny.' He tossed the coin at Laura and she snatched it out of the air. 'Now get away to bed.'

'Aye, Da.' Laura stowed the penny in the pocket of her pinny and went with her mother. She washed in an enamel bowl set on the kitchen table then went to her bed. The family had upstairs rooms, so besides the kitchen there was a bedroom for Albert and Kitty and another, quite small and over the stairwell and ground-floor passage, for Laura.

Kitty tucked her in and picked up her discarded clothes. 'You've been playing with that Addy Seaton, haven't you? How do the pair o' you get so mucky?' But it was said with affection and Laura recognised it as a rhetorical question she had heard often before and did not answer.

Instead, she asked, 'Can I go and see Aunt Cath tomorrow?'

This was routine, too, and Kitty answered, 'As long as you're back in time for your dinner.'

Laura snuggled down in her bed and in her last few minutes of wakefulness thought over the events of a good day: the cheering and singing, the marching and the bands; the penny won from Albert Grimshaw, won because she already knew with a child's instinct how to play him. Her own reckless nerve enabled her to exploit the knowledge.

Then sleep came suddenly, without dreams, to wrap her round till morning.

In Sunday school Laura wore her Sunday best. That meant a clean pinny, beribboned straw hat and black stockings without holes. She listened attentively, obedient to her mother's wishes, but once it was over she shot out into the street. She ran down towards the North Dock and the sea, but swung left to cut inland. She passed Uncle George Finley's timber yard, on her left and locked on the Sabbath, and raced on with one hand holding her straw hat on her head. She ducked under the nodding heads of the pair of horses pulling a cart and the driver bawled at her and waved his whip. Laura put out her tongue and ran on still, until she brought up at the front gate of Aunt Cath's house, a cottage in a long terrace of them. Uncle George owned it and while small, only three rooms and kitchen, it was decidedly better than that in which Laura lived. All those houses were rented, with two families in each, one up, one down. Only George and Cath lived in their cottage. Cath's front door stood ajar. Laura had expected this and walked along the passage to the kitchen at the rear of the cottage.

Catherine Finley, short and sturdy, her hair drawn back into a businesslike bun, had also been expecting Laura. She straightened, red-faced from stooping over the oven and laughed. 'I left the door because I thought you were about due. Sit yourself down and get your breath back.'

Laura plumped down on a kitchen chair and fanned herself with the straw hat. 'I ran all the way.'

'Here you are.' Cath poured the glass of home-made ginger beer and set it on the table before Laura. 'Help yourself to a biscuit.' And as the little girl stood on tiptoe to delve into the tin with its picture of Queen Victoria: 'Just one, or you won't be able to eat your dinner and your mother will tell me off.'

'Thanks, Aunt Cath,' Laura answered through a mouthful of crumbs.

'Sit still while you put that lot away, then say hello to your Uncle George. But only a minute; he's reading the paper.'

Laura obeyed in due course. George Finley sat in the parlour, the front room of the house. Cath, unlike her sister Kitty, had married a man who had got on. George had started as a shipyard joiner but was hard-working and astute. He now had his own timber yard where he employed two men, bought and sold timber and made ladders and other joinery for the shipyards. When the schools were on holiday Laura would often visit Uncle George in his yard to watch the work and ask a week's worth of questions in a day. He was tall, thin and laid down his newspaper to grin at Laura. 'Now then, bonny lass! What cheer?'

They talked happily for a few minutes, Laura leaning on the arm of his chair. Then she returned to Aunt Cath to chat again until it was time for her to go home. It was a Sunday ritual that Laura followed eagerly every week.

Aunt Cath saw her off at the front door. 'Mind how you go now. Be careful o' them trams.'

'Aye, I will, Aunt Cath.' Laura ran off up the street, hand clapped to head and hat again.

Her aunt watched her go, smiling fondly. Cath was childless and always would be.

As she returned to her kitchen she paused at the open door of the parlour to say, 'I worry about that lass.' And as George looked up at her over the paper, she explained, 'Because that Albert Grimshaw is far too strict with her.'

George only partially agreed: 'Aye, but you've said yourself that she needs a firm hand.'

'But not picking her up for every little thing!' Cath argued. 'If she's a minute late for owt or gets a bit dirty he shouts the house down and takes his belt to her.' She shook her head. 'No, he's too hard. She takes it all now, poor little bairn, but one of these days she'll break out.'

George said, grinning, 'Or talk her way round him, like she does wi' you. She's as cute as a cage full o' monkeys.'

Cath had to laugh. 'Aye, but I can see what she's up to.' She walked on to the kitchen.

George called after her, correcting, 'Maybe you do — most of the time.'

Laura played late into the evening with her friend, Adeline Seaton, in the street which swarmed with children at their games. Their cheeks were whipped red by the cold wind coming in off the sea. The two girls took it in turns to bounce three rubber balls against a blank wall with the deftness of circus jugglers. Laura chanted as she fielded and flicked the balls: 'Raspberry, strawberry, marmalade and jam, tell me the name of my young man! A . . . B . . . C . . .' She broke off at 'W' as one ball bounced awry from an uneven brick in the wall and flew past her clutching hand.

Adeline, fair and plump, a jolly girl, called, 'W! That's William! Billy!' The two girls giggled. Little Billy Gatenby, a boy of their age in a ragged jersey and shorts, grinned sheepishly. Billy often watched the two girls at their games, had always been shyly fond and admiring of Laura — and the girls knew it. Adeline squealed, 'Look! He's blushing, gone all red! He'll end up courting you!' She glanced at Laura and squealed again, 'So are you!'

Laura fiercely denied it: 'No, I'm not!' But her cheeks were pink. She turned away from the other two and began juggling the balls against the wall again. Adeline giggled but Laura ignored her. Billy sidled off a few yards and pretended to be watching some of the boys playing marbles, but he was soon back to sneaking glances at Laura. Adeline saw her friend's annoyance, ceased her sniggering and the game went on. They played happily together as the dusk closed around them and the lamp-lighter came with his long pole to switch on the gas lamps. When Laura finally realised the passage of time the sky was dark above them.

Laura tossed the balls to Adeline. 'I'm off, Addy! I

should ha' been in long ago! Me da will kill me!' And she ran.

Albert Grimshaw waited for her, standing with his back to the fire, his thumbs hooked in his braces, baleful. Saturday's drinking had been succeeded by Sunday's temperance and he had been bad-tempered all day. Now as his small stepdaughter edged in around the kitchen door he beckoned with a crooked finger, 'C'mere, you.'

Laura went to him, frightened and alert, and Kitty Grimshaw pleaded, 'No, Albert, please.'

'She's got to learn what's right and what's wrong.' He scowled, unbuckled his leather belt and coiled it around one hand. 'Now then, where have you been till this time?'

Laura whispered, 'Playing, Da, with Addy.' And she added quickly, a forlorn hope that the excuse would be accepted, 'I didn't know the time.' And she slid her feet until she stood close by the kitchen table.

'You could have *asked*!' Grimshaw shouted. 'You know you shouldn't be playing on a Sunday, not on the Lord's day! It's only because of your mother's soft heart that I let you! You've sinned and now you must repent!' He pulled back his arm, fist clenching on the belt. It hissed through the air and Laura shrieked as it landed, though it scarcely touched her. She felt a split-second of pain as its tongue licked her legs but that was all. Most of the force of the blow was taken by the table leg with a fearsome-sounding '*Thwack!*'.

Laura had learned this trick early and quickly. She

knew that the sound of the belt and her screams would convince Grimshaw that she was suffering her punishment. As the belt rose and fell again and again she begged, 'Please, Da, no more! I won't do it again!'

Kitty added her pleas, with more determination wrung out of her. 'That's enough, Albert! Let the bairn be now.'

'All right.' He unwound the belt and strapped it around his middle again. 'I just hope you've learned your lesson. Now get away to bed. There'll be no supper for you.'

Laura went with her mother. Undressed, there were red marks on her legs but she did not complain. 'Can I have a drink, Mam, please?'

'O' course, you can.' And Kitty fetched a cup of water.

Laura said, 'I'll drink it in a minute, Mam. Thank you.'

So Kitty set the drink on the chair by the bedside. She looked down at her happy-go-lucky daughter and said, puzzled but with a touch of admiration and relief, 'You take after your grandma, like Aunt Cath.' Grandma was a family legend, a bold woman who had married a ship's captain and had gone to sea with him. They had perished together when his ship sank off the Horn.

Laura's brows creased, puzzled in her turn. 'You said I had your hair.' And she did have the lustrous chestnut tresses of her mother.

Kitty smiled. 'I didn't mean that. It's just that your Aunt Cath doesn't worry about anything.' She was wrong about that, but then she left her daughter to sleep. Laura took from the pocket of her pinny the biscuits she had wheedled from Aunt Cath Finley and munched them for her supper. She was thinking already of the day to come and what she would do at school, the thrashing forgotten. She knew she had broken the rules and she had paid for it. Not so badly as Albert thought or had intended but that was all part of the game, a fact of life. Young though she was, most of the time she outwitted him or simply kept out of his way when the black mood was on him. She sighed contentedly, washed down her biscuits and slept.

And Cath Finley, lying next to George in their feather bed, stared up at the ceiling and said worriedly, 'We're going to have to look out for that lass.'

Dragged back from the edge of sleep, George mumbled, 'Wha' lass?' Then realising, he agreed automatically, 'Oh, aye.' He turned over and slept while his wife lay wakeful.

Chapter Two

AUGUST 1909. MONKWEARMOUTH.

'It's money wasted on a lass!' Albert Grimshaw grumbled. He stood with his back to the kitchen fire that was only a few glowing coals in the heat of summer. 'Sending her to this commercial college to learn shorthand and typing, it's a lot o' daftness. What does she want wi' more schooling? Her mother got on all right without it. She'd be just as happy and fetching in some money if she got out to work now.'

Cath Finley did not agree that Kitty had 'got on all right'. Out of the corner of her eye she could see her sister sitting by the kitchen fire and thought she looked old and worn, tired. But Cath did not argue. She also forbore to mention that the money Albert deemed to be wasted was not his but hers. She had paid the fees and fitted out the fourteen-year-old Laura for the shorthand and typing course. Cath did not dispute these points because she had decided on her objective. She wanted Albert's permission for Laura to take the course and was determined to get it, was angling for it now. Laura was kneeling beside her mother, her eyes fixed hopefully on Cath, who played her fish: 'Laura will bring in more money when she gets a job as a shorthand typist – a lot more than if she was in a shop or at the ropery.' She knew both of those avenues were in Albert's mind.

He queried, 'Aye?'

Cath could see the glint of avarice in his eyes now. She urged, 'It's an investment, like putting money in the bank to get the interest.' But she knew Albert would not appreciate that thinking and so she added, ' "Cast thy bread upon the waters, for thou shalt find it after many days." Doesn't it say that in the Bible?'

'Aye,' Albert agreed reluctantly. He had never heard the quotation but would not admit it.

So Cath coaxed his agreement out of him and Laura went on to the commercial college. She enjoyed learning, liked the other girls, and soon had a reputation as independent-minded but hard-working and accurate. She made new friends and one of them was Sybil Johnson, a tall, slim and shy girl who was both shocked by, and admiring of, Laura's dare-devil ways. When one acid-tongued teacher bullied Sybil sarcastically, it was Laura who found a dead mouse and put it in her desk.

Out of school there was the stirring of romance. Now Laura and Addy were part of a foursome with Billy

Gatenby and Joe Gibson. Billy had lost his shyness but was a gangling, awkward youth. He still doted on Laura, was eager to be passionate but Laura slipped away from his advances. Joe was the youngest of a large family and was often called the runt of the litter. He was pale, thin and dubbed 'delicate', but there were also rumours that he was very clever. The neighbours said that Joe Gibson would go a long way if he lived long enough to grow up.

The four of them sat in the back row of the picture palace to laugh or thrill to the jerky silent images on the screen while the piano jangled appropriate music in the background. Or they wandered along the sea-front or sat on the sand and watched the ships steaming in and out of the port of Sunderland. It was on one of those days, a brightly sunny Sunday when the beach was crowded, that Addy was unusually silent and withdrawn.

Laura took her away from the boys and asked, 'Is there something wrong, Addy?'

Adeline shook her fair head. 'No.'

Laura eyed her, then persisted, 'Yes, there is. What is it?'

Adeline would not return her gaze. She muttered, 'I can't tell you.'

She maintained her silence despite Laura pressing her: 'Why can't you tell me?'

Adeline would only shake her head. 'Just leave me alone.'

Her mother had told her, 'Don't you tell Laura you saw her dad with another woman.'

'But, Mam, she's my friend!'

'All the more reason. You'll only upset her and there's nowt the lass can do.'

'She could tell her mother.'

'I reckon she probably knows.'

'Mam!' Adeline could not believe it.

But her mother nodded. 'And she's staying quiet to keep the peace.'

So Adeline learned to live with this knowledge of betrayal and kept it to herself.

Laura had to give up her probing in the end. It was a long time before she learned what had upset Adeline so much.

In her happiness Laura did not notice her mother's wasting away. Then one day she came home from the college and found Kitty doubled up in pain in one of the old armchairs. Kitty whispered, 'I haven't been able to cook your dad's dinner. You'll have to do it, lass.'

'Aye, I will.' But then Laura knelt by her mother. 'What's the matter, Mam? You're looking awful badly.'

'It's just a bit o' stomach ache. I get them now and again. I expect it's my age.' But then her face twisted in pain.

Laura said, 'You just sit still.' She hurriedly made her mother a cup of tea: 'See if that eases it.' Then she prepared the pie for the dinner, put it in the oven at the side of the fire and raked hot coals under it to start the cooking. She told Kitty, 'I'm just going out for a few minutes, Mam. I'll peel the taties and put them on when I get back. You sit and rest.'

'Aye,' Kitty promised, 'I will. I'm sorry to be a nuisance. You're a good little lass.'

Laura kissed her and ran. She fetched up, panting, at Cath Finley's cottage and told her, 'Me mam's very bad, Aunt Cath. Can you come and see her?'

Cath kicked off her slippers, pulled on her shoes and reached for her coat where it hung on a hook behind the kitchen door. 'This has been coming on for a long time. I told her she should see the doctor but she wouldn't have it.'

They hurried to Kitty's house and found her curled down in the chair and twisted by suffering. She whispered, 'Oh, Laura, you shouldn't have bothered Cath. I'll be fine in a bit.'

Cath put an arm around her. 'I've heard that tale before and you know it's not true. You wouldn't let me get the doctor in then, but I'm sending for him now.'

Kitty protested weakly, 'No, Cath. Albert gets so bad-tempered—'

Cath cut her off: 'Let him. Laura, run and fetch the doctor.'

Laura fled, frightened, but before she returned with the doctor the shipyard hooters blared, signalling the end of the working day, and Albert came home.

Cath told him, 'Kitty's bad and needs the doctor.'

'Doctor?' Albert scowled. 'I'm having no doctor here. That would be money tossed away. There's nowt wrong wi' Kitty but the change o' life. Probably it's never bothered you because you've never had a bairn, but it's nature and we just have to put up with it.'

'It's Kitty that's putting up with it, and has been for too long!' Cath was outraged. 'But I won't argue. I've sent Laura to fetch the doctor and he'll be here in a minute.'

Albert glared. 'You take too much on yourself.' He slammed his bait box, that had held his lunchtime sandwiches, down on the table and followed it with the can that had held his tea. He demanded, 'Anyway, where's my dinner?'

'It's not ready,' Cath replied. Then she added maliciously, 'You'll just have to put up with it.'

Kitty pleaded weakly, 'Don't fight, you two. I'm sorry, Albert. Laura's baked the pie and she'll soon finish the taties.'

Albert grumbled, 'And a right balls she'll have made of it. She might ha' done better if she'd not had her head filled with that bloody college daftness.' He glared at Cath again. 'And that was your idea!'

They were on the verge of a blazing row but at that point Laura returned with the doctor. He was sixty and portly and came puffing, 'There's no call to rush me like this, my girl! Your mother's probably only got a touch o' colic.' He sought to calm and cheer Laura, but he became grave after he had examined Kitty. 'I think we'll have you into the hospital for a more thorough examination.'

Albert grumbled, 'Hospital? Can't you give her a bottle o' tonic?'

The doctor eyed him, summed him up in that glance and answered, 'No.'

So Kitty was taken to the hospital in Roker Avenue, where the surgeons operated but found they were too late. Kitty did not survive and Laura wept on a winter's day as her mother's wasted body was lowered into the grave.

After the funeral, Albert told Laura curtly, 'You can finish wi' that college daftness. This is a woman's place — at home. Now you'll get down to some work proper for a lass, looking after the house.'

Laura, grieving, miserably accepted this but Cath came storming to tell Albert: 'We've got the lass this far and it won't be long to her examinations. You can't stop her now. I'll see that you don't suffer and your dinner is ready when you get in, your washing done and the house clean. Me and the lass will see to that together.'

Albert argued, 'It's none o' your business!'

'She's my sister's bairn and owt to do with that lass is my business! Kitty isn't here to stand up for her, but I will. If she'd listened to me instead o' you she'd still be alive today. And I'll tell the street that if you force me to it.'

Albert snarled and fumed but backed down in the face of her anger — and her threat. He knew she meant it.

So when Laura came home from the Dundas Street shops she found Cath waiting at the front door to tell her: 'Your father's changed his mind. He says you can stay on to sit your exams. You'd better go and thank him.'

Laura looked after her father and the house very well, with only a minimum of help from Cath, who told George proudly, 'She could manage it all on her own but I like to give her a bit of a hand.'

It was not for long. Albert married again, bringing home Doris, who was florid and blowsy, as his bride. The wedding reception was held in the Frigate, a public house meal of ham sandwiches, beer and port. While Doris smirked, self-assured, at Laura, the girl remained unsmiling. Dislike was mutual. Doris hissed at Albert, 'That lass of yours wants putting through her paces and I'll see to it.'

Albert pointed out, 'She's not mine. I told you, she's Kitty's bairn by her first husband.'

'All the more reason she should show gratitude. Is she bringing owt in?'

'Not yet, but when she passes her exams . . .'

'The sooner the better.' Doris nodded grimly, and smiled across the room again at Laura, who stuck by the side of her Aunt Cath through that miserably long day.

Laura still had some fondness for her stepfather, coaxed into her by her mother. So she whispered to Cath, 'Dad will be pleased when I start work and bring in some money.' Then added with doubt born of experience, 'Won't he?'

Cath lied, 'O' course he will!' And hugged the girl.

But when Laura finally heard she had passed her exams it was Cath she ran to first to break the news, flying through the cobbled streets to her aunt's door to gasp out, shrill with excitement, '*I've passed!*'

Cath swung her off her feet and around delightedly. 'I knew you would! Well done, bonny lass!' And then, setting her down, 'Have you given your dad the news yet?'

Some of Laura's exuberance left her. 'No.'

'I think you should, straight away.' Then she added tactfully, 'Don't tell him you've already told me. And wait till he has his dinner.'

Laura obeyed, served up the dinner Doris claimed to have cooked – though Laura had done most of the work, while Doris had only put the casserole into the oven. Laura set Albert's loaded plate before him and then could wait no longer. She burst out with pride, 'I've passed my exams, Dad!'

He paused with his fork before his open mouth, but only to glare and warn her, 'So you should, the money it's cost. Don't get above yourself.' And he snapped at the food.

Doris, seated at his side, agreed. 'Aye. And where's my dinner? After me slaving over it I'm sitting here starving!'

Laura brought Doris's meal, but thought, You don't look to be starving to me! Because her stepmother bulged over the top of her tight corsets.

Doris muttered, 'About time. And there's no call for you to be boasting until you've got a job and bring some money into this house.'

Laura was looking forward to it and did not have to wait long. She started work in the office of a firm of solicitors, Wallace and Turner, and at the end of her first week brought home her pay packet.

An hour later Cath answered a knock at her front door to find Laura standing forlornly on the doorstep – or rather just short of it. She would never stand on her aunt's whitened step.

Cath greeted her cheerily. 'Come in, lass. What are you doing here? I thought you'd be out with Addy and the lads tonight.'

Laura trailed into the kitchen and sat down. 'I didn't feel like it.'

Cath smelled a rat and asked, 'Are you getting on all right at work?'

'Oh, aye.' That brought a brief, proud smile. 'They said so.' But then it faded.

Cath poured tea for them and took a cup through to George, hidden behind the *Echo* in the sitting-room. She returned to ask with foreboding, 'And I suppose you were paid today. Is the money good?'

Laura whispered, 'They took it all.' She was white-faced but her eyes blazed anger. 'I didn't have a full week because it was my first so Dad said I shouldn't have any pocket money out of it but I can have some next week. I thought I would get something, you know? For them to do that – it can't be right!'

'Your dad knows what's right,' answered Cath. But to herself she added, But he doesn't live by it. She bit her lip, looking down at the girl smouldering with temper. 'Did you have a row?'

Laura shook her head. Her chestnut hair no longer hung down her back, had been put up now she was at work. 'I remembered what you said, not to let my temper get the better of me.'

'Good girl. Least said, soonest mended.' Cath thought that a good principle for a young girl to follow. When she was grown into a woman it would be another matter. But what now? Her own lips twitched with anger; something would have to be done. She took her purse from the drawer in the sideboard and pressed a shilling into Laura's hand. 'There's a bob to tide you over till you're paid for a full week. Now run away, find Addy and enjoy yourselves.'

Laura gaped at the shilling, then threw her arms around Cath. 'Thank you! But I'll pay you back. Promise.'

Cath knew she would get her money back, but for now only said, 'Right you are. Now get away with you.'

She smiled as Laura danced out of the door, calling back over her shoulder, 'Goodnight, Uncle George!'

His grunted reply was lost on the air; Laura had raced off up the street. He had hardly lifted his paper again when Cath looked around the door as she pulled on her coat. She said, 'I'm going out for a bit. Won't be long. You fetch some more coal from the coalhouse and make that fire up afore it goes out.' There was nothing wrong with the fire; Cath was just coming to the boil. But George got up from his chair as the front door slammed behind her.

When Cath banged on the Grimshaws' kitchen door it was opened by Doris. Cath walked in past her, followed by Doris's startled, 'Here! What do you want?'

'A word with you two, for a start.' Cath saw Albert

sitting in his usual armchair. An empty pint bottle of stout stood on the table, with two half-full tumblers. 'I see you're celebrating early.'

Albert started to get up from his chair. 'Celebrating? What're you on about?'

'Having a drink out of Laura's wages, that's what I'm on about.'

Albert sneered, 'So she went crying to you.'

'Not crying.' Cath eyed him. 'The day you bring her to tears will be the day you'll regret.'

Doris put in, 'It's about time she brought some money in. What's wrong wi' that?'

Cath swung on her. 'No harm in her paying her way, but you two took the lot.'

Albert argued defensively, 'She only had a part week—'

Cath cut him off: 'She'd worked five days out of the six!'

He shrugged. 'I'll give her a bit o' pocket money out o' next week's pay.'

Cath exploded, 'My oath! You'll give her more than a bit! She'll pay her board and that's *all*! The rest she'll keep. And the same for this week. You can take her board but you'll give back the rest. It'll be little enough, God knows!'

'Never!' Albert took a step towards her. 'That money is mine by right.'

Doris joined him: 'Aye! That's ours.'

They loomed over Cath, threatening, but she faced them and said with searing contempt, 'If either one o' you lays so much as a finger on me I'll shout for the pollis and drag you through the courts and the papers. And you'll do just as I said. I want a fair deal for that lass. I don't want to come between a man and his stepdaughter, but if I have to I'll make a home for Laura and a better one than this. Then you'll get nothing, not a farthing!'

She waited, returning glare for glare, as she saw it sink in. Their eyes shifted. Albert was thinking of losing Laura's board money. Frustrated male pride made him spit out, 'You've got too much bloody mouth!'

Doris sided with him sullenly. 'Aye.'

But Cath knew the matter was settled. 'I'm glad we all agree — don't we?'

They nodded. Cath turned her back on them and walked away down the stairs. As she stepped out of the front door reaction set in, she began to shake and did not stop until she was almost home. But she was ready to go through it all again if she had to and swore to herself, 'I'll see that lass gets a fair crack o' the whip.

When Laura returned home that night, her stepfather, sprawled in his chair, did not look at her but pointed at the table. 'I've kept back your board but the rest there is yours.'

Laura saw the little pile of coins and scooped them up. 'Thank you, Dad.' It was said politely and out of politeness because Laura was no fool. She saw that Albert had been forced into this, that it was not out of generosity that the money was given and the bargain made. She suspected Cath had taken a hand.

Doris snapped, 'You should be grateful! It's more than you deserve.'

Laura made no answer but was still in silent rebellion.

As the weeks, months and years rolled by she settled into her job and into the changed household – after a fashion. She missed her mother, looked to Cath and mentally defied Albert and Doris. She grew up quickly but Cath said worriedly, 'She's flighty, George, restless. It's as if she's looking for something and she's not sure what.'

He stared at her, mystified. 'What can we do about it?'

Cath sighed. 'I don't know. But she's becoming more and more independent and I wonder sometimes how long she'll listen to me.'

She had the right of it, that Laura did not know what she sought. The girl only knew there must be a better life than she had with Albert and Doris.

And then she thought she had found it.

Chapter Three

'You look like a little tart! Dressing up like that on a Saturday night!' Doris Grimshaw snarled the words. 'You spend every penny you've got on clothes to act the fine lady, but that you'll never be.'

Laura, standing before the mirror above the kitchen mantelpiece, did not argue the point. She could not deny that a large part of her money was spent on clothes, in fact she was proud of it. She put Doris's denunciation down to envy, and there was certainly a deal of that. Laura knew that the objective was to goad her into a shouting match, into anger and later maybe tears. She would not give Doris that satisfaction, though the accusations hurt, wounded her like a knife thrust. It made no difference that they were not true. She dressed up because she liked it and it turned the boys' heads, because she was eighteen now. None of the other girls in the street dressed as stylishly as Laura. That was not because she had more money, for Laura was left with little after paying her board money to Albert. He and Doris took more than they should but Laura did not complain to them or her aunt. She felt Cath had done enough. But Laura dressed well simply because she had flair. All her finery was bought cheaply in sales or second-hand. She refused to believe that made her a loose woman.

She spun on her toes, watching the way her long skirt floated up to show the lace of petticoat and the glistening black patent leather shoes with their pointed toes and louis heels. Her high-necked blouse was of fragile muslin and showed off her young figure. She had washed her hair in water from the rainwater butt, always better than that drawn from the tap across the back yard. Now she clapped the cheeky lacquered straw boater trimmed with ribbon on to her piled chestnut tresses. It had cost almost ten shillings to dress her, but if she had gone to the big Fawcett Street and High Street shops it would have been at least twice as much, well over a pound. She was well pleased with the result, knew she would draw some disapproving glances from older women but did not care. The look of frustrated fury on Doris's bitter face only added spice. Laura slung her long-strapped beige leather handbag over her shoulder and danced out into a fine summer evening. She felt the sense of freedom that always came when she left that house, Albert and Doris.

Adeline Seaton lived only a few doors along the street and they met halfway, laughing. Adeline felt her usual slight twinge of envy and large one of admiration for Laura. 'Is that a new skirt?'

'I bought it today.' Laura twirled again. 'Do you like it?'

'Um!' Adeline nodded enthusiastically. Then she got down to business and asked, 'Where are we going?' Because Laura always led.

'Across the ferry and up into Crowtree Road.'

'Ooh!' Adeline giggled, because Crowtree Road was where the boys and girls paraded, seeking to 'click'.

They set off arm-in-arm, talking of boys, work, clothes, shops. Adeline made casual references to her happy home life but Laura did not.

They were still fifty yards from the ferry when they turned the last corner and Adeline shrieked, 'She's going!' The deckhand was casting off the mooring lines from the little steamer lying at the foot of the boarding steps, with her stubby funnel spilling a thread of smoke.

Laura cried, 'We can catch her!' She hitched up her skirt and ran. Adeline followed but more sedately.

The mooring lines had been tossed ashore and the ferry was going astern to ease away from the steps. Adeline slowed, squeaking, 'It's too late! You can't catch her!'

That was a challenge to Laura. She plunged down the steps, legs flying in a froth of lace and black stockings. The ferry was going ahead now, bow turning to point out into the river. Her stern was below Laura and four feet away with the gap widening. Adeline shrieked, frightened now: 'The propellers will get you!' They were churning the water to foam under the ferry's stern when Laura jumped. Her momentum carried her over the gap and the ferry's rail to land on the deck, but she would have sprawled her length if she had not been caught. She fetched up against a broad chest and two arms went around her. For a few seconds she lay there, gasping for breath and speechless. Then she eased back from her saviour's arms and shook down her skirts. A group of elderly women shook their heads and clicked their tongues. Laura tossed her head defiantly. She glanced behind over the ferry's wake and saw Adeline still standing disconsolately alone on the steps. Laura waved, then her gaze came down to the white water torn up by the ferry's screws and recalled Adeline's warning: 'The propellers will get you!' She shivered and thought that she had been a reckless fool.

Then a voice grumbled, 'You shouldn't ha' done that, my girl. You could ha' got yourself killed. I've a mind to bring charges.' It was the deckhand collecting fares.

Laura was ready to apologise, contrite now, but her saviour put in quickly, 'That's all right. The young lady is with me. I'll vouch for her good behaviour from now on. Here, keep the change for your trouble.' And he proffered a sixpence. The fare for two was only a penny.

Now Laura had time to look at him. He was tall and slim with wavy hair the colour of butter and a wide, confident smile that showed white teeth. His well-cut suit with its fashionably narrow trousers fitted him like a glove. His stiff white collar was closed by a silk tie and he held a soft felt hat in his hand.

The deckhand coughed. 'Ah! Well, I suppose no harm was done.' He took the sixpence and put it in his leather pouch but pocketed the fivepence change he took out. 'Thank ye, sir.' And he passed on.

Laura realised she was staring and that this handsome young man was admiring. She turned her head to look at him from the corner of her eye. 'So you'll vouch for me?'

'If you'll let me.'

He was different from the boys she saw in her street and engaged in repartee in Crowtree Road. She had seen his sort going by in carriages, and occasionally in the solicitors' offices where she worked. He was gentry. But did that matter? She recognised the look in his eye and knew she had 'clicked' – if she wanted to. And there was something attractive about his smile . . .

Her heart thumped and Laura said, 'All right, then.'

His smile widened. 'Good.' They were nearing the southern shore, the engines slowing. 'Was that your friend we left behind?'

'Oh, aye, but she'll be fine.' Laura decided Adeline would no more want to play gooseberry than she would herself.

He held out his hand. 'I'm Ralph Hillier.'

Laura stretched out her own hand to take his. 'Laura Stanfield.'

The ferry slid in to the quay and bumped against the timber pilings. Laura staggered, caught unawares and

Ralph steadied her, his arm around her waist. She was aware of the tight lips of the watching women.

Ralph said, 'It's a pleasant evening for a stroll. Had you any plans?'

Laura shook her head. 'No.'

'Then perhaps I may escort you?'

'Thank you.' Laura slipped her arm through his and they stepped ashore.

They walked up to Mowbray Park and around its winding paths. Laura saw several glances cast their way and guessed it was because they were a smart-looking couple. She was sure it was Ralph who was turning the heads of the women. He admitted as they wandered, 'I'm just getting used to this place. My mother remarried a year ago and we moved here then, but I've been up at Oxford.'

'Oh, aye?' Laura did not know anyone who had been to university.

Ralph said dismissively, 'I met some decent chaps there but apart from that it was a bit stuffy, so I came away.' In fact he had been sent down for not working but he preferred his own explanation.

Laura looked up at him, curious. 'What do you mean: stuffy?'

He pulled a face. 'Oh, lots of piddling rules. I wouldn't put up with it.'

'Ah! I know what you mean.'

He smiled down at her. 'Do you?'

'Aye.' Laura lived a life of defiance of rules, but she would not tell him about Albert and Doris.

Ralph squeezed her hand. 'I think we have a lot in common.'

Laura blushed, smiled and asked to cover her confusion, 'Do you like living here?'

He shrugged. 'Oh, Ashbrooke is well enough, I suppose.'

'Ashbrooke!' Laura exclaimed. She only knew it as a part of the town with big houses where the wealthy lived, shipbuilders and shipowners, businessmen.

'That's right.' Ralph wrinkled his nose. 'It's a bit stuffy, too.' Then he went on, 'I prefer travelling, France and Italy, Paris and Rome. St Peter's Square . . .' Laura listened avidly. The furthest she had travelled had been to Cox Green, just a few miles away, on the train with the Sunday school for the summer treat. They had run races in a farmer's field and eaten the bags of buns given to them as they sat in rows on the grass.

Laura had some questions to ask about this foreign travel but dusk was closing in and it was time to leave the park.

Ralph said, 'I say, I'm hungry. What about a spot of supper? Can I tempt you?'

He could and she yielded readily, hoping for a hot pie bought from one of the shops still open and eaten on the street. Instead he dumbfounded her by taking her to the restaurant in the Palace Hotel, high-ceilinged and opulent. As they ate, Laura both self-conscious and excited – she had never before had so much as a cup of tea in a café – finally put her question: 'How do you get time off work for all this travelling?'

Ralph became sombre: 'That was before Mother lost her money. Father left her plenty but she gambled on the Stock Exchange to make more and instead she lost it.'

'Oh, that's sad.' Laura was sorry for him.

He smiled bravely. 'Oh, well: "The slings and arrows of outrageous fortune." Life goes on. And she married again a year ago, to a chap called Corrigan. The only trouble about that is that he insists I should work in his shipyard, thinks I could take it up as a profession.'

'Corrigan's!' Laura exclaimed. It was one of the biggest yards on the river.

'That's the one.' Ralph grimaced. 'It bores me stiff. He thinks it's marvellous but I don't. He makes me an allowance, not enough but better than nothing, so I'll stick it for a while but then I'll be off to make my own way. It's not as if I would inherit the yard if I stayed, though I don't want it anyway. He has a son who's as keen on the shipbuilding as his father. He's on a sort of grand tour at the moment, going round the world looking at shipyards – I think he's in Japan now – but he'll come home some time and take the lot when old man Corrigan snuffs it.'

'You don't like him.'

Ralph gave a wry laugh. 'I don't dislike him. It's just that we don't get on. He wants to run my life and I won't have that.'

Laura was sympathetic; wasn't she in the same position with Albert trying to run her life? She agreed with new-found loyalty, 'I think you're right.'

Ralph gave her that charming smile and reached out across the table to take her hand. 'I told you we had a lot in common.'

Laura blushed, was sure people were looking at them but didn't care. She had never known anyone like this before. Then she remembered and gasped, 'What time is it?'

Ralph shot his cuff to glance at the gold watch on his wrist. 'Nine thirty.'

'Oh! I have to go home. I'm late!' Laura jerked up out of her chair.

Ralph said, 'I say! Wait a second. I have to settle with the waiter.' He called for the bill and paid while Laura shifted from one foot to the other. She knew she was going to face Albert in his wrath. And this was Saturday, so he and Doris would be drunk.

As they passed through the foyer, she whispered, 'I've got to run and catch a tram.'

But Ralph gripped her arm firmly. 'Oh, no. I can't have you getting into trouble when it was my fault for keeping you out. *Cabbie!*' The cab swung across the road as the driver hauled on the reins.

'Where to, sir?'

Ralph glanced questioningly at Laura and she imagined what Albert would say and do if she returned home in a cab – and with a young man. She answered quickly, 'The Frigate.' It would only take her two minutes to walk home from there. But she saw the look on the cabbie's face when she asked for the public house down by the river and the shipyards. Angered, she tossed her head as Ralph handed her into the cab — and she had never had that little courtesy before. She whispered, 'Can you make him hurry?'

Ralph called, 'Whip him up a bit, cabbie! Fast as you can! There'll be a shilling in it for you!'

'Right y'are, sir!' The cab started away with a clatter of hooves and raced across the bridge. Laura always thought the river an enchanted place at this time with the night hiding the smoke and grime — for this was a working town — and instead the lights were twinkling on the ships lying on the dark glass of the water, the towering jibs of the cranes standing like sentinels, black against the sky. She had no time for that now, only aware of the minutes ticking away. She was conscious of Ralph gently rubbing his face against hers in the darkness of the cab, but before she needed to stop his wandering hands the horse was reined in.

' 'Ere you are, sir!'

Laura was out on the street as the cabbie called and Ralph jumped down beside her. She was eager to get away but also looking about her to see if anyone who knew her was watching. If so, then Albert would soon hear that his flighty stepdaughter had been brought home in a cab by a young man. She saw no one and heard Ralph call to the cabbie, 'Wait!' Then he was gazing down at her, smiling and pleading. 'When will I see you again? I must! Tomorrow?'

'No!' He was going too quickly for her. This evening

had been an entirely new experience for her. She had never known anyone like this, was shy and just a little frightened now, out of her depth. Besides, she was sure she would not be allowed to go out in the town for the rest of the week. Like every other girl of her age and class, she was expected to be home long before this. She said, 'Next week.'

'I have to wait a week!' Ralph's reply was tortured but he smiled still.

Laura insisted, 'Yes.'

'Where?'

'In the park.' She was about to dash off but he held her hand a moment longer.

He bowed over it to kiss it. 'Until next week. Goodnight.'

'Goodnight.' Laura turned away but then swung back to kiss his cheek. Then she did run, her face burning.

Albert stood before the fire in the kitchen, hands in his pockets, glowering as she came panting in at the door. 'What bloody time d'ye call this?'

'I didn't realise how late it was.'

'Didn't that Adeline know? Were you both bloody daydreaming?'

Laura thought that she had been, but now she had to answer, 'Adeline wasn't with me. She missed the ferry.' It would be no use spinning some tale that would need Addy's backing because Albert would confirm it with Addy's parents only a few doors away.

He was suspicious as well as angry now: 'Who were you with then, till this time o' night?'

She hated lying but would have to because she dared not tell him the truth. 'Nobody. I just walked round looking at the shops on my own.'

Doris, sitting by the fire, sucked in her breath with a hiss. She said, voice slurred by drink, 'There's only one sort o' young lass goes walking the streets on her own like that late at night.'

Albert said darkly, 'Aye.' His hands went to the buckle of his belt.

Laura knew she would not let him use it on her, not now. She said quickly, 'I just wanted to see all the fashions; there's all kinds o' nice things in the High Street and Fawcett Street. I saw a costume in Binns I'm sure Aunt Cath would like, not dear, and I'll tell her about it tomorrow.'

That mention of seeing Cath Finley the following day made Albert reconsider; he had a fear of Cath's sharp tongue, could guess at her reaction if she learned he had taken his belt to Laura. He let go of it, jammed his hands back in his pockets and scowled at her. 'Aye, well, it's too bloody late for you to be out and you'll not get the chance again this week. And don't look for any supper, just get yourself away to bed.'

'And count yourself lucky,' Doris grumbled, disappointed that she was not to see a flogging. 'If I had my way you'd get a leathering to show you how to behave.' And to Albert, 'I tell you, flaunting herself dressed up to the nines, she'll bring disgrace on all of us one o' these days!'

Laura knew Doris's opinion of her very well. She also knew Doris and Albert and had cunningly manipulated them for years now. She said, 'Goodnight,' humbly and went to bed. She had been punished but no more than she thought fair; she had talked her way out of worse. She lay in her bed and thought that it would be a long week before she saw Ralph again. She went over the evening in her mind, again and again, recalling what he had said, how he had looked, how handsome he was when he smiled. She both remembered and looked forward with excitement.

He had said they had a lot in common and she agreed.

She would have to be careful, must not be caught by Albert and Doris, must not be late, must not come home or back to her own neighbourhood in a cab or there would be trouble.

Ralph had shown her there was a life away from her step-parents, waiting for her out there.

This had been her lucky day, her luckiest, luckiest day.

'Where did you get to till this time? You've been with some woman, I suppose!' Melissa Hillier was darkly attractive, sultry, but usually presented a picture of decorous modesty with shy, downcast eyes and low voice. Now she was flushed with rage and hard-eyed.

'Don't be damned silly.' Ralph walked past his wife to slouch into a leather armchair before the fire. 'I went for a walk to get some exercise, took a ride across the river and back again on the ferry, then had a couple of drinks.' He stretched his legs to rest his booted feet on the fender. 'And there was no question of going with a woman. I've had enough of women.'

Melissa kicked his feet off the fender. 'I've had enough of *you*! Drinking, gambling, lazing about the place! Dan Corrigan gave you a job but you won't hold it for long because you're always taking time off for the races! You could make something of yourself, we could have a place in society, if you tried! But I get a new dress once a month if I'm lucky, we never go out together, and this house is Dan Corrigan's, let to you rent-free! And it was your mother who got that for you!'

Ralph was red-faced now. Stung, he threw back at her, 'That's why you married me! Because that drunken father of yours told you I was connected to the Corrigan money! He was wrong about that as he was wrong about everything, but you jumped at the chance! "Yes, Ralph! Thank you, Ralph! Whatever you say, Ralph!" ' He mimicked her in falsetto tones. It struck home because it was true. Melissa's father had failed in business and drunk away what was left of his fortune. Almost his last act before he died six months earlier was to manoeuvre her into marrying Ralph, whose mother had married into the Corrigan family. Melissa had hoped she was doing the same but had found that to be untrue. Now she nearly choked with rage. She was about to lash out at him when the maid tapped at the door and then entered bearing a tray. 'I've brought the whisky, sir.' The tray held a decanter, a glass and a soda syphon.

Ralph said curtly, 'Put it there.' He pointed to a small table and the maid obeyed.

She asked, 'Will there be anything else tonight, ma'am?'

Melissa answered with an instant smile. 'No, thank you, Mary Ann. You can go home now.'

She and Ralph were silent until the girl had left the room and closed the door behind her. They kept up the performance of a happily married couple in front of the servants and the Corrigans but now Melissa snarled, 'That's one blessing of our poverty: we only have one girl to be maid and cook but, thank God, she doesn't live in. If she did I'd have to watch you with *her*! But you'll sleep in your own room from now on. You'll not get into my bed!'

Ralph snapped back at her, 'I haven't for long enough, you frigid bitch!'

The first part of that statement was true but not the last because their early lovemaking had been passionate. But now they parted with cold glares and the door slammed behind Melissa.

Ralph splashed whisky into the glass, gulped it neat and scowled into the fire. He regarded this comfortable little house as a prison and Melissa as his gaoler. He yearned to be rid of both — and the job at the Corrigan shipyard. If only his fool of a mother had held on to their money. If only he could have that little girl he met tonight . . .

Chapter Four

'What happened to you last night?' Adeline asked when she met Laura on Sunday morning.

Laura gave a deliberately careless shrug. 'I met a feller. Got a "click".'

Addy stared, mouth open. 'You never!' And when Laura nodded, Addy asked excitedly, 'Where? Crowtree Road?'

This time Laura shook her head. 'No. On the ferry.'

'How?'

Laura thought, I fell into his arms. But that sounded worse than it was. 'He was on the ferry and we just got talking.'

Adeline was both thrilled and curious. 'Who is he, then?'

But Laura was not prepared to say – yet. Adeline was

59

her closest friend but she wasn't sure how Addy would feel about Ralph Hillier. 'Just a feller.'

Adeline asked, reproving, 'Don't you know his name?'

'Oh, aye.' And when Adeline waited, Laura added, 'Ralph.'

'Ralph!' Adeline wondered. 'That's a nice name. I've never known anybody called Ralph before. Ralph what?'

But Laura felt she had told enough: 'I can't stop. I'm off to see Aunt Cath.'

Albert had grudgingly allowed that: 'Because it's Sunday. You'll not get out in the week.'

Laura left Adeline still curious and one final question followed her as she hurried away: 'Are you seeing him again?'

'I might.' For the first time she thought, What if he doesn't turn up? Suppose he thought I was boring? He probably meets lots of girls in those big houses.

But when she got to Aunt Cath's cosy house she talked ruefully of how she was not to be allowed out in the town for the next week because she had been late home the night before. 'But it was my fault, Aunt Cath. I just forgot about the time, looking in all the shop windows.' She pulled a face but cheerfully. She did not mention the fictitious costume in the window of Binns, nor Ralph Hillier, connected to the Corrigan family. Uncle George did a lot of contracted joinery work for Corrigan's shipyard, making ladders and so forth. Laura told herself there was plenty of time to talk of Ralph and she was not sure how Cath would react.

She thought of Ralph that evening as she sat by the fire with Doris on one side of her and Albert, sober and pious, on the other. Albert had spent most of the day in the chapel and was regurgitating what he had heard. Laura had cooked the Sunday dinner at midday, and Doris washed it down with a bottle of stout. Then Doris had slept in the afternoon while Albert sat through the men's Bible class. Now Laura let his sonorous preaching wash over her. She was not sure what she disliked most, his religious posturing or his Saturday drunkenness.

She wondered what Ralph was doing now. Was he in the Corrigans' big house, turning the pages of the music for some rich young girl playing the piano?

Laura was not far wrong.

'Beautifully played, lass.' Dan Corrigan applauded softly with his big hands. He called them 'gentlemen's hands' now because they were clean and uncalloused, but they still bore scars from his youth spent working on ships in the yard. He was a big man in his fifties, heavy but still active and flat-bellied.

There was a scattering of applause from the guests, a half-dozen local businessmen and their wives, and Dan demanded, 'What d'ye say, Jess?'

Jessica Corrigan, Dan's second wife and Ralph's mother, smiled vaguely and agreed, 'Yes, lovely.' She was a shallow woman, gentle and kindly. She loved Dan and was grateful to him for the wealth he had brought to their marriage. She passed her days quite happily by devoting them to pleasing him. Blonde and blue-eyed, in her forties now but with an hour-glass figure that was natural and owed nothing to corsets, she was an attractive partner for Dan. They were both well-satisfied.

Now she tapped with her fan the chesterfield on which she sat and called, 'Come and sit down, my dears.'

Ralph Hillier, who had been turning the pages of the music while Melissa played, now handed his wife up from the stool and led her across to sit by his mother while he sat on Jessica's other side. Both were smiling, Melissa modestly as Jessica said, 'You do play beautifully, my dear.'

Melissa laughed softly. 'My teacher was not compli-mentary. But I'm glad if I can play for my supper.'

Now Jessica laughed. 'You've certainly done that!'

Dan echoed her, 'Hear, hear!' And to the man beside him, in an undertone that carried through the room, 'Charming girl.'

It was an apt description. Melissa wore a decorously high-necked silken gown with black silk stockings and satin shoes. Her eyes were shyly cast down under the gaze of those present, but she raised them to smile across at Ralph. The smile was returned. They were the picture of a devoted couple.

Melissa acted her part because of her wish to be part of the Corrigan family, to get into the Corrigan money. Ralph played his because he knew Dan doted on this daughter-in-law he had acquired through marrying Jessica.

Ralph could not afford to offend Dan, his benefactor. The shouting and mutual recriminations they saved for their return to the little house let to them by Dan. As their cab set them down at their front door and pulled away, Melissa snapped, 'You still haven't seen to that fence that needs mending!' It ran down the side of the house to where the stable stood at the rear, unused except to store a few old items of furniture.

Ralph growled, 'I'll ask Dan about it at work tomorrow.'

'You'll have to!' Melissa jeered. 'It's his house, his fence and he'll pay for it! We're living on relief!'

They were inside the house now and Ralph cursed her: 'Damn your eyes!'

Melissa shrugged out of her stole and threw it at him. He tossed it aside to fall on the floor.

And so they went to their beds.

'I'll never see Ralph again!' By mid-week Laura was certain of it. She could not tell Adeline, fearing her friend would only say, 'That's the best thing. He's too forward if you ask me.' But she had to tell someone, so she bought two bottles of stout from the Bottle and Jug of the Frigate and begged Albert to let her visit her aunt. He accepted the stout and grudgingly agreed, though Doris shrilled, 'Ye're far ower soft wi' that lass!'

So Laura set out in the early evening to talk to Cath Finley. In the still warmth she dressed in a thin cotton frock that showed off her neat ankles, small waist and curvy figure. She passed the timber yard on the way and saw a light was on in the sawmill that housed the big saw and other joinery equipment. She wondered at that, because work was long over for the day, and thought that Uncle George might be there and Aunt Cath with him. So she passed through between the gates which stood open and walked up the yard to the sawmill. There was only one light inside, casting its gleam on the big circular saw, but no one to be seen.

Laura moved further into the sawmill, wondering nervously now if some thief had broken in. Then she heard a movement behind her, swung around and saw a looming figure. She snatched a breath, mouth opened to scream, then recognised Seth Bullock. He was a thick-set, burly man of thirty, ape-like and powerful, who had recently come to work for Uncle George Finley. He said, 'Scared you, did I?' And he grinned, relishing it.

'I wasn't expecting anybody to creep up behind me,' Laura protested. And angry with herself, she demanded, 'What are you doing here? Where's Uncle George and Frank?' Frank Pearson was a young man who also worked for George Finley.

Seth was eyeing her and he made Laura uneasy. He said, 'They went home an hour ago and left me to finish off this rush job that'll be collected tomorrow.' He nodded to a corner and Laura saw a brand-new ladder standing there. Now he asked, 'And what are you after?'

Laura explained, 'I didn't think anyone would be working now. I thought somebody had broken in.'

Seth chuckled unpleasantly. 'What could you do about a burglar?' He brushed past her to a nearby bench. There he lifted his hand and Laura saw he held his open clasp-knife. With a quick jerk of the wrist he drove it into the bench. Laura knew the knife, with its handle of bone, carved into a replica of a bare-breasted mermaid. She was uneasily aware of Seth's eyes on her and that here in the sawmill she would not be heard outside if . . . She started to edge away but found her back against another bench. She searched for something to say: 'I've never seen a knife like that.'

'And you won't see another.' Seth fondled the bone handle, his eyes still on Laura. 'An Arab feller living in Shields carved it for me.' He let go of the knife and moved towards Laura. 'You come in here a lot.'

'To see my Uncle George or Auntie Cath,' said Laura.

'Aye?' Seth put his arm around her waist and drew her to him. 'That's not all, though. I know what a young lass like you is after.'

Laura had frozen, shocked, but now she came to life. As Seth lowered his face towards hers she slapped him, his head jerking from the power of the blow. For a second he was thrown off guard and Laura tore free and ran to the door. Seth's voice followed her: 'You're a bloody teaser! Coming round here in your fancy clothes! You came here after me!'

Laura screamed back at him, frightened but furious,

'*No! Never!*' Then she ran, but once out of the gates and in the safety of the busy streets, she slowed. At first she headed for Cath's house but then she changed her mind. She wanted comfort and consolation and she would get those from Cath, but it would not end there. Her aunt would be furious but Seth would lie to defend himself. Albert and Doris would be dragged in and they would take Seth's part, Laura was sickeningly sure of that. She recalled Doris's accusation: 'You look like a little tart!' Now she would say triumphantly, 'I told you so!'

Laura halted. She felt ashamed, and angry because she knew she should not feel ashamed; *it was not her fault*. She felt the tears welling and they ran down her cheeks as she turned away from Cath Finley's and walked back home.

The rest of the week passed miserably. She had been frightened by Seth but not harmed and her youthful high spirits helped her to shrug off the experience. But she worried more and more that she would not see Ralph Hillier again.

On Saturday evening she dressed in the long skirt and muslin blouse she had worn before – because he had liked her in them. She adjusted the angle of the lacquered straw boater carefully then sought out Adeline Seaton to tell her, 'I can't come with you tonight.'

Adeline's mouth drooped. 'I thought they were going to let you out tonight. You're all dressed up.'

'They are.' Though they had issued grumbled warnings: 'You be home at a proper time.' Laura said awkwardly, 'But I'm seeing that feller again.' She prayed that would be true.

Adeline studied her shrewdly. 'What's he like, this Ralph? You've not told me much about him.'

Laura said, 'He's – nice.' But thought it an inadequate word.

So did Adeline, who said drily, 'That's what I mean. Still, I expect I'll hear some more about him one of these days.' She went on, 'Joe asked me to go to the pictures with him. I thought you and Billy could come along.'

Laura shook her head. 'Billy's a nice lad, but . . .' She left that unfinished.

Adeline sighed. 'Aye. I thought that was how it was. But this feller you're seeing, you want to be careful. You grew up wi' Billy but you've only met this chap once. You don't know what he's really like.'

Laura smiled confidently. 'I think I do.'

She walked up Church Street, took a tram into the town and got off at Mowbray Park. She tried to compose herself, to walk sedately as she passed through the gate, but then she saw Ralph waiting for her and ran into his arms.

Their courting progressed over the next weeks as summer turned into autumn. With familiarity Ralph became more ardent and Laura infatuated. She admired his pose of rebellion, liked his clothes, expensive and casually worn, his careless generosity when tipping waiters, the way he treated her like a lady. She had not met his like before, thought him a man of the world, and could not believe her luck, that he should care for her. Soon she admitted to herself that she loved him.

There were problems. Laura knew she could not tell Albert and Doris she was being courted by a young man like this – a 'toff'. She had to be careful not to go out more often than she had before, not to be late. On the other hand, Ralph said he could only see her infrequently during the week because of his work: 'Old Corrigan wants to get his money's worth out of me.' But they usually managed to spend Saturday evenings together. They would see an early show at the Empire Theatre, or have supper at the Palace Hotel. Not both because there wasn't time; Laura had to go home. Ralph began to call her, jokingly but with an element of exasperation that upset her: Cinderella.

'You know how I'm placed,' Laura pleaded. She had told him of her background. He had guessed at it already, though surprised that this stylish girl came from the crowded streets down by the river. She went on wistfully, 'I wish I could see you more often.'

'One day,' he promised her softly.

That day was brought much closer on a Saturday evening at the Palace. They had met by Mackie's clock in the centre of the town and because it was raining heavily they ran to the hotel for shelter. They were too early for supper and Ralph urged, 'Let's wait in here.' He indicated a small alcove off the foyer where a couple could sit, hold hands and steal kisses, hidden by palms and unseen except by someone who actually entered.

'Aye,' Laura agreed, but then added, 'I must tidy myself first.' She pushed at her piled bronze tresses which threatened to come down after running through the rain. 'I won't be long.' She was familiar with the Palace now and headed for the ladies' room.

She returned a few minutes later, weaving through the groups of people now filling the foyer to escape the rain. At the mouth of the alcove she checked her stride as she heard: 'You came in here with a woman! I was in a cab but I saw you!' The woman's voice was shrill with rage. 'We never go out but you've money to spend on some little whore!' Her back was half turned to Laura who could see her only in profile, a handsomely dark-haired, sultry woman. Laura could just see beyond her to where Ralph sat with his long legs stretched out and eyes studying the ceiling, but his cheeks were flushed.

He answered impatiently, 'I came in here on my own! There was a chap in front of me with a girl. She went upstairs and he walked through to the men's bar. Ask him if you like.' He knew she could not because no woman was allowed in the men's bar.

Melissa retorted furiously, 'I don't believe you.' Then, when Ralph did not answer, 'I'd put nothing past you! When you proposed you virtually lied to me, talking about your money and position, your well-connected family! And you swore you loved me! There's been no sign of it for a long time now!' Ralph had kept silent all through this diatribe and said nothing now. Infuriated, Melissa demanded, 'Haven't you anything to say for yourself?'

Ralph's reply was dignified and sorrowful: 'I answered you. I won't take part in an exchange of insults.'

A group of four, two men and their wives, had eased out of the crowded foyer to stand between Laura and the alcove. Now they turned as they heard the altercation. Melissa took a stride towards him and Laura thought for a moment that the woman was about to attack Ralph. But instead she fumed, frustrated, 'You've not heard the last of this!' She spun on her heel and thrust past the little group without glancing at Laura, taking her to be one of them. Melissa stormed across the foyer and vanished into the street. Laura stood, her face drained of blood, heart faltering.

Ralph came to her side, took her arm, and she tried to pull away but he pleaded, 'Just let me explain! This is the last thing I wanted. I would never hurt you.' His grip was firm and she was shocked and weak. She wanted to hide and weep. He led her into the alcove and sat her down beside him, held her hands in his. 'I never meant to lie to you, but the first time I saw you, I fell.'

Laura whispered, 'I didn't know you were married. You never said—'

Ralph cut in, 'I didn't tell you I was married because I knew that if I did you wouldn't have any truck with me, you're not that kind of girl. And I was afraid I'd lose you, when I'd just found you.'

Laura's eyes searched his face. 'Were you?'

'Yes, and it's not as if I'm properly wedded; it's a marriage in name only. You heard her.' He winced at the memory.

Laura shuddered. That awful woman.

Ralph sighed. 'She married me because of the Corrigan money; she thought that, as my wife, she would get into the Corrigan family. When she realised I was just a poor relation, she hated me. Those hard words tonight were nothing compared to some of the things she's said. My life was so miserable – until you came into it.' Ralph held her gaze, his fingers tightening on hers. 'Please don't turn me away. If you do, I will understand. I won't make a scene or threaten to kill myself or anything stupid like that. But my life will be empty again.'

Laura struggled, 'I can't . . .'

Ralph pleaded, 'I'm not asking you to be my mistress, just a friend, someone I can talk to, who understands.' He paused, then went on, 'No, that's not true. I love you, I've always loved you and I would hope you would love me too, one day. But if you will give me – give *us* time, I'll settle for friendship. I'm so alone.'

Laura shook her head, lips compressed to keep them from quivering. 'I – I don't know. I can't think. Please, let me go home.'

He walked with her as far as the end of the bridge over the river. There she stopped and said, 'I can go on my own from here.'

He wrapped his arms around her and kissed her, held

her face in his hands and said, 'Think kindly of me. And meet me next week. Please. If only to say goodbye.'

Laura could not refuse him. 'Yes.'

She walked on alone, her thoughts in a turmoil, but essentially she believed Ralph because she wanted to, did not want to lose him any more than he did her.

And as he strode back to the Palace for supper, Ralph thought he had handled that pretty well. He did not know what would happen next but thought that was the exciting part of the affair, as always.

Melissa spoke no word to her husband for three days. On the Wednesday they went their separate ways, again without speaking, he to his job and she to visit Jessica Corrigan. In common with her friends, Jessica 'received' chosen ladies for lunch and tea on two mornings a week. Melissa passed the day there in conversation with Jessica and other ladies and returned to her own house in the late afternoon. Mary Ann, the maid who also cooked, had been allowed to leave a cold collation for dinner that evening and having done this had gone home. So Melissa was about to put her latch key into the lock on the front door when she saw some new timber had been added to the fence. She walked down the side of the house to inspect it and then heard hammering in the stable. The half-doors were open and she stepped inside.

Seth Bullock was hammering, nailing together a section of fencing. He was using the stable as a workroom, an

old table as a bench. He stopped when he saw Melissa
enter, her back against the light. The day was mild and in
the confines of the stable it was warm, so he had stripped
off his shirt and was naked to the waist. Melissa stared at
him, then said, 'You're mending the fence.'

'That's right, ma'am.' His eyes roved over her. 'Mr
Corrigan told my boss, George Finley, that he wanted it
done. George has gone on his holidays but he gave the job
to me.'

Melissa was aware of the insolence of his gaze but only
breathed more quickly. Seth turned back to his work and
hammered again. Melissa watched him. She had denied
her favours to Ralph but had also frustrated her own
hunger. The thin blouse she wore was suddenly constricting and she unbuttoned the neck of it. Seth detected the
movement from the corner of his eye, glanced her way,
saw and grinned. He turned again to drive in one last nail
and Melissa stretched out her hands to run her fingers
down his back. For a moment he was still and she reached
around him, seeking his manhood, and he turned and took
her savagely.

Ralph found a letter by his plate at breakfast next day. He
read it with increasing excitement but then hurriedly
stuffed it in his pocket before Melissa came down. She
was dressed to go out, in a silk frock, one of her best.
Ralph, his thoughts elsewhere, did not notice nor ask
where she was going that day. Melissa did not speak. As

they ate breakfast they could hear the hammering coming from the stable.

Ralph emptied his coffee cup, glanced at his watch and rose hurriedly. He wore a blue serge suit instead of overalls because his work in Corrigan's yard was in the office. A minute or two later he left the house. Melissa waited until Mary Ann had cleared away the breakfast crockery then sought her out in the kitchen at the back of the house and told her, 'You can have today off as well, Mary Ann.'

The girl, startled, warned worriedly, 'What about the dinner, ma'am? I haven't had no time to do anything towards it yet.'

'There's no need for you to worry; the master and I are dining out this evening.'

'Oh! I see. Thank you, ma'am.' The girl whipped off her apron and pulled on her coat. 'Hope you enjoy yourselves, ma'am.' Then she was gone.

Melissa followed her through the kitchen door a few minutes later and walked across the yard to the stable. Seth looked around as she stood in the doorway and she said, 'Come into the house.' He threw down his hammer and followed her.

When Ralph returned home that night Melissa told him, 'I've given the maid the day off. You can take me to dinner at the Palace.' She had changed her dress of necessity and stretched lazily, with a malicious smile.

Ralph did not notice nor argue. He had spent an hour in a solicitor's office that morning in response to the letter he had received and was still absorbing what he had learned. He did not mention the visit or letter to Melissa, but said only, 'If that is what you wish.'

So they went forth amicably for once, though for purely personal reasons, each celebrating a victory over the other.

Laura had no reason to celebrate.

Albert bellowed, 'Doris was right all along! You're no more than a young tart!' He was still in the old clothes he wore for work in the shipyard, stiff with the oil and dirt that also smeared his hands and his face with its weekday stubble. He stood by the fire, glaring down at Laura where she sat at the table.

Doris tossed coal on the fire from a bucket and turned to ask, 'What's she been up to?'

'Blackening my name, that's what she's been up to!' Albert slammed his tea-can down on to the table. 'Geordie Fearon from down the street, he saw me tonight on my way home. "What cheer, Holy Joe," he says, sarcastic bugger! Then he asks, "What's that young lass o' yours doing wi' that toff?" "What toff?" I says. "That one she was kissing on the bridge afore everybody last Saturday night," he says, laughing all over his ugly mug. So I asked, "Are you sure it was her? She's not the only lass in the town." And he laughed again. "Certain," he said. "The

75

wife was with me and saw her an' all. We passed her only a few feet away but she wasn't seeing anybody. Too busy wi' this toff." He said, "We'd ha' told you sooner but we were on our way to the station, going down to York to bury the wife's mother and sort out her place. Didn't you know?" he said. And me gawping like a fyul!'

Doris raised her hands. 'Don't say I didn't warn you! I told you from the start she'd bring all of us down. But you let that Cath Finley talk you round.'

'Aye, well, there's going to be some changes now,' said Albert grimly. 'And George Finley and his missus are on their holidays in Scarborough.' George, being self-employed, could take another holiday when he wished. 'So we won't have her poking her nose in.' Albert eyed Laura. 'Who was this bloody feller you were slobbering over?'

Laura would only say, 'He's a gentleman.' She had already spent days being torn apart by her love for Ralph and her feelings of guilt because he was married. She knew what adultery meant. Her sense of guilt was only moderated by her experience of Melissa as a hate-spitting harridan; she could feel no sympathy for her and a lot for Ralph.

'A *gentleman*!' Albert sneered. 'Did he give you money?'

'No!' Laura denied that fiercely.

'What then? Some o' those fancy clothes you wear?'

'No! Nothing!'

Doris put in, eyes slitted, 'You've been up to something. There's guilt written all over your face. It's about time you showed some shame.'

'I've done nothing wrong!' Laura knew her cheeks flamed now but that was from embarrassment.

'I'll make bloody sure of that from now on.' Albert turned to Doris: 'Clear out that wardrobe of hers. Every stitch! She keeps what she needs for work but the rest goes.'

Laura cried, 'No!'

But Albert was implacable: '*Now!*'

So Doris yanked back the curtain that made a wardrobe out of one corner of Laura's tiny room. She pulled out all Laura's clothes save for the blouses and skirts she wore to the office. She gathered up the carefully ironed and hung garments, rolled them carelessly into a ball and tied the shapeless parcel with string. 'There! I'll take them down to the tagareen shop in the morning.' The tagareen shop bought old clothes and rags.

Laura refused to cry, would not let them see she was hurt. But she turned her back on them and ran from the house. As she burst out of the front door she almost collided with Adeline.

Adeline caught her, laughing, but then became serious when she saw Laura's face. 'Here, what's the matter?'

Laura would not tell her at first, only shook her head and walked rapidly down the street towards the sea. But Adeline hurried alongside her and pressed her until finally she stopped and said, 'Oh, Addy! They found out about Ralph – that feller I was going with.'

Adeline pursed her lips. 'I told you to be careful with him.'

Laura leaped to his defence. 'It wasn't his fault. He only kissed me. But somebody saw him do it and told Albert. He called me a tart!'

Adeline drew a quick intake of breath, shocked. 'He never!'

'He did.'

Adeline sniffed. 'He's one to talk.' She shut her mouth then but it was too late.

Laura challenged, 'What do you mean?' Adeline shook her head, refusing to answer. Laura pressed: 'It's something about Albert. Why won't you tell me?' Adeline still stayed mute and refused to meet Laura's eye. She pulled Adeline round so the silent girl had to face her. The silence struck a chord of memory in Laura and she said, 'You were upset about something once before and wouldn't tell me. Is this the same? Is it about me? Albert?' She shook Adeline. 'Tell me! You're supposed to be my friend! Tell me or I'll never speak to you again! *Tell me!*'

Adeline pleaded, 'My mam said I wasn't to tell you because it would only upset you.'

'I'm upset now!'

Adeline could see that. Laura was white to the lips with anger and distress. So she told her, 'I saw your dad out with another woman.'

Laura, puzzled, asked, 'You mean, not Doris?'

Adeline could not look at her again, but said, 'It was Doris. This was before your mam died, not long before, when she was poorly. Him and Doris were arm-in-arm and laughing. They went into a pub together.'

FANCY WOMAN

Laura could not take in the enormity of it at first, that Albert could be unfaithful while her mother lay dying. How could anyone sink so low? But as acceptance came, anger and distress were multiplied.

Adeline said softly, 'I'm sorry. I didn't want to tell you, but I suppose it's better that you know.'

Laura whispered, 'Aye.'

'What are you going to do now?' Adeline asked anxiously, for Laura was thin-lipped with fury and her friend recognised the signs.

'I'm going to tell them what I think about them.' Laura turned back to go home.

'No, Laura!' Adeline seized her sleeve. 'They're just as likely to knock you about.'

But Laura shook her off. 'They won't touch me.' It was said with careless confidence. 'I'll see you tomorrow, Addy. You're a good pal.'

Adeline kissed her and Laura walked away, back to the house and climbed the stairs. She heard the ground-floor neighbours talking as she passed their door. In the kitchen, Albert and Doris sat before the fire. The parcel of Laura's clothes stood by the door, ready to go to the tagareen shop the following day. They did not matter now.

Laura addressed Albert coldly. 'I hear you were courting this woman while my mother was on her deathbed.'

Albert gaped and Doris, taken aback, complained, 'Here! Don't call me "woman"!'

'I'll call you what I like,' Laura dismissed her. Still talking to Albert, meeting his gaze with her own, she accused him: 'You couldn't wait until she was in her grave. You had to be off with Doris.'

'Don't you talk to me like that!' Albert blustered, but he could not meet her cold gaze that bored into him. Instead he resorted to the only language he knew for this situation and started to unbuckle his belt. 'You should ha' had this hiding early on tonight but you'll get it now.'

Laura stood her ground. 'Keep the belt to hold your trousers up. If either of you two lays so much as a finger on me I'll scream this house down and bring everybody in the street round here. I'll tell them what you did and give them your character. Come Sunday I'll be at the chapel and any marks you leave on me I'll strip to my shift and show them. By the time I've finished you won't be able to stay in this town, never mind this street. You talked to me about shame. I'm ashamed now, that I have anything to do with you.' Laura picked up the bundle of clothes and walked into her room. The door slammed behind her.

Albert's mouth worked. 'I'm not putting up with this.'

'No. The very idea, talking to us like that.' Doris added indignantly, 'After all we've done for her.'

'Aye.'

But Laura's threats had frightened them and they did nothing.

She lay in her narrow bed and wept. In her heart she knew her threats were just that. She would never carry them out because of the gossip they would cause that would sully the memory of her mother, who should be allowed to rest in peace.

Laura was unwontedly silent at work next day. The other girl in the typists' room asked, 'Are you all right? You're very quiet.'

Laura could not tell her the whole truth, only part of it: 'I didn't sleep well last night.' That was certainly true; she had tossed and turned for hours and heard the town hall clock across the river chime midnight before she slept.

It was at mid-morning that she took some letters to one of the solicitors in the partnership. As she walked along the passage a door opened and Ralph Hillier emerged. She checked at sight of him, surprised. She had told him she worked in the offices of Wallace and Turner, had gently boasted of it, in fact. Now she wondered if he had come looking for her – and she found herself smiling. 'What are you doing here?'

Ralph closed the door behind him and gave a backward jerk of the head towards it. 'I've been to see your Mr Wallace. He wrote to me. Tremendous news! I was hoping to see you tomorrow but this is better.'

Laura clutched the letters to her breast. 'I can't talk to you here.'

Ralph laughed at that but nodded agreement. 'When do you stop for lunch?'

'At twelve. I have a sandwich in the park.' Though she thought she would probably feed it to the birds that day. She had no appetite.

Ralph said, 'We can do better than that. But will you meet me?'

Laura hesitated, had still not made up her mind about Ralph. 'My father found out about you. Someone saw us on the bridge that day and told him. He called me awful names.' Her voice shook as she remembered.

Ralph saw her anguish and said gently, 'Meet me and tell me all about it.'

How she wanted to tell someone. Laura said, 'Yes.'

He took her to the Palace for lunch but while he ate heartily Laura only picked at the food. At his urging she told him of the row with Albert and Doris, and of Albert's infidelity. Laura was almost in tears again when she finished, 'I can't bear to look at them, let alone live under the same roof.'

Ralph saw his chance: 'I told you that your Mr Wallace had written to me. I came in and saw him yesterday. He told me that my Great-Aunt Beatrice on my father's side had died. I haven't seen her in years because she and my mother never got on. She blamed my mother for losing Father's money. I suppose she was right there. Anyway, she's left a pile of investments in trust for me. I get an income until I'm twenty-five and then I inherit the lot.'

'That's marvellous.' Laura smiled, glad for him.

'Isn't it? When I saw him yesterday, I asked Wallace if I could have an advance and he coughed up today.' Ralph reached inside his smart jacket, pulled out his bulging wallet and opened it. Laura saw it was crammed with banknotes. Ralph laughed. 'See.' He tucked the wallet back in his pocket then reached out to take Laura's hand. He said softly, 'You know how Melissa treats me. I can't stand it any longer and I'm going to get out – now. Come away with me, my darling. I can't offer you marriage but I'll give you love and try to make you happy, a long way from here.'

Laura stared at him, open-mouthed, bereft of speech.

He said, 'Please! We can be together, leave them behind: Melissa, Albert, Doris, all of them. Come away with me, my darling.'

Laura said dazedly, trying to come to grips with this proposal, 'I don't know. I've never thought . . .'

Ralph urged, 'It will be a new life for both of us. You could never be happy with them now. Say you will come.'

'I – I'll have to think.' Laura did not find that easy, her mind in a whirl, being confronted suddenly with a situation she had never dreamed of, to go away with this young man. She would leave behind what family she had, her friends, the only home she knew, to live in another place among strangers.

As if he read her thoughts, Ralph pressed her. 'Wherever we go we'll have each other and our love. Don't turn me down. Don't break my heart.'

'Give me some time, *please!*' Laura held her hands to her head, eyes closed but in her mind's eye she could still see him smiling, pleading, promising. She could ask advice of no one; Cath Finley was in Scarborough on holiday with George. Laura hesitated long over this enormous decision, doubted as they sat on over coffee. She fought huge temptation as Ralph begged, vowed, smiled with all his charm. She was still not sure until they were back outside the offices where she worked — and she would have to leave him. She thought, what if he's leaving me for ever? And with that, Laura said, 'Yes.'

Ralph watched her slight figure walk into the office then turned away, exultant. He wrote a postcard to Melissa, saying, 'I won't be home tonight. Writing.' She would receive it in the late afternoon. Then he bought a suitcase.

Laura resigned from Wallace and Turner, giving as her reason that she was leaving the area. Her employers thought it very odd and tut-tutted because she had not worked her notice. But she was contrite and had always been a good worker, so they paid her up to date and gave her a reference.

From there she took a tram over the river, looking down on the ships lying in the Wear and being built on the slips in the yards on either side. She thought that she might not see them again for a long time and again she had pangs of doubt. But then she climbed the stairs and found Doris in the kitchen, cooking the dinner. Her stepmother screeched, 'What are you doing here? Why aren't you at work?' But Laura passed the kitchen door without a word and went into her own little room. She made a parcel of the clothes still in her wardrobe and picked up the other bundle which Doris had tied up the night before. Laura did not have a suitcase because she had never been away.

She cast one last glance around the little room where she had grown up then stepped out on to the landing carrying the two parcels. Doris was at the kitchen door now, wiping her meaty hands on her apron. She challenged, bullying, 'What are you doing? Where are you going wi' them?'

Laura looked past her into the kitchen that had once been home, with its shining brass fire-irons, dull now, the clock on the mantelpiece, the pictures of George V and his Queen. And that of her mother. She pushed past Doris and took that but nothing else. The place had changed and there was nothing there for her now. All doubt gone, she turned to the stairs.

Doris called, voice rising with anger and uneasiness, 'Where are you going?'

'Away. With the man I love.' She was ready to declare it now, her mind made up. Laura walked down the stairs and into the street with all she owned in her two hands.

She heard Doris calling after her: 'It's that toff, isn't it? You're selling yourself for his money. You'll regret it and come crawling back but you'll not get in here . . . !' The curses and empty threats hurt Laura but receded behind her.

Ralph was waiting for her at the station. She kissed him, not caring who was watching, and took the new suitcase from him. In the almost empty ladies' room she put her bundles on the table and untied them. She folded her clothes neatly and packed them in the case along with her mother's photograph and the few articles Ralph had bought. Two elderly ladies watched her, curious, but she left them wondering and rejoined Ralph. 'I'm ready.' He took the case from her and snapped his fingers to attract a porter who came hurrying to take it. They all went down to the train.

On the long journey south Laura quickly recovered from the trauma of the past few days. She felt she was embarking on a great adventure, a new life of freedom and love. She had made her choice and there was no turning back. She could not have second thoughts and closed her mind to everything but her need for Ralph. There was relaxation and peace of mind in that acceptance.

In London they took a hansom-cab, pulled by a trotting horse. It took them to a hotel and Ralph signed the register for 'Mr & Mrs Hillier', while the plain, thin gold ring he had bought in Sunderland slipped back and forth, too big, on Laura's finger. He had promised, 'I'll buy you an engagement ring in London.'

If the manager or the receptionist had any doubts about this slip of a girl they kept them to themselves. Ralph's money and casual confidence persuaded them not to ask questions. But it was a very good hotel, not some squalid place of assignation. Laura had eaten in the Palace but had never expected to sleep in a hotel like this. Still, she knew how to behave, had listened to girls who worked at the Palace, telling their stories of guests and their doings.

She felt like a princess as maids dipped in curtseys and a porter carried their case. Once in their room she said, awed and voice hushed, 'It's very posh. And very expensive, I suppose.'

Ralph chuckled and kissed her. 'Don't worry about that.'

Laura said, 'Just the same, we'll have to look for something cheaper.'

She yielded, breathlessly and willingly, to his seduction, at first shy but never stinting, reckless now the die was cast, drunk with happiness and passion. Then she slept curled into his arms.

It did not seem like sin.

Chapter Five

'Oh! Ralph, it's beautiful!' Laura clapped her hands in delight.

'It's not bad,' said Ralph disparagingly. 'It'll do till we find somewhere better.'

Berkeley Mansions was a terrace of big, old houses in a tree-lined Chelsea square. Several had been divided into flats and bed-sitting-rooms. The apartment in which they stood was high-ceilinged with tall windows. It had a huge drawing-room, a bedroom, a kitchen and a *bathroom*. Laura had always bathed in the tin bath in her cold little bedroom. She and Ralph now looked out of the drawing-room window at the tree-lined square before them, the leaves already turning. Other houses like Berkeley Mansions ringed a garden where children played and mothers sat in the sunshine, while nearby a milkman was delivering from a churn on his horse-drawn float.

Laura had found it. She had asked the porter at the hotel where they stayed where they might find a flat, and he had suggested, 'You could try Berkeley Mansions, ma'am. It's a big house in a nice part, owned by a theatrical lady as was. I know the chap who's the caretaker there, had a drink with him just last night. He said there was a furnished flat coming vacant. It's only a ten-minute cab ride from here.'

'That sounds nice. Thank you,' said Laura.

'You're welcome, ma'am.' He liked Laura and had told the night porter, 'She's a good sort, always got a smile for you. Not like that husband of hers. It's a tip today and a curse tomorrow with him.'

Now she looked at Ralph with doubt and hope. 'Can we afford it?'

'I think so.' Ralph laughed as she pulled his head down to kiss him.

'You're so good to me!' Laura danced away excitedly. 'We could hold a *ball* in here!' She pirouetted around the floor, on the rather worn old rug and weaving through the equally shabby furniture – but Laura did not care about that – she fetched up in Ralph's arms again. 'And those windows! We'll want new curtains with a twelve-foot drop!' Because the curtains she did care about. She would no more live behind those curtains than she would go out in some dowdy old dress. She looked up at him. 'Shall we tell Miss Ingleby now?'

'May as well,' Ralph said tolerantly, still generous with his new-found wealth.

So they descended the linoleum-covered stairs through the smell of floor polish to the ground floor, and told their new landlord, 'We would like to take the flat.'

Venetia Ingleby was something over sixty, a thin little woman with silver-grey hair, watery blue eyes and seeming fragile. She drifted gentle and watchful through life in a fragrance of rose water. Her own flat was crowded with furniture, bowls of artificial flowers and fruit under glass, and photographs of numerous gentlemen. It was by the front door of the building, with a bay window where she could sit with a very straight back. From there she could see past the aspidistra and through the lace curtains, watching all that went on in the square. For that she wore spectacles with gold wire frames, set aside now as not suitable for entertaining a gentleman.

She smiled and pointed them to chairs with a thin finger, the skin like paper with a web of blue veins. 'I'm so glad. You'll be happy there, I'm sure. It's cosy and such a nice outlook.'

Laura thought, But it needs new curtains. She only said, 'Aye.'

Miss Ingleby said, 'You are from the north-east, aren't you, my dear?' And when Laura nodded, continued, 'I thought I recognised your accent earlier. I came from those parts myself, Newcastle way. Then I moved south when I was offered parts. I was in the theatre.' She nodded towards a photograph on the wall, a portrait of a young woman reclining on a couch in flimsy draperies. Despite the unnatural colouring, the girl's beauty showed through.

Laura said, 'That's lovely.'

Venetia smiled faintly. 'So are you, my dear.' And to Ralph, 'You're lucky to have such a beautiful bride.'

Laura blushed at that, still not comfortable with the part she was playing, and wondered if this professional saw through it. But Miss Ingleby only smiled to herself.

Ralph paid a month's rent in advance and that night, while Laura slept, he wrote to his wife and his mother. The next day he and Laura moved into Berkeley Mansions and put a card on the door of their flat: Mr & Mrs Ralph Hillier.

The bastard! The letter shook in Melissa's hands. Ralph had written on the hotel stationery:

> We're leaving here tomorrow and not leaving a forwarding address so don't bother looking for me. I've had enough of your nagging and frigidity and from now on I am a free man. You're welcome to anything I have left behind because they would only remind me of you.

Melissa screamed with rage and Mary Ann, the cook/housemaid, came running. But the girl only got a flea in her ear when she enquired, 'Are you all right, ma'am?'

'Yes!' Melissa shouted at her. 'Mind your own damned business!'

Mary Ann fled. Melissa realised she had crumpled the letter into a tight ball. She was about to hurl it into the fire but then thought better of it. She might find a use for it later, if only as a reminder to stoke her rage and her determination to be avenged, on Ralph and the trollop who had run off with him.

She dressed carefully. That is to say she dressed to appear like a woman torn by grief and shock, who had carelessly put on any clothes that came to hand. At the big Corrigan house she found, as she had expected, that another letter from Ralph had arrived. When the maid showed her into the morning-room where Jessica Corrigan was seated, Melissa burst into tears. 'The most awful thing has happened,' she began.

'Yes, I know, dear.' Jessica hurried to put her arms around her daughter-in-law. 'We're so sorry.' She sat Melissa down and eventually showed her the letter Ralph had written to his mother: 'Dearest Mummy . . .' Melissa read it, picked out the phrases: 'loveless marriage . . . deeply unhappy . . . terrible mistake . . . cannot go on . . . new love.'

Melissa pushed the letter away. 'Oh! How could he say such things? I've tried so hard to make him happy.'

Jessica soothed her. 'Of course, we all know that. This girl has obviously turned his head. The pair of them are guilty, that's why they ran away. He will soon see through the little minx and come home, never fear.'

Melissa hoped so. She would be ready for him.

Meanwhile she had the comfort of knowing that the Corrigan family was on her side.

Dan Corrigan assured her of that when he spoke to her later. 'Couldn't believe it! Ralph must have gone out of his mind! He's treated you very badly. Now, you don't want to be in that house alone. You come and stay here where Jessica can look after you.'

Melissa thought, Oh, damn! But there was no help for it. She put on a weak smile. 'Thank you. That's so kind of you.'

She settled into the Corrigan house the same night, consoling herself that there was always Seth Bullock. That was her secret. And when Ralph finally came home, by God! She would make him suffer!

Laura settled down to domestic life – with new curtains she had sewed herself – and happily cooked and cleaned. One morning in the third week of their life together she hesitantly asked Ralph, 'Aren't you going to look for a job?'

He looked up from the newspaper he was reading, his legs stretched out before the fire, and corrected: 'A position?' Then he dismissed the question: 'No need. Don't you worry.' And when he saw the doubt on her face: 'I've plenty of money, but if I come across some work that attracts me I'll look into it.' He glanced at his wristwatch and rose to his feet. 'I think I'll take a walk.'

Laura offered eagerly, 'Do you want me to come?'

Ralph kissed her. 'No, thanks, you get on with cooking lunch. I'll be back for that.' He rubbed his cheek against hers and whispered, 'And for you.'

Laura blushed and laughed, then stood at the window holding her new curtains and watched her handsome young man saunter away around the square.

He returned for lunch but only in the early afternoon. Laura had tried to keep the meal hot but it was past its best, a sad affair. Ralph was in a cheerful mood. 'I met some chaps in the Duke of Wellington. It's just round the corner.'

'Yes, I know.' Laura had seen the public house. 'I—'

Ralph went on, 'Good chaps, sportsmen, good company. I lost track of the time.'

Laura explained, 'I worried a bit when you were late.'

Ralph's smile slipped. 'I hope you aren't going to whinge about me not being on time for this, that and the other. I had enough of that from Melissa.'

Laura flinched and she protested, 'I'm not whingeing. But you said you would be back for your dinner—'

Ralph corrected her: 'Lunch.'

'Lunch then, but it was always dinner at home. And when it got around to two—'

'Well, it doesn't matter. I'm here now.' He sat down and ate with appetite, and afterwards grinned at Laura. 'There, happier now.'

She smiled back at him. 'Always happy with you.'

He came around the table and put his arms around her from behind. 'Come to bed.'

'Oh! Ralph!'

Early that evening he ran out to catch a paper boy crying a late edition and returned scanning the racing results. 'I think I'll go out for a bit.'

Laura said, 'I'll come.'

'Afraid you can't, my dear. I'm going to the Duke and it's gentlemen only in the bar.' He stooped over Laura where she sat by the fire and kissed her. 'Won't be too late, I promise.'

Laura sat on. She would have liked to have gone out but was reluctant to venture forth in this strange city at night. After a while she took down the two letters, received a few days ago, from their place on the mantelpiece. She had written home, to Cath Finley and Adeline, the day she and Ralph moved into the flat in Berkeley Mansions. She had given them her new name and address but asked them not to pass the information on to Albert and Doris. 'I am very happy,' she wrote, 'and have no regrets. Ralph is very good to me and his marriage was a sham. I am not ashamed of anything I have done. I hope you will think kindly of me.'

Adeline had replied:

Just a few lines to say I'm sorry to have to tell you that you are the talk of the neighbourhood. I can understand why you ran away from Albert and Doris but with that young toff! And he's *married*! I fear you've made a terrible mistake but I hope I am wrong. I am glad you are happy. It was a terrible shock when we heard what you had done and another shock when Albert dropped down dead. Doris is saying some terrible things about you. I don't think you will be able to come home for a long time.

That news was no more than Laura had expected but it hurt none the less. She could well imagine the talk on the street and how she would be labelled. And return home? She would never go back. This was her home which she shared with Ralph.

Laura turned to Cath's letter:

When I read your letter I couldn't believe it, that Kitty's daughter had run off with a married man. But while I'm certain she would have been upset, I'm sure your mother would be glad that you are happy. She knew that kind of happiness once, before your father was killed. I've never met this young man and I just hope you've made the right choice. As for Albert Grimshaw being struck down, God forgive me but I can't feel sorry. The doctor put it down that he died of a stroke and heart attack. Doris said it was because you had run away but to my mind his own filthy temper killed him and serve him right. He was a sanctimonious bully and tried all he could to make your life miserable. He was guilty, more than anyone, of driving you out so you must not blame yourself for Albert. I wish I'd been home at the time instead of at Scarborough. I might have been able to help. You need not have run away to find a home. You would always have that with me.

Laura wept at that point, tears of thankfulness that she had such good friends. She returned to Cath's letter:

George is keeping well and sends his love. He had to sack Seth Bullock because he caught Seth selling timber out of the yard and pocketing the money. George felt let down because he had paid Seth well and trusted him. Now Seth has set up in a timber yard of his own and taken some of our customers with him. George was annoyed at first but says, 'Cheats never prosper.' He could have had Seth arrested but you know how soft-hearted George is. Anyway, we still have Frank Pearson, he is a good lad, and George has taken on another boy to learn.

That's all for now except to wish you all the best and don't forget us. You are always in our thoughts. Hoping this finds you as it leaves me,
    Your loving aunt,
    Cath

Laura folded the letters and replaced them carefully behind the clock on the mantelpiece. They were her link with the life she had left behind, the parts of that life she remembered with pleasure. Seth Bullock was not one of them. She was not surprised by his action and had never liked the man. She recalled his hands on her body and shuddered.

Melissa panted under the weight of Seth's body then clutched him to her. She had not had time to give him her news; he had seized her as she entered the house he had rented near his timber yard. It was little more than a cottage but Seth had boasted, 'I'll have a house among the nobs in Ashbrooke before long.'

Now, after their lovemaking, Melissa complained bitterly, 'That miserable, cowardly husband of mine has left me without a roof over my head.'

Seth stared at her. 'You mean he's sold the place?'

'No!' Melissa was scornful. 'He couldn't because he didn't own it. The house belongs to Dan Corrigan, but now Ralph has left, Dan says he can't have me left alone there and I've got to live in the big house with him and Jessica. "Like one of the family," he said. But I think that Jessica put him up to it, interfering old cow. It means I won't be able to move without telling them where I'm going or what I'm doing. When I left to come here I told them I was going for some exercise.'

Seth grinned. 'That sounds all right to me.' Then he advised, 'There's plenty o' money in the Corrigan family. You should be able to get your hands on some of it.'

'No chance of that. Master Nicholas will inherit the lot.' Melissa sneered, 'He's the blue-eyed boy and they're expecting him home from Japan or wherever he is before too long.'

Seth advised, 'Well, you keep your eyes and ears open. We might see our way to make a few quid. I can use it.' He went on to grumble about the difficulty of starting up a business but Melissa did not listen.

She dressed and left, saying, 'They'll be full of questions if I'm late back.' She mimicked Jessica, simpering, ' "We were worried about you, dear." That's what I meant. I can't call my life my own.'

However, when she returned to the Corrigan house she was all shyness and gratitude. 'It's so good of you and Dan to take me in,' she told Jessica. 'I felt so alone in that house now Ralph . . .' She stopped and dabbed at her eyes with a scrap of handkerchief.

Jessica was dressed to go out to dinner – to some function attended by local businessmen – and turning this way and that before the mirror as her maid watched anxiously. But she was quick to sympathise when she saw Melissa's tears, and took her hand. 'Don't cry, my dear, that son of mine – I'm ashamed to call him a son of mine – he's not worth it. Dan and I, we know the guilty parties. Ralph's made you suffer dreadfully and it's mainly his fault. It's obvious that baggage seduced him but he should have seen through her. She's after his money, of course.'

Melissa asked, puzzled, 'What money?'

Jessica was embarrassed. 'I didn't intend that to slip out, but you see he had a great-aunt on his father's side, Matilda, and she died recently. We never got on and I must admit I expected only a little bequest, but five pounds! That was an insult and she meant it to be. But Ralph was always a favourite of hers and he had a lot of money left to him in trust. *That's* how he was able to throw up his job and — and you, dear, and go gallivanting off to London.' She interpreted Melissa's silence as due to shock at Ralph's callousness, laid a hand on her sleeve and consoled, 'Never mind, he'll come crawling back to you one day, just you wait. Now, be brave and smile.' She squeezed and jollied, 'I know! You can help me choose my jewels for tonight.'

At that moment Dan Corrigan bellowed from his room next door, 'Don't forget your gewgaws, m'dear! No sense hiding them. Might as well wear them!'

Jessica gave a falsetto trill of laughter. 'You see?' She sat down at her dressing-table and took a key from her evening bag to open a locked drawer. She lifted the lid of the tortoiseshell box within to reveal necklaces, rings and other jewellery. 'What do you think of this, dear? And this? Or this?'

Melissa feigned admiration and interest, but thought bitterly that she was being humoured like a child and was now the poor relation. She would have murdered Ralph and that chit of a girl, given the chance, and if he did crawl back she would put her boot on his neck!

The Snug in the Duke of Wellington was aptly named, a small room with the entrance at one end and a polished counter at the other. There were leather benches down each side and a cheerful fire burned in the grate. It was comfortable and select. Where the bar of the Duke was reserved for gentlemen, the Snug was the province of ladies of a certain maturity. There they could reminisce about times long past and deplore the brazen habits of the young girls of the day.

Venetia Ingleby occupied her regular position at regular times, for an hour at noon and again for two hours in the evening. It was a seat near the warmth of the fire but from which she could see, over the counter, what was going on in the gentlemen's bar. She could also, by turning her head, with the gold-wire-framed spectacles perched on her nose, witness whoever passed by in the street outside. Venetia sometimes thought as she sipped her port and lemon that it was as good as the theatre.

She had seen Ralph drinking with the young bloods earlier in the day and again in the evening. Venetia had known a lot of men in her time and now she pursed her lips and thought, Well now . . .

And she saw him much later as he left the Duke, saw him lift his hat to the young woman who passed, full-bosomed and hips swinging. He watched her, as if hoping she would look back, until she turned the corner and was lost to sight. He shrugged then, clapped on his hat and walked away.

Venetia thought, Oh, dear. And sighed.

Chapter Six

'Damn them for their impudence! The bloody people want wage slaves to be tied to a desk all day! That's no occupation for a gentleman.' Ralph tossed his hat at the rack in the little hall but it missed and fell on the floor. He left it there, walked on into the drawing-room of the flat and flung himself into an armchair.

Laura sympathised. 'What a shame! I was becoming hopeful because you had been so long; it's past lunchtime. I thought you must have got the job.'

'No.' Ralph wrinkled his nose in disdain. 'I was in and out of that office in five minutes. I made it clear that I was a gentleman of means, not some peasant to be hired for a few pounds a month. On the way back I looked in at the Duke and had one or two with the chaps in there. But did we have any post this morning?'

'There's a letter for you, on the mantelpiece.' Laura went on eagerly, 'I made a pie and it's still in the oven, keeping warm. I'll serve it up now.'

Ralph was not listening, had ripped open the envelope and was scanning the letter. '*Blast!*' He screwed it into a ball, threw it into the fire and glared at Laura. 'That bloody solicitor you worked for says I can't have a rise in my allowance! He says the terms of my great-aunt's will were precise. I am to have the income of the estate for life but he can't release any of the capital to me until I'm twenty-five. That means he'll be sitting on *my* money for another two years!'

Laura tried to soothe him: 'I'm sure we can manage, if we're a bit more careful, and—'

Ralph stormed, 'I don't want to *manage!* Scrimping and saving! I want to get some fun out of life! The chaps are going to a race meeting tomorrow and I wanted to go along! *Hell!*' He stood at the window glowering out at the square.

Laura had become used to these tantrums, knowing that afterwards Ralph would be apologetic. She did not know how much Ralph received each month from his aunt's estate, but for the last three months he had complained of a shortage of money, and only reluctantly gave her the housekeeping allowance he had agreed to when they first set up home in the flat. So Laura had decided to do something about it. As she began to serve up the lunch she said shyly, 'I've a bit of news for you.'

'Oh?' Ralph's reply was politely disinterested.

Laura said, 'I got a job today, as a shorthand typist in the offices of some solicitors, Greenlaw, Norton and Field, and I start tomorrow. That should make things easier.'

'*What!*' Ralph frowned at her. 'I don't want you going out to work! I have my pride!'

Laura put her arms around his neck and smiled at him. 'I know, and you want me to live like a lady and I love you for it, but it will be better if we don't have this worry over the bills at the end of every month. And I do get bored, sitting in here while you are out with your friends. I'm looking forward to talking to some other lasses.' She kissed him. 'Now cheer up and tell me I'm a clever girl.'

'Well, if it makes you happy . . .' Ralph yielded grudgingly.

'Come and eat your dinner – lunch.' Laura pulled him to the table.

As he sat down, Ralph said, 'As you've got this job now, d'you think you could lend me a few bob out of the housekeeping? Just till the end of the month?'

Laura laughed, seeing the storm was over. She said affectionately, 'I'll see what I have in my purse.'

'I've got to get some money from somewhere.' Seth Bullock lay beside Melissa, both of them naked. 'I've the payments on the mortgage to keep up and I need more cash to buy machinery. I can't borrow any more.' He had also stolen a fair sum from George Finley over the years, but he had found it was nowhere near enough to get his business off the ground.

Melissa said bitterly, 'Don't ask me to try to borrow from Dan Corrigan. I'm living on charity there already.'

Seth did not care; he had his own problems: 'I can't borrow any more because the interest would ruin me.' Melissa's hand came, fondling, and he turned towards her but then seized the fingers of her left hand. 'Here! What about these rings o' yours? You've got rid o' that husband of yours so you won't need them now. You could pop 'em and lend me the money.'

Melissa pulled her hand away. 'I can't pawn them because Jessica's bloody son gave them to me and she'd soon notice if they went missing. Now if you had *her* rings . . . She's got a drawer full of rings, bracelets, necklaces.'

Seth sat up with a jerk: 'Where?'

They planned the theft carefully, chose an evening when Dan and Jessica Corrigan were to be out until midnight. It was ten o'clock on that moonless night when Seth scaled the wall surrounding the grounds of the Corrigan house and wound his way through the trees. When the belt of woodland ended he waited, looking out over the acre of rolling lawn at the side of the house beyond. It stood, a grey pile in the darkness, seeming to rise out of a sea of shadows that was the undergrowth about its walls. He was nervous and muttered impatiently, 'Come on!' He watched one particular window, found by counting from the left as Melissa had told him. And now a light glowed there faintly and he swallowed and moved forward.

Melissa held the light in the house. It was one of the new-fangled electric torches, usually called a 'flashlight'. She shone the beam of the torch around Jessica's bedroom, as if afraid some guard might be hiding there. Then she told herself not to be a fool and moved to the window, drew back the curtains and flashed the beam of the torch towards the trees for that one quick signal to Seth, then switched it off. The window was in fact a big bay holding three windows in line. She opened one, leaned out and lowered one end of the length of cord she had brought with her, secreted around her waist under her skirt. Seth's face was a pale moon in the darkness below at the foot of the ivy clad wall. She felt the gentle tugging at the string as he worked with it, then the two sharp jerks that told her he was done. She hauled in on the cord and seconds later the jemmy was in her hand.

Melissa paused then, hesitating. She knew what she had to do; Seth had schooled her. But the night was so quiet, she felt sure the slightest noise would bring the household about her ears. She had believed Seth when he had told her, 'Nobody will hear you. They'll all be down in the kitchen or in their bedrooms at the back of the house.' He was talking of the servants because there was no one else in the house, and she had believed him then. Now she was not sure. But he would be waiting down there, becoming impatient. She took a deep breath, leaned out of the window again and jammed the jemmy into the frame of the next window in the bay. She yanked on the jemmy and forced the latch on the window with a *screech* and a *crack!*

Melissa froze, breath held, but when no alarm was raised she let it out in a sigh. Now she opened the jemmied window, closed and latched the one she had opened before. It would now appear that some burglar had forced his way into Jessica's bedroom by way of the ivy. Melissa crossed to the dressing-table and used the jemmy again to lever open the drawer. The tortoiseshell box was there. She lifted the lid to confirm the contents and the jewellery glittered in the light of the torch. At the window again, she tied the cord around the box, making a secure parcel of it, and lowered it down to Seth.

At that moment Dan Corrigan's carriage, drawn by two greys, wheeled into the drive leading up to the front of the house with a crunching of gravel.

Seth, round the side of the house, could not see the carriage, nor could its passengers see him, but he heard its arrival and took fright. He snatched at the box, found it securely tied to the cord and fumbled frantically at the invisible knots for a second or two. He was on the point of leaving it there when he remembered his knife. He whipped it out and severed the cord then fled with the box under his arm. Away from the deep darkness under the house, he felt terribly exposed and ran flat out for the belt of trees. He plunged into them and almost immediately tripped over a root in the new-found gloom and sprawled his length.

He moaned, cursed and sobbed but was on his feet again at once and wending his way through the trees. When he came to the wall he buttoned the box inside his shirt and vest where its sharp corners tore his skin, but it left his hands free to climb over the wall. From there he trotted, sobbing for breath, for the last two hundred yards to where a culvert ran under the road. He hid the box inside the culvert and then set off home. He avoided main roads and always walked at the side, so he was ready to duck into the ditch if any searcher pursued, but none did.

Arrived at his house by his timber yard, he took to his bed. If the pollis came then he would swear he had never been out. If Melissa had talked he would deny all knowledge of the cow.

She, too, had heard the return of the carriage and had stood frozen at the window for some seconds. Then she saw Seth run for the woods and she came to life. She dropped the cord and the jemmy into the undergrowth below then whisked out of the room and into her own only a few yards away. There she stripped and put on her nightdress, let down her hair and braided it, then jumped into bed and waited, her light out.

Soon she heard activity in the house below, voices and movement. There was a tramping of feet in the corridor outside and Dan's voice: 'Madame was fine until we sat down to eat, then she felt faint so I decided to bring her home. Here you are, my dear. The girls will put you to bed. *Good God!* We've been burgled!'

Melissa arose, put on her dressing-gown and ran to the room she had robbed. There she found a distraught Jessica, attended by two of the maids, and a furious Dan Corrigan. Melissa listened to accounts of what had happened, and herself breathlessly explained that she had been asleep: 'I heard nothing.'

Dan said, 'Good thing you didn't. Lord knows what the feller would have done if you'd come on him. Something must have disturbed him; likely it was us returning, and he'd only had time to break in here. It was just our bad luck he picked the room with Jessica's jewels.'

He went off to telephone the police and Melissa comforted Jessica, who was not minded to sleep in the bedroom the burglar had just forced. Melissa organised the maids to put their mistress to bed in one of the guest rooms and generally added to her good reputation. Jessica would say later, 'She is a fine girl, one you can rely on. So calm about the whole awful incident. How Ralph could leave her, I don't know. He was out of his wits, of course.'

In fact, Melissa's nerves were jangling. Suppose Dan had come home earlier? Suppose she had not heard the carriage and he had walked in on her when she stood with the jewellery by the ripped-open drawer?

The police arrived and she steeled herself to answer them as a frightened innocent. She answered all their questions with just the right inflection of nervousness. The inspector confided to Dan, 'I think whoever did it had help from inside, sir. I doubt that a passing thief would have been lucky enough to choose the right room and the right drawer.' But suspicion fell on the servants and not the respectable young woman, a member of the family. Later, however, the inspector admitted, 'All the members of the staff have witnesses, other members, as to where they were.'

Dan stoutly confirmed, 'I don't believe any of them were involved. I've known them all for years. There's plenty around here worth stealing but we've never had any trouble of that sort. They're all totally honest. No, Inspector, with all due respect, I think this was a burglar who climbed up the ivy and struck lucky. The jewellery was insured so I'll claim and that will be an end of it.'

Seth collected the jewellery the following night. He drove out in a borrowed pony and trap and found the road empty. It was the work of only a few seconds to retrieve the tortoiseshell box from the culvert and hide it in a sack on the floor of the trap. He drove back to his house and found Melissa waiting for him there. She stood by him eagerly as he went to open the box. Seth grumbled, 'You made a good job o' this.' Because the box was still tightly bound with cord. He fumbled for his knife and then whispered, 'Hell and damnation!'

Melissa demanded impatiently, 'What's the matter?'

'I've lost me knife. Left it in the grounds.' He could recall falling in the trees, the knife in his hand, then scrambling to his feet and running again in panic.

'What about it?' Melissa asked.

'Suppose somebody finds it?'

'Why should they? I've never seen anybody walking down among the trees. And what if somebody did come on it? It hasn't got your name on it – has it?'

Seth shook his head, and grinned, seeing her logic. 'That's right. No need to worry. I'll just buy another one.'

He took a carving knife from a drawer, cut away the cord and spilled the contents of the box on to the table. They both gloated over the pile of glittering baubles and Seth said hoarsely, 'I'm all right now.'

Melissa corrected him. '*We* are all right.'

'O' course – us.' He reached out to her. 'There's money to pay off some o' the mortgage *and* buy machinery. Now we're in business!'

He took the jewellery to a pawnbroker in Newcastle who bought it without question and sure of a handsome profit, but Seth was satisfied because the price was good enough for him. He shrugged off the loss of his knife as of no importance.

*   *   *

Dan Corrigan was passing through the hall of his home some weeks later when a maid opened the front door, answering the ring of its bell. Dan stared, then grinned delightedly at his son.

'Nick! It's grand to see you!'

Chapter Seven

'Thank you, Miss Stanfield.' Adrian Norton smiled at her. He was a man of fifty, a partner in the firm of solicitors where Laura had worked for nearly three months now. She had to use her own name because her reference from her job in Sunderland referred to her as Laura Stanfield. She had given her address as: 'c/o Mr and Mrs Hillier, Berkeley Mansions'.

She smiled in return now, closed her notebook and picked up the file and draft contract from the desk. 'Thank you, Mr Norton.' As she left his office a young girl passed her and went in. Laura admired her summer costume in blue cotton with a narrow, ankle-length skirt. She thought, That will have cost her father a pretty penny. And she heard the girl say, 'Hello, Daddy.'

His voice came fondly, 'Now what do you want? Not

another advance on your allowance? Out of the question.'
Then the door closed.

Laura smiled because she knew Thelma from seeing
her in the office when calling on her father, overhearing
their conversations – and from listening to the other
typists. She also knew Thelma would get the money she
asked for. And that reminded her . . .

In the typists' room with its rattling machines she
dumped the file, contract and her notebook on her table.
She saw Miss Briggs, the typing supervisor, was intent on
her own work so Laura picked up her handbag and slipped
out of the room. She found Ralph waiting just outside the
front door of the office, as they had arranged, where they
could not be seen from the office windows. She gave him
the ten shilling note she took from her bag – most of the
pay she had received that morning. 'There you are.'

He stuffed it into his pocket. 'Thanks. You're a brick.
It's just till my cash comes through.'

Laura laughed. 'I know.' Thinking that he did pay back
the money he borrowed from her – most of the time,
anyway. 'Now get on with you.' She pecked him on the
cheek and then squeaked as he clasped his hands around
her waist and pulled her to him. 'Ralph! Let *go!*' She
laughed.

'Will you excuse me, please.' The voice was cool. She
realised she and Ralph blocked the steps to the office and
a lady waited to pass. She was pink-cheeked, in her late
thirties and elegant in a cream silk day dress with dolman
sleeves, and a neat little yellow felt hat. She could have

attended any *salon* yet there was an air of the country about her. Her glance, like her tone, was cool.

Laura had seen a look like that on Cath Finley's face when she had disapproved of some antic of Laura's. She moved aside hastily, dragging Ralph with her, and the lady passed with a stiff nod, climbed the steps and disappeared into the office.

Laura reproached him, 'That's naughty, Ralph.' But she could not help smiling. She pushed him on his way and darted back into the office before her absence could be noticed. On the way she passed Thelma Norton again, and thought with a grin that Thelma and Ralph were a pair; neither could make their allowance last out the month.

As she sat down at her desk, Eva Perkins came over from hers to whisper, 'Was that your boyfriend?' She was also a shorthand typist, a year or so older than Laura, brown-eyed, slim and pretty.

Startled, Laura asked, 'How do you know?'

Eva giggled. 'I was in the store, getting out some old files. I could see you and him from down there.' The store was in a narrow tower on the corner of the office building.

'Oh!' Laura had not realised she could be seen from there. 'Did anyone else see—'

Eva was already shaking her head. 'Nobody but me.' And then shyly, 'I've never seen your chap before. He looks ever so handsome.'

'Yes.' Laura knew of Ralph's effect on women. 'Yours is nice.' She had seen him meet Eva after work on some evenings, a stolid young man in a bowler hat and dark suit, a clerk in the City. Then she warned, 'Look out – Ma Briggs!' The supervisor had raised her greying head and was eyeing the girls over her half-moon spectacles. They parted, to Laura's relief. She was always uncomfortable when Eva wanted to chat, always afraid she would give away that she was living with Ralph. It was one of the many subterfuges forced on her, like changing her 'wedding' ring to her right hand before going to the office and replacing it when she left. But they bothered her less and less as time went by and she became used to acting her part.

Now she typed the contract Adrian Norton had drafted then took it to his office. She knocked at the door and entered when Norton called, 'Come in!'

Laura entered and he smiled at her. 'Ah! I think this is your contract, Mrs Beare.' He had mentioned casually to Laura that Mrs Edwina Beare was the wife of a captain in the Royal Navy. He had finished a tour of duty at the Admiralty and was now going back to sea, so they were selling their house in London and buying another in Portsmouth. Now Laura saw that Mrs Beare was the lady with the frosty stare who had passed her on the steps.

Norton glanced at the contract, saying, 'Miss Stanfield is very quick and accurate – reliable.'

Mrs Beare's gaze was on Laura, her tone sardonic when she drawled, 'Is – she – in – deed.'

Laura waited miserably for her to go on, to say that they had already met – and how. But Mrs Beare stayed silent, though studying Laura where she stood, wishing she could apologise and explain. But would this chilly lady understand?

Norton said, 'That looks fine.' And glancing up at Laura, 'Thank you.'

She backed out but paused at the door to say, 'Thank you, ma'am.' She saw Norton was puzzled by that but didn't care. Edwina Bearc gave her stiff little nod of the head again, but was there an amused twitch of her lips? Laura remembered Cath was always fair.

Laura returned to Berkeley Mansions at the end of that working day and called, 'Hello! Ralph?' as she let herself in with her key.

'In here.' His voice came from the drawing-room and she entered it after hanging up her coat in the small hall. She was startled to see a khaki-clad figure standing at the window, his back to her. At first Laura thought it was a stranger, but then he turned and grinned at her.

Laura took in the uniform, the visored cap cocked on the side of his head, the puttees wound amateurishly loose and not matching. She whispered, 'Ralph! What have you done?'

He saw the shock in her face and laughed, was quick to reassure her: 'I haven't joined the Regular Army! I'm a Territorial. You know the drill hall just a couple of streets away. One of their recruiting sergeants came into the Duke a few nights ago. He made a dead set for us chaps and we'd been celebrating our wins at the races — remember?' Laura did; he had not come home until past midnight. He went on, 'Vince Tully said, "It'll be a bit of a lark, boys." So we all joined.'

Laura laughed with relief. So he was not being sent off to India or some other far distant part of the empire.

Ralph went on, 'The battalion is going to camp on Salisbury Plain for two weeks in August.'

Laura smiled. 'I can spare you for that long!'

Ralph added, 'I have to go and train at the drill hall this evening after we've eaten. Then I'll be bringing the boys around for a game of cards and a drink or two.'

He did. It was after midnight again when the party broke up and next day Venetia met Laura in the hall as the girl hurried off to her work. 'I've had complaints from a number of the residents about the noise late last night. I do hope it won't happen again.'

Laura, crimson with embarrassment, assured her, 'Oh, no. I'm sorry.'

That night when she returned from the office she told Ralph about the meeting that morning but he dismissed it: 'Take no notice! Noise? We were only playing cards, for God's sake!'

'There was singing, too.'

'Pretty good singing, I thought.'

'It was coarse and too loud.' Laura was becoming angry. 'If you do it again then you can answer for it to the neighbours and Miss Ingleby. I won't. And I won't clear up the mess afterwards, either.'

He saw her anger and was quick to soothe her: 'All right, we will be quiet and no singing.' He slid his arm around her. 'Don't let's fight. I'd do anything for you, anything to please you. And I know a better way to spend the time.'

Laura resisted his advances for a while but he was charming, affectionate and patient and she gave in to him, as always.

It was in the early evening, a week later, that Laura came home, hurrying and excited, to find Ralph seated gloomily before the fire. Always sensitive to his moods now, she asked with foreboding, 'What's wrong?'

'I'm broke,' he complained, petulant. 'I had a bad day with the gee-gees. Every one lost. I told the chaps I'd see them tonight but I haven't a penny. Can you lend me a few shillings until my allowance comes through?'

So that was all! Laura was relieved. She said lightly, 'I can't; I've only a few coppers to last me until I get paid. But just wait till you hear my news.' She had to break off there to answer a knock at the door of the flat. She opened it to stare up at the young man who filled the doorway. He was in his middle twenties, in a well-cut tweed suit and carrying his cap in his hand. His hair was a thick, black thatch that looked as if he had combed it with his fingers. His dark eyes were hostile as he pointed to the card on their door, its legend clear. He stated grimly, voice deep, 'Mr and Mrs Hillier, I'm told.'

Laura saw the antipathy in that look and was sure it threatened trouble of some sort. She held on to the door and answered guardedly, 'It is. Why?'

Ralph's voice came from the drawing-room: 'Who is it?'

'Nick Corrigan,' called the stranger. He thought that Ralph's presence was enough to prove this girl's guilt. She was attractive but she would not make a fool out of him. 'I'm by way of being a relative of yours by marriage.'

Nick Corrigan! Now Laura was sure there was going to be trouble, knew why he had eyed her with such dislike on first sight. She did not want him airing the fact that she and Ralph had run away. She was not ashamed but she had to face the other people in Berkeley Mansions every day and did not want the reputation of being a loose woman. She held the door wide and gestured. 'You'd better come in.'

'Thank you.' He eased past her, Laura staring into his broad chest, and entered the drawing-room. She followed and saw Ralph still sprawled in his armchair before the fire, but watchful now. Laura indicated the armchair she had just vacated and invited, 'Please sit down, Mr Corrigan.'

'No, thank you. I won't be staying long.' He was not looking at her but at Ralph, running that gaze over him from head to foot. 'Ralph Hillier, I take it. We've never met but I was shown a photograph.'

'I saw one of yours.' Ralph's grin was tight now. 'Heard about you, too, till I was sick. From your father, everybody in the house, and in the shipyard. They all thought you were bloody marvellous.' But then he demanded, 'How did you find us here?' And he glowered accusingly at Laura.

Nick explained, 'Your letter had the address of a hotel. My father hired a detective and he talked to the staff.'

Laura bit her lip, then wondered how Nick had got past that sentry, Venetia Ingleby? She decided the old lady must have been distracted or dozing not to see him entering the house. It was too early for Venetia to be at the Duke of Wellington.

But now Ralph, flushed because it had been his carelessness that had given away his address, retorted, 'Bloody gossiping peasants.' Then he sighed with heavy patience. 'Well, anyway, you're here. What do you want? As if I didn't know.'

Nick was unmoved. 'What the family, or you, think of me doesn't matter. What does is the fact that you left your wife and ran off with this — lady.' He did not look at Laura but she felt tears come to her eyes at this cold accusation. She did not reply and he was going on: 'Your mother asked me to talk to you, to ask you to reconsider, honour your vows and go back to your wife. Melissa wants you at home, despite the hurt you've caused her.'

'The hurt I've caused her? What about how she's hurt *me*!' Ralph jerked forward in his chair. 'You've been running around the world looking at ships and you don't know her! You haven't heard her when her temper takes her, not as some of us have.' He shot a meaning glance at Laura and she recalled Melissa's savage attack in the foyer of the Palace Hotel. Ralph threw himself back in the chair again and said disgustedly, 'But you don't believe me. I didn't expect you to. She's a clever one, is Melissa.'

Nick was not impressed. 'I don't know the lady very well but I don't think I need to. I've got the answer I expected.'

Ralph demanded, 'So that's all you want?'

'Yes. Is there anything you wish to ask me?' Nick paused, then added, 'As to how your mother is, for example? Or Melissa?'

'My mother is well enough.' Ralph flapped a hand in dismissal. 'She's married to a rich man and that was her ambition, but she'll make a good wife for your father. She won't worry about me unless I sully the Hillier name. Melissa only wants me to wreak her revenge and I won't give her the chance.'

Nick nodded then added, 'Your mother had a nasty shock a couple of months back. Somebody broke into her room and stole a lot of her jewellery.'

Ralph was concerned for once: 'Was she hurt?'

'No. The theft took place while she and my father were at a dinner. She was upset, no more than that.'

Ralph said, relieved, 'That's all right, then.' He laughed. 'And you can't blame me for that. I've never been back since we came down here before Christmas. Did you think I might have done it?'

'No, not that at any rate.' Nick's bald statement

seemed to suggest there were other sins of which Ralph could be guilty.

Or so it appeared to Laura. He had shown his disapproval when he first saw her and after entering the room had ignored her save for that one scathing reference. Now she said coldly, 'I think you've said enough. I'll show you out.' She walked through the hall to the front door of the flat and held it open.

He followed her, then paused just outside the door. She moved to close it but he rested a restraining hand against it. Laura saw with surprise that the hand was broad, thick-fingered and calloused, a working man's hand. He said quietly, 'May I ask who you are?'

'Laura Hillier.' But he waited patiently and after a second or two she added, 'Laura Stanfield. From Monkwearmouth. One of the streets down by the river. You won't know it.' And because she thought she knew what he was driving at: 'I came with him for love, not money. I would marry him if I could, but I can't so I'm here anyway.'

He did not answer that or argue, but said, still quietly, 'I wish you would go home. I never saw Ralph before today but I think he is a wrong 'un and you're going to be badly hurt one day.'

Laura shook her head and answered him firmly and with passion because of what she knew now: 'You came here with your mind made up. You believed I'd made a set at him. *They* told you that, his wife and his mother. They sent you to try to come between us so you could take him back but it won't work. Ralph will stick by me and I'll stay with him. He's the only man in the world for me. But I don't think you can understand that.' That last was said with contempt.

Nick did not blink. 'I think I can but I must admit I have not met the only woman for me. I hope you're right about him. I've tried to warn you but you have a lot to learn, Miss Stanfield.' He turned away then and descended the stairs. Laura watched his broad back until he rounded a turn in the stairwell and was lost to sight.

She closed the door then and rested her back against it, for a moment exhausted by her emotions of shock, anger, hurt. But not fear; she had never thought that Ralph might be persuaded to leave her. With that thought she walked back into the drawing-room where Ralph sat scowling into the fire. She put her arms around him and said softly, 'Never mind. He's gone now. They can't touch us. And I have some news for you.'

Nick had been disconcerted. His father had told him: 'Melissa has been in tears. Some harpy has twisted Ralph round her little finger. Will you go down to London and try to talk some sense into him?' So he had come, though not liking the job, and expecting to confront a hard-faced adventuress. Instead he had found a smiling, pretty girl with a soft and vulnerable mouth. But then he reminded himself that beauty was only skin-deep, and the girl's behaviour, not her looks, marked her for what she was.

And Ralph? Jessica had said, 'He's really a good boy.'

Melissa had nodded and added with a catch in her voice, 'Tell Ralph I love him – still.'

They had asked Nick to try to persuade Ralph to return. Dan had taken Nick aside and muttered, 'To tell the truth I'm not sure about the chap, but do what you can.'

So Nick had tried. Now, walking away from Berkeley Mansions, he thought that he had achieved nothing. Ralph was determined not to go back to his wife. The girl was determined to stay with him. Nick thought she was heading for trouble and he had tried to warn her but she would not heed him. Laura Stanfield . . . A pretty girl. Pity.

He returned to Sunderland and reported his lack of success. Melissa, her eyes red from rubbing and mouth drooping to order, asked, 'Who is the girl?'

'She told me she was called Laura Stanfield.' And Nick added, awkwardly, trying to be fair, 'She's – not what you'd expect.'

Dan demanded, 'How d'ye mean?'

'She didn't look the kind who would do this.'

'That's her act,' said Jessica. 'That kind of woman can hide what she is, but never mind her. Is Ralph coming home?'

That was an easier question to answer: 'No.'

Melissa dabbed her handkerchief at her eyes and

Jessica put her arm around her. 'Don't cry. She'll soon tire of him, that kind always does, then she'll be off with someone else and Ralph will be back.'

Nick had only met Laura Stanfield once but he did not think she was 'that kind'. Ralph was another matter.

Chapter Eight

July 1914. London.

Laura told herself that – probably – all men were like that.
Ralph had been no more than mildly pleased when she
told him that he was to be a father. He had kissed her and
said, 'That's wonderful, darling. Are you all right?'

Laura had laughed. 'Of course I am!'

But soon he had reverted to his money problems, and
he had found the answer. 'Let me have that engagement
ring I gave you just before Christmas.' He had given it to
her to wear with the 'wedding' band.

Laura took it off, but only with difficulty. She joked, 'I
think it's on for life!'

But Ralph did not laugh: 'It will come off.' In the end
it did and then he asked, 'And the necklace.' He had given
that to her only a month ago.

Laura undid it but asked, 'What do you want them for?'

'I'll pop them.' Ralph stuffed them in his pocket. 'Never fear, I'll give them back to you when my cash comes through. I thought of putting my watch up the spout but a chap isn't dressed without a watch.' He kissed her. 'I'll do it now. Won't be long. It's just around the corner.'

Laura knew where the pawnshop was with its sign of the three brass balls.

Ralph returned very soon, whistling cheerfully. He jingled a handful of coins from his pocket and handed two shillings to Laura. 'There you are. You'd better have something. Can't have you with an empty purse.' He put the pawn tickets under the clock on the mantelpiece. 'I'll reclaim them when I get my remittance from that skinflint solicitor up in Sunderland.'

Laura thought that was an example of his generous nature, to give her some of the money he got from the pawnbroker, although she had already had her house-keeping allowance. She knew Albert would never have given money to her mother like that.

There was a letter from Cath Finley that said, among other things, that Seth Bullock was doing well since he had bought a lot of brand-new machinery for his timber yard. 'We think he must have had a good win on the horses, to have the money to pay for that.' Laura thought sadly that Ralph seemed to lose more than he won.

*　　*　,　*

Melissa stormed into Seth's house. 'That so-called bloody husband of mine!'

Seth looked up from the kipper he was eating for his tea. 'What's he done now, then?'

'Nothing! We sent Nick Corrigan down to London to fetch him back but he said he wasn't moving. He's staying with the little bitch he ran off with, some Monkwearmouth slut by the name of Laura Stanfield.'

Seth spat out a bone and grinned. 'Laura Stanfield? Well, I'll be buggered!'

He often walked down Dundas Street with its shops but over the next few days he did so searching. On the third day his patience was rewarded and he saw Cath on the opposite pavement. He hailed her, 'Hello, Mrs Finley! How's George?'

'Very canny,' Cath replied, suspicious of his enquiry and his smirk. 'Thank you.'

Seth bawled across the street, causing heads to turn, 'Glad to hear it. That was a shock about your niece, though, Laura Stanfield, running off to London with a married man.'

Cath's lips tightened. So that was it. She could not guess how he had found out but she took a breath and replied clearly, 'That's her business and none of yours. You'd do well to look after your own.' Then she turned her back on him, but thought, Oh, Laura, my little lass!

Ralph trained with his Territorial battalion at the drill hall on two evenings each week. On one occasion a friend of his came to the flat to meet him. Vince Tully stood an inch or two shorter than Ralph, but was broader, with a square face under neatly clipped hair. He stood in his khaki, cap in hand, just inside the drawing-room door, and said shyly, 'Evening, Mrs Hillier.'

Laura remembered him from times he had come to the flat with the others. Ralph had introduced them before they settled down to their cards. She recalled that Vince was quieter than the rest of the 'chaps'.

Now he reddened, plainly embarrassed, when Ralph boasted, 'Laura is blooming, don't you think, Vince?' He laughed and added, 'We're expecting a blessing on our union soon.' And then, eyeing her, 'Doesn't show yet, though.'

Laura could feel her own cheeks burning, but smiled forgivingly for Vince's sake. She kissed Ralph, he put on his cap, and he and Vince left. But before the door closed behind them she heard: 'That was a rotten way to treat your wife, Ralph.'

And Ralph's reply: 'Just in fun, old boy, just a joke!'

Laura did not think it funny, but she thought nothing could destroy her happiness now.

It suffered some blows as time went on. In late July her employers lent her to an associate in another office, whose typist had fallen ill. Laura soon adjusted to his machine and rattled through the work by the early afternoon. So he told her, 'No need for you to go back to your office or wait here. You may as well go home.' It was on her way back to Berkeley Mansions that Laura saw Ralph. He was standing outside the Duke of Wellington with its brass-handled doors and hanging sign of a picture of the duke, big-nosed and austere in his cocked hat. Ralph had his arm around the waist of a girl. His cap was on the back of his head, which was bent over her. Laura could see him talking, smiling. The girl, or rather woman — she was thirty or more — had a hard-faced, overt sexuality and was smiling up at him. She wore a barmaid's white apron.

Laura had stopped dead and now the woman saw her staring. Her smile slipped and she said something to Ralph with a nod of the head in Laura's direction. Ralph glanced that way, irritated now, but that turned to shock and then anger. He released the woman with a few words and a shove towards the door of the public house. She turned away and hurried inside. Ralph marched up to Laura and demanded, 'What are you doing here?'

'I might ask the same.' Laura's face was stiff. 'I finished work early and I was on my way home. Then I saw . . .' She nodded dumbly towards the pub.

'Oh, *that!*' Ralph laughed. 'That was Bella. I was trying to cheer her up a bit because she's got the sack.' Laura waited, wanting to believe but doubting. He saw that, and added reproachfully, 'It's a sad little story but one you hear every now and then. Don't repeat this because I've only Bella's word for it, but she was sacked because the publican wanted extra favours and she isn't that sort. She's a respectable married woman. Ask her yourself, if you don't believe me.'

Laura wanted to, but: 'Then there wasn't anything between—'

Ralph laughed. 'Never!' He bent to her and said softly, 'There's no one but you for me – ever.'

That was what Laura wanted to hear. She could still remember how he had bent this way to talk to Bella, but she told herself that he was just lured by an attractive face, and one in need of comfort. Laura was his only love as he was hers.

Ralph saw her acceptance in her face and tucked her arm through his. 'Let's go home.'

Laura believed him, but she took to meeting him outside the drill hall after he had finished his training. He still left her to go with his friends to the Duke of Wellington but they were not parted for so long. She was waiting outside the drill hall on the evening when Captain Jack Daubney visited the battalion on a tour of inspection. He was a regular officer, blue-chinned, black-moustached and darkly handsome. Tall and powerful, he strutted straight-backed in the red coat of his regimentals. He was bored stiff with the 'peasantry' in the Territorials and resented the duty in the evening when a chap was entitled to some relaxation – or sport. That boredom left him when he saw Laura.

He had just left the drill hall to board the cab waiting for him, the horse head-hanging, when he saw the little group of men gathered around a laughing girl. Her dark eyes flashed and the breeze that threatened to blow out the chestnut hair piled on her head moulded her thin cotton summer dress to her body. Daubney ran his eyes over her, seeing through the fabric, and told the cabbie harshly, 'Wait!'

He strode to the group. When they saw him approaching they fell back and stood to attention. He saluted: 'Good evening, ma'am. D'you mind if I have a word with these chaps?'

Laura blushed. 'Why, no.'

Ralph stepped forward and saluted. 'May I present my wife, sir? Laura Hillier.'

Daubney bowed over her hand. 'My pleasure, ma'am. You're a true companion to your husband and not one of those shrill career women one hears too much about.'

Laura answered defiantly, 'I have a job.'

He smiled good-humouredly. 'That puts me in my place.'

Laura said with pride, 'I'm a shorthand typist with Greenlaw, Norton and Field.'

He liked defiance and pride in a woman; it added excitement to the breaking. 'You're a clever girl.' He smiled at her, then turned to the men: 'I thought you all looked very well tonight . . .' He chatted to them for a minute, but mainly to Ralph, then finished by asking, 'And you are all local men, I take it?' Again, he was looking at Ralph.

He answered promptly, 'Yes, sir. I'm from just around the corner.' He would not admit to living in just a flat, presumed this officer had a house in town and another in the country.

But Laura supplied, 'In Berkeley Mansions.'

Daubney had learned enough. He said in feigned surprise, 'Good Lord! My cab's waiting.' He lifted a hand to his cap in salute to Laura and climbed into the cab. The driver shook the reins and the horse broke into a trot.

Ralph said, 'Seems a nice chap.'

The group agreed, but Vince Tully said, 'Joe Wilson, the steward in the officers' mess, says he heard our officers talking about Daubney, saying he was known in the Regular Army as Black Jack.'

'Why do they call him that?'

'Because of that black chin, I suppose. I don't know. That's just what Joe heard.'

Ralph shrugged. 'Well, he looks like a decent chap to me.'

He and his friends retired to the Duke of Wellington and Laura walked home. She was not sure she shared Ralph's opinion of Captain Daubney, had been uncertain when she had caught his gaze on her. But then she forgot him and let her thoughts drift to the child to be born.

Daubney carried the memory of her away with him, but next day he was posted to Ireland on duties that would keep him away from London for some time, to his annoyance.

He had been missed in his own regimental mess that

night. One officer said to another, 'Haven't seen Jack Daubney this evening.'

'He's inspecting some Territorials.'

'Makes a change. He's usually inspecting somebody's wife or daughter.'

He guffawed but the other said, 'He really is too bad. It beats me how he keeps his commission.'

'Because he doesn't get caught and he's a good officer.' That was true. Daubney cared for his men, in the same way that he cared for his charger, because he needed them. 'And if a war comes . . .'

The last days of peace were happy ones for Laura, content with her life and secure in her love. Venetia Ingleby, redolent of rose water, intercepted her in the hall one day. That lady eyed her shrewdly and asked, 'Are you keeping well?'

Laura blushingly admitted, 'I'm going to have a baby.' So then she had to take tea with Venetia and enter into details.

'Will you be able to manage those stairs?' Venetia asked anxiously.

Laura laughed. 'Oh, aye! I'm fine!'

The old lady smiled dreamily. 'I'm so happy for you, dear. I never had a child, I made sure—' She stopped abruptly and Laura wondered, With something unsaid? But Venetia went on, 'My profession, you know, the stage. Still, I had lots of gentlemen friends and that's almost the same thing, isn't it?' She giggled conspiratorially, then said, 'But I mustn't laugh. They were all most kind.' She was daydreaming again, now, a smile on her lips. 'The first young man who took me out – I loved him. I could have had my pick in those days but I was true to him. He was married to a slut who bedded every man she met. Then he went out to Africa – he was in the army – and was killed there.' Venetia's pale blue eyes were damp now.

Laura went away, but thinking over the conversation later she had reservations about Venetia's profession and the numerous pictures of her gentlemen. She recalled the phrase: 'Stage-door Johnnies', describing the men who waited at stage doors of theatres with a hansom-cab to take an actress or chorus girl to supper, and afterwards . . . Laura thought, amused and slightly shocked, Why, Miss Ingleby!

War came suddenly. There was a distant, small threat, an assassination in Sarajevo, that rapidly loomed larger and closer. Then an excited Ralph was ordered to join his battalion, dressed in his uniform and packed his kit. 'Don't you worry,' he told Laura. 'It'll all be over by Christmas. And I've left instructions with that solicitor in Sunderland. He'll pay you half of my allowance while I'm away, so you'll be all right.'

'I'm worried about you!' Laura tried to hold back the tears.

'Nothing will happen to me,' Ralph asserted confidently. 'Now, come on.'

So she walked with him to the drill hall and waited interminably outside in the summer's heat until the battalion formed up and marched off to the station to entrain. That was her last glimpse of him, and he was not looking at her. Vince Tully, and several of the others she remembered from their coming to the flat, grinned and waved, but Ralph's eyes roved elsewhere. Then he receded into the distance, just one more khaki doll in long ranks of them, blurred by her tears.

It was only the following evening that Laura answered a knock at the door and confronted a tall figure standing outside. For a moment of soaring happiness she thought it was Ralph, then the man's head turned fractionally towards the dim light on the landing and she recognised Captain Daubney – Black Jack. He was not in uniform but instead was dressed in a lounge suit and he carried a parcel in one hand. In the gloom his teeth gleamed white under the black bar of his moustache as he smiled. 'Good evening, ma'am.'

Now Laura plummeted from joy to fear: 'Has Ralph been hurt?'

'Ralph?' Daubney dismissed him with a wave of the hand, 'He's on Salisbury Plain with the rest of his battalion. I came to make sure you were all right.' He stepped towards her, automatically she gave way and he strode past her into the drawing-room. He glanced around him. 'Jolly nice place you have here.'

Laura had closed the door and followed him, relieved that he had not brought dire news of Ralph, but bemused. 'How did you know where we live?'

'You told me — remember?' He grinned. 'So it was easy. The cabbie knew where to come. I walked in at the front door and then looked at the names on the doors.'

'Oh!' Usually Venetia Ingleby intercepted strangers and residents alike, to satisfy her curiosity or just to gossip. But Laura remembered that at this time the old lady would be sipping port and lemon in the Snug of the Duke of Wellington.

Daubney was unwrapping the parcel, producing from the layers of brown paper a bottle of wine. 'An officer isn't supposed to be seen on the street carrying a parcel, let alone a bottle, so I kept it hidden. Have you some glasses?'

Laura did not like the way this was going. 'I don't want wine, thank you. Will you leave now, please.'

Daubney flashed a smile at her. 'I've only just arrived. And I do want a drop or two.' He produced a corkscrew from his pocket and started to open the bottle.

Laura threatened, 'If you don't leave I'll call the police.'

Daubney laughed at her: 'How? By smoke signal?' The cork was drawn and he ordered, 'Fetch a couple of glasses, there's a good girl.'

Laura did not know where the police station was and doubted if there would be a constable on duty in the square now. She tried to edge past him to reach the door but he put out one hand, gripped her arm and forced her back with easy strength. She gasped, 'I'll scream.'

'That would be silly.' He said it casually and his smile was still there but now it was cruel. Laura did not know what he threatened but was frightened. He went on, reasonably, 'And if you screamed or called the police, what would happen? I should say I was here by invitation. The door hasn't been forced, has it? I would say you demanded money and a jury would conclude you lured me here for that purpose.' Laura flinched at that, he saw it and knew he had scored a point. But he did not realise how strong it was. Laura knew she could never go to court, to admit to a jury that she had run off with a married man. They would find her guilty at once.

Now he said, soothing, 'I'm off to France tomorrow and all I want is the – company – of a very attractive woman.' He was forcing her to retreat now and she felt the edge of the table bite against her thighs. He bent her back, set the bottle on the table to free that hand and reached for her. Before he could seize her free arm Laura snatched up the bottle by the neck and smashed it over his head.

He staggered, stunned. '*Damn you!*' He released her so he could wipe wine and blood from his eyes and Laura was quick to put the table between them. She was panting, swallowing her fear but still holding the neck of the shattered bottle like a knife. There was a second or two of hard-breathing silence, then they heard the distant slam of the front door down in the hall and the tread of several feet as some other residents climbed the stairs.

Daubney was bleeding from a cut scalp, staunching the flow with a handkerchief turning crimson. His jacket was spattered with blood and stained by wine. He glared at Laura and said only, 'Another time.' Then he walked out of the flat and the door slammed behind him.

Laura went to the door and locked it, then sank down into a chair. She was shaking and cried a little, but after a while she set to and cleaned up the broken glass and the spilled wine. Later she decided to say nothing to Ralph. If she did he would want to make an issue of it. Then, when Daubney was acquitted and she was found guilty, as he had prophesied, Ralph would also be in trouble in the army. No, it was better just to forget. Laura took comfort from the thought that Daubney had said he was going to France the next day.

But then she remembered he had promised: 'Another time.' It was a long while before she slept.

Daubney was frustrated and enraged but not deterred by her determination to fight. That only added an extra spice to the seduction. And he assured himself, 'Some day I'll break her.'

It was a week later that Laura returned home and found Venetia in the hall, dwarfed by an officer in the blue of the

Royal Naval Volunteer Reserve. Miss Ingleby was smiling up at him, but turned as Laura entered to say, 'Oh, there you are! I told Lieutenant Corrigan you were out. He's come to see how you are, being a relative of yours. I said you were quite well, considering your condition.'

Laura managed to smile for Venetia. 'Thank you.' She kept the smile in place as she turned on Nick and said, 'You'd better come upstairs.' They left Venetia smiling — Laura thought of it as simpering — after Nick.

As they climbed the stairs, Laura promised herself she would have words with the old lady about discussing her 'condition' with strangers. She knew this Nick Corrigan had got in before by telling Venetia he was a relative, but she said no word to him until they were in the drawing-room. She rounded on him then, not offering him a seat but demanding, outraged, 'How dare you come here prying into my affairs! And you are *not* a relative of mine!'

Nick answered calmly, 'She stepped out into the hall as I came in. I gather she guards the entrance to some extent.' Laura could not deny that. But he was going on, 'The first time I came I said I was calling on you and she asked if I was a friend. I said I was related to Ralph by marriage. I could hardly qualify it by saying I was no relative of yours. As to my coming here now, I'm on my way to Portsmouth to join my ship and thought I'd look in to see how you were. Ralph had written to his mother to say his battalion was being mobilised.'

Laura knew that was true because she had prompted

Ralph to write a short note and he had complied, grumbling all the time because he was busy packing his kit.

Nick said now, 'I wanted to be sure you had no financial worries. A soldier's pay is small—'

'There is no need for you to concern yourself!' Laura cut him off. Nick had explained his presence but not to her satisfaction. He was looking down on her and, she felt, not just physically. She stared back at his polite lack of expression. 'I am quite well and Ralph has provided for me. You have wormed out of Miss Ingleby my "condition" but I can assure you it does not discommode me.' She was pleased with that phrase.

Nick was silent a moment, black brows knitted in anger now, then he answered flatly: 'I didn't "worm" anything out of Miss Ingleby. She volunteered the information but in all innocence. I expect she thought there was nothing to hide.'

Laura had expected that was the case. No matter; she thought she had landed a blow and now she would put him in his place: 'Either way, it was none of your business. Now I'll thank you to leave.'

'I must. I have to catch a train to join my ship.' He glanced at the clock on the mantelpiece and Laura was reminded that, while Ralph had reclaimed his watch and her necklace, the pawn ticket for her ring was still under the clock.

Nick was on his way to the door: 'I'll let myself out.' But in the hall he waited until she came to close the door.

Then he said, 'If ever you need help, please write.' He raised the cap in his hand in salute then strode away down the stairs. Laura watched him go and swore she would never appeal to him, no matter what extremity she was in. He heard the slam of her door.

Laura did not carry out her intention of taking Miss Ingleby to task. She decided it would only upset the old lady and possibly make her talk about Laura's 'condition' to more outsiders. But Venetia met her in the hall the next day and told her, 'I enjoyed talking with your relative yesterday. A real gentleman. A real *man!*'

Laura decided there was no point in trying to explain that, in her opinion, Nick Corrigan was a patronising busybody. Venetia was obviously infatuated. Laura thought, But God knows why! She smiled and went on.

She wrote to Ralph every day as August passed into September and he replied weekly. Her letters were of several pages, relating her doings, her love and beseeching him to take care. His were brief accounts of the training: 'They're keeping us hard at it.' Two letters asked for money by postal order: 'We spend all our cash on food.' Laura duly sent it by return of post.

It was on a Sunday morning towards the end of October that she was walking past the Duke of Wellington when Vince Tully came out of the bar, pulling on his cap. He looked smart in his khaki uniform, fresh-faced and fit, with an outdoor look about him. Laura called, 'Hello, Vince!'

He turned, startled, and for a moment Laura thought

he looked guilty. He smiled then, but it seemed half-hearted: 'Hello, Laura. How are you?' He was politely not looking at her obvious pregnancy.

Laura smiled. 'I'm well. But what are you doing here?'

'I'm on leave, a weekend pass.'

'Leave!' Laura said excitedly. 'Then Ralph will be coming home soon!'

Vince said hesitantly, 'I suppose so . . . I don't know . . . They aren't giving a pass to everybody. There's no system about it.' He started to edge away: 'If you'll excuse me, I have to meet someone.' He lifted his hand in salute again and then he was gone, striding away down the street.

Laura stared after him and thought it was as if he were running away.

The leave train was crowded on that Sunday night but Vince Tully strode up and down the length of the platform, shouldering through the crowds of soldiers who milled there. He found Ralph at last, sitting in the corner of a carriage. He waved a hand at Vince. 'Come on in! I've saved you a seat.'

Vince thumped down into the seat beside him. There was just enough room because the carriage was crowded with men in khaki. Under the noisy buzz of conversation, Vince leaned close to Ralph and hissed, 'I met your wife and she wanted to know when you would be home for a weekend. I had to lie to her, told her I didn't know, said you hadn't got a pass! You're being rotten to her.'

Ralph's contented grin faded. 'What Laura doesn't know won't hurt her. I'm supporting her. Isn't that enough?'

'No! It bloody well isn't!' That came from a heated Vince loudly enough to cut through the joking, laughing hum. Heads turned, staring curiously. Vince glared back at them and went on, but more quietly, now speaking into Ralph's ear: 'You're betraying your wife. And not only her – what about Bella?'

Ralph shrugged impatiently. 'That girl knows a thing or two. She'll survive. I wasn't the first with Bella, I'd bet on that, and I won't be the last, either. What has it got to do with you, anyway?'

'Nothing!' Vince's glare was for Ralph now. 'But you asked me to make your excuses to Bella at the Duke and then I had to lie to Laura for you. From now on you do your own dirty work.'

Ralph clapped him on the shoulder. 'I thought you were my friend.'

'I am,' Vince answered, still scowling. 'But I'm not making your excuses again.'

'Fair enough.' Then Ralph argued, 'Give me my due: I didn't know you would run into Laura. That was just bad luck.'

'No,' Vince admitted, 'that's true.'

'I'll apologise for any embarrassment I've caused you.' Ralph held out his hand, 'Shake on it?' Then, as Vince shook the proffered hand, 'Enjoy your leave?'

Vince nodded, silent now, wondering if that was the

last weekend he would spend with his parents. The lists of casualties, killed or wounded in Flanders, were long.

Ralph smirked, remembering Thelma. 'So did I.'

Vince sighed. 'Ralph, you really are the bloody limit.'

The train carrying young men bound for the war rolled steadily on.

Davey Milburn was a driver's mate, working at that time – he moved regularly for the sake of the change – for a High Street store; he helped the driver load and unload the van. He knew he was soon to go to the war. He had signed on and had to report to the barracks the next day. He was a jaunty, carrot-topped young man with a fetching grin and a way with the girls. That was why he now stood in the shade of the wall of the Corrigan house and estate. He had a liking for housemaids and had courted several, more than one from this house. The wall was high but it had not kept out Seth Bullock, nor would it deter Davey. He had an 'understanding' with his current girl. They had met on her days off during the past summer months and tonight she had promised to sneak out to see him. Davey's ardour carried him up and over the wall.

It was darker under the trees that ran close to the wall but he picked his way through them. The long, wide sweep of the shaven lawn was in sight when his toe stubbed against something in the long grass among the trees. He glanced down and saw the sheen of metal, reflecting the moonlight filtering through the boughs above him. He stooped, picked it up and saw it was a clasp-knife. He thought, That might be useful, Davey lad. But then he saw the girl running to meet him so he stowed it in his jacket pocket then opened his arms to her.

She fell into them. 'Oh, Davey, Davey!'

Chapter Nine

November 1914. London.

'Please, lady, can you tell me where I can find some cheap lodgings?'

Laura, hurrying homeward around the square, umbrella lifted against the rain driven on a cold wind, paused reluctantly. It was early evening and the gas lamps shed a wavering yellow light that was reflected in the puddles. The girl who had put the question was of her own height but probably younger. She carried a small, battered suitcase. Rain dripped from the hat clapped on over her piled brown hair and some tendrils had come loose to hang like rats' tails, or stuck soddenly to her pale face. Wide, frightened brown eyes looked back at Laura.

She answered, 'I'm sorry, I don't. I live in Berkeley Mansions there, but I wouldn't say it was cheap.' She had given up her job because of her pregnancy but had not mentioned it to Greenlaw, Norton and Field, her employers, who still knew her as the unmarried Laura Stanfield. Instead she had said she was returning to the north-east for family reasons. Her half of Ralph's allowance from his great-aunt's will was more than enough to keep her in Berkeley Mansions. She wondered how he had squandered so much of it while she had to husband her housekeeping allowance and take a job to eke it out.

Laura recognised the girl's accent, an echo of her own and a reminder of home. 'You've come a long way.'

'Aye, from Newcastle. I got off the train this morning.' The girl shivered. 'I'd heard of Chelsea so I thought I'd try to get a room here, but . . .' Her voice trailed away despairingly.

Laura asked, 'Do you know anybody in London?'

'No.' A shake of the head and another soaked lock of hair fell wetly. Her shoulders slumped and she looked like a disconsolate child. Laura hesitated and thought, She's not much more than a child, anyway. And alone in this teeming capital city. She made up her mind on the spur of the moment and invited, 'It's too wet for either of us to be out here. Come home with me now.'

'Well . . .' It was the girl's turn to hesitate. Possibly remembering stories she had heard of the city, warnings of its dangers?

Laura said firmly, 'My husband's away in the army.' Ralph had been in Flanders for the past two months. He wrote to her haphazardly, twice in one week, sometimes not for a week or two. 'There's just me in the flat. Come back with me and I'll make you a hot cup of tea.'

That decided the matter. The girl managed a weak smile. 'Thank you.'

Laura made tea and they sat in the armchairs before a glowing fire. The coal had been dug from Monkwearmouth colliery, less than a mile from where Laura hailed. In the comforting warmth of fire and tea the girl said her name was Sally Barnes.

Laura asked, 'What made you come to London?'

Sally explained simply, 'My dad was killed down the pit two years ago, then my mam died a month back. I could have lived with my auntie but she didn't really want me, and my uncle – watched me.' She hurried on, ashamed: 'I thought I'd come down to London and get a job. I heard there were a lot of lasses working in the munitions factories now.'

There were, but not near Berkeley Mansions. Laura said, 'You could try for a job at Woolwich arsenal and you might find lodgings cheaper there.' She glanced out of the window at the sullen clouds, the rain streaming down the panes. 'But it's right over the other side of London. Why don't you stay here for the night and go there in the morning?'

Sally, relieved and grateful, replied, 'Thank you. That's kind.' She hesitated, then admitted, 'I can't pay you anything except a few coppers.'

Laura said definitely, 'You hold on to your money.' She thought it was little enough, and – if Laura had not met her – this girl might soon have faced a choice, between starvation or a life on the streets. And thinking of starvation, she thought it likely that Sally had not eaten this day, saving her few pennies. 'I'll cook some supper now and make up a bed for you on the sofa in front of the fire. Then you can dry your clothes there when you're tucked up for the night.'

The next morning Sally was brighter with the optimism of youth. As they ate breakfast she chatted eagerly of her hopes for the future: 'A job on the munitions would be a start but I thought I might join one of the women's services, the VADs or something like that.'

Laura smiled at the girl's confidence but remembered how she had been yesterday when they met. Sally's confidence was fragile and she would need help. 'You'd better leave your case here until you have a job and lodgings. You don't want to be dragging it about and you can stay here tonight if you haven't found lodgings by then.'

'Thank you,' said Sally gratefully.

Laura, easier in her own mind with that arranged, saw her to the door. She opened it but only to find a woman with her fist poised to knock. Laura's surprise changed to instant recognition: it was Bella, the barmaid from the Duke of Wellington. She wore a tight-fitting coat, her bosom straining its buttons, a feather-bedecked hat and a fur tippet wrapped around her neck. Laura noted that and summed it up: mangy.

Bella was startled for a second or two but then her

coarse features set in belligerence and she demanded, 'I want a few bob.'

'What did you say?' Bewilderment jerked the words out of Laura. She had heard clearly enough.

'I said I'd come for a few shillings. I got the sack from the Duke. Ralph said he would see me right if ever I was wanting and I am now. I saw his address on a letter I once found in his pocket and I've seen him with you.' Laura recalled when she had found Ralph talking to Bella. But she was going on, 'He said he lived with his mother and his sister so if you haven't got the cash you can get it from his ma.'

Laura, still stunned by this confrontation, could only answer, 'I'm not his sister; I'm his wife.' Then she remembered she was not. The statement had come glibly, from practice. But then she decided she would stand on it; in her own mind she had always considered she was Ralph's wife, in his bed or out of it, and whatever it entailed.

'*Wife!*' Now it was Bella who was lost for words. She gaped, but only for a moment. Then she recovered: 'Never mind. He promised before he went off to the war that he'd look after me, so you can see me right — or I'll write to his Commanding Officer.' She stood with hands on hips, the feathers on her hat waving as she talked, boldly confident.

Bold as brass, thought Laura, outrage fuelling anger now, and she snapped, 'You can want all you like but you'll get nothing from me.'

'What?' The feathers shook. 'He promised—'

'I don't believe he promised you anything,' Laura flared. 'He was always open-handed with his money. You know all those lads who used to meet in the Duke are away in the army and you thought this would be a soft touch.'

Bella countered furiously, 'Are you calling me a liar?'

'Aye! And I'll call you a sight worse than that! So you can get it into your head that you won't worm any money out of me!'

The barmaid persisted: 'I tell you he said—'

'I don't care what *you* say. You won't get a penny from me!'

'I'll send a letter to the army.' But it was a weak threat, the fight going out of her as she saw Laura was implacable.

Now she rubbed it in: 'You can write to Kitchener or the King for all I care!'

The postman, in his fifties, had come puffing up the stairs behind Bella and now asked her, 'Excuse me, gel, I just have to deliver this.' And as she automatically stepped backwards and aside, he said, 'Here y'are, missus,' and handed the letter to Laura. Then he turned and clattered off down the linoleum-covered stairs.

Laura did not open the envelope but slammed the door in Bella's face and sank back against it. Her heart was pounding and she nodded when Sally said anxiously, 'You've gone a bad colour. Come and sit down.' Laura let Sally take her arm and lead her on wobbly legs to a chair in the drawing-room. As she sat down she remembered the letter clutched in her hand. It was addressed to:

Mrs R. Hillier. She tore open the envelope and took out the single sheet of folded paper. She spread it out and saw from the date at its head that it had been written two days before.

Laura still raged at Bella's insolence. She knew the barmaid had told a pack of lies, as Laura knew Ralph was a man who attracted some women. But he loved *her*! Bella was one of those women, had probably received some kindness from him, of word or deed, and misinterpreted it as a token of a deeper interest in her. But there Bella had fooled herself because there was no one for Ralph but Laura, she was sure of that.

The address at the top of the letter was that of a military hospital in Hampshire. Laura thought, Oh, God! Not Ralph! But the writing was not his. Her eyes sought the signature and she breathed again; it had been written by Vince Tully. He said:

> You will have been given the news by now and all I can say is how sorry I am. We were in an attack and a few of our old gang from the Duke were killed. I was caught in machine-gun fire, wounded twice and held up on the wire. Ralph lifted me off and dragged me back to our trenches. He saved my life but then he was hit. It may be some consolation for you to know that he died instantly and did not suffer.

The letter fell from Laura's fingers and she cried in anguish, '*Ralph!*' She realised that he had been dead for days.

Laura only learned much later that he had given his mother's name and address as 'next-of-kin', so the official notification of his death had gone to her. Now Laura was only dimly aware of a frightened Sally crying, 'I'll fetch some help!'

Then she and Venetia were helping Laura into the bedroom and the old woman was telling the girl, 'Run and bring the doctor.' But he was too late and Venetia delivered the child, a little girl. She was several weeks premature and survived for only a few hours.

Laura registered her child's name as Catherine Stanfield and the surname meant she had to explain to Venetia and Sally. 'I wasn't married to Ralph.'

The girl was surprised and a little shocked: 'You mean . . .'

Laura said weakly, wearily, not caring now, 'We were living in sin.'

Venetia only shrugged. 'I thought that was the way it was but I took to you as soon as I saw you, so pretty and so happy.' She paused, was about to add a rider but decided against it. Laura had suffered enough and, besides, you should not speak ill of the dead.

Sally and Venetia cared for Laura. When she was well enough they took her to the cemetery where her child had been buried. Laura stood at the foot of the grave, marked by its small headstone. The day was bitterly cold and the trees blackened by rain to match her mourning dress. Laura had wept until she was dry-eyed. She could go home to her Aunt Cath who would be loyal, but Laura could not ask her to face the disapproval she was sure she would meet. That was not just in Monkwearmouth but a fact of life at that time. If Ralph had been alive to comfort her in her loss . . . But he was not and she was alone in the world.

Chapter Ten

'There's a letter for you,' said Sally Barnes. She handed it to Laura and sat down again opposite her at the breakfast table. The room was lit by pale winter sunshine, the sky a pale blue and Laura could see children playing in the square, wrapped up against the cold. Their voices came to her thinly, laughing, a painful reminder of her own daughter. Physically she was recovered but she still grieved at times like this. Now she turned to the letter.

It came from the Sunderland solicitors, Wallace and Turner, who had paid Ralph's allowance, and later, half of it to Laura. They wrote, stiffly sympathetic, but saying that now Ralph was dead the income from his great-aunt's trust fund would, under the terms of her will, pass to another, more distant cousin. Laura would not receive any more money.

She laid the letter down. She grieved for Ralph as she did for little Catherine. She conceded that he had his faults – he was careless, a gambler and attracted by a pretty face – but he had been her lover, the only man for her, and she loved him still. He had provided for her while he could but now she must fend for herself. She had saved some money from her earnings at Greenlaw, Norton and Field and she could go back to them now, but this flat was an extravagance she could no longer afford.

Laura grinned at Sally. 'We're both looking for cheaper digs now.'

Sally said tactfully, 'I thought you might, after . . .' She did not finish but inferred that Ralph's death meant a loss of income to Laura as well as the deeper hurt. 'Now you're better I can go out looking for a job and a room.'

'Look for two of us.' Laura was grateful for the way the girl had cared for her during and after the birth. She thought that they needed each other now. 'It will be cheaper if we share.'

Sally's face lit up. 'I hoped you might say that.' Then she admitted, 'I didn't fancy being on my own.' And soon afterwards she called, 'Ta-ra!' and set out to find work in the arsenal at Woolwich.

Venetia Ingleby looked in at mid-morning, accepted a cup of tea and gossiped for a while. Then, happy that Laura was fully recovered, she went off to the Duke of Wellington: 'To get something to keep out the cold.' And she coughed in ladylike fashion. She had offered, 'I'll lower your rent so you can stay on.' But Laura suspected the old lady needed the money so she refused, with thanks for that and Venetia's help when she collapsed.

Laura was not expecting any caller when there came a knock at the door. She opened it, smiling, and Nick Corrigan towered over her, saying, 'Good morning.' He was in uniform again, dark blue with the two wavy gold rings embroidered on his cuff of a lieutenant in the Royal Naval Volunteer Reserve.

Laura's smile vanished. 'What do you want?'

Nick saw that and was angered, but kept it under control. 'I'm on my way to the Gunnery School. I had a letter from my father. He told me about Ralph and said Jessica was very upset. I'm sorry.'

'Are you?' Laura questioned. 'You never liked him.'

'I didn't wish him dead,' Nick replied, 'for your sake as well as his.'

'You made it clear how you felt about the pair of us, that he'd run away from his wife and I was after his money, just his fancy woman. I bet you haven't changed your mind.' Then she said with bitter triumph, 'I thought so. I can see it in your face. Now go away.'

Nick cursed to himself because he had not been able to hide his feelings. 'Wait!' He jammed his foot in the closing door and added quickly, 'If you want an honest answer then, yes, I didn't trust Ralph and I haven't changed my opinion of him – or you. But now you're left on your own, I'm concerned. Do you need any help – or the child?'

'No! I'd never take anything from you!' Laura knew

that wasn't true. If little Catherine had survived and she had needed help with the child she would have taken it from anyone rather than let her suffer. But Catherine had not survived. She was left with only her memories and her pride and she would not mention the loss of her child to this man. She saw she had hurt him, though not as much as he had wounded her. 'Now leave me alone.'

'I'm sorry.' Nick withdrew his foot. 'But if ever you are in need—'

Laura slammed the door on him, walked back into the drawing-room on shaky legs and sat down at the table. She stared out at the square, at first unseeing but then he appeared, long-striding, straight in the back, and head and shoulders above the other men he passed. Laura thought that Venetia, sitting in the Snug of the Duke of Wellington, would be sorry she had missed him. Laura did not want to see him again, would not mention his visit to Venetia. She watched him walk away from her and then the tears came.

Laura was brighter when Sally came home in the late afternoon to say, 'I've found a nice room with a little kitchenette.' She paused then for effect, then announced, 'And I've got a job making fuses for the guns, in Wandsworth! I went to the labour exchange and the clerk there sent me to this factory. I start tomorrow!'

'That's wonderful!' Laura greeted the news with enthusiasm. 'When can we move into the room?'

'Any time from next Monday.' Sally added anxiously, 'I paid a week's rent in advance. Is that all right?'

'Yes.' Laura was firm on that. She had thought to stay at Berkeley Mansions until the end of the month when her lease ran out, but now she wanted to get away, so Nick Corrigan could not find her. She wanted no more of him, censorious and disapproving. She would not let him mar the love and happiness she and Ralph had shared.

Vince Tully called the next day. He appeared hesitantly in the evening, dressed in the baggy, royal-blue uniform of the convalescent wounded. Sally Barnes opened to him, dropped her gaze before his and called to Laura, 'There's a soldier asking for you!'

Laura recognised him and invited, 'Come in!' And to Sally, 'This is Vince Tully, a friend of Ralph – and me.'

Vince had been transferred to a local hospital and this was his first day out. He came to offer his condolences and reassurance. As he drank the cup of tea they pressed on him he said, 'Ralph was as happy as anyone could be out there.' Like all the veterans come back from the front he did not describe the full horrors of trench life. 'He was a good soldier, a good mate when things got rough. He saved my life and he didn't suffer.' He thought, Not when he was shot, anyway. Before that, when they were living in rat-infested holes cut in the side of the trench, was another matter.

'Thank you for coming to tell me,' Laura said chokily. 'You've made me so proud of Ralph. I'm so lucky to have had him for a while.'

Vince left then, with another — there had been several — shy glance at Sally. She, equally shyly, blushed and looked away. As he descended the stairs he told himself guiltily, 'Well, you couldn't tell her all the truth about him.' He shrank from the thought. Instead he recalled the girl he had just left: Sally Barnes. He would remember her . . .

The new room was small with only one window which looked out on to a dark and dismal alley and the opposite blank, brick wall. The glass was coated white with frost when Laura called, 'Sally! Wake up!' She shook the girl, who had slept through the strident jangle of the alarm clock, and now she groaned and turned over. Laura got out of the bed they shared and took the bedclothes with her. Sally yelped and hugged herself, curled up in her nightgown, but Laura knew her by now and said without mercy, 'If you're late they'll dock some of your pay.'

That jerked Sally awake; the munitions factory only paid her fivepence halfpenny an hour — twenty-two shillings for a forty-eight-hour week. She could not afford to lose any of it and now rolled from the bed. 'Oh, God! Bless you, Laura.'

They washed and dressed, breakfasted hastily on tea and bread and butter — not toast because the fire had gone out — and made the bed. As they shrugged into their coats, Sally's dragged on over an overall, she said, 'You do always turn yourself out smart.' Laura's coat was black as she was still in mourning, cheap because it was bought second-hand, but well fitting. Together they clattered along the uncarpeted wooden floor of the passage and out into the street. There they parted, Sally to hurry away to the fuse factory, Laura to climb aboard a bus to become again Miss Laura Stanfield, shorthand typist for Adrian Norton and the other members of the partnership. She still grieved and would for a long time. She was trying to pick up the pieces of her life again but finding it hard. There were too many memories.

As Laura stepped down from the bus and crossed the road to the office she remembered how Ralph sometimes came to meet her there. She often thought of him, though without tears now. This time she was reminded of Nick Corrigan's visit not long ago. That memory angered her. He had said he was going on a gunnery course and Laura wondered if he would look for her again when the course was finished. She thought with satisfaction that he would not find her in Berkeley Mansions. She had left her new address with Venetia to forward any mail, but with strict instructions to give it to no one. That would rid her of him.

Nick had sought her when the course was done and had to admit defeat. Venetia had peered up at him out of watery blue eyes and said sadly, 'I haven't an address I can give you.' She had watched him go then sighed and shut her door.

He returned home for a short leave, to be welcomed heartily by Dan: 'It's good to see you again!' That was followed by the inevitable question: 'How much leave have you got?'

'Just a week.' Nick grinned ruefully. 'Lucky to get that. I only wangled it through being on the course. Lots of men on foreign stations go years without home leave.'

Jessica fussed over him and Melissa hovered coyly in the background. She quickly reassessed her situation. 'It's lovely to have you home again, Nick.'

His grin shifted to her then faded and he said gravely, 'Sorry about Ralph.'

Melissa smiled bravely. As a dependent member of the family by marriage she had, out of Dan's generosity, a comfortable home and security. But she found it constricting. She sought her pleasure with Seth Bullock but had to indulge it secretly. She knew that if word of that got out then the Corrigans would wash their hands of her. 'Let me take your coat, Nick. Can I fetch you a drink?'

Seth had progressed, and was progressing rapidly in business. The war had brought a huge demand for ships and Seth supplied a lot of joinery such as ladders. He had taken on a half-dozen men who were certified unfit for the army. They were working in shifts, eighteen hours a day, and he was now considering a night shift.

'No, don't get up, Nick. Here's your whisky and just a splash of soda.' Melissa would find a home and satisfaction of her desires with Seth but while she was passionate she was also cautious. She would not throw in her lot with

Seth, and lose her place in the Corrigan household, until she was sure he was bound for the top.

'I'll just sit here.' Melissa sank down gracefully at his feet on the rug before the fire. 'There we are, all comfy.' She smiled up at him. There was a way for her to achieve fortune and position. If she was to marry the only son of the house . . .

Melissa courted Nick. They met daily and all day, she saw to that. If Nick took a walk she accompanied him. She was always ready to talk or listen. She made sure the maids washed and cleaned all his kit then presented it to him herself. She partnered him at whist, was serious when need be but otherwise a smiling, cheerful companion. She wore her widow's weeds as she must but saw that they enhanced her figure. She casually, but with seeming innocence, moved so that she hinted at the sensual body inside the black silk.

Nick accepted her as one of the family and her innocence at face value. He thought of her as a sister and a widow grieving but bravely trying to hide her pain. And that was all.

Melissa's patience ran out on the night before he returned to duty. She retired to bed in the evening but waited in her room until he came to pass her — slightly open — door on the way to his own. She saw him through the crack and swung the door wide as he drew level. With pretended surprise she put a hand to her mouth: 'Oh, Nick! I thought I heard Jessica.' She wore a thin cotton nightdress and the light behind her shone through it to show the lines of her body. Melissa knew he could also see the bed behind her, and said huskily, a break in her voice, 'I wish you weren't going.' She fell against the broad strength of him.

Nick was startled, aroused and his arms went around her, could feel her warm suppleness. But then he remembered this young woman had been deserted by her husband and then widowed. She had come to this house as a refuge and he must not betray that trust, though temptation was strong. It would be easy to take her, use her, and his body wanted her. But he would also hurt her because she was looking for love and he could not give her that.

He eased her away from him and said gently, 'You've suffered too much and you're overwrought. You've made my leave pleasant. Thank you.'

Melissa knew she had gambled and lost. It was time to recover as much as she could. She brushed at imaginary tears with the heel of her hands, blinked and smiled weakly at him. 'You must think I'm a silly neurotic woman.' She looked down at herself and acted surprised and confused. 'Oh!' She hurriedly stepped back into her room and peered out from behind the part-closed door. 'I must have embarrassed you. I'm sorry, and sorry to have broken down like that. We've had such good times. I even managed to think about dear Ralph without crying. Now I've spoiled it.'

'No,' Nick denied gallantly. 'Think no more of it.'

Melissa asked tremulously, 'Still friends?' And when he

nodded, 'Be careful, Nick. Come back to us.' She closed the door and he walked on.

Nick knew she had offered herself to him but decided it was because she was lonely and heartbroken, seeking comfort at any price. But later there was still a small germ of doubt in his mind about Melissa and it would not go away. He recalled Ralph complaining about his wife – for what his word was worth. And following that train of thought he wondered about the Stanfield girl – Laura. He realised he knew little about her, except that she hated him.

Laura met Sally by chance that evening. The fog had come down in the afternoon, a London 'pea-souper' so thick you could see only a few feet ahead. Buses and cars just crawled along, their headlights shedding only a flat glow that reflected back on itself and showed the drivers little. The journey seemed to Laura to last a year before the conductor bawled out the name of her stop. She squeezed out of the bus, crammed with office workers returning home, as the girl was walking by. Sally greeted her glumly, 'I'm glad that's over for the day.'

Laura glanced at her. 'Another bad one? I think that factory is getting you down.' Then she asked herself, What about you?

'We-ell.' Sally dragged out the word, hesitating as they linked arms while they walked. 'It's – boring now, doing the same thing over and over again, hour after hour . . .'

Her voice trailed away but Laura thought she had not finished, and waited. Sally lowered her voice so Laura could barely hear her: 'And that foreman, he touches me, whispers in my ear. I wanted to get away from all that.'

Angered, Laura asked, 'Can't you complain to the manager?'

Sally shook her head. 'I think they would believe him sooner than me. He's an engineer and practically runs the place. They could find a girl to do my job any time.'

Laura guessed tears were not far away, squeezed the arm linked through hers and ordered, 'Don't go back. Write and tell them you're finished.'

'But I'm owed two days' pay,' Sally protested.

'We'll manage without that, between us,' Laura assured her.

Sally, relieved already with the threat of the morrow removed, said, 'I'll write tonight.' Then she added, 'I'll have to find another job.' Laura stopped in her tracks, staring, and Sally asked, 'What is it?'

Laura said frustratedly, 'I feel I'm just sitting on the side and watching this war.' She stood under a street lamp that shed a cone of light, and pointed. The glow just reached the poster she had seen daily for the past week: a young woman in drab uniform beckoned, inviting girls to join the Voluntary Aid Detachments.

Sally said doubtfully, 'Do you think I should try to get in?'

'Both of us.' Laura would not send the girl away while staying in her own job. But would this be any different?

As if to point this out, Sally said, 'It says they want cooks and typists . . .'

So Laura might well end up in some government office in London and still typing. She did not want that, wanted to get away, start again.

As she hesitated a woman appeared out of the fog, a silk scarf wrapped across her face against the dampness, heels clicking on the wet pavement. She was about to pass by but stopped. Laura saw the eyes above the scarf were fixed on her, then its wearer lowered it to say, 'Good Lord! Aren't you the girl from Adrian Norton's office?'

Laura recognised and remembered Mrs Edwina Beare, wife of a Royal Navy captain, who had moved to Portsmouth. Who had seen her with Ralph on the steps of the office – and held her tongue. 'Yes, ma'am.'

Edwina Beare smiled. 'The last time I had reason to visit Adrian he told me you'd left to go up north. Are you back with him now?'

'Yes.' Laura did not want to tell her story again, least of all to a stranger. She glanced at the poster: 'We were thinking . . .' She stopped, unsure about the VADs now.

Mrs Beare had followed her gaze. 'They do need girls; but you're not sure?'

'I – I don't want just to move to another office. I want to get away.'

Mrs Beare thought, From what? Who? But that was not her business and she got down briskly to what was: 'I'm organising an ambulance column. It's not army, but funded by public subscription like Lady Paget's column. I have doctors and nurses but still need some drivers.'

Laura had heard of Lady Paget's hospital for wounded soldiers, but admitted, 'We can't drive.'

'Matthew Bellamy will soon teach you to drive.' That was said confidently. Mrs Beare went on, 'He's a mechanic and owns a garage. He tried to join the army but they told him he was too old. That annoyed him and he came to me. And I promise you won't be in another office. Are you game?'

Laura looked at Sally and they nodded together.

Laura did not care but Sally asked, anxious, 'Where?'

Black Jack Daubney came to Berkeley Mansions on his first leave and Venetia told him, 'I don't know where she's gone.' Then he tried the offices of Greenlaw, Norton and Field and was told, 'We don't have a Mrs Hillier on the staff.' He cursed at that, but then shrugged and went after other prey. But he was determined to hunt down the Hillier girl one day.

Chapter Eleven

Spring 1915. Serbia.

'Oh, no!' Sally said wearily, soft brown eyes mournful. She and Laura were in the middle of the column of seven Ford motor ambulances, all painted slate grey and with big red crosses on their sides. 'Is this it?' The 'hospital' was an ancient, two-storey building that might once have been a school. Now it was derelict, cold and forbidding under the rain. That had started on the day they disembarked. On the voyage out on a great troopship, garish with dazzle paint to confuse a U-boat's aim, they had practised first-aid out on the deck all of every day. The sun shone and the temperature steadily rose. There had been a holiday atmosphere despite the training and the war awaiting them. The rain had begun to fall on the day they came ashore and had not stopped. They had driven the Ford motor ambulances inland through the deluge and over the awful pot-holed roads but now it seemed they had halted at their destination.

Laura sat behind the wheel and wiped at the rain that blew in between the windscreen and tilt of the Ford. She smiled to try to cheer the younger girl. 'It could be worse.'

'How?' Sally said mournfully. Laura had no answer ready so held her peace. Sally pointed. 'Look, tents.' There were, two rows of them, each sporting a red cross on its roof. 'I bet that's where we live.'

'We'll soon know. Here comes Teddy,' said Laura. The ambulance column had soon rechristened their commander and Laura leaned out over the side door to greet Mrs Edwina Beare. She came trudging back from the front of the little column, splashing through the mud of the dirt road in her cord breeches and laced-up boots that came to her knees. Her brown greatcoat flapped soddenly around her legs.

She hailed Laura cheerfully. 'Here we are, girls, home sweet home at last. We'll park in a line in the lee of the hospital.' Laura grinned to herself, noting that use of 'lee', marking Mrs Beare as the wife of a Royal Navy captain. But she was going on, 'All the drivers – except Mr Bellamy – will be in the same tent, so you can sort yourselves out.'

'Thank you, ma'am,' said Laura, and Mrs Beare splashed away to the next Ford.

They parked as ordered and now the grinding of engines had ceased they could hear the gunfire, desultory because there was a lull in the fighting. The reports came dully flat as if muffled by the low hanging clouds, but they were a reminder of the nearness of the firing line. This was a field hospital.

The Fords disgorged their loads. Besides the drivers they carried between them two surgeons and fifteen nurses. There were also a score of Serbian orderlies, recruited by Mrs Beare and still on their way from the coast by bullock cart.

Laura hauled her valise out of the back of the ambulance and followed Sally into their tent. It held eight cots set close together and it was just possible to stand up in the middle. Laura dropped her valise on a cot. Outwardly it appeared to be a khaki canvas case with pockets on the sides but it opened out into a sleeping bag. She and Sally had each bought one, on Mrs Beare's recommendation, in London only the day before leaving.

A male voice bawled, 'Are you girls decent?'

'We'd have closed the flap if we weren't, Matt,' replied Laura, and pushed her head out into the rain again.

Matthew Bellamy was close on fifty years of age, pale-faced from a life spent in workshop or office and grey-haired where he wasn't bald. He had a mechanic's hands, the oil and grime engrained in his skin that no washing could clean. He was protective of the girls and had taught Laura and Sally to drive and also basic maintenance and servicing. Now he grinned at Laura. 'Lovely weather for ducks. Will you girls give me a hand to unload some of this stuff?'

Laura jammed her wide-brimmed, felt hat back on her head. That, with the brown greatcoat and tunic, the laced-up knee-boots and cord breeches, formed the unofficial uniform of Mrs Beare's ambulance column. 'Right you are.' And she stepped out into the rain. They all, doctors and nurses too, worked through what was left of the day and into the night. Then they cooked an improvised meal on primus stoves, ate it by the light of oil lamps and dragged themselves off to bed.

Laura was glad of the fatigue. She always managed to smile and joke through the days no matter what happened, her own self-imposed anaesthetic to numb the pain and keep remembrance at bay. But the deaths of Ralph and their child had hurt her cruelly. Despite all she had learned of him she still clung desperately to her love for him. She had never been able to understand that in other women who had been betrayed by their men in one way or another, but now she did. In the cold, dark dampness of the tent, listening to the breathing of the other girl drivers, memory haunted her. But after a while exhaustion came to set her free and she slept.

'That's better!' Mrs Beare was buoyantly cheerful the next morning. 'We can get some work done today. Come on, girls.' The rain had stopped and the sun shone. The greatcoats and jackets were hung up to dry in the sudden heat that set steam rising from the tents. It reminded Laura of the washing strung across the back streets in Monkwearmouth, a world away. The girls rolled up the sleeves of their shirts but with only one button undone at the neck. They washed walls, scrubbed floors and cleaned windows. Then the Serbian orderlies arrived by bullock cart and with them came one hundred and fifty iron cots. They were unloaded and laboriously hauled inside and set up in the various wards, as the rooms were now called. And at last Mrs Beare declared the hospital ready for patients.

They came. The fine weather brought more fighting, the Austrian enemy increasing his attacks on the Serbs. The ambulances would go out, a driver and nurse in each one, and bring back seven wounded packed into each boxy body. That was six stretchers and a 'sitter', a 'walking wounded' who sat by the driver. There were more drivers than ambulances so they rotated. Often Laura and Sally were in separate vehicles but they went as a pair when they could, one driving while the other acted as a nurse. As such they would squeeze into the back of the Ford with the men, coated in the mud and grime of the battlefield, with their bandages showing bright white and red. They would ease the men's pain as best they could while the Ford bounced and rocked over the ten miles back to the hospital. The roads were no better than tracks, where the mud had dried into bone-shaking ruts and ridges.

They learned to accept the dirt and smells of the wounded, gangrene and antiseptic, vomit and blood, the moans and shrieks of men in unbearable agony and the sudden sigh and chill silence as breath left the body. They worked ten, twelve, fourteen hours at a stretch and slept when and where they could.

Then there were the funerals, when the ambulances carried coffins to be interred. Standing in the cemetery, brand-new that summer and filling so rapidly with dusty mounds. Wincing as a volley cracked out from the firing party, shivering in the summer's heat at the plaintive call of the bugle playing the last post. Driving back in silence, the ambulance empty, knowing it would all need to be done again, yesterday, today and for ever. Trying to put a brave face on it, to smile no matter how low you felt because that was the way to do your job and survive. In the heat and the dirt they hacked off their hair with scissors until they looked like boys, and laughed wryly at the 'new fashion'. Wherever they went they smelled of antiseptic. Laura was reminded of Venetia Ingleby but this was not rose water.

'We'll just have light to fill up with petrol and check the oil.' In the late dusk of high summer, Laura drove into the hospital vehicle park, carbide headlamps glowing and Sally by her side. Sally had taken to the nursing, whereas Laura did it because it had to be done. But the men were glad to see her smile. Now she switched off the engine, climbed down and turned off the lamps. The two girls busied themselves wearily about the Ford and were almost done when Matthew Bellamy came striding up to them.

'Hello, girls. Is everything all right?'

'Fine.' Laura smiled. 'She's running like a clock.'

'Don't go shouting about it' — Matthew lowered his voice — 'but have you seen any disreputable people wandering around while you were driving?' He looked from one to the other, and when they shook their heads, went on, 'There are rumours of deserters attacking women they find on their own. Here.' He handed Laura a cloth-wrapped bundle. 'It's a gun. I've managed to buy one for each car. Just in case, you understand. But don't tell Mrs Beare because I don't think she'd like the idea of you girls carrying firearms.'

Laura did not think so, either, and could see her point: there might be an accident. On the other hand . . . In her mind she went over some of the runs they had made through desolate country, when she had thought, What if we break down here? And she had thought of Black Jack Daubney. She took the bundle. 'Thank you.'

'I'll give you a lesson on how to use it later on,' said Matthew. 'It's not loaded; best not to keep it loaded.' He hesitated, then added, 'The others have pistols but I couldn't get any more. What you have is just as good, though, maybe better.'

He strode off and left the two girls eyeing the bundle. Sally declared, 'I don't want it near *me*.'

Laura soothed, 'No harm in looking.' She unwrapped the parcel. 'Funny sort of gun . . .' It had two stubby barrels and a handgrip like a pistol. There was also a box holding a score of cartridges. Laura said, 'Oh, well.' She stowed it away, wrapped in its cloth, by the side of her seat. 'Out of sight, out of mind.' She smiled at Sally, who looked doubtful. But Laura did manage to keep it out of her mind for most of the time, though now and again she would notice the bundle and recall its grim contents.

The summer wore on into autumn and in September the Germans and Austrians unleashed their attack on

Belgrade and northern Serbia. The number of casualties increased. On a fine morning with the sun blazing down, Laura and Sally set out to fetch some wounded back to the hospital. They were driving through wooded country with a steep drop on one side, Laura at the wheel and jackets discarded in the heat. Their hats were hung up in the cab to let the wind blow through their cropped hair. They rounded a bend and saw a man lying in the middle of the track. They had to stop because there was no room to edge past him: on one side were trees and on the other the ground fell steeply away into a valley. But they could not have driven by and left him, anyway. Laura braked and the Ford skidded to a halt in a cloud of fine dust. As it settled around them, Laura said doubtfully, 'Is he asleep?'

But Sally was already getting down from the Ford. 'He's unconscious. Probably sunstroke.'

That was quite possible; they had had to deal with several cases and Laura could feel the sun strike on her neck and the back of her head as she slipped from her seat. She followed Sally to where the man lay. He was spreadeagled on his back, eyes closed and dressed in Serbian uniform but he did not have a rifle. That raised Laura's suspicions but too late to warn Sally. As the girl stooped over him his eyes snapped open and his arms clamped around her.

Sally screamed and, as if it were a signal, two more men burst out of the wood. One joined the first in holding Sally while the other made for Laura. She turned to run but he was on her, grabbing at her arm. She fought him and he swung at her, flat-handed, a blow she partially avoided but it still caught the side of her head and set it ringing. Then he tried to grab her other arm but she kicked out and her boot hit his shin. He yelped and hopped, trying to escape from another kick, and Laura saw the edge of the track was close. He was leaning forward on her, his legs back, and still trying to seize her other arm. She backed away, taking him with her, then swung him. His own impetus took him forward and he fell over the edge, tearing off the sleeve of her shirt, worn thin by washing.

Laura staggered back as he slid down over the rocks and shale, some twenty feet or more before a small bush halted him. He bawled something and shook his fist. She guessed he was threatening revenge and turned to run. She saw the other two kneeling, pinning Sally to the ground. One of them looked round and laughed at his fallen friend's discomfiture. He was already climbing back up to the track.

Laura ran back to the ambulance. She pulled out the cloth-wrapped bundle stowed between the seats and unwrapped it. The cartridges juggled in her hands as she sought to load, but at last they were in and she closed the breech. Her attacker was up on the track and running towards her now. She held the gun in both shaking hands and pointed it at him as Matthew had taught her. The twin stubby barrels wavered but as they jerked past his eyes she saw his mouth gape as he stared down the muzzles, his hands coming up as some sort of defence.

She pulled the trigger, the gun kicked against her hand, and one barrel spat flame and a wisp of smoke. Laura was ready to fire the second barrel but it was not needed. The deserter shrieked in pain, she saw his hands now smeared red and he turned and ran.

Laura followed, carrying the gun and with some spare cartridges in her shirt pocket. She ran at the two holding Sally down. They were staring at her and their friend – and at the gun. Then suddenly they were on their feet and fleeing. Laura watched them go, the barrels of the gun pointed skyward, until they plunged off the track into the woods and were lost to sight. Laura unloaded the gun with trembling fingers and helped Sally to her feet. The girl clung to her, sobbing and eyes frightened. Laura soothed her. 'All right now. Come on, let's get away from here.' They climbed back into the Ford and drove on, but with a wary eye open for more deserters, nerves on edge and the gun handy.

They told Mrs Beare of their ordeal and she was both relieved and worried, the first because they had escaped none the worse, the second because it might happen again. She called the drivers together that evening and warned all of them of the danger. 'And I'll turn a blind eye to the weapons Mr Bellamy bought for you.'

Laura could not. She asked Matthew Bellamy for reassurance and he gave it: 'That feller will have no more than a scattering of birdshot to pick out of his hands. He deserved a lot worse.' Laura still did not like the gun but accepted that it had its uses. She took more care of it, cleaned and oiled it, finally came to look on it as just one more part of her kit in a dangerous land.

It became more dangerous. The deserters proved to be an isolated incident but the war came closer every day. They left the hospital as the Serbs were forced back, retreated with their stores and cots stacked on the ambulances or the bullock carts. They worked in a succession of smaller and smaller, poorer and poorer buildings, sometimes for a week or two, sometimes for only a few days. And all the while there were wounded to care for.

In October Mrs Beare told them gravely, 'The Bulgarians have invaded . . .' As Laura listened she could picture the map in her mind, the Germans and Austrians attacking in the north, and now the Bulgarians in the south. Serbia was caught in a trap.

The war went on but Serbia's end was in sight. On 5 November the Germans joined up with the Bulgarians and Serbia was cut in two. The rain came again and the column drove south in the ambulances, the bullock carts and the cots abandoned. All their wounded had been committed to hospitals and now they were fleeing to avoid capture. Laura clung to the wheel as the Ford slithered this way and that on the road. It was inches deep in mud and thronged with refugees so the ambulance was barely making a walking speed. The light was poor on this early evening under a lowering sky. Sally slept exhaustedly, head lolling and slumped in her seat. Laura glanced at her now and again but mostly strained her eyes, intent on the ambulance in front. Hers was the last in the column.

The people in front of her moved across the road to avoid a small lake that had formed, as they had done a hundred times that day, and Laura swung the wheel to avoid them, as she had also done. The Ford slid into the pool but then lurched and sank deeper. The wheels spun but obtained no traction and the Ford remained stuck in the mud. Sally woke up, blinked blearily and asked, 'Why have we stopped? Is it my turn to drive?'

'No. We're stuck. We'll have to get someone to give us a shove.' So Laura got down, stepping into the pool and waving at the refugees, vacant-faced with misery, and asked, 'Will you help?' She made a gesture of shoving at the tail of the ambulance. If any of them understood, none showed it. They stared through her and walked around her and on. After some minutes of this Laura sighed. 'It's no use. We'll have to get her out ourselves.'

They found some rocks by the side of the road and thrust these behind the rear wheels of the Ford. Then Laura dug into the back of the ambulance and pulled out a worn old blanket and spread this in front of the wheels. She climbed in behind the steering wheel and drove the Ford forward. Mud spurted from the pool, churned up by the spinning wheels, but then the Ford moved, rocked forward and clawed up out of the pool on to the road. Laura wiped rain and mud from her face. 'We'll have to get on now and catch up.'

She made the best time she could on that crowded

road for some minutes without sighting the other ambulances, but then saw the crowd now milling in the road ahead of her. Some instinctive caution made her brake and she said to Sally, 'There's something going on. I'll just have a look.' She found that the road forked. There was a turning to the right but her road went straight on. The crowd was halted, turning back, and now she could see the men on trotting horses in the middle distance.

Laura ran back to the ambulance, splashing through the mud and slid in behind the wheel.

Sally, alarmed, cried, 'What's wrong?'

'Austrian cavalry ahead,' panted Laura. 'Somehow they've got across our route. That's why all those people are coming back.' Some of them were running now. Laura drove on then swung right into the fork. The traffic here was thinner but she thought it would soon thicken up. The cavalry would see to that, driving the refugees before them.

After ten minutes she stopped the Ford again. 'Let's take a look at the map.' They pored over it in the dark by the light of a torch. Laura's finger pointed. 'That's the road we were on and we're now on this track here. It goes on . . .' Her finger traced it: 'It seems to go up over the mountains and into Albania.' She was silent for a while, trying to make a decision on very little knowledge. She knew nothing of what a winter would be like in those mountains, nor of the country around them, except that it was now occupied by the enemy, who would make them prisoners or worse. 'I think that's the way we have to go, over the mountains.'

'All right,' Sally agreed, trusting. Then she asked, 'How much petrol have we?'

'Not much,' Laura admitted.

The column had halted when the driver of the last ambulance squeezed the rubber bulb of her horn: *honk-honk* and the signal was passed, vehicle to vehicle, to the front of the column. Mrs Beare and Matthew Bellamy walked its length to be told by that last driver, 'We haven't seen Laura for ten minutes or more.' The road behind was crowded but straight and there was no sign of an ambulance. And then Matthew breathed, 'Oh, no!' Men on horseback had appeared at the end of the road. They were tiny with distance but Mrs Beare used her binoculars – bought for when she went racing at Ascot or Epsom – and said, 'Austrian cavalry.'

Matthew offered, 'I'll go back and see if I can find them.'

'No.' She shook her head. 'I can't allow that. And I have to think of the other girls. We must get on.' She led the way, but she wept.

Laura sighed. 'We'll have to walk from here.' The petrol ran out when they reached the foot of the mountains. Night had fallen and they were grinding along the track when the engine faltered and died. Laura tried to be cheerful: 'At least we have somewhere to sleep.' And as

Sally stared, went on to explain, 'We can turf out all the stuff we're carrying in the back. We'll have to leave it. Whatever we want we'll have to carry.'

So they emptied the ambulance of the stores it held as the river of refugees washed past the stranded Ford. There were stretchers, blankets, bandages and dressings, two or three boxes of rations, four tents and a primus stove. Sally started the primus and heated up a stew from a tin of corned beef and some potatoes. Meanwhile Laura sorted out what they would take with them on the morrow. They each had their valises and she packed these with as much food as she thought they could carry. She hesitated, longingly, over the tents but then remembered the looming mountains, some seven thousand feet high, and decided they could not carry one. Instead she cut off a side from one to make a waterproof canvas sheet about eight feet by six. She sat back on her heels as Sally said, 'Supper's ready.'

Laura drew a weary hand over a damp brow. 'So am I. And so are we — for tomorrow.'

They ate hungrily and then crawled into their sleeping bags, lying on a mattress of blankets spread on the floor of the ambulance. Ahead and behind there were others fleeing from the Austrians but now seeking shelter for the night. They snatched at the articles Laura had discarded, carried them away or threw them aside with a curse. But they did not try to enter the ambulance. Sally soon slept but Laura lay awake for some time with the shotgun, loaded but with the breech open for safety, in the bag beside her. She stared at her breath that steamed on the cold night air and wondered what lay ahead of them.

They woke to a world of white snow under a leaden sky, broke their fast with tea and bread with a smear of potted meat and then set out. Their valises were slung on their backs, and one carried the primus, the other the waterproof sheet. It was the beginning of a journey that was to prove a nightmare. On that first day the snow came again and thickened to a blizzard. The track was steep, snaking narrow and icy. Early on they came across a man who was selling donkeys and had a few words of English. Laura tried to bargain with him but he demanded the equivalent of twelve pounds for a donkey and they did not have half that between them.

They climbed all day, with a long line of refugees coiling away ahead of them to disappear in the driving snow. When Laura paused for a moment to rest and looked back she saw another line winding up behind them from the valley. They were encountering casualties now, those who had died in flight, now become just mounds under the snow with here and there a limb projecting like a dead bough or a hand outstretched in mute supplication. Laura and Sally passed them shuddering, eyes averted. When night brought the toiling procession to a halt the summit was still far above them. Between them they stretched the canvas sheet across a fissure to make a rude shelter, held it in place with rocks and shoved their kit inside.

'I can't *feel* this!' Sally moaned as she tried to light the primus stove, her fingers blue with cold.

'Let me try.' Laura put down the tin and opener, rubbed her own numbed hands together and reached for the stove. She struggled with it as the canvas slapped and banged in the wind but finally had it roaring nicely. They warmed their hands around its flame as it cooked their meal then ate and slept fitfully. The wind woke them as it tore the canvas sheet from its moorings and exposed them to the blast. Laura grabbed a corner of the sheet before it was lost entirely. In the howling darkness the best they could do was to wrap the sheet around them and huddle together. They dozed for a few minutes at a time until the dawn came, bringing the snow again.

They joined the straggling procession once more, and now there were some donkeys ahead of them, riders or baggage on their backs. The track ran through a pass with the mountain lifting on one side, falling away in scree on the other. Laura was reminded of the road where the deserters had set their trap for her and Sally, but that had been on the plain on a hot September day. Here and now the wind wailed, driving snow into their faces. The track was treacherous with ice and narrowed so scarcely two could walk together.

Sally shrieked, 'They're going!' Laura did not need telling. A score of yards ahead the edge of the track crumbled under the hooves of two donkeys walking in single file. The man leading one of them hung on to its tail and managed to keep it on what was left of the path. The other fell, taking an entire family with it. They slithered together, donkey and people in a screaming, bawling, braying group, ploughing through the snow until a ledge halted them.

Laura called, 'Wait here and watch our kit!' And she hauled the gun out of her valise and loaded it, set the safety and thrust it into Sally's hands. 'Fire it in the air if anyone tries to steal.' Then she ran along the track and climbed down to where the donkey stood and its owners lay on the ledge. The man of the family, young, stocky and heavily moustached, seemed dazed. The two women, one young, one old, wailed, as did the three children, one little more than a babe in arms. Laura made sure none was seriously hurt, only bruised and frightened. Then she urged the man to climb up, leading the donkey. Laura made several trips, up and down the steep drop, slipping and sliding in the snow, bringing up the women and children. The man seemed to offer thanks, loaded the children on to the donkey then set off again with the women trailing behind. They looked scarcely able to stand.

Sally said, 'They won't get far.'

Laura nodded her head in agreement but there was nothing she could do.

Now Sally admitted miserably, 'I don't think I can carry all this kit any longer.'

Laura had sat down to rest. She looked at the two valises and the canvas sheet that held the stove and some of their rations. Take up that load again? She knew she could not. They talked it over briefly and when they went on it was without Sally's valise.

That night they spent in a rest-house that was no more than a stone-built shack. It was crowded so there was barely room to turn over. Laura and Sally huddled in the one valise, cuddling the stove and what was left of their food, and slept like the dead. In the morning they found some of their companions in the shack had died.

The ordeal continued. Now they were on the downward path but their legs were loose under them. Every time they halted to rest it was harder for Laura to start again, harder still to wake Sally. 'No!' she would mew, turning away to huddle down into the snow to sleep. 'No!'

'You can't stay here. Got to go on. Come on!' Laura would urge her, drag her to her feet and shove her along with a hand in her back. Laura was carrying the valise, the stove and the sheet. There was only a scrap of bread and a little water left. She thought later that she must have slept as she walked. Certainly she was almost on the village before she realised it. She was aware of whitened walls with trailing vines, that the snow had stopped, the sky had cleared. There was a shop with a window through which she could see a few tables. She staggered out of the trailing crowd of refugees to seat Sally at a table then slumped beside her and called for coffee. The proprietor was wary until Laura showed him her money, when he not only brought coffee but also bread and sausage. Laura had to wake Sally to eat it.

There was a mirror on one wall and Laura caught a glimpse of herself. Her thin face was pale under the battered, wide-brimmed hat tied on to her head. She was waif-like in the brown greatcoat and covered in mud from hat to boots. She recalled how fashionably she had dressed in the days before the war and thought wryly, If they could see me now!

Laura managed to make the proprietor understand where they were headed and that they wanted transport. Money changed hands again but here the prices were within Laura's reach. Within the hour she and Sally lay on straw in the back of a two-wheeled ox cart, bumping along the road to Scutari. It was not a comfortable ride but they slept nevertheless.

At Scutari they met the rest – or what remained – of the column. They had escaped through a different pass. The ambulances had been abandoned because they could not cross the mountains but all the staff were present and welcomed Laura and Sally. 'We're a fearsome-looking crew,' said Mrs Beare drily. They had all been on the road for six weeks of bad weather and scant rations and it showed. 'I've talked to the British consul here. He's found us accommodation and arranged passage on a ship. She sails in a couple of days' time, for Italy, but then we'll re-equip. There'll be work for us, but I don't know where.'

So there was a day of blessed rest, of bathing, changing and washing clothes. Then another day's slow travel down to the coast. They rode all the way, luxuriously, by their standards now, in ox carts. Laura and Sally kept dozing; it would take more than one day of rest to make up for the ordeal of their climb. Lighters – huge barges with an engine at the stern – carried them out to the Italian vessel that awaited them. As the lighter pitched and rolled under Laura she saw a warship steaming close inshore and flying the White Ensign of the Royal Navy. And out of the recesses of her mind emerged a memory of a tall young man in naval uniform. She wondered what Nick Corrigan was doing now? And then wondered wearily, bitterly, why she should think of him?

He was aboard the warship, standing on her bridge, looking down as the lighter bucketed past on its way to the Italian ship. Nick had not been ashore but his captain had, and had talked with the consul. Now he said, 'Those are British girls, Mrs Beare's ambulance column.'

'Good God!' exclaimed Nick. 'I know Mrs Beare and her husband, met them before the war. I heard they had a house in Portsmouth now.'

His captain grinned. 'The lady is a character, bags of determination, and it seems her people take after her. They were caring for wounded Serbs and damn near got caught. They had to walk out over the mountains. Marvellous girls.'

Nick silently agreed, did not connect these women with Laura Stanfield, did not even see her. She was tucked down on the rusty deck in the belly of the lighter to avoid the spray that burst inboard, sleeping with her head on her valise.

*   *   *

JANUARY 1918. ALEXANDRIA.

'And now, ladies and gentlemen, we proudly present: Salome, flower of the desert and pick of the harem. Salome!' The long, colonnaded hall of the hospital was packed with men, seated on rows of chairs or propped up on stretchers while more stood lining the walls. Sprinkled among them were the white caps and aprons of the nurses. The ceiling fans whirred and whirled slowly. Mrs Beare's ambulance column had served two years in Palestine but had now been brought back to this big base hospital, preparatory to returning to Britain. They were needed on the Western front.

The Medical Corps sergeant who was acting as MC now walked from the stage. As he did so the curtains, made of blankets, opened jerkily, dragged by the two 'walking wounded' who had volunteered for the task. The improvised 'Jazz Band' — one trumpet, several mouth organs and drums made from biscuit tins — struck up. Laura, standing in the wings and shaking with nervousness, drew a deep breath and ran out on to the stage to a roar of applause — and laughter.

She was barefoot, wore a suit of silk pyjamas and, over the jacket, a 'brassière' made out of pan lids and string. She danced around the stage, pirouetting, arms extended so the numerous tin bangles she wore clashed to rival the pan lids as they bounced. It was simple entertainment, 'home-grown' in the hospital, but a delight to men who had spent months in the desert. Laura could dance, she was young — and happy then — and the men had seen nothing like her for a long time. They cheered.

Nick heard the cheering as he passed the building which housed the hall, but he went on, seeking the man he had come to see. This was Leading Seaman 'Dusty' Miller, who had been severely wounded when Nick's ship had exchanged fire with enemy guns on the Palestinian shore, up the coast from Tel Aviv. He found the young man in the long, cool ward but he was sleeping. Nick talked quietly with the nurse on duty, who told him Miller was seriously hurt and suggested he talk to the surgeon. 'He was going to the concert but I think it will be over now and I expect you'll find him in the officers' mess.'

Nick did as she said and found the surgeon in the mess. He was sitting in a little room, writing a letter to his wife in England, but welcomed Nick. He was unable to set Nick's mind at ease and said tiredly, 'There's no chance that he will pull through, I'm afraid. We operated today, but it was a forlorn hope.' He had been ten hours in the theatre. 'We've given him something to make him sleep. We won't let him suffer, I promise you that.'

Nick thanked him and left with a heavy heart; 'Dusty' Miller had been a good man. As he walked past the door to the anteroom he saw the officers crowded in there in a circle, drinks in their hands. Then he paused as there was a break in the circle and he saw at the centre of it — the Stanfield girl! He could not believe it, thought he had to be mistaken, but as he stood and stared he knew he was not. She was wearing what looked like — silk pyjamas! The men were thick around her like bees round a honeypot. They were laughing and she was laughing with them, her head thrown back. A young officer, his arm in a sling, said, 'Excuse me?' Nick moved aside to let him pass. When he looked again for the girl he found the circle had shifted and closed, hiding her.

He wondered how she had got to Alexandria; he had last seen her in London. He recalled that there was a saying, that if you sat in Shepheard's Hotel in Cairo, sooner or later you would meet everyone you knew. But this was not Shepheard's. And Laura Stanfield! Was she the property of some officer? The girl seemed to be no better than an adventuress. The sight of her laughing while young Miller was dying was an affront to him.

Nick returned to his cruiser. As the pinnace took him out to where she lay he saw a ship taking aboard troops from lighters lying alongside and the sight brought back a memory of the craft bringing off the girls of Mrs Beare's ambulance column. Remembering them restored his faith in human nature. But for some time afterwards he recalled Laura Stanfield laughing, head back.

Laura had seen him. All the cast of the concert had been invited into the officers' mess when the show ended. She had gone with Mrs Beare and with her blessing. The older woman had been in a different circle when Laura saw Nick, and he had seen her. She spotted him through the gap as he let the young officer pass. He was not looking at her but she caught his expression of disapproval. Defiantly, she laughed. But she left the impromptu party soon afterwards, pleading tiredness.

She lay sleepless in the room she shared with Sally and the other drivers, cursing the coincidence that had brought Nick into the mess that night. She thought she knew what he had thought of her, did not care but was angry because it was so unfair. Why him? Damn the man!

Chapter Twelve

MAY 1918. LONDON.

'Bloody 'ell! It's Laura!' He had staggered out of the bar in the Strand, almost fallen, reeled across the pavement and pulled up short of her. Mrs Beare's ambulance column had been shipped back to England prior to going to France. Laura was on leave in London with Sally but the girl had gone to a show. Laura had not because the last time she had been to a theatre she had been with Ralph. She did not want to bring back painful memories.

This man wavering unsteadily before her now was a sergeant, his uniform neatly pressed but the jacket open with the buttons undone, his cap on the back of his head. His webbing equipment of belt, ammunition pouches and pack hung loose on him and his kitbag was slung over one shoulder. He was very drunk and swayed as he stood before her. For a moment Laura did not recognise him in the dusk as the people passing on the crowded pavement washed around her. Then she saw through the changes of the past five years. He was more thick-set, bulky in the khaki, no longer a slender youth, but . . .

'Billy Gatenby!' Laura smiled with fond recollection of times past. Then she grabbed at him as he overbalanced and blundered into a well-dressed woman who shrank from him in disgust.

He mumbled, 'Sorry, missus. Sorry.' He put a finger to his cap.

Laura held him, steadying and anxious now, peered into his face. 'What are you doing here? Where are you going?'

He squinted at her, trying to focus. 'Jus' having a drink 'fore I catch the train. Going back off leave.'

Laura had guessed that because his uniform was clean and the men coming from Flanders were always muddied and filthy. But catch a train? There were redcaps – Military Policemen – at every mainline station. If they saw him like this they would arrest him. Laura said, 'You'd better come with me.'

Billy swayed and objected, 'Going to have a drink. Train's tomorrow. Thought I'd make a night of it, catch it in the morning.'

'No. You've had enough to drink.' And as if to prove her right Billy belched then vomited. It covered him, splashed on Laura and the passers-by scurried aside. Billy moaned and let his kitbag fall and Laura whispered to herself, 'Oh, God!' She held on to him and somehow contrived to hoist up the kitbag and sling it on her shoulder. 'Come on, Billy.'

He went where she led him, on wobbly legs, her hand under his arm. She tried to watch out for redcaps but it was all she could do to handle him and the kitbag. She managed to steer him – through side streets as much as she could – to the flat where she and Sally were staying. It was owned by Mrs Beare and she allowed any of her girls to use it when on leave in London. Its only drawback was a shrill woman living in the ground-floor flat. Like Venetia Ingleby, she watched who came and went, but unlike Venetia she always disapproved, saying the girls were too noisy or too late, or just looking down her sharply pointed nose. She appeared now, peering suspiciously round the edge of her door as Laura led Billy across the hall to the stairs.

Laura explained briefly, 'This is an old friend of mine. He's been taken ill.'

The woman stared, lip curled, and sniffed. Suspicion hardened into disapproval. '*Friend! Really!*' She slammed the door.

Laura manoeuvred Billy up the stairs and into the flat then closed the door behind her and dropped the kitbag. Billy stood wavering, his uniform soiled. The smell had been bad enough out in the air. In the confines of the flat Laura retched but told herself to get on with it. She steered Billy into the bedroom, unbuckled his equipment and tossed it aside. Then she stripped him down to his shirt and underwear, pushed him into the bed and covered him up.

He said, shivering, 'Oh, Laura, it's bad over there, awful bad.'

She was able to answer softly, 'Aye, I know.' Because she really did. She stroked his hair, kissed him and sat with him on the side of the bed until, in a minute or two, he fell asleep. Laura left him then. In the small kitchenette she boiled a kettle on the gas ring and poured a bowlful of hot water. Then she sponged Billy's uniform clean and hung it by the coal fire to dry.

She was just finishing this job when Sally knocked at the door – Laura had the only key. She let the girl in and Sally entered. She had matured in the four years of war, was no longer the frightened waif Laura had taken under her wing. Now she said cheerfully, 'The old girl downstairs is in a bad mood. I said, "Goodnight," and all I got was a dirty look.'

'That was my fault.' Laura hung Billy's trousers by his jacket and saw Sally's startled expression. 'I brought an old friend back. He wasn't very well so I've put him to bed. D'you mind sleeping in one of the armchairs tonight?'

Sally grinned. 'We've done worse than that in the last few years.'

Laura thought back over their shared hardships: 'Yes.' Then she told Sally all about Billy Gatenby.

They slept in the chairs under their greatcoats. In the morning Laura woke Billy with tea and toast. It was all they had because of the war; there were food shortages and many items were rationed. He was not hungry but drank the tea thirstily. Laura gave him his uniform and soon he came out of the bedroom, dressed but embarrassed. He shuffled his feet in their big boots and muttered, 'Sorry about last night, Laura. I was bad. I remember you took my things off. I'm sorry if I—'

'You were a perfect gentleman,' Laura broke in to save him further blushes. 'Now, what have you been doing all these years I've been away?' She sat him down at the table with another cup of tea and exchanged accounts of their doings while Sally listened.

Then Billy harked back: 'I was lucky you came along or the redcaps would ha' got me for sure. Not that they could do anything to me, unless they shot me right off.'

'You'll still be in trouble if you don't catch your train.' Laura shrugged into her coat. 'Come on, I'll see you off.'

'Aye,' he said heavily, 'I've got to go back.' And softly, so Sally out in the kitchenette could not hear, 'I'd left the other lads. I was going to desert and that would have shamed me. Are you ashamed of me now?'

'No, Billy. If you don't want to go back, I'll help you—'

He was shaking his head. 'No, Laura. I couldn't let those lads go on their own. It's just that I get so bloody scared now.'

'I know,' Laura said again.

They went with him in a taxi-cab to Victoria station. After passing through the barrier he was hailed by a little clutch of soldiers, one of many groups crowding the platform. They gathered around him and slapped his back: 'We wondered where you'd got to, Sarge.' 'Like your escort, Sarge, lucky devil!'

Billy stood straighter and took on authority, addressed one of them with the single chevron of a lance-corporal on his sleeve, 'Now then, young Peter, canny lad! Have ye got them all here?' His eye roved over them, counting. 'All got your kit?'

Every one was from Sunderland, voices out of Laura's past. For a moment she had a fierce yearning for the faces and places of her youth but then she quelled it. She would not go back, ever, to face the accusing stares, to be regarded as no better than a whore, her love as something dirty. Her conscience was clear and she would not beg for understanding.

The lance-corporal came to her and introduced himself. 'He calls me young Peter but I'm really Peter Young.' He added, relieved, 'We were worried he might miss the train and be charged. He'd had a few drinks when we lost him. God knows, nobody could blame him for having a drink. It's bad enough for the rest of us but he's been out there nearly from the beginning and wounded twice.'

The train pulled in then and they all climbed aboard. The two girls waited until it pulled away and Laura's last sight of Billy was with his head and shoulders out of the window as he waved to her.

They returned to the flat, heavy-hearted, suffering the hard-eyed stare of the woman on the ground floor.

An hour later Vince Tully was at Victoria, his leave over. At the start of it he had gone seeking the girls at Berkeley

Mansions and had asked Venetia where they were. Venetia smiled sadly. 'I'm sorry, I'm sure, Mr Tully, but I can't tell you.' That was not because of Laura's injunction not to divulge the address she had given Venetia, but because she had left it long ago. Venetia explained, 'The last letter I had came from Egypt. I wrote back but I've heard nothing since then.'

Vince said heavily, 'Thank you,' and went on his way. The few of his friends who had survived the war thus far were making the most of their time with wives or sweethearts. He did not get drunk though that would have been easy enough; there were plenty of civilians ready to buy a soldier a drink. Before the war he had lived in lodgings near the office where he worked. Now he returned to his parents' home in Middlesex. A lot of young men were away in the services so there were plenty of unattached young girls but not the one he was seeking.

He caught his train at Victoria, sober and fearful. There was talk of another 'big push' in Flanders. He knew what that meant and he would be in it.

'*Ship bearing green two oh!*' The bridge lookout shouted it.

Nick had been first lieutenant in the old destroyer *Vengeance* only a month and now she was a battered wreck under his feet. This night action had lasted barely ten minutes but his captain lay dead and Nick now had command. He peered into the darkness, a black backdrop slashed by the muzzle-flashes of the guns, and saw the enemy destroyer, one of the big, new vessels.

'Starboard twenty!' He shouted the change of course and the bow of *Vengeance* came around. 'Steady! Midships! Steer that!' She was already making her full speed.

The bridge lifted under his feet as his ship was hit aft by another salvo. He clung to the guardrail to keep his balance and shouted down the voice-pipe, 'Stand by to ram!' The captain of the enemy destroyer now saw Nick's intention and tried to swing away but only succeeded in turning broadside to *Vengeance*. Her bow struck the other craft amidships and *Vengeance* changed from twenty-five knots to stationary. The shock almost tore Nick from his hold but he clung on. The bow of his ship was stabbed into the side of the other like a knife, heeling her over, but now that bigger vessel's speed pulled her clear. She blundered on, leaving *Vengeance* astern of her, but the sea was rushing in through that cavernous hole in her side and she listed over.

The cox'n bawled, 'She's sinking, sir!'

Nick knew that but now was concerned for his own ship. Her bow was crumpled, there were wounded — and dead. He had to take her home and in the grey light of dawn he conned her into Portsmouth harbour.

A day later he called on Captain Beare at his house on Portsdown Hill but only to find the captain was at sea. Mrs Beare, ruddy-cheeked and in tweeds, greeted him. 'Why, Nick! It's good to see you.' They talked and she called the maid and ordered tea.

After a while Nick asked, 'Are you still running your ambulance column?'

'My word! Yes, I am. We're in France now. I'm only here for a few days. We take it in turns to have leave. And that reminds me, isn't your home in Sunderland?'

Nick wondered what was the connection: 'Yes, it is.'

'One of my girls comes from there: Laura Stanfield.'

Now Nick stared: 'She's one of your girls? Laura Stanfield?'

Edwina Beare laughed. 'That's exactly what I said. You seem taken aback. Do you know her?'

Nick fished out the phrase he had used before: 'She's by way of being a relative of mine.' Edwina thought that was an odd choice of words, but Nick was still trying to come to terms with this. 'How long has she been with you?'

'From the start – January 1915, all through Serbia, Egypt, Palestine and now France.' She read the expression on his face: 'You seem surprised.'

'I – didn't know.'

'She's a very good type.'

Nick started, 'I was in Alexandria four or five months back. I went to the hospital to see one of my men and there was some sort of concert—'

'I think I know the show you mean,' Edwina broke in. 'Laura organised that. Did a turn herself, too, rigged up as a dancing girl. Quite respectable really but it gave the boys a chance to whistle. Did you see it?'

'No,' said Nick. 'No, I didn't.' He hesitated, then

asked, 'Do you know anything of her life before she joined your ambulance column?'

'Only that she worked for my solicitors. Why? Is there something I should know?'

'No, I just wondered.' He would not gossip but he concluded Mrs Beare's ignorance doubtless accounted for her approval of Laura Stanfield. The girl had charmed her as she had Ralph – and Nick himself, he had to admit it. But he would not be fooled. The record showed she was an adventuress.

Edwina wondered if he was – interested? 'Well, if you want to say hello she's in London now. I keep a flat up there in case Bob and I want to go to a show, but the girls are using it as a leave centre now. I'll give you the address.'

Nick began uncertainly, 'I don't think—'

'Note it down, anyway.' She thought, He's not exactly the eager swain but one never knows.

Nick explained, '*Vengeance* will be in the dockyard for a long time so I'm going on leave before they give me another ship. I may look in on her, just to make sure she's all right. You know how it is.'

Edwina Beare grinned. 'Oh, yes, I know how it is.'

Nick was annoyed because it wasn't like that at all, but took the address and thanked her.

He broke his journey north at London, taking a motor taxi to the flat. He had an hour or so to spare before catching the night train from King's Cross. He climbed the stairs and tapped at the door. A voice called distantly, 'Coming!' Then some seconds later and just on the other side of the door: 'You should have taken the key!' The door of the flat opened and Laura faced him. He saw she clutched a greatcoat about her and her lower legs and feet were bare. He thought that she was naked under the coat.

She was, had been bathing in the hip bath before the fire and had snatched up the coat when he knocked at the door. She had thought Sally had returned. The bath was out of Nick's sight and he did not know of Sally.

They stared at each other then the door opened on the flat below and the vinegary woman peered up the stairwell at them. They heard the sharp intake of breath, then: 'Another one! Disgraceful! A few days ago it was a drunken soldier and he stayed the night. I know because I saw him go off with them the next morning. I'll write to the landlord about this! It's lowering the tone of these apartments!' She disappeared and her door slammed.

Nick was tongue-tied for a moment, taking in the implications. Laura guessed at them and he saw the flush rise up from the valley between her breasts. Laura exploded, '*Damn* that woman! And you! What are you doing here?'

He said stiffly, 'I wondered if you were all right. I just wanted to be sure——'

Laura cut him off: 'I don't care what you want! What *I* want is for you to leave me alone!'

'Very well.' He was angry and outraged. The evidence of his eyes and the woman's accusation only confirmed the label tied to this girl. She still should not be denigrated by the harridan. 'But I'll have a word with that woman, stop her saying things—'

'*No!*'

He wondered, was she afraid of what he might learn? 'She said she would write—'

'I don't care what she says! Why should you?'

But he did. 'I care about your reputation.'

'It's mine and none of your business! Now get out of my life!'

The door closed with a crash that shook it on its hinges. Nick stood facing it for some seconds then turned and walked slowly down the stairs. He knocked at the door at the bottom and it was opened by the sharp-nosed woman. She peered up at him around the edge of it, bitter but nervous now. He said, 'I am related to the lady upstairs by marriage. If you continue to make slanderous remarks I will sue you for damages. Do you understand?' And when she nodded, wordlessly, he advised, 'You would do well to remember it.' Then he left her and strode away.

He was angry and told himself the girl was impossible. He had hesitated over calling, anticipating this welcome, but Mrs Beare's report had persuaded him to try. Now he saw he had been right all along and he had been a fool to come. He had done his best and could do no more for her.

Laura wept behind her closed door. She cared about her reputation, if only because she wanted the respect of her friends and the likes of Cath Finley. But it was obvious Nick Corrigan had made up his mind about her and nothing she could say would change him. His persistence had angered her, his judgement of her had hurt. She thought that this time she had seen the last of him and good riddance.

When Sally returned Laura told her about Nick: 'I'd just pulled my coat on and he didn't see the bath and he didn't know about you. He thought I'd opened up for a man, and that woman downstairs was shouting about Billy staying all night.'

Sally held her, for once supplying the strength and the comfort. And the gentle girl breathed, 'I'll wring her neck.'

Laura dried her eyes. 'She's not worth bothering about. And we're off to France the day after tomorrow. Let's get dressed and go out tonight.'

It was a week later, on the third night of torrential rain, that the trench suffered a direct hit from a big gun. The bursting of the shell collapsed the walls of the trench for some twenty yards. Two men disappeared, blasted into eternity without trace. Four more were buried but were dug out from under the glutinous mud. Three survived but Sergeant Billy Gatenby was dying of his wounds and he knew it. As they carried him back along the communication trench on a stretcher he whispered to the lance-corporal, 'Listen. I wish I could ha' seen that lass again . . .' Peter Young listened, until Billy had finished and ceased breathing.

In her next letter to Laura, Cath Finley told her that Billy Gatenby's name — 'You remember Billy?' — had been listed among the casualties as killed in action. Laura blinked back the tears; Billy had been a part of her youth.

Cath also said:

Your Uncle George has aged with the war – he's keeping well but he's seventy now – and working long hours. He's having trouble keeping up with orders without any help. The shipyards are taking all the labour. Seth Bullock has plenty of men working for him but they're all rogues like he is. They all have doctors' notes to keep them out of the army. There's something funny there. And Florrie has died. It was sudden, just took bad and passed away. She had a hard time with that man of hers getting shot and I'm sorry for her lad, poor little bairn.

Cath's letters were always a jumble of bits of news, opinions, questions, names appearing out of context and out of time. This was another example; the name had never been mentioned before.

Laura wondered, Who was Florrie?

Chapter Thirteen

November 1918. Flanders.

'It's true, Laura! It's true! The war's over! They've signed an armistice! Isn't it wonderful?' Sally hugged her. They stood on duckboards that were laid on, almost floated on, the squelchy mud. The canvas tents of the Field Dressing Station, with their big Red Cross markings, were ranked behind them. The tents echoed with cheers as the news spread. Some of the wounded, those not in agony, sang the old songs, 'Tipperary', 'Pack up your Troubles' and the rest. The walking wounded danced with the nurses and the girls who drove the ambulances. They all sang, cheered, danced, laughed, cried.

Laura said that night, 'I've had enough.' She was sick of the sight, sound and smell of war.

Sally agreed, but added, 'I want to carry on nursing, train to do the job properly. Mrs Beare said she would put a word in for me, but I don't like leaving you.'

Laura smiled. 'I'll miss you but we can keep in touch.' And Sally no longer needed her.

The younger girl asked, 'What will you do?'

'I don't know. Go back to my job, I suppose.' Laura could see no further than that. With the war over and Ralph dead these past four years, her life lacked direction. But she would not return to the north country as a prodigal, would not go back to Nick and the Corrigan family, and all the rest who would condemn her.

Mrs Beare had asked Laura, 'Did your relative call while you were on leave in London – Nick Corrigan?'

Laura remembered his visit and her embarrassment only too well and would not admit it. She lied, tight-lipped, 'No.'

Mrs Beare said, 'I'm sorry.' She detected the anger and thought, Oh, dear. But left it there.

But Laura's outrage and bitterness were directed against the Corrigan family and Nick in particular, its visible presence. She knew only too well how they had treated Ralph. He had told her.

Laura talked to Mrs Beare, who found Sally Barnes a position as a trainee nurse in a Sussex hospital. She also pulled strings for Laura, who was back in her job with Greenlaw, Norton and Field within weeks and living in a bed-sitting-room.

Life had already treated her badly but there was worse to come.

*　　*　　*

Vince Tully stamped the snow from his boots and pushed through the brass-handled, swing doors of the Duke of Wellington. This was the middle of the day and there were only a dozen or so men in the bar. He knew none of them. Vince was on his demobilisation leave and wearing civilian clothes for the first time in four years: a navy blue suit and a dark grey overcoat, with a cap pulled down on his head against the cold. They felt light and loose after the khaki.

He ordered a half-pint of bitter and drank, savouring it. He thought it was cold comfort. The landlord paused in passing to say, 'You're the first one of your old gang I've seen for the last year.'

Vince said, 'No.' He had not come to talk about that. The 'old gang' were buried in Flanders or lying in hospitals from which they would never emerge. He asked, 'There were two girls, they never came in here as far as I know but they used to live in the square — in Berkeley Mansions. You might have seen them passing. Have you seen them lately?'

The landlord shook his bald head. 'I think I know the two you mean but they haven't been around here for years.'

Vince had expected the answer. He had been to see Venetia Ingleby again but the old lady, remembering her promise to Laura and Sally, had said she could not help him.

The landlord finished polishing one glass and picked up another. 'Have you done with the army, then?' And when Vince nodded, 'So what are you going to do now?'

Vince looked around the bar, not at the men who were there but the ones who were not, seeing their grins and hearing their laughter. He said, 'I'm going to move.'

'Ah? Where to? Got a job there?'

'I haven't a job and I don't know where I'm going, but I'm off.' His parents had died, one only weeks after the other, not long before the Armistice. Their doctor had told Vince that worry over him at the front had hastened their end. He couldn't stay here with his life filled by ghosts, and it was no use his wasting time looking for Sally Barnes; if she had wanted him she would have left an address for him. He had just been fooling himself.

He finished the beer and walked out.

It was less than a week later that the landlord saw a new customer standing at the little bar of the Snug, with its polished dark wood and two leather-seated benches. This was a slight girl with soft brown hair and eyes. Sally Barnes had also sought help from Venetia Ingleby, who had told her, 'There *was* a young feller asking for you just a few days ago! He said his name was Vince Tully. I remember him from the Duke, before the war. He wanted to know where you were but I told him I couldn't tell him. Did I do wrong?'

Sally had replied, 'No.' She remembered she and Laura had asked Venetia not to give their address to anyone. Sally told herself it was her own fault. She had been cautious, wary of having her heart broken. And now?

She asked the landlord, 'Do you remember a Vince Tully, please? He used to come in here.'

'He was in only last week.' He peered at her, remembering the purpose of Vince's visit and putting two and two together: 'Are you one o' the two girls as used to pass here? Did you live in Berkeley Mansions then?'

'That's right,' replied Sally, then pressed, 'But Vince—'

He cut her off: 'He was asking after you, leastways he was asking after the pair o' you.'

'Do you know where I can find him?' Sally was smiling now, eager.

But the landlord admitted, 'Sorry, gal, I can't. The last words he said to me was that he was going away, so I doubt if I'll see him in here again. See, he was down in the mouth because he was the only one left out of the old gang he used to meet in here.' He saw her disappointment and offered, 'Tell you what, though, just in case he does come in, if you want to leave a message I'll see he gets it.'

Sally forced a smile. 'Thank you.' She thought, hoped, there might be a chance . . . She took the sheet of paper and the envelope the landlord gave her. After writing her address at the head of her note, she hesitated, thinking that she did not want to throw herself at him. But then she decided that if the alternative was losing him, then honesty would be the best policy. 'Dear Mr Tully, I would like to see you again and you can find me at the above address.' She signed it, and added, in case he did not remember who Sally Barnes was: 'The girl from Berkeley Mansions.'

She sealed the envelope, addressed it to Mr Vince Tully and handed it to the landlord. He stood it on a shelf behind the bar and told her, 'There y'are. I'll see he gets it if he comes in.' He said it cheerfully, but privately had little hope that Vince would appear.

His doubt was shared by Sally as she walked disconsolately away.

Laura spent Christmas with Eva Tait, née Perkins, who was now married to her Charlie and living happily in a little house of her own. In the New Year two letters arrived belatedly from Cath Finley, one of them holding a Christmas card. They had followed Laura to France and back again. The writing wavered and sprawled, the phrases disjointed. At one point Cath said, 'George is trying to keep the business going but he is looking very old.' Laura was concerned and wrote to her.

Adrian Norton had welcomed Laura, smiling, 'Miss Stanfield! It's good to see you back safe and sound.'

Laura had never told her employers of Ralph or his death and did not do so now. That was in the past. 'I'm pleased to be back in the office again.' That was partly true. She hoped that there she would be able to sort out her life again.

Laura thought Norton looked older, and not just by

the four years of war. He had been a hale and hearty man of fifty, who could have passed for forty when it started. Now his once thick dark hair was grey and thinning, his face was drawn and his suit hung on him. There was a general lack of life about him. It was some weeks later, at the start of January, that Laura found out the reason.

Eva whisked into the typists' room with a swirl of black skirt. She sighed, 'Poor old Mr Norton. It's an awful job to take dictation from him now. He's having one of his bad days and his mind is wandering.'

Laura questioned, 'Bad days? I've noticed that sometimes he loses the thread of what he's saying.'

'He has one or two every week.' Eva shook her head. 'That girl has a lot to answer for.'

'Girl?' Laura looked up from her Remington. 'What girl?'

Eva said, stating what was obvious to her, 'That Thelma, his daughter.' Then she put a hand to her mouth, 'Oh! Of course, you don't know!' She crossed to stand by Laura's desk. There were only the two of them in the room — Miss Briggs, the supervisor, was taking dictation from a partner — but Eva lowered her voice. 'Well, it happened some time after you left. I was in Mr Norton's office, taking dictation, when the door flies open without a knock and in comes Thelma! She bangs this newspaper down on the desk and says, "He's dead! Daddy, he's been killed!" Then she falls down on her knees with her head in his lap and starts bawling her eyes out. Mr Norton says,

"Oh, my God!" And he tells me, "Get the brandy!" So I tear off and, just by chance, old mother Briggs had the medicine cupboard unlocked already, getting a bandage for one of the clerks that had cut himself, and I grabbed the brandy and dashed back.'

Eva paused to take a breath, then lowered her voice even further: 'The door of his office was open and I was about to go in when Thelma says, "Daddy, it's worse than that. I'm expecting! I only found out last week and I wrote to tell him he would have to get compassionate leave to marry me, and now . . ." Well, I tiptoed away, then went back again but making plenty of noise about it, shouting, "Here's the brandy, Mr Norton!" He looked hard at me but I kept my face straight and he took the bottle and said, "That will be all for now." So I picked up my pad and the files and came back here. It was only then I found I'd brought the newspaper with me as well.'

Laura said, 'Poor Thelma. How awful for her.'

Eva nodded solemnly. 'That's right. To tell the truth, I was never that fond of her, always felt she was looking down on us, but I'll tell you some more in a minute. And I wouldn't wish that luck on anybody.'

She paused, glancing over her shoulder, then faced Laura again and spoke now in a whisper: 'He took her off home and we didn't see her for months. Then one day she comes in here and all chummy – I couldn't believe it! Asking how we all were, and saying how she'd been staying with her aunt in Dorset, never a mention of any baby, but she rambled on, giggling, full of herself and as I say, all matey. Then I twigged: she was squiffy! Eleven in the morning and she was pie-eyed! She came in two or three times after that, until one day — there was that flu going about and there was only me here — she was worse than ever. Her hat was on one side and she could hardly walk. She wasn't happy with the drink, either, not that time. She sat in your chair, that very chair, and cried, said how sad she was. She said, "I wanted to keep my little boy but they had him adopted. I wanted him to remind me of his father." She went on about how she'd met him just outside of here, how he was a gentleman but his family were mean with money and so Thelma paid when he took her out.' Eva leaned closer to Laura: 'She said he was married but he was going to get a divorce and marry her! I think she was silly, believing that tale! Then he was called up for the army and killed. "I wanted the baby to remind me of Ralph," she said. But then Mr Norton came in and took her off and she hasn't been in since.'

Laura said, 'Ralph?' Her voice was almost steady, her face without expression, numb. She told herself it couldn't be true, it had been another young man called Ralph.

Eva nodded. 'That's right. I told you I brought that newspaper out by mistake. It had a casualty list in it. There were a dozen or so wounded, all from London regiments, but only one killed: Private Ralph Hillier.'

Laura could say nothing, but at that point Miss Briggs entered with notebook and files in her arms, pencil jammed in her grey bun. Eva skipped back to her own desk and sat down at her typewriter. Laura forced herself to work for the rest of that interminable day, managed somehow to act as normal, but at the end of it she almost ran out into the street.

Eva called after her, 'What's the matter?'

Laura replied over her shoulder, not wanting to show her face now racked in anguish, 'I have to catch a bus! Goodnight!'

'Goodnight!'

Laura hurried on, not boarding the bus which pulled away without her, seeking only a hiding place. She walked the streets for a long time and finally found it in the bed-sitter, with its gas ring on which she made a cup of tea. She had the use of the kitchen to cook meals for herself but did not bother this evening. The ashes of the fire of the previous night still lay in the grate. She cleaned them out and lit a new fire then sat, still wearing her coat, until the little room warmed through. She did not. She felt she would never be warm again.

Laura stared into the fire and slowly accepted that she had been a fool – or rather, that Ralph had made a fool of her. She had loved him and he had used her. Over time she had thought she had discovered his faults and had accepted them as she had his generosity and kindness. But there was a limit to what she could live with. She had made excuses for him, for Bella the barmaid at the Duke, for his wandering eye on other occasions. She had thought he had been right to leave Melissa, his wife, but now Laura wondered, did Melissa have good reason to suspect his infidelity?

As for what she had now learned from Eva . . . Laura could not find excuse for this. She had loved him even while she mourned him, *but he had been unfaithful to her while she carried his child!* Laura's love had died and Ralph had killed it. The 'wedding' ring she had worn had been a fraud. She had never married and had lost her child. He had never returned the 'engagement' ring he had taken from her to pawn. She slipped off the gold band and hurled it into the fire.

Blinking into the flames blurred by tears, she saw the face of Nick Corrigan, seemed to hear his voice: 'He's a wrong 'un. I told you so.' She felt resentment bordering on hatred and knew the antipathy was mutual. He had shown that on their first meeting and since then had not changed one whit, she was sure of that. She pulled the coat around her as if it were a shroud, shivering.

Major Jack Daubney had returned to London, on leave from the army of occupation in Germany. He read the private detective's report before going to his club for dinner. Laura had told him that she worked for Greenlaw, Norton and Field. That had been four years ago but he remembered her very clearly because he had a score to settle. He had thought it at least possible that she was still in that job.

He waited for her outside the office next day, sitting in his open Vauxhall tourer. As the clerks and typists hurried out when work was done he saw her as she ran down the steps. She walked along the street towards a bus stop and he drove after her at walking pace. As she reached the waiting bus he stopped just behind it. So when she turned to board she saw him scant feet away, smiling. Her lips parted in shock and a hand went to her mouth. The bus conductor rang his bell and the bus pulled away. Daubney could see her standing just inside the crowded vehicle, staring back at him, wide-eyed. He laughed, but did not try to follow. There was no need.

The report had said there was no Laura Hillier at that office but there was a Laura Stanfield. Hillier or Stanfield, this was the girl he sought, had mentally seduced for four years. The detective had followed her home from the office and supplied her address. Daubney could lay his hands on her whenever he wanted. He was promised to spend a fortnight in the country, at the Wiltshire home of a brother officer, who was now conveniently still on duty in Germany, and unaware of the proposed visit. Daubney could wait another two weeks. First the eager Josephine, then he could pursue this girl at his leisure.

She was frightened, shocked. This monster had come out of her past without warning and caught her unprepared. She had not recovered from learning the truth about Ralph, her nerves raw, and Daubney's sudden appearance had set them jangling. She clung to the roof strap in the bus as it pulled away and the Vauxhall was left behind. She watched, white-faced, and saw it did not follow. She looked for it when she changed buses and again at the end of her journey. It was not to be seen and her nerves steadied; she told herself she had escaped him.

She knew how he had found her, recalled how she had told him where she worked and concluded he had waited for her on the off-chance. In the immediate future she would use the rear entrance to the office and change her route for getting there. And she would look for another job. She decided not to go to the police, doubting what they could do, if anything. She was also afraid Daubney would accuse her of enticing him, as he had threatened before.

Then that evening her landlady sheepishly asked, 'Could I ask you to look elsewhere? Y'see, my boy Harry, he's getting married and they're going to want a place to live . . .' Her voice trailed away apologetically.

Laura smiled. 'Of course.' She had not been happy there. Harry was a feckless, idle young man who had cast glances at Laura. She had ignored him, to his annoyance. Now she thought a change of surroundings, a new bed-sitting-room besides a new job, might be a good idea. Like starting a new life?

As she spoke another was ending.

George Finley peered into the gloom as the door of the sawmill was yanked open. He was seventy years old now, thinner and shrunken with age, and while indignantly declaring, 'I can still do a day's work,' he admitted to himself, Your eyes aren't what they were, George. And it was dark outside while the gas lights in the sawmill were focused on the saws, machines and work-benches. He could only make out the visitor in silhouette but that was enough, and he demanded, 'What the hell do you want here?'

'Just a chat, George.' Seth Bullock lounged towards him, grinning, hands dug into the pockets of his smartly cut suit. A good tailor had laboured long and hard so it fitted well. It could not disguise the power of the man, lumpy with muscle. As he moved into the light where George worked, the old man noted the suit. He knew already that Seth was a wealthy man now, rich from wartime contracting to the shipyards and the navy. George was not impressed. For him the man inside the suit had not changed. He said curtly, 'You'll get nothing from me,' and he returned to his work.

Seth's grin did not flicker. He had the confidence of money behind him. 'We'll see.' He stood straddle-legged and watched George. The old man had lifted several of the timbers that covered the trench beneath. While the full length of it was eight feet he had only uncovered about half of it. So as the trench was four feet wide he had a hole four feet square. From where Seth stood he could just see into the hole, brick-lined, and the cold, black, shimmering surface of the water within. It was believed at the time that seasoning timber in salted water prevented 'checking' – the splitting of the surface of the wood – later on. George was using a line with a grappling hook on one end to fish for timber. He had already hauled out one six-foot length and was trawling for another.

Seth had seen all this before, in his own sawmills – he

had three now – and when he had worked for George. He knew what George was doing and why. He said, 'I've come to make you an offer for this place.'

'No.' George did not look up from his job. He had hooked another length and began to haul it up, but then it slipped away from the hook and slid into the water again.

Seth wheedled, 'You're long past the age of retiring. You could put up your feet and live in luxury on what I'll give you. And remember, there won't be so much work about now the war is over.'

George gave him a glance of contempt. 'You did well out of it.'

Seth still grinned. 'I couldn't go. My back wasn't up to it. I've got a certificate to prove it.' The certificate, from a doctor who would soon be struck off, had cost him a lot of money but he thought it well spent.

George muttered under his breath as the timber slipped from the hook again. Aloud, he said, 'As I hear it, all the fellers working for you have flat feet or something to keep them safe at home.'

Seth was unperturbed, thick-skinned. 'They're on war work, George, government contracts. Where would the country be without us, eh?' He laughed. 'Now then, I'll give you—'

'No!' George barked it this time.

That needled Seth and he snapped, 'You don't know what I'm ready to pay—'

George faced him now: 'I don't give a bugger what you want to pay me! You could offer me a million and I'd still tell you to go to hell! I treated you fair and you robbed me! So you'll never get this yard so long as there's breath in my body! Now get out of here!'

Seth's smile had gone and now he glared hatred at George. 'You stupid old fool! Can't you see I'm being kind to you? If I want I can put you out of business and you and that bitch you're married to would starve!'

'Shut your foul mouth!' George started towards him, outraged.

Seth put up a hand to fend him off contemptuously but George took him by surprise and landed a punch on Seth's jaw. It was more of a push than a blow but it stung Seth's pride. He grabbed George, with two hands gripping his collar, and hurled him away. The old man staggered backwards, fell into the trench and the water burst up around his body. It splashed into Seth's face and he rubbed it away and peered into the hole. The water was six feet deep and its surface was four feet below the level of the floor. George rose into sight, his arms threshing, but sank again. He could not swim.

Seth knew that, too, and waited. The body surfaced and this time George scrabbled at the side of the trench, seeking hopelessly for a purchase. His fingers tore great trails in the moss and weed that covered the brickwork, then he slid under once more. Seth waited, breathing fast. George surfaced a third time, but his arms were only moving feebly now. He was close to the side, almost at Seth's feet, and he stared up and tried to speak but the water had now soaked into his clothes and the dead weight of them dragged him down. The black water closed over his head and he did not appear again.

Seth looked around him, frightened now and sweating, his breath rasping loud in the silence, the water still as black glass. He wiped his face and looked about him. He was sure no one had seen him come in – there were few people about. Certainly no one would have heard he and George shouting because they were inside the sawmill with the empty yard surrounding it. No sound would escape to the streets. He spotted the line and hook which George had been using to fish in the trench and he threw hook and line into the hole. Then he left the lights burning, closed the shed door behind him and looked to see that no one was watching before he hurried away. He made his way home using back streets and avoiding street lights.

He kept a bottle of whisky in the sideboard and he uncorked this and sucked greedily from its neck. His hands were steadier. He swallowed another mouthful and now he grinned. He had done it, not as he had intended but more effectively – and cheaper. Soon the sawmill would belong to him and his only competition be gone.

He drank again, this time in celebration.

Each day Laura went to work and returned to her bed-sitter, all the while with her head turning like a hunted animal. She thought she saw Black Jack Daubney a score of times, but realised her mistake in seconds. She was afraid, ashamed and angry at her fear.

IRENE CARR

She told Eva she was moving but said nothing of
Daubney. Eva immediately offered, 'Come and stay with
us until you get fixed up.' Laura knew what Eva meant by
'fixed up'; the girl kept introducing her to young men.
Laura was sure they would all make good husbands – but
not for her. Still, she was grateful for Eva's offer and
accepted it.

The letter was delivered on the morning she was to
move. Her landlady came puffing up the stairs with it just
as Laura was finishing her breakfast of tea and toast.
'Letter for you, dear. What shall I do with any others what
come for you?'

Laura took the envelope and saw it was from Aunt
Cath; there was no mistaking that wavering scrawl.
Abstractedly, she said, 'I'll leave a forwarding address
with you. Thank you.'

'You're welcome, dear. It's been lovely having you,
only wish I could have kept you, but needing the room for
my son and his intended . . .'

Laura smiled at her. 'Of course, they have to have
somewhere to live.'

When the landlady left, puffing down the stairs, Laura
ripped open the envelope, scanned the single sheet of
paper within and whispered, 'Oh, no!' Uncle George was
dead, had drowned in the water-filled trench in his
sawmill a week ago. Laura knew that dark hole. He
had slipped and fallen in and there had been marks
showing where he had fought to get out but failed. Cath
said she could not believe he was dead but she could not

234

manage now with the timber yard and everything else: '. . . and I told you about him.' Laura wondered, About who? She turned over the sheet and now Cath was talking vaguely of a curse on the timber yard: 'Nothing's gone right for years. I could see George getting older and feared for him but he wouldn't give up the business. It's been bad luck all the way.'

Laura wondered at that, so unlike her aunt, but was it because of her age? She decided to put that aside for the time being. She wrote at once to Cath, hurriedly because she had to go to work and because Cath would be waiting for the letter. She wrote it with her case and her old valise packed and standing by the door. 'I am coming home.' What else could she do? She would help her old aunt to straighten out her affairs and see her as comfortably settled as possible. She wanted to do that but would not stay longer than needs be. She could guess at the reception she would receive from people who knew her and what she had done. At best it would be hostile, and it was likely she would be jeered at in the street.

And Nick Corrigan would be in Sunderland. She thought, I don't want any more of him!

She read Cath's letter again. It seemed to Laura like the meanderings of an old woman losing touch with reality. Tears came to her eyes as she remembered how Cath had been a tower of strength for her. Now it was Laura's turn. She would have to face those waiting for her, for a time at least. She owed Cath so much.

She also owed some loyalty to Greenlaw, Norton and

Field. So she added to her letter: 'I have to work a week's notice and will travel up when that is done.'

The letter finished, she took another sheet of paper and jotted down Cath's address in Sunderland. She handed that to her landlady as she left the house, saying, 'That's where I'll be a week from today.' She thought there was no point in giving Eva's address when she would be leaving so soon. She added, Daubney in mind, though she was sure he did not have her present address, 'Don't give it to anyone, please.'

The landlady assured her, 'No, love, I won't.'

Laura posted the letter to Cath on her way to work and then handed in her notice. Adrian Norton was disappointed: 'I'd hoped to keep you longer this time. I'm sorry to hear of the death of your uncle, but we'll keep your position open for a while. Do you think you might come back?'

'I don't think so.' She was certain she would not return to this office, if only because Black Jack Daubney would look for her there.

Laura thought again that Adrian Norton had aged more than just the five years since they first met, and knew that was due to his daughter, Thelma. It brought back to the surface memories she would rather forget and she told herself that part of her life was over.

There was one more farewell. Laura spent an hour tending the grave of little Catherine, her daughter, and laid fresh flowers. Then she turned her face to the north.

Time she went home.

BOOK II

Chapter Fourteen

A wind off the sea breathed coldly up the street, shredding the fog. It brought with it a spit of rain that lay on Laura's face like icy tears. The singer had gone, the front doors had closed and swallowed the rectangles of light and suggested warmth. Laura shivered and Addy saw it: 'Come on in, Laura, and get warm. You can stay with us tonight.' She stepped back, opening the door wide.

Laura followed her in and set the boy down, though still holding his hand. 'Thanks, Addy, but I'll sleep in Aunt Cath's – my own place.' She thought it would not be easy but she would start as she meant to go on. And Addy's cottage was cosy but comfortably full with her, Joe and their children.

'Well, you'll have a bite of something,' said Addy. 'The bedlinen in there is all clean, I saw to that, and I can let you have a brick to warm the sheets for you. Now sit down beside the fire and I'll get the supper ready.'

Laura was glad to take off her coat in the sitting-room and sink into one of the two armchairs. The fire was surrounded by a fender, its brass winking in the light from the blazing coals, and there was a guard to keep out the children. She talked with Joe, and Addy as she chattered away in the kitchen next door, appearing now and again in the doorway to wave a spoon or ladle as she made a point.

'I would have done a bit more for Cath if she'd have let me, although these bairns keep me busy, but she was always one for looking after her own place. I tidied it a bit when she died but you'll find it's in a rare state . . .'

Laura let the words wash over her, weary now as the heat relaxed her. The boy sat on a cracket, hugging his knees and nervously rocking back and forth on the low stool. He was thin-faced, big-eyed, wiry in shorts and a worn, blue woollen jersey. His brown hair was neatly cut but finger-rumpled. He stared into the fire but every now and again he would glance uncertainly at Laura, then quickly away.

She said, 'So it's Tommy Taylor? Like little Tommy Tucker, that sang for his supper? I bet you could eat some supper as well!' He nodded, eyes flicking to her, then back to the flames. Laura did not press him.

Addy emerged from the kitchen with a brick, taken from the oven and wrapped in a piece of old blanket. 'I'll just run in next door and put this in your bed.' She returned minutes later, shivering. 'It's bitter cold out there now.' Then she served supper of a steaming broth of meat and vegetables, nearly thick enough for the spoon to stand up in. And all the time they talked. Addy said, 'We've got nearly six years to make up.' They laughed. But she never asked about Ralph, the man with whom Laura had run away, and Laura offered no explanation.

The meal over, the children were allowed to climb down from the table and were soon absorbed in some game while the adults sat on over a cup of tea. Laura said quietly, so the children would not hear, 'It was a shock to find out that Aunt Cath was dead as well as Uncle George.'

Addy sighed. 'She'd been worried about George and the sawmill, had lost a lot of weight and was having trouble with her heart. We weren't really surprised when she slipped away. What killed her was hearing that he was dead.'

Joe nodded. 'Aye. And George seemed to be keeping well, getting on in years and working too hard, but good for a few more years. It was an accident with him. He fell into that pit and drowned. You can still see the marks on the wall where he tried to claw his way out.'

Both Laura and Addy shivered and Laura changed the subject: 'How are you getting on at work, Joe? And what ship are you building now?'

Later Laura helped clear away and wash up then said, 'I think I need my bed now.' She picked up her valise and suitcase, laughingly declining Joe's aid now: 'I'm only going next door.' The baby was asleep in her cot but the two girls and Tommy came with Joe and Addy to see her to the door. Laura said, 'Goodnight.'

'Will you be coming tomorrow?' Tommy asked in a small voice.

Laura stooped and kissed him. 'I'll be coming for you.' But he still watched her doubtfully as she walked away.

The door of Cath's cottage opened easily and Laura entered, setting the valise and suitcase down and closing the door behind her. She stood there for long seconds, listening to the silence but in her head she could hear Cath's voice: 'Come in, pet. I've been expecting you.' The silence was not complete, though there was no ticking of a clock and Laura concluded it would need winding. There were the creaks and groans of an old house as she stood with her gaze wandering in the dimness; some light came in through the open curtains from the street lights outside.

She moved forward as she made out the door to the kitchen at the end of the passage. It stood open and she passed through to sit on the kitchen chair at the table, the valise on the floor at her side. Here she had sat as a child, legs swinging, nibbling at a biscuit as Cath bustled about the kitchen. She had always been there when Laura needed her. This was the reason Laura had wanted to spend this night in Cath's old house. She had a vigil to keep with Cath Finley, who was still there. Laura thought she could sense her presence. She whispered, 'I came back too late but I'm here, Cath. Help me.' And then cold, frightened and alone, she wept, head down on the table.

After a time she stirred herself to light the gas lamp to

undress. Then she turned it off and slid into the welcome warmth of the bed heated by the brick. Now she was at peace and she slept the night through to be wakened by the church bells on Sunday morning.

Laura rose and dressed as the Boy Scouts' band of bugles and drums marched by outside, tooting and rattling. She ate breakfast with Addy, Joe and their brood, Tommy Taylor watching silently. The meal done, Laura said, 'I'm going to be busy this morning.' She eyed him: 'What about you giving me a hand?' He nodded, still uncertain, and she prodded gently, 'Cat got your tongue?'

'Aye,' he whispered, and stopped there, mouth open, hesitant.

She guessed at his problem and stroked his hair. 'Call me Aunt Laura.'

He was at her side when she went back to her cottage, laid and lit the fire. As she dusted and swept he copied her with a rag she gave him. Laura saw that the house had been neglected for some time, a sign of Cath's loss of ability to cope. As she worked she collected a mass of paper – and bank-books – found in various drawers. Among the photographs crowding the mantelpiece were several of herself at various stages of growing up. There was also a small studio portrait of a couple, the girl seated, the young man in khaki standing beside her. Both stared into the camera. Tommy ventured, 'That's my mam and dad.'

Laura smiled brightly. 'We'll be extra careful with that, then. I bet they're pleased with you.' He said nothing but watched Laura set the photograph in a prominent position.

After a while Tommy showed signs of boredom and Laura called over the back yard wall to Addy next door. 'Would the lasses like to come round and play?' They jumped at the chance, so the rest of the day Laura cleaned, though sometimes she had to join in the games of 'Shops' and 'Houses' as the children imitated their elders.

Addy brought round a neat, small pile of clothing: 'These are Tommy's.'

'Thanks.' Laura carefully sorted them into a drawer. Among the shorts and socks were two worn royal-blue woollen jerseys and a third in green that looked new.

Addy said softly, 'I bought that for him but he won't wear it.' And when Laura looked the question at her, explained, 'His mother always dressed him in blue.'

Laura said, 'I see.' And she put the green jersey aside. 'We might find some little lad who'll be glad of it.'

That was more than likely; most children's jerseys were worn ragged.

That night the pair of them made up a bed for Tommy in the spare bedroom. When he was in it and sleeping soundly Laura set out the papers on the kitchen table and sat down to read.

Cath's bank-book was for a deposit account and showed a small balance after a succession of withdrawals. George's business account showed a similar picture. He had not done much business in the past year. Some of the papers were Cath's old shopping lists or notes to remind her of things to do. There was a pack of letters written to her by Laura, all in order and wrapped round with a rubber band. Laura bit her lip and shook her head over those. But the bulk of the papers were old invoices and receipts, all annotated in Cath's now shaky handwriting, all connected to Uncle George's sawmill business. Laura had cause to shake her head again. Her old aunt had tried to take the burden of the office work from George's shoulders. It was no wonder the house had needed dusting.

Laura sorted these into date order and found they were spread over the past year, all but a few weeks. Among the thick wad of accounts noted as settled there were also unpaid bills and invoices not sent out for payment. She sat with head in hands. There was a mountain of work before her and she almost despaired again, but she had said she would make a home and a life here for her and Tommy.

She wondered, as she peered in at him then slipped into her own bed: If this was the house, what will I find at the sawmill?

That Monday morning she saw Tommy off to school then walked down to the timber yard. Rain and mist had gone, leaving a blue sky and bright sunshine, but it was not enough to melt the frost this early and Laura's breath steamed on the air. As she unlocked the door in the gate she remembered Seth on Saturday night. He had uttered threats and she knew he meant them. She would have to beware of him. Laura reflected bitterly that she had just got away from Black Jack Daubney only to find another enemy here.

She opened the double gates and set them wide, just in case some business came her way, though she was far from sure how she would deal with it. The office was on the left of the yard, blank walls of it facing her. The door and window were in the wall out of her sight, facing up the yard and so not receiving the morning sun. In the evening it would shine directly into the office window but now, as she walked round to that side and in at the door, there was enough light to show her the dust and cobwebs. It was just as she remembered it, with a battered desk and a hard chair softened by an old cushion; she had sat there and sucked humbugs given to her by Uncle George. There was a cupboard, a cast-iron stove and a sagging armchair where he had sat when business was slack. His overalls hung from a nail behind the door as if waiting for him.

A clock hung on the wall facing the desk but it had stopped. Laura found the key where she remembered it, in a drawer of the desk. She opened the glass face of the clock, wound it and set it right by her watch and it ticked solemnly. With that heartbeat some life came back into the office. An old newspaper lay by the chair and a bucket of coal and a pile of sticks by the stove. Laura cleaned it out and lit it. Her hands were dirty now but there was a tap in the yard and she found an iron bowl and a bucket beside it. She washed in the bowl and was ready to start in the office.

Laura had brought with her the papers from the

cottage and now she found more of the same in the desk. But this time most of the bills were not noted and still outstanding, some amounts due, others to be paid. Laura sorted them all, listed them with a stub of pencil she found, and by noon she had a rough idea of the overall financial position. When all outstanding accounts were settled the mill would just be in profit. But she would have to see the solicitor and the bank manager about her taking over. And then what would she do? She knew Uncle George had made joinery for ships, had watched him at work, but she was ignorant of the inner workings of his business.

Addy had invited her to the midday meal. Laura decided she would look in at the mill itself for a minute or two before leaving. As she walked up the yard towards it she thought that the windows, set high in the walls, needed cleaning for a start. She could see the cobwebs inside them were covered in sawdust. She opened one of the big gates, setting it ajar as it had been on the Saturday night when she had come upon Seth Bullock. She entered through the gap, scolding herself for being nervous, telling herself there was nothing to fear. But she could not help remembering Seth in there and the threats he had hurled at her.

There was no one waiting for her in the mill, but there were scents out of the past: the resiny smell of the timber, the coal smoke and oil of the steam engine. And there were memories. Of Uncle George warning her as a child in a white pinny: 'Don't you touch any o' these machines, nor get near them!' There were no guards on them at that time. She remembered standing with her hands to her ears as the circular saw spun with its high-pitched, rasping whine. Its vicious teeth would sever a man's finger or arm. The sawdust squirted from under the blade so the floor was carpeted with it.

The trench was still partly uncovered. Now, in the light of day, she could see into it. Its brick walls were covered with green slime and weed but in places there were grooves torn in it. Laura recalled the conversation with Addy and Joe the previous night and realised that was where George Finley had tried to climb out of the pit. She shuddered and fetched the baulks of timber, like railway sleepers over four feet long, that fitted on to the brick ledges either side of the pit. With these in place the pit was covered with a timber floor.

That done, Laura set the memories aside. There was work to be done here. The windows, the floor, the saw, the lathe and the other wood-working machines all needed cleaning and it would be dirty work. She looked it all over with a calculating eye. It would be dirty work but it had to be done and now she decided how to do it. There had not been a customer or even an enquiry all morning. From what she had gleaned from the paperwork it was unlikely there would be any such this afternoon. She had an idea how to do something about that but first the place had to be made ready for customers.

Laura left then, walked back to Addy's house and ate lunch there. Tommy quietly tucked himself in at her side.

When he set out for school again he asked, 'Will you be here tonight?'

Laura bent and kissed him. 'Yes.' She glanced up at Addy. 'But I'll probably be a bit late.'

'We'll keep yours hot,' Addy assured her serenely.

Laura returned to the sawmill, taking with her a change of clothes and two towels she had found among others in Cath's linen cupboard. In the office she slipped out of her dress and donned an old overall of Cath's. It was short-skirted on Laura's long legs but clean and serviceable, with a deep pocket in which to carry a handkerchief. Then, with her hair wrapped in one of the towels she set to work. With a brush tied on the end of a clothes prop – Uncle George had a stock of those for sale – she cleared the cobwebs dangling from the roof and about the windows. Then she dusted all the machinery and washed the windows, took a broom and swept the floor. Laura worked furiously, taking on the job as a challenge, a chance for her to defy the malign fates that seemed set against her. She would make a success of this task and then of the sawmill – and Tommy.

The only note she took of the time was when the winter sun sank early behind the sawmill and she had to light the gas lamps to see. But she laboured on until she could stand back and survey what she had done with satisfaction and pride. I could bring anyone in here now, she thought. Her next job would be to make sure someone did come.

Laura wiped the back of her hand across her wet brow

and grimaced because her fingers were coated with sawdust and dirt. She knew the rest of her was the same, could feel the itching, and thought, You certainly can't walk home like that. And was glad she had foreseen this. She turned off the lights in the sawmill and walked back across the dark yard to the office and lit the gas lamp in there. The stove was still hot and she set a bowl of water on top of it to heat. The bucket full of water she set alongside. She drew the curtains across the window, making a mental note to take them home and wash them, and bolted the door. Then she hesitated, wondering. Just to be sure, she unbolted the door again and stepped out into the yard to confirm that the window was properly covered. She saw the curtains were doing their job, returned to the office and shot the bolt again. Now she was able to undress and wash off the worst of the dirt in the bucket of cold water. She shivered, but had done this in Serbia and the desert in the interests of cleanliness. Then she set the bowl on the floor, stood in it and washed down with the hot water, luxuriating in it and content in her mind that she had done a good day's work.

She reached for the clean towel and a voice called, 'Hello, there, George!' The door burst open and Nick Corrigan walked in.

Laura saw him smiling, saw the smile slip away, his eyes widening. She clutched the towel to her and shrieked, '*Get out!*'

He turned about, trying to explain. 'I came to see George, saw the light—'

'Get *out* and shut the door!'

He obeyed but his voice came through to her, apologising but growing angry. 'I'm sorry, but you should have locked it.'

'I bolted it!' But she could see the screws that had ripped out of the jamb of the door where it was rotten.

'It didn't feel like it. And I didn't expect to find you – washing. I came to see George.'

Laura was hurriedly drying herself, thanking Providence that she had held the towel. If he had walked in seconds earlier he would have seen her naked. *Him!* Of all people! He was probably smirking outside now and would be telling all his friends tomorrow. She would like to wipe that smirk off his face. As she began to struggle into her clothes: 'What did you want with Uncle George?'

'He's your uncle?'

'That's right.'

'I didn't know.'

'You don't know everything.'

He ignored that and it annoyed her further. Instead he asked, 'I want to see him. Is he in the sawmill?'

'He died a fortnight ago.'

There was silence for some seconds, then he said quietly, 'I'm sorry. He was an old friend.'

Laura was damp but dressed. She whipped at her hair with a brush and peeped into the small mirror in her bag. She was ready. She yanked the door open and found Nick standing a yard away. Demobilised from the Navy now, he wore a Norfolk jacket and carried a motorist's cap in one hand. A motor car, an Arrol-Johnston coupé, open-topped now and brand-new, stood gleaming close by. Its huge headlights looked like big eyes staring at her. Laura guessed it belonged to Nick and she was right. He had bought it that day, for seven hundred pounds, the price of a sizeable house. She was not impressed, looked him in the eye and asked crisply, 'Now, Mr Corrigan, you haven't told me what you wanted with my uncle.'

He returned her gaze straightly and she could see his antagonism, sense his disapproval. He countered, 'You haven't told me why you are here.'

'My Aunt Cath died as well, just a few days ago. They left this place and their house to me.'

Nick said, 'I see.'

'No, you don't,' Laura contradicted, her face burning again. 'You think that's why I came up here, like a vulture, to see what pickings there were. And you're wrong. I came because—' But she stopped there and said instead, 'No. That's nothing to do with you, so you can think what you like.'

He had been surprised to see her in the station, not surprised when she told him to mind his own business. He thought that was in tune with their stormy relationship and she was right. It was her affair if she chose to come home. But it showed she had guts – or impudence. He said, his voice harsh, 'I'll do that anyway, without your permission. I didn't make any guess as to why you came back here, but if I have a certain picture of you in my mind it's because you put it there. I came to steer some work

George's way. I'll wait now to deal with the new owners.'

'Then you will have to deal with me,' snapped Laura. And when he stared at her: 'I am going to carry on the yard.'

'*You?*'

'Aye. Have you any objection? Not that it's any of your business.'

'No objection, but – do you know anything about it?'

'A bit – and what I don't, I'll learn.'

'That could prove expensive.' Laura knew that, and more, that it could be ruinous. She did not answer so he asked, 'Why?'

'To make a home and a living for Tommy and me.'

'Tommy?' Nick blinked, startled. 'Is that Ralph's son?'

'No!' Bitterness welled up in Laura again. 'His child was born prematurely and died. I found out Ralph was bedding another woman while I was carrying his daughter. And she was not the first.'

Nick was stricken silent and as they faced each other in the gloom they heard the tread of boots as a man crossed the yard. They faced him as he came up, stocky in over-big overalls and with his cap pushed back on his head. He looked from one to the other: 'I heard the auld feller had died but I saw the light as I was passing. Has somebody else got the business now?'

Laura was still angry and upset by Nick. She stared blankly at the stranger for some seconds, then found Nick's gaze on her, curious, and was spurred into life. 'Yes, I have.'

'You?' He looked from her to Nick and asked, 'The two of you?'

Laura kept a hold on her temper, told herself that this Corrigan man would be thinking: I told you so. But she would not be provoked because this was business. 'No. This' – she glanced at Nick – 'gentleman is just a visitor. I am running the yard. What can I do for you?'

'I don't know.' He said it uncertainly, lifted the cap from the back of his head and scratched the cropped poll it had covered. 'They call me Chris Marley and I bought timber from George. Now – I don't know.'

Laura said, 'Let me show you what timber I've got.' And she led him across the yard to the open-fronted shed where the timber was stored. 'Can you see what you want?'

'Well, I think so,' he started.

'Take a look,' said Laura promptly.

'Righto.' He put on the cap again, peered at the various stacks of timber and selected two or three lengths. He slung them over his shoulder. 'They'll do me. How much?'

'The same as you paid George. I'm not reducing prices till I know where I am.'

'Aye? Right y'are, then.' And he dug in his pocket and paid with a handful of coins. 'Thanks, miss. Goodnight t'ye.'

'Goodnight.' Laura watched him trudge away down the yard to load the timber on to his cart that waited outside the gate, the horse in its shafts turning its head to greet him. Then she returned to Nick, defiantly, having made her point. 'Can I show you anything?' Then she realised what she had said.

So did Nick, and as she felt the blood flooding her face again he said neutrally, 'I've seen enough for one day. Goodnight to you.' He lifted a hand to the peak of his cap in salute and marched away down the yard.

Laura, fuming again, thought, Damn the man! He had a genius for catching her at her worst. He had seen her wrapped in nothing but an old greatcoat and now – this! He probably thought of her as a slattern as well as a fancy woman. She locked up the office and the yard and walked home, her anger slowly dying. Nick Corrigan had said he would wait to do business with the new owners of the sawmill. He would change his tune now he knew she was carrying on with it. That was fine. She didn't want his business. The less she saw of him, the better. He had seen too much of her already. *Damn* him!

Nick drove his Arrol-Johnston out to the Corrigan house in Ashbrooke. He admitted that he had learned something new about the Stanfield girl this night – and about Ralph Hillier. He had betrayed her, treated her abominably. So maybe she was not entirely the scarlet woman she was painted. He could picture her as she had stood with only the towel held to her. He would never forget that. It would be set beside the other pictures of her that persisted in intruding into his thoughts at odd moments. He did not understand her, but now he had seen, though he did not sympathise, why Ralph Hillier had been tempted and deserted Melissa.

And there had been that incident when he had thought that Melissa was inviting him . . . He stopped short there and told himself he had misinterpreted her approach. There had certainly been no other such incident and now she took tea with Jessica Corrigan and her 'ladies' circle', browsed in the public library, was shyly deferential when she took part in the family conversations. Melissa was the model of a virtuous woman.

It was as well he could not see her at that moment, writhing and moaning in the arms of Seth Bullock. They had come some way from the dusty stable. He lived in a four-bedroomed detached house now that he rented for thirty pounds a year. A good cook in service was earning less than that. Afterwards Melissa lay naked by his side, stroking him as he stared up at the ceiling and growled, 'I want that yard of old Finley's!'

'You'll get it,' Melissa soothed, but her tone and thoughts were vicious as she assured him, 'She's only a lass. Ralph only wanted her for her innocence. She'll soon be glad to get out of that place.'

'I'll make sure of it.'

Melissa lifted on one elbow: 'How?'

'One way – or another.'

Melissa still lived in Dan Corrigan's house as one of the family though she frequently shared Seth's bed. She had established a pattern to her life that left large amounts of time for her to slip in through the back door of his house. She occasionally found this restricting but Seth had never suggested marriage. Further, he had advised, 'You never know when it might be handy, you living there.'

Melissa warned, 'I'm not burgling again.'

Seth thought, You'll do as you're told, lass. But he agreed. 'No. I meant you could pick up bits o' news.'

Melissa was willing to accept these terms – for the time being, at any rate. Seth was doing well and would do even better when he took over the Finley yard.

And that night Laura lay in the darkness and thought that she had boasted to Nick Corrigan of running the business but she had a lot to do and she could not make ladders or joinery work at all. She had ideas about getting the work but someone else would have to do it. She needed a man, and not a Corrigan.

But it was Nick she dreamed of.

Chapter Fifteen

JANUARY 1919. MONKWEARMOUTH.

'I'm looking for a man,' said Laura. She was helping Addy to wash up the breakfast crockery, having sent Tommy off to school with a kiss. Joe Gibson had fitted a china sink in the kitchen for Addy, a big improvement. Laura recalled washing up for Doris Grimshaw in a bowl set on the kitchen table.

Addy giggled. 'You shouldn't have any trouble finding one.'

'Now then,' said Laura with mock severity, 'you know I didn't mean like that.' And thought, Maybe no trouble finding, but after . . . 'I need a joiner for the sawmill. I was thinking, there was Frank Pearson who used to work for Uncle George. Do you know what happened to him?' She asked while fearing the answer because too many young men had died in the war.

But Addy replied, 'He joined up in the Durham Light Infantry and was twice wounded, but when I last saw his wife she said he was still in a big hospital down south. That was a week or two ago and she said he'd been in for a month or more. She said his nerves were awful bad now because he'd been shell-shocked. She couldn't see him working again and she was crying to me because she wants to have him home with her.'

Laura said quietly, 'Oh, dear.' She knew something of shell-shock, brought on by spending too long under fire and under stress. That ruled out Frank Pearson, but: 'He worked a good few years for Uncle George. Do you know their address? I'd like to call on his wife and see if there's anything I can do.' She thought, But that will be precious little. You'll have your work cut out to make your own way.

It was barely a ten-minute walk to the little terraced house with its polished brass knocker. The door was opened by a thin-faced young woman, drying her hands on her apron. She looked tired and unhappy. Laura could see past her and right through the passage and the kitchen beyond. The window there looked out on the back yard, where a line of washing snapped on the wind like bunting. 'Mrs Pearson?'

'Aye, I'm Norah Pearson.' The weariness gave way, slightly, to curiosity. 'What do you want?'

'I just came to say that I hope Frank will soon be home, and if there's anything I can help with, just let me know.' And then explained, 'He worked for my Uncle George. I'm his niece, Laura Stanfield.'

'Oh! Pleased to meet you . . .' That tailed away as Laura saw Norah remember what she had heard of Laura Stanfield. The curiosity turned to a blank-faced hostility. There was a pause and then Norah went on, 'Frank's home, came back a few days ago.' She hesitated, then added reluctantly, 'Would you like to see him?'

Laura smiled at that cold stare, had expected nothing else: 'Aye. And I'll bet you're pleased to have him here again.'

Norah made no answer to that and Laura followed her along the short passage to the kitchen. Once through its door she could see the fire and the man slumped in the armchair before it. Norah said, 'Someone come to see you, Frank.' He struggled to his feet, thin and little taller than his wife, clean-shaven and seeming fit. He wore clean pullover and trousers, new carpet slippers, but looked carelessly dishevelled.

'Hello, Frank. Do you remember me? George Finley's niece, Laura.' She held out her hand.

'Aye!' Frank's solemn features broke into a smile and he automatically reached out to her but then his hand began to shake and he thrust it behind his back. 'S-sorry. Can't help it. They say I'll get better but it'll take time.' He nodded to the other armchair that faced his: 'Sit down, then. Norah told me about George and your Aunt Cath. I remember you coming to the sawmill when you were a little lass.' Then his smile slipped, embarrassed, as he recalled more about her.

Norah said with cold disapproval, 'I'll just put out this bit o' washing, then I'll make you a cup o' tea.'

Laura said quickly, 'I'll give you a hand. You sit still, Frank, and we'll have a chat in a minute.'

Outside in the yard, passing pegs and clothes from the basket to Norah, Laura said, 'He's not the Frank I remember. He was full of life.'

'He just sits in that chair all day, won't go out, doesn't want to meet people because of that shaking, says he can't work any more and he's useless.' Norah fumbled with a peg, dropped it and sobbed as she ran back into the house. Laura pegged out what was left of the washing and went back into the kitchen. Norah was busying herself with making the tea and Laura talked with Frank of days gone by, memories of George and Cath Finley.

Until Laura asked casually, 'How do you shave, Frank?'

Norah answered, managing a smile, 'When he sets the razor to his face it's as steady as a rock. Isn't that funny?'

'Aye,' Laura agreed. But her gaze was still on Frank: 'I'm keeping on the sawmill, going to run it.'

He stared at her, doubtful: 'What – on your own?'

Laura laughed. 'I've done some funny jobs these last few years but I can't see me working the lathes and saws. I can cope with the office side but I need somebody for the mill. What about you? Will you help me out?'

Frank started to shake his head. 'I couldn't. You've seen the way I am.'

'You look pretty fit to me, and you can handle a razor. I'll lay odds you could handle the saws and machines as well.' Laura pressed him. 'I need somebody, Frank. Will you try, anyway? For old times' sake.'

Frank hesitated still but then his gaze shifted to Norah and she nodded eagerly. He took a breath and said nervously, 'Well, I'll give it a go. When do you want me to start?'

'Now!' Laura stood up and grinned at him. 'Here's the key to the yard. I have to go to see the bank manager and I'll be along to join you later. I've had a clean-up in the mill but if you could make a start on sorting out the timber? I need to know what I have to order.'

'Right y'are.' Frank was on his feet. 'Where's my dungarees, Norah?'

'You fetch your boots,' she told him. 'I'll see Miss Stanfield out then I'll find your overalls.' At the front door she said, 'I'm sorry if I was a bit short when you first came.' She was blushing now.

Laura took the bull by the horns: 'I expect there was talk; there always is.'

'Aye.' Norah did not expand on that but looked away, recalling what had been said.

'There are a lot of things I'd do differently if I had my time over again, but I'm ready to answer for anything I've done. All I ask is that you make up your own mind about me.'

'I will.' That was said firmly, but then she became hesitant again and asked anxiously, 'Do you think you will be able to use Frank?'

'I'm sure.' Laura said that definitely too.

There came a cry from inside the house, frustrated and complaining: 'Norah!'

She laughed. 'That's his lordship. I suppose he can't find his boots. He's sounding better already.' And called: 'Coming!'

Laura left them and went on to the solicitor and then the bank. One confirmed her outright ownership of the yard, the other that she had a small balance in George Finley's account, enough, she thought wryly, to keep the yard going for two to three weeks. Neither solicitor nor bank manager liked the idea of her running the sawmill and timber yard. The one pursed his lips while the other shook his head. Laura swore under her breath.

She was back at the yard before lunch and found Frank, in clean but ancient overalls, whistling as he pottered around the timber store, measuring, counting and noting. Laura settled down in the office with the pile of invoices and receipts covering the past twelve months. A quick study enabled her to work out how a few of the various items made in the sawmill had been costed. After another hour she had an idea, albeit sketchy, of the prices to quote. She had also listed a dozen customers who had done regular business with the yard and another dozen who had not figured in the accounts for the past six months. The first group she wanted to keep and the second to bring back.

She told Frank, 'I'm going for my dinner then I'll be making a few calls. I'll be back late but I have another key so lock up when you finish. Oh! And talking of locks, the bolt on the office door needs mending. Will you do it, please.'

He broke off whistling to call, 'Righto, boss!' They both laughed and Laura went off to make sandwiches for herself and Tommy, home from school. In the afternoon she set out on her calls. One of the names on her first list was that of the Corrigan shipyard. She had crossed it out as a waste of her time.

Dan Corrigan had spent the morning in Newcastle on business but Nick, glancing into his father's office, saw him at his desk. He entered and sat down opposite Dan: 'I was talking to a – lady – last night.'

Dan noted the momentary hesitation, raised bushy eyebrows and grinned. 'Behaved yourself, I hope.'

Nick pictured Laura sheltering behind the skimpy towel and answered seriously, 'Yes.'

Dan signed a typewritten letter, reached for another and asked, only mildly curious, 'Anyone I know?'

'Someone you know of.'

A big, bold signature. 'Who?'

'Laura Stanfield.'

'Who?' Dan looked up, brows wrinkling now as he searched his memory. Then he remembered and threw down his pen: 'That loose woman? Good God!'

Nick said, 'She's back in Monkwearmouth. Her aunt died—'

'Ah!' Dan interrupted. 'And she's come for the funeral. The sooner she clears off again, the better.'

'No. Her uncle died as well – George Finley.'

'The one that runs the sawmill?'

'Ran it, yes. He left the sawmill and the timber yard to the girl and she's going to stay here and keep it going. I dropped in there expecting to see George . . .' Nick explained, tactfully making no mention of how he had walked in on Laura.

Dan heard him out, sitting back in his chair and scowling. At the end he said, 'A woman like her to manage a business like that? She'll never do it.'

'She had one customer while I was there. She dealt with him all right but she'll need more than one to keep going.'

'She'll need a hell of a lot more than one and she'll get no work from this yard,' Dan snorted and picked up his pen again.

Laura worked through half of her list that day. Some of those she contacted said they would give her work, others said they might. The rest made various quickly fabricated excuses and Laura knew she could count them out. But she told herself, 'I'm not finished yet,' and set out again the next morning.

She returned in the late afternoon, tired and dispirited, with more promises but not a single order. As she turned into the yard she saw Nick Corrigan's motor car standing before the office. He and Frank Pearson were in conversation. Depression turned to anger as she stalked up to them and asked Frank, 'What does this gentleman want?'

He stuttered, 'I d-don't know. He just g-got here.'

So Laura rounded on Nick: 'What do you want?'

He took off his cap. 'I came to see you.' Then he amended hurriedly, 'Talk to you.' That only made the gaffe worse.

Laura remembered how he had last seen her and snapped, 'I don't want to talk to you.' She turned to Frank and asked, 'Is everything all right?'

'N-no, lass, it isn't.' He was obviously upset, his hands trembling.

Laura took his arm gently. 'Tell me what's the matter.'

'I mended the bolt on the office door. While I was at it a couple o' chaps came in, big fellers. They said I was b-backing a loser and I should pack in and go home. I told them to g-go to hell. They laughed but they went, only they shouted that I should get out because there wouldn't be any yard or sawmill left afore long.' He had dug his hands into the pockets of his overalls but he went on, 'They didn't frighten me. I'm stopping.'

Nick asked, 'Do you know them?'

Frank shook his head. 'Never saw them afore.'

Laura patted his back. 'It's about your finishing time. You may as well go home now.'

'Aye.' And he added, 'I've got the timber sorted out and I've left a list in the office of what we want.' He shrugged into his jacket, called, 'I'll see you tomorrow,' and trudged off out of the yard.

Laura turned on Nick: 'I'll thank you to leave.'

'I'll leave when I'm ready.' And before Laura could

explode, he went on, 'In my dealings with you I've always tried to be polite. A little common courtesy from you wouldn't come amiss.'

Laura fumed at this accusation. 'I *have* been polite!'

'I said I'd come to talk to you but you try to send me off without hearing me.'

She grudgingly accepted the truth of this and demanded, 'So what is it? Another lecture?'

Nick was silent a moment. He thought that he had never struck a woman but he was coming close.

Then something of this must have shown in his face, or there was some transference of thought, because Laura whispered, 'Don't you *dare* lay a finger on me!'

That made him laugh, at her and himself because he could have picked her up with one hand. As she stared at him, bewildered and suspicious, he said, 'Yesterday you claimed to be open for business.'

He had told his father, 'Ralph Hillier was unfaithful to her and treated her badly.'

Dan grumbled, 'She wasn't married to him, stole him from his wife. I suspected he was no good but that doesn't excuse her running off with him. I won't deal with a woman like that.'

Nick pointed out, 'We deal with Seth Bullock.'

'So?'

'I don't like him or the way he treats women – and men when he can get away with it.'

Dan shrugged. 'Neither do I but that is business.'

'And he hasn't any competition now — if Laura Stanfield fails,' Nick said. 'I think competition is desirable.'

'There's that, I suppose,' Dan admitted, yet still argued, 'But after what she did?'

'True,' said Nick, and quoted Dan's words back at him: 'But that's business.'

Now he told Laura, 'I want to place an order for ladders for ships we're building in the yard. Are you interested?'

At first she did not believe him, then she was suspicious and almost asked, 'What are you up to?' But she held her tongue and after a second or two let relief wash over her. An order for ladders! She was being thrown a lifeline. She did not let it show but said calmly, 'Thank you. You'd better come into the office.'

There he gave her the specifications of the various ladders. Then he prepared to leave, but said first, 'You'll be telling the police about those fellows who tried to frighten Frank Pearson.'

Laura shook her head. 'No, I won't.'

He warned, 'I think they mean trouble.'

'I'm sure they do,' Laura agreed. 'And I'm sure Seth Bullock sent them because he wants me to sell this yard to him. So he sent his bully-boys to frighten me out. But if I told the police they would put a constable outside. That would keep the bully-boys away, but as soon as the policeman was taken off, they would be back.'

'So what do you intend to do?'

But that was one question too many. She was grateful for the order which was saving her from ruin, but she thought she had suffered too much in the past at the hands of this man. 'Thank you, but that's my affair. Goodnight, Mr Corrigan.'

His lips tightened, but he said only, 'Goodnight.'

Laura watched him climb into his motor car and drive away. She wondered why he had come to her aid and never considered the obvious answer. Nor did he.

She collected some old oil cans she had found in a corner of the sawmill. They still smelled of the paraffin used in the lamps out in the yard. She spread them across the ground close to the wall where it had broken down. Then she locked up the yard and walked home to cook dinner for Tommy and herself.

Afterwards she asked Addy if she could put up Tommy for the night, then packed her valise and returned to the yard. The office was chilly, prey to cold draughts but she built up the fire in the stove, then unrolled her valise and slipped into the sleeping bag, still fully dressed. She turned off the lamp and tried to sleep but lay wide awake and restless for a long time, staring into the darkness. She thought that now, with the order for ladders, there was hope for the yard, but while one order would set them moving, more were needed. Tomorrow . . . Nick Corrigan . . .

She woke, struggling out of sleep, vaguely aware that some noise – but then it came again, an empty clanking, and she knew someone had kicked into the oil cans set by the breach in the wall. Laura fumbled for the electric torch left handily by her sleeping bag, found it and shaded its narrow conical beam with her hand as she focused it on the alarm clock. That was also by her side, there to wake her in the morning but now telling her it was just past midnight. The clanking had stopped and there was movement outside, a low mutter of voices. Someone tried the door, there was a muttered oath and then a boot crashed against it and it burst open.

Laura thought, farcically annoyed, Frank has just mended that! Then the two shoved into the office, to halt inside the door, tall and menacing as she shone the torch on them and demanded, 'Who's that? What are you doing here?' She kept her voice from shaking but it came out high.

One of the two, both with their hands up now to shade their eyes, said, 'She's here!'

The other laughed. 'Don't worry about her. We might even have a bit o' fun.'

He took a pace towards Laura and she slipped her hand under her pillow and found – nothing. She scrabbled frantically, searching, the beam of the torch dancing while he leered at her and made an obscene gesture showing what he intended. Then she found what she sought, closed the breech, eased off the safety catch and squeezed the trigger. The shotgun she had brought back from Serbia, that had weighed so heavily in her valise, bucked in her hand, flamed and bellowed. The birdshot whipcracked between the two men and smashed into the roof. They cowered for a shocked second and then ran. Laura struggled out of her sleeping bag, muttering as its folds held on to her, but she could see them, and another figure come running and lash out. One of the runners fell and the other tripped over him. The third arrival seemed to jump on to the other two. Then Laura was out of the bag and the office. She shone her torch on the group and Nick Corrigan snapped, 'Take that light out of my eyes!'

Laura lowered the beam, seeing that one of the men lay across the legs of the other, both face down. Nick stood over them and held one arm of the uppermost, the wrist twisted and his boot lodged in the small of the man's back. He squinted at Laura and asked, 'What was that noise? I thought they'd used a gun!'

'No, I did.' Laura held it up to show him.

'Good God!' Nick had a lot of questions he wanted to ask but settled for saying, 'You can't do that. You might have killed them.'

'I don't know what they intended to do to me. One of them was talking about having "a bit of fun".' She crouched so she could look into the faces of the two men, now turned to squint into the beam of the torch. She shoved the stubby barrels of the shotgun, unloaded and its safety catch securely on now, into the beam so they could see it. 'Now, who are you?'

The one underneath was bleeding from the nose. He snuffled, 'Joe Garvey.' The other licked his lips, eyes fixed on the shotgun: 'Les Morton.' They both smelled of rum.

Laura thought, They've been taking Dutch courage. She asked, 'Who sent you?' Though she thought she knew the answer.

For a second neither answered, but then Laura moved the muzzle of the shotgun so it pointed, almost, at Les Morton's head. She had thought he seemed the most frightened and now he admitted, voice rising shakily, 'Seth Bullock.'

'You'd better tell him to do his own dirty work. I let you off tonight, but if there is a next time, I won't, God help me.' She stood up and back, then looked at Nick: 'You can kick them out the way they came in.' And pointed.

Nick allowed them to climb unsteadily to their feet, both big men, though he topped them by some inches. He herded them to the broken stretch of wall. There he said softly, 'Say a word to the police and I'll see you go down for this night's work. Now get out.' They shambled away.

Nick walked back to Laura where she stood outside the office, hugging herself in the cold night air, but that was not why she shivered. She was thinking how the affair might have ended if . . . She asked him, 'How did you come to be here?'

'I didn't like the sound of those chaps who threatened Frank and thought I would keep an eye on the place tonight.' He had stood in the darkness of a shop doorway and watched. When he saw the intruders he had followed them in. He had heard the clanking of the empty oil cans and was just picking his way through them himself when the shot was fired. He ran towards the office and when the two figures fled from it he hit the first and the second fell over his accomplice. He did not explain any of this but Laura guessed at what happened.

She said, quietly, 'I'm glad you came. I'm grateful to you.' She had found the gun just in time. Another second and she would have been in the clutches of Garvey and Morton. She would have needed Nick Corrigan then.

He asked, 'Where did you get that gun? And what are you going to do with it?'

'A friend gave it to me in Serbia, in case I needed it – and I did. I'm keeping it for the same reason.' She met his gaze squarely and he knew there was no point in arguing, especially after the events of that night.

He said, 'What are you going to do now?'

'Go back to bed.' Laura added to herself: And try to sleep. But she was sure she would not, though she was tired enough.

He thought that there was no doubting her courage. 'Then I'll bid you goodnight.'

Laura accompanied him to the gate and unlocked the small door in it. Nick ducked his head to pass through into the street and Laura bade him: 'Goodnight, Mr Corrigan.'

He put his finger to his cap in salute and strode off down the street. Laura watched his tall figure pass through the pool of light from a street lamp then fade into the darkness.

She locked the gate again and returned to the office.

There she jammed the door shut with a chair wedged against it and settled down in her sleeping bag, after making sure, again, that the safety catch of the shotgun was on and the breech open. As she had expected, she lay awake, tired but unable to sleep, the events of the day running through her mind. She thought that Nick Corrigan had redeemed himself to some extent but he had a long way to go to make up for the anguish he had caused her, unwittingly or no.

And she had always known she would meet with some hostility, coming back to this place, but to be attacked in this way! She comforted herself that the two who had come this night would not come again. She was sure of that.

Laura was right. They shifted uncertainly before Seth Bullock — they had gone to him at once — and he stood squat in a dressing-gown, called down from his bed. He was not pleased: 'What the hell d'ye mean, waking me in the middle of the night?'

Garvey, his face still smeared with blood from his nose, said, 'We got in all right, but she was there.'

'All the better,' said Seth, grinning now. 'You threw a fright into her, eh?'

'Like hell we did,' mumbled Morton, loose-lipped. 'She had a gun.'

Seth gaped. 'A *gun*?'

'Aye, and she fired at us.'

Seth dismissed that: 'A blank.'

Morton sniffed. 'Blank be buggered. It blew a hole in the roof.'

Garvey added, 'And when we tried to clear out, there was this big feller waiting. He just showed up in front o' me and never gave me a chance. I think he's broken my nose.'

Seth glared from one to the other. 'So — what then?' The two exchanged glances, neither willing to give the message. Seth snapped impatiently, 'Well?'

Garvey said, 'She told us not to go in again, said she'd do for us if we did.'

Seth snorted. 'You let a lass chase you off the place! She was bluffing!'

Stung, Garvey snapped back, 'No, she wasn't. And she said to tell you to do your own dirty work.'

'*What!*' Seth swore, a torrent of obscenities. The other two waited glumly.

He finally ran out of breath and Morton said, 'If that's all right we'll get away to bed.'

'All *right?* Get out o' my sight, the pair o' ye!'

Garvey whined, 'What about my nose, boss?'

'Damn your nose! That's your own fault! Out!'

When they had gone Seth paced the floor. What should he do now? Send an anonymous letter to the police, telling them that the Stanfield girl had a gun? But he did not like the idea of involving them. Suppose that provoked that lass to complain about him? He did not want the law investigating his dealings.

But he was still determined to have that yard from her. He would think of a way. And meanwhile he would try to force her out by competition.

Laura knew none of this but was intuitively apprehensive. She finally fell asleep wondering uneasily what the next day might bring.

Chapter Sixteen

'We're not used to dealing with ladies, particularly young ladies.'

The next day began well with a blue sky and sunshine and warm for the time of year. Laura put on a mid-calf, white silk dress that showed off her legs and a red linen edge-to-edge jacket. Silk stockings and black court shoes went on her feet, a large straw boater on her bobbed chestnut hair. They were all clothes, like those she had worn to return home, that she had bought out of a gratuity given to her on account of her service in the ambulance column. She turned this way and that before the mirror and thought, That will do.

Tommy stared, his mouth an O, then said, 'You're like a princess.'

Laura laughed and kissed him. 'You get away to school, young man.'

She had set out to call, with more determination than hope, on some former customers who had not given business to the yard for some time. Now she was closeted with the first, manager of a small engineering shop employing a score of men, all of whom had ogled Laura as she walked through the clangorous din and oily smell of the shop to his glass-sided office. He smiled at her, a man of forty stroking a silky moustache. Laura could read that smile: 'By! She's a little cracker!' She thought, Well, all's fair in business. She returned his smile brilliantly and saw the effect of that. 'Corrigan's are dealing with me.'

That impressed him and his eyebrows lifted. 'Are they, by Jove!'

'We're working on an order from them now but seeking more business. My uncle was getting on in years and I think he was finding it hard to keep some of his valued customers, like yourself. I'm here today to tell you we are ready to accept commissions from you again. If I could quote you one or two prices . . .'

She found that her work of the previous day, pricing various items, while it was sketchy, helped her to offer terms with more confidence. He listened, and after a while with as much attention to business as to the vibrant young girl just the other side of his desk. Laura came away with a firm promise of a future order and a mental note that she would remind him of that promise.

At the end of the morning she was humming happily

to herself, on her way home to lunch with Tommy. She had other promises *and* three firm orders in her bag. This had surprised as much as pleased her. Then the last customer she saw had let slip: 'Your prices are quite a bit less than Bullock's yards are charging now.'

Laura said non-committally, 'Really?' She had no idea what Seth was charging.

'Aye.' He grimaced. 'He put them up as soon as George died. Before then he was undercutting the old feller, and, besides, George wasn't able to handle as much work as he used to.' He explained guiltily, 'You had to wait for him.' Then he grinned at Laura. 'But it's good to see a bit o' competition.' And he gave her an order.

Laura thought that possibly explained her success that morning, but welcomed that success for itself. She was happy as she turned into Dundas Street. Carts and a brewer's dray drawn by patient horses, with here and there a motor lorry, all trundled back and forth. Its two sides were lined with small shops and its pavements busy with people.

'*You fancy woman!*' The shriek rose high above the sound of traffic and chatter. The streams of people passing slowed and halted, startled and curious. Then the voice screamed again: 'You've got no right here! Adulterer! Harlot! Murderer!' Doris Grimshaw lurched from one pavement to cross to the other where Laura stood but halted out in the street and pointed a black-nailed finger. 'You'll find no forgiveness here! Trollop! These are all decent people. You come here flaunting your finery, all bought with the wages of sin!'

Laura saw the glances of disapproval aimed at her by some of the women, and knew she stood out in that crowd. And there was Seth Bullock, grinning, a lounging spectator. Laura knew she was blushing, would have liked to hide but knew she could not. This had to be faced. She cried, 'Anything I have was paid for by honest work! It was bought with money I didn't spend on gin and beer.' That told and some glances were levelled at Doris now. Her slurred speech and her swaying testified to her drunkenness.

She started, 'Your poor father—'

Laura cut across her, not slurred but rising clear as a bell: 'My poor father was killed at work when I was three years old! The man who took his place – God help me – was the victim of his own bad temper, not any of my doing. I ran away with a man. I would have married him but I couldn't. I was a fool but not the first to be used by a man. I'm not whingeing or making excuses. This woman who is accusing me was walking out, and worse, with that stepfather of mine while my mother was dying in agony.'

Laura's voice broke then and Doris tried to get in: 'That's lies she's telling—'

But the crowd shouted her down: 'Let her have her say!'

Laura shook her head as if to clear it and went on: 'I've not forgotten and I'll not forgive. You're an evil woman and you'll come to a bad end.' She looked past Doris to the ring of faces, three or four deep around her now while others crowded out of the shops to listen. Seth was no longer grinning and instead glared hatred. 'I made a mistake but I'm not the only one.' She recognised most of the faces in that crowd, as they would remember her. She let her gaze focus on some of them, one after another as she continued, 'It's been known for lasses to walk down the aisle in white and the bairn moving inside them but nothing was said. There's lasses had a bairn when their man had been away at sea nearly a year but there was forgiveness.' They knew who she was talking about without her naming them. 'I was born and bred here and I've come home. I'm not asking for help or sympathy, just that you leave me alone.'

She finished then and into the quiet a woman called, 'That's right, bonny lass!' Laura saw the owner of the voice, a tall girl at the back of the ranks of spectators, and knew her at once. That cry of approval broke the silence and voiced the feelings of the gathering. The crowd shredded away, talking among themselves, avoiding Doris Grimshaw and turning their glances of disapproval on her now. Doris lurched away, shaking her fist at Laura and muttering, to stagger round a corner and out of sight.

Doris was soon overtaken by Seth Bullock and he said, 'It wants a few more like you to show her up. That lot back there don't know what she's like.'

Doris peered at him suspiciously. 'What's it got to do wi' you?'

'I'm Seth Bullock.' And he boasted, 'I own the Bullock sawmills and timber yards.' He was gratified to see her impressed and went on, 'Old George Finley left his yard to her when he died. I offered to buy it at a fair price — it's no use to a lass like her — but she turned me down out of spite on account of I know how she ran off with a married feller.'

'She's got plenty o' that,' muttered Doris. 'I'd like to murder the bitch.'

'Listen!' Seth gripped her arm and lowered his voice. 'If you find out anything that will help me get her out of that yard, let me know. It'll be worth your while.' He told her where she could find him and went on his way. He had found an ally of sorts. Anyone who hated Laura Stanfield was a friend to Seth.

Laura went to the girl who had cried out, and who had been her friend when she was training to be a shorthand typist: 'Sybil Johnson!'

They hugged each other and Sybil said, 'It's Payton now, not Johnson.'

'And Mrs, too, I hope,' teased Laura, for Sybil pushed a pram holding a sleeping baby while a two-year-old sat on top.

'Aye,' said Sybil. They laughed together, then Sybil asked, 'When did you get back?'

'Just a few days ago. Thanks for backing me up.'

'There are a few of us who know that woman.' Sybil

jerked her head indicating the direction taken by the departed Doris. 'Have you had much of that?'

'A bit, but I knew I would.'

'It's not fair because I'm sure it wasn't your fault.'

'It was – half of it. Ralph was married when I ran off with him. There was a lot I didn't know about him, but I knew that.'

Sybil said, 'Oh,' uncertainly.

Laura's smile was lopsided. 'I should have seen through him but I didn't.' She pressed on to save them both embarrassment: 'How are you getting on?'

Sybil brightened. 'Fine! My Steve came home safe from the war, thank God! We've got rooms in Dock Street. The bairns are lovely and there's another on the way.'

'So you've no worries.'

'Well, making ends meet – that's not always easy, especially if Steve hasn't got any overtime, and there's not much of that now the war is over. I'd get a job if I could but we've nobody to look after the bairns. And who would give me a job when I have three to care for?'

That was always a problem. Laura managed with Tommy because she had no boss but herself, and there was always Addy next door to help. And that reminded her: 'I've got to go. There's a little boy waiting for me to give him his dinner.' Then, seeing Sybil's delighted surprise, 'No! He's not mine, but his mother died so I've taken him on. I'll call round to Dock Street to see you as soon as I can, but I'm pretty busy. Uncle George and Aunt Cath left me the timber yard and sawmill.'

'Ooh!' Sybil said with delighted surprise. 'I'm glad for you. What you get for that could set you up in a little shop. Or you could save the money for your bottom drawer and go back to typing.'

Laura wondered why she had not thought of that. Then she knew: she did not want a little shop – or marriage. 'I'm not selling.' And as Sybil stared, perplexed: 'I'm going to run it – I hope.'

Her friend shook her head. 'You're a funny one. I'd love a steady job and can't get one. You could walk into one and you don't want it. You're always different.'

Laura didn't agree but couldn't argue. 'Anyway, I have to get along.'

They embraced then Laura hurried away, Sybil calling after her, 'Lovely to have you back!' Laura cherished that welcome after the row with Doris and it restored her cheerful, optimistic mood.

She ate with Tommy and later saw him off to school again. Then she happily returned to the yard and found Frank had mended the office door again and was surveying the broken-down stretch of wall. He grimaced as she joined him: 'Just having a look, boss, but I'm not much of a hand as a bricklayer.'

Laura shook her head. 'Don't worry about that. It's more important for you to make a start on those ladders for Corrigan's.'

'Right y'are, boss.' He trudged off into the sawmill and Laura heard the steam engine start up.

She thought that the wall would have to wait because

she had to count her pennies until the sawmill began to make money. She went to the office, stirred up the fire in the stove and added some cast-off pieces of wood to make a cheerful blaze. Then she got out of the desk Frank's list of timber required, to make out an order. She looked in the cupboard where she knew there was paper with the letterhead: Geo. Finley, Timber and Joinery Supplied, above the address. There was also a pen but the nib was bent. The bottle of ink was almost dry. Laura muttered under her breath, annoyed, but only mildly so, still in a happy mood. It was bad enough having to *write* the damned list anyway. And she hoped there would be a lot more of that work to do – but with these tools? It would make a far better job if––

She looked up as the knock came at the door. 'Come in!' It opened to reveal Nick Corrigan. He stepped in and closed the door behind him, but first inspected the repair. 'Nice job. So you're a carpenter as well.'

Laura grinned. 'Not me. Frank did it, as I expect you guessed.'

He stared before he went on, because he had not seen her smile since she had come home, and rarely before that. 'How are you today?'

'Fine.' She thought, Now I have some orders and I might have a fighting chance.

'Good.' He was reluctant to proceed with his errand because this was a side of her he had not seen before. But it had to be done. 'What are you going to do about that shotgun? Because you could get into very serious trouble for having it, let alone discharging it. I take it you don't have a licence?'

'I haven't,' said Laura. Then she asked, 'Have you?'

Nick was taken aback for a moment, but, 'Yes, I have. My father bought a gun after we were burgled.'

Laura could still picture him looming out of the darkness the night before. Suppose she had seen him before the others – and fired? That possibility had cost her some sleep. This man had infuriated her more than once, had caused her embarrassment, but if she had shot him . . . On impulse she asked, 'Will you take it?'

He was not prepared for that question, but was quick in his reply: 'I'll buy it from you. How much do you want?'

Laura recalled looking hungrily at the Armstrong typewriter in a shop window only that morning. 'Five guineas.' A new machine would have cost twice that, over ten pounds.

'Done.'

'I'll fetch it.' Laura rose from her chair. 'It's at home. Make yourself comfortable. I won't be long.'

Nick offered, 'My car is outside. Can I—'

'No, thank you.' Laura was not going to be seen riding around with any young man in his car, let alone that of Nick Corrigan.

'I'll walk with you.'

'No.' Nor that, either. 'Just wait here.' She saw his lips tighten at the snub. She did not want to explain but did so: 'For my sake, please. I've heard enough talk about me already. I don't want any more.'

He almost answered: 'And whose fault is that?' But instead he bowed his head in a stiff acknowledgement and kept his thoughts to himself. As he waited he wandered about the yard, exchanged a few words with Frank and finally returned to sit in the office. He took note of the desk, empty save for the broken old pen and almost dry ink bottle. He sighed and shook his head, told himself he had done what he could to help — admittedly for the sake of the memory of George and Cath Finley, but . . .

Laura returned with the gun, wrapped unrecognisably as such in an old sack she had found. After cautiously reaching inside the sack to confirm the ugly weapon was not loaded, Nick paid her.

Laura said drily, 'Does that ease your conscience?'

'Yes. And yours?'

Laura admitted, 'It does.' But then asked apparently seriously, but mischievously, 'What if I need it and want it back?'

Nick saw through that: 'I'll treat that as a joke. But you'd have to talk to my father and I doubt if he'd listen.' He paused in the doorway of the office, filling it. 'Good luck. You're going to need it. Running a place like this is a man's job.'

'People keep telling me that. I don't need your advice but thank you for your good wishes. Goodbye, Mr Corrigan.'

He only grinned at that, his temper in hand now, and strode away. Laura watched him stride across the yard to his car and thought, Why do I let him annoy me? And was annoyed at the fact.

He drove off and thought that it might be easy to like the girl — if she was always as he had found her earlier today. Then, it had been hard to believe her record. But after the later waspish exchanges . . .

Laura bought her typewriter and had it delivered by a horse-drawn van late that same afternoon. Frank had finished work for the day and gone home but she wanted to try out her new toy. She was typing out the order for timber and humming happily to herself when she had another visitor. This time she opened the door to a burly, red-faced man. He lifted the battered trilby hat he wore and introduced himself in a flat Yorkshire accent: 'Benson, Abel Benson, Abel by name and able by nature. I'll build owt you like. How do.' He held out a big, broken-nailed hand to crush Laura's briefly. 'I was talking to Chris Marley and he said a lass had taken on ould George's place.'

'That's right.' Laura smiled at him. 'I have.'

'Right, then, I want some timber — wrote it down.' He pulled a scrap of paper from the pocket of a grubby waistcoat.

'Come in.' Laura seated him in the sagging armchair and it creaked and sagged further. She slipped back behind her desk and scanned the slip of paper. 'I can't supply all of this but I'm just making out an order now.' Which would need amending if she could win this business. She asked, 'When do you want it?'

'Next Monday morning.' Benson eyed her doubtfully. 'Can you do it?'

'Oh, aye.' Laura would make sure she could. 'I'll just add it to this order.' She whipped it out of the typewriter, inserted fresh paper and carbon and tapped rapidly at the keys.

Abel Benson watched her flying fingers and said, 'By, lass! You can't half work that machine. Ah could do wi' somebody like you one or two days a week.'

Laura had seen a lot of men like Benson in her time with the army. She paused to grin and flutter her eyelashes at him. 'Why, Mr Benson, what would Mrs Benson say?'

He guffawed. 'Say? Ah, booger, she'd kill me! Nay, what I meant was somebody to type up my letters and bills and so forth. I don't have enough work to keep a lass like you busy all week, and not a proper office neither, just a shed in the corner o' my yard.'

Laura, intent on her work and in full spate now, said, 'Hold on a minute.' But when she finished she whipped the completed order from her machine and smiled at Benson. 'We might be able to do each other a good turn, Abel.' She led him out of the office and to the section of wall that had collapsed. 'Could you build that up again?'

He inspected the wall: 'Oh, aye. D'ye want an estimate?'

'In a way. How much typing would you want done to cover the cost of the job?'

Benson blinked. 'Boogered if I know.'

'Well, you work it out — after you've seen how much

typing you want done.' That to encourage him to get on with the deal.

'Right y'are. I'll fetch the stuff round tomorrow and send a bricklayer next week – Tuesday.' He held out his hand again and they shook on it.

He left and Laura returned to her desk well pleased. She had got another order, saved some of her precious cash and she knew she would deal with his typing in an idle hour or so.

But next morning, when Benson brought his work for her – in a brown paper bag – he was accompanied by Laura's first customer, Chris Marley. Benson started, 'Ah was telling Chris about our arrangement.'

Chris spoke up for himself then: 'I've got some bills to send out. Neither me nor our lass are much as scholars and she has enough to do to look after the bairns. Then when I come in of a night I want to put me feet up. Will you take it on, like you have for Abel here?'

Laura said, 'I haven't got another wall to build.'

'Oh, aye, I know that! I'll pay cash, same as Abel will have to if he ever gets that wall done.'

Abel said amiably, 'Cheeky booger. I was building when you were still in infants school.'

Laura accepted. 'Done. Drop it in next time you're passing.'

After they had gone Laura sat in thought, a half-smile on her lips. Then she left the office, pulling on her coat, and crossed the yard to the sawmill. The steam engine was clunking away and the circular saw whining as Frank cut timber into lengths for ladders. Laura stood by his side and shouted above the din, 'I'm going out! See you later!' He nodded and smiled and she left him and walked round to the Carnegie library in Church Street. There she borrowed a Sunderland directory and began another list, this time of small businesses. Then she set out to make her calls. At noon she ate lunch with Tommy, answering his questions when she could, hugging and kissing him before his return to school.

Laura set out again in the afternoon. As she trudged the streets her thoughts harked back to Nick Corrigan, who had said she was trying to do a man's job: 'Good luck.' She would show him!

At the end of the afternoon Laura fetched up at the front door of a house in Dock Street. She rapped with the polished brass knocker and moments later heard childish voices. Then Sybil Payton opened to her, one child in her arms and another clinging to her skirt. She beamed and held the door wide: 'Come in, lass. I'll make a cup o' tea.'

Laura asked, 'Did you mean it the other day?'

Chapter Seventeen

Laura was being watched. She came out of the office, the post for that day dealt with, and started across the yard. There had been frost in the night and it lingered still as a silver skin in the shadows. Out in the open it was now only a dampness that glittered on the cobbles in the morning sun, that was low so it blazed blindingly into her eyes. But it was over the back of the sawmill and she saw quite clearly in the other direction, out through the open gates. There was no mistaking Doris Grimshaw.

Laura's sudden appearance had taken Doris by surprise. She stood on the pavement across the street from the yard, gaping at Laura. She wore the same black coat, greasy with age, and her hat clapped anyhow on her head. A horse and cart drove by then, loaded with coal, the driver perched on the front of his load, his scales and shovel beside him. The horse was trotting and the iron-rimmed wheels of the cart bounced on the cobbles, making a thunderous clangour. For a moment it hid Doris, then it had passed and Laura saw her scurrying away.

There was no doubt that Doris was watching the yard. She was not 'just passing'. It was not near where she lived and there was no reason for her to be there. The area round the timber yard was taken up by little workshops and the only shop as such, almost opposite the gates of the yard, was closed and shuttered. Besides, this was the second time Laura had caught her, had similarly surprised her just a week earlier. Now she went on, but wondered uneasily, Why?

Doris muttered to herself bad-temperedly as she fled, 'Gawping at me like I had no business there! Bloody cheek!' But later, more reasonably, she decided, 'She might tell the pollis if she catches me at it again.' She knew Seth wouldn't want that, and what she wanted herself was information he might pay for. So she went poking and peering about at the rear of the closed shop. She found it down a lane. Several of the little workshops backed on to it but had no overlooking windows, nor did they ever use it, if the piles of rubbish were any indication. She tried the back gate and found it unbolted. The yard inside was again littered with rubbish and she shoved it aside to reach the back door of the shop. That was locked but Doris smashed the window beside it with a half-brick, reached in and turned the key. Seconds later she was looking out of the shop window through the narrow slit between the shutters. No one in the timber yard could see her. There was even an old chair so she could sit while she kept watch. Doris settled into it.

Meanwhile Laura had gone on and told Frank Pearson, 'I'm going to collect some typing from Sybil and take it on to the clients. I should be back about one o'clock.' And she voiced the thought she had entertained for the past few days, 'I could do with some help, really.'

Frank started doubtfully, blinking down at the work on his bench. 'W-well, I can't type but—'

Laura interrupted him, laughing, 'No! Not you! You have enough to do here. In fact, the way the work is piling up, I think we may need to get some help for you.' She waved to him and set out. As she walked she thought about what she had said. Both the timber yard and the sawmill had steadily gained orders since she started up a month earlier, but she decided it was no use just sitting back. She had to strive to keep the customers she had and attract more. Laura knew what she intended to do about that.

In Dock Street Laura collected the typing Sybil had done the previous day. The typewriter she had bought for Sybil's use, second-hand but a Remington this time, stood on a high shelf out of reach of the children. Laura said, 'So you managed to finish all of it. I thought there would be two days' work in what I gave you.'

Sybil laughed and admitted, 'Janet came in and did a lot of it. I told her I was stuck and said we could share the money and she jumped at the chance. You remember her, in our class?'

'I do, a little blonde lass that looked about twelve.'

'That's the one, and she only looks to be fifteen now but she's tied to the house with two little bairns, the same as me.'

Laura saw opportunity there: 'Would she like to do some more?'

'I'm sure she would.'

Laura drank the cup of tea Sybil had made her and went on her way. Walking briskly she delivered the work she had taken from Sybil, some of it to little businesses across the river in the centre of Sunderland. At most of them she collected more typing to be done; at all she asked, 'Do you know anyone else who might want work typed?' She wrote down in a notebook the several names and addresses she was given.

The shopping bag in which she carried work completed or to be typed weighed heavily, so she took a tram to ride back over the bridge to the Monkwearmouth side of the river. As usual the Wear was crammed with shipping, building or lying at the fitting-out quays, moored to buoys or being hustled up or down river by bustling tugboats. There was a drift of smoke from a dozen funnels and a score of tall chimneys, and gulls wheeled through it screaming. This was the biggest shipbuilding town in the world.

Sight of Corrigan's yard brought Nick Corrigan to mind. Not for the first time she thought that she had not seen him for some weeks, though there was no reason why she should see him, and that suited her.

Laura delivered the thick sheaf of new work to be typed to Sybil and then ate the midday meal with Addy – and Tommy close alongside. Laura joked, but with serious intent, 'That bag nearly broke my arm this morning. I'll have to arrange something different – or find somebody else to do it. A young lad, maybe.'

Addy said, 'I know Mrs Wheeler's boy is looking for a job. He's not long finished school. They live just round the corner but you won't find his mother home now because she goes out cleaning. She'll be in tonight, though, after five o'clock.'

Afterwards, as usual, Laura sat with Tommy on her knee, his arms around her neck, and talked to him: 'What did you do at school this morning?' She listened to him intently, smiling or solemn as needs be, as he told her his little adventures. When it was time she kissed him and sent him off: 'Away you go, back to school. There's my little man.'

Laura returned to the timber yard and her office. She spent the rest of that day poring over figures relating to the sawmill and looking to see how each account was made up, how much it cost to make ladders, doors and other items of joinery, including labour and other over-heads. She was trying to find ways of cutting costs and so reducing prices. A week later she interrupted the exercise to draw up a hasty balance sheet on the typing. At the end of it she spent most of her working capital of that little venture on a third second-hand typewriter, this time another Remington, that cost her four pounds fifteen shillings; she had haggled for a discount because of her earlier purchases and won one. She needed this machine for Janet, the new recruit.

March went out like a lion with North Sea gales. As they eased at the end of the month Laura was blown up the yard from the gates to the office with the wind at her back. It was because of that prevailing wind that George Finley had sited the office as he had. The window and door were turned away from the gates and the wind and looked up past the side of the sawmill to the wall at the back of the yard.

Laura looked in on Frank in the sawmill and he offered, 'I was talking to a f-feller in the Wheatsheaf last night.' The Wheatsheaf was a public house. 'He was a joiner in a yard in Hartlepool but it went bust. He said the owner b-boozed it away. Anyway, he's looking for a job and the way he talked he knows his trade. I said I'd see him tonight if you wanted anybody.'

'I do,' said Laura. 'You can't cope with all the work now.' And as Frank nodded agreement she said, 'Ask him to come round tomorrow and I'll talk to him. What's his name?'

'Walter Skidmore.'

Laura returned to the office and settled down to her analysis of costings, a task that was almost complete now. There was no typing for her to do as it was all being done by Sybil and Janet while delivery and collection were now the province of Mrs Wheeler's Ernest. He was a large and lively fourteen-year-old, proud as punch at the responsibility given to him. He was equally proud of the delivery boy's bicycle Laura had bought for him on hire purchase, with its big steel basket over the little front wheel. He shuttled all day between Laura, Sybil, Janet and the clients, carrying work to be done or completed. Now Laura had only to make the round once every Friday to settle up accounts.

At the end of the morning she visited the shops in Dundas Street to buy a few articles. Wherever Laura went, butcher, baker or greengrocer all greeted her with a smile and: 'What are you wantin' today, hinny?' She knew she must have been talked about, but also knew that after talking they had made up their minds about her. She was content with that.

Laura ate lunch with Tommy and asked innocently, already knowing the answer, 'What are you doing at school this afternoon?'

He wriggled excitedly. 'The teacher said she would take us down to the river to see the launch!'

'Ooh!' said Laura. It was common knowledge that a ship was to be launched. She listened, copying his expressions, as he told her about it. Then she sent him off: 'Mind you behave yourself, and watch out for me. I might be there!'

In the afternoon she walked down to the river with Addy. The Buchanan yard was launching the ship and as usual at these ceremonies there were crowds of people lining the quayside upriver of the launching. Some were men but most were housewives, or children from local schools brought down by their teachers to watch the event. Tommy was there and Laura asked permission for him to stand with her, and his teacher agreed. Tommy came to her eagerly, slipping his hand into hers. He cast proud glances over his shoulder at his school-mates that said plainly: This is my Auntie Laura. She knew she was being examined by the children and the women. She had dressed in her red edge-to-edge jacket over a white skirt and knew she stood out as a consequence, knew it might have been wiser to have appeared in more sedate garb. Laura wore it defiantly anyway.

The ship on the stocks was moving! Laura cheered excitedly with all of them as the vessel slid down into the river. Its momentum nearly carried it across to the other side but the retaining hawsers checked it. Nothing checked the wave it set up, however. That came humping across the river and swelled up on to the quay. Laura ran back with the rest, all fleeing to keep their feet dry, Tommy and the children shrieking and giggling. Laura was laughing like any bairn as the water receded and she halted. Then she saw Nick Corrigan watching her.

He stood some fifty yards away where his motor car was standing, his tall, broad figure seen clear above the heads between them, his thatch of black hair tousled by the wind. She could not read his expression – was it censorious? She thought it likely and flashed him a defiant glance before turning away.

He registered that and thought, wryly amused, No change there! He had had no reason to visit the sawmill except — curiosity? He had concluded that when he wanted a fight he knew where to find one, though in an odd way he had missed her. But he had heard the business was doing well, and she seemed happy. He climbed into the Arrol-Johnston and drove off but he took with him the memory of a laughing girl.

Laura returned to the timber yard and the office to finish her day's work. She concentrated on the figures on the desk; she had almost completed her review of pricing, had established where numerous cuts could be made and still make a profit. When Frank called, 'Goodnight,' she decided it was time to go home and put away her books. She sat back and looked at the result. It seemed she had overcharged for some jobs, undercharged for others. No matter; she had had to get the business started. She was sure her efforts would win her more customers and orders. As she stepped out of the office and turned round its corner to walk down the yard to the gate, she took in the road and pavement outside in one swift glance. She was relieved to see that Doris was not watching the yard now, but not surprised after Laura had caught her at it. She locked the gate and walked home contentedly.

But Doris was there, sitting on her old chair, peering out through the window of the closed shop like some brooding, malevolent spirit intent on evil.

Chapter Eighteen

SUMMER 1919. MONKWEARMOUTH.

Laura was restless and in a mood for mischief. She sat outside the office in the afternoon sunshine because there was nothing for her to do. In four months of hard work she had built up a customer base of dozens of small businesses, all of whom wanted typing done. But she had also recruited four girls — two more besides Sybil and Janet — now industriously typing at home on machines Laura had loaned to them. They did it all. Even the organisation had been taken over by Sybil Payton.

Laura yawned. Walter Skidmore, skinny and smirking, stepped out between the wide-open doors of the sawmill and crossed to the timber racks. He sorted out the length he wanted, carried it back and called to Laura: 'Nice day, boss.' He disappeared into the sawmill again.

Laura smiled in return, then scowled. Walter was

another one. She had taken him on a month ago, when Frank had admitted they were taking more orders than he could cope with. Walter had jumped at the chance when Laura offered him the job of running the sawmill. Frank had said flatly that he did not want that responsibility, would be happier working with the machines and leaving the organisation and office work to someone else. He was still sensitive about his stammer and shaking hands, brought on by his suffering in the war.

Walter was a skinny whippet of a man, sandy hair carefully parted and slicked into a quiff on his brow. His pale eyes perpetually blinked. He made frequent reference to his service in the army during the war but was vague as to details. Neither Frank nor Laura knew he had spent the whole of it in a quartermaster's store in Yorkshire. He seemed eager to please, was always brisk and busy and had soon shown himself capable of running the yard – and the office as well. He had started by looking after it when Laura went out to drum up fresh business but now he did it all.

Laura could tell herself she had made a success of the place but she felt no joy in it now. She was not rich, far from it. Her two little enterprises were showing a net profit that was enough to keep her and Tommy and still save a few shillings each week. But that was all. She wanted to earn more, if she could. And she was bored. She did not want the sort of excitement of the early days when Seth Bullock had tried to force her out, but she was not used to sitting in idleness and it irked her.

'Ekweoh!' A boy in ragged shorts and shirt trotted across the gateway, shrill voice crying again, 'Ekweoh!' He carried a bundle of the *Sunderland Daily Echo* and Laura called him over, opened her purse and bought a copy.

'Ta, missus.' As he trotted away, Laura glanced over the front page lethargically. Blacketts had summer blouses on sale for thirteen shillings; she would have to look at them. Then she turned a page and the name Corrigan caught her eye. She thought absently that Nick had never returned after their last abrasive parting in January when he had bought the gun from her, except for that exchange of glances at the launch. She decided it was hardly surprising because she had rebuffed him more than once, though he had deserved it for how he had treated her. She read on. When she saw the advertisement she almost passed it over, but then she thought this would be a chance to satisfy her desire for more money and a remedy for her boredom. She grinned. Well, why not?

That evening she called in at the house next door to ask Addy: 'I'm thinking of applying for a job. If I get it – and if I decide to take it – could you help out with Tommy? Look after him for an hour or two each day?'

'O' course I could,' said Addy. 'Where is it?'

It was two days later that Dan Corrigan, seated in his office, asked his son, 'All ready?'

'I've cleared my desk,' said Nick. 'I'm going home in a minute or two to finish packing, but it's only the stuff I'll need on the way. My heavy luggage is locked and ready.'

Dan advised, 'Take as long as you need in France and Italy. There have been a lot of developments in this industry here, during the four years of war. There's doubtless been others out there and we need to know what they are.'

Nick nodded; they had discussed this and planned his trip for weeks. He reached out to pick up the small clock on his father's blotter: 'Nice little timepiece.'

'For one of the typists: Betty Armitage. She's resigned to get married; her husband has landed a plum job in Canada and, of course, she is going with him. So we've advertised for a replacement; had a lot of replies and Cheyney is interviewing them all now. I'll see the one he selects. I like to know the people I meet about the place.' He knew most of the men in his yard by sight.

Nick said, 'Cheyney is getting on very well.'

Dan nodded. 'Very well. He's a good man.' Cheyney was the chief clerk and had come from the Tyne to take over the job when the former chief had retired.

Nick rose. 'I'd better be getting on.'

There was a tap at the door and Dan called, 'Come in!'

Cheyney entered, forty, dapper and briskly efficient. 'I've sorted out the best applicant, in my opinion, Mr Corrigan. Will you see her now?'

'You sound enthusiastic.' Dan grinned. 'I trust your judgement but I'll see the young lady in a minute.' And as Cheyney retreated, 'What's her name?'

'Laura Stanfield.'

'What did you say?' Dan gaped at him.

Cheyney hesitated in the doorway: 'Miss Laura Stanfield, sir.'

Dan's mouth clamped shut for a moment, then he said curtly, 'Wait — outside, please.'

As the door closed on Cheyney's black-suited back, Dan turned on Nick. 'Did you hear that?' And when Nick nodded Dan exploded, 'She's doing this out of devilment!'

Nick could not deny it.

His father growled, 'Cheyney came from Newcastle so he's never heard about her. But *we* know her, only too well, and I'll not employ that sort of woman.'

Nick asked, 'What sort?'

'Hey?' Dan glared. 'That sort, of course. Immoral.'

'We employ that sort of man. We never ask whose bed they got out of to come to work.'

'No, but that's different.'

'Is it? But anyway, I think we may be condemning her without proof.'

'*Proof!*' Dan threw up his hands. 'She ran away with a married man! What more proof d'ye want?'

'She was only eighteen.'

'Old enough to know right from wrong.'

'Young enough to be exploited,' Nick countered. 'I told you I thought Ralph was a bad lot, and that he'd been unfaithful to her.'

'Yes, but—'

'There was more than one woman, and this while she was carrying his child.'

Dan whispered, 'Good God!' He stared across at the closed door for some time, then: 'You think we should give her a chance?'

'Yes. It may be that she's trying to annoy us.' He was sure she was, but . . . 'It's possible she needs the job. She took on the care of a boy, inherited him when she inherited the sawmill.'

'Aye?' Dan was silent again, then: 'There could be talk.'

Tongue in cheek, Nick said, 'There was talk about Great-uncle Fergus.'

'Aye,' Dan admitted. His Uncle Fergus had had several mistresses and died in the arms of one of them. 'He worked hard and . . . Quite.'

Nick argued, using the terms taught him by his father, 'If the ship is right and the price is right – talk won't matter.'

Dan acknowledged the quote with a wry grin, and gave in. 'Very well.' He had one other thought then: 'We've had a chat like this before, when I didn't want to give her some business. You stick up for this lass.'

Nick shrugged. 'I just think she deserves a fair deal.'

'You're not falling for her?'

'Good God, no!' Nick laughed. He was quite sure of that.

Dan called, 'Mr Cheyney!' And when he opened the door: 'Bring in Miss Stanfield, please.' And as Nick crossed to the door, his father thought, He's ready to run the yard now.

Nick stood aside as Laura appeared in the doorway.

She had chosen to wear a decorous, high-necked, crisp white blouse with a full black skirt that swirled ten inches from the floor to show silk stockings and neat court shoes. A wide belt accentuated her slim waist. Her expression was meek and modest, but when only he could see she grinned mischievously, provoking. He gave her a nod of the head, unsmiling, and went on his way, but Laura thought, I bet you're wild!

Dan said, 'Sit down, Miss Stanfield.' He was standing, almost a mirror image of his son, not so tall but a big, broad bear of a man, hair greying and a welcoming smile on his face. He waved a thick-fingered hand at the single chair set before the desk and Laura sat down on it, straight-backed, knees together and hands in her lap. She was disconcerted by her reception, had not expected to progress this far, had thought she would be sent off with coldly concealed outrage. She had not seen Dan Corrigan before and he was neither cold nor – apparently – outraged.

He seated himself, relaxed back in his chair, and said jovially, 'So you want to help us build ships.' And thinking, She's a damned pretty girl, and well turned out.

'I'll just type if I may, sir. Any ship I built might not float very long.'

He grinned. 'Ours don't sink – but I'll touch wood.' He reached out to tap the surface of the desk and thought, She has a sense of humour and doesn't titter. Looks you straight in the eye.

He asked her a few more questions, affably, and Laura

replied modestly but to the point. She detected he was wary, measuring her, but no more than any prospective employer would have done. She found that surprising, considering how they both knew her reputation. As the interview went on she decided he was like his son only in appearance. He was warmer and kinder. In fact, by the end of the short interview, she thought with some surprise, I *like* him.

As she left the office Dan thought, with equal surprise, I believe she'll do well here.

Laura was determined to do so, in the first place because that was her nature. She did not meet Nick and soon learned where he had gone. She would have liked to have seen his face when he found she was going to be working at Corrigan's yard, but she would have to be content with that grin she had given him as he had left his father's office.

She threw herself into her work at Corrigan's. The other typists were all Sunderland 'girls', an all-embracing title because they ranged from little Betty, fifteen, shy and in her first job, to Ganny (the local term for Granny) Bates, the silver-haired office 'mother', who remembered Nick when he was a very small boy in shorts. All had heard gossip about Laura. Six years had passed since she had run away with Ralph Hillier but it had not been forgotten. When faced with her, however, and challenged by her smile, curiosity overcame disapproval. They wondered what she was really like and were ready to accept her as she was. They found her cheerful, always ready to help and to take her turn at making the tea. Before the first week was out she was accepted.

News of her arrival and rumours about her past soon leaked out to the men in the yard and were embroidered. But one argued, 'You've got to speak as you find. Give the lass a chance.'

A riveter challenged, 'Now then, young Peter, what d'you know about it?'

'I know she looked after Billy Gatenby when he was paralytic, took him home so the redcaps wouldn't get him, fed him and got him to the train so he wasn't posted as a deserter. I know that much. So like I said, give her a chance.'

They did.

For her part, Laura liked them all, but more importantly she found a romance in her job. She had always been interested in the ships, as everyone was in the town, and now to be involved in their building was exciting.

She guessed, was sure, she was being watched by Dan, and welcomed it. She had confidence in her ability, had shown his son that she could run one business and start another; now she would show him. But while with Nick it had been *just* to show him, with Dan she wanted his approbation.

He called for a report from Cheyney and the chief clerk said, 'She's certainly lived up to my expectations. Her shorthand and typing are both faster and more accurate than any of the other girls. She learns quickly; I don't have to tell her anything twice. And she thinks for herself, organises her time.'

Dan raised thick eyebrows. 'D'ye think she might be after your job?'

Cheyney grinned. 'I hope not, sir. I wouldn't want to compete with her. For a start, I can't type.'

Dan was able to form his own opinion soon afterwards. Late one Saturday morning, Cheyney looked around the door of the room where the typists worked and saw only Laura, standing before the little mirror to put on her hat. He said, 'Everybody else gone, then?'

'It's past twelve,' Laura pointed out, albeit respectfully.

He pulled a face. 'The old man wants to dictate a letter to post to be delivered Monday. It'll have to be you.'

'Yes, Mr Cheyney,' Laura replied dutifully. She was glad Addy had taken her children, and Tommy, walking down to the beach, with sandwiches and a bottle of home-made ginger beer. It would not matter that she was late in joining them. So Laura reported to Dan with pencil, pad and smiling face.

He thought again, Damned pretty girl. But we'll see if that's influencing Cheyney or if she is as good as he says.

The letter was a long one of several pages and involving tables of figures and calculations. When Laura brought it back to him – in a surprisingly short time – he pored over it carefully and found it neatly laid out and perfectly typed.

He said, 'Well done.' And thought, There's my answer.

Cheyney spoke nothing but the truth. The memory stayed with him.

When Nick returned after several weeks Dan greeted him: 'Good to have you back.' He riffled the edges of Nick's report, several neatly handwritten foolscap sheets. 'I've read this; good work. I'll have it typed. And that reminds me: the girl we took on just as you went away – Stanfield – has justified her choice.' He pursed his lips. 'Don't know about her morals but we've had no cause for complaint and we can't fault her work.'

Nick said only, 'Good.' But he thought with relief, What if I'd been wrong? Suppose she'd made a mess of the job and caused all sorts of trouble? But then he realised, with some surprise, that he had always been sure Laura Stanfield would be all right.

Dan slapped the report down on his desk. 'Now then, I've had a letter from Desoutter.'

Nick's eyebrows raised, because Desoutter was a French shipowner, three brothers in partnership. 'The last vessel they bought was built in St Nazaire.'

'And I'll bet St Nazaire are tendering again,' Dan said grimly. 'But I want the contract so I'm going out there. You can hold the fort until I get back.' Then he added, 'But if you want a few days off then Jennings can look after the shop.'

Nick knew Jennings, the manager, was quite capable of that. But he said, 'I can stand in for you.'

Dan nodded. 'Good.'

'Who are you taking with you?'

'A draughtsman, Tallentyre, and a clerk, Makepeace. He's fussy and dogmatic, dots the "i"s and crosses the "t"s, but he knows his stuff. And Miss Stanfield to type. Cheyney said none of the other girls was prepared to go; didn't want to leave their husbands or were just nervous.'

In fact they had been put off by Makepeace. One girl summed up: 'I couldn't stick a week with him watching everything I did and finding fault.' Laura had laughed and decided she would deal with Makepeace.

Now Nick said, 'She's been abroad so she's no stranger to travel.'

Dan agreed. 'That's a big point in her favour.' None of the other girls had been further than Newcastle. He added, 'We don't have to worry about a chaperone now, either. The war put an end to that.'

Laura was delighted at the prospect of the trip. She had been to France but only in wartime and close behind the lines. Her memories were mainly of a moonscape of shell-torn ground and blasted trees, mud and dirt, dead and wounded. This would be different.

So she arranged with Sybil Payton and Walter Skidmore that they would look after the typing agency and the sawmill respectively, as they were doing already. Laura had a pang of conscience then, seeing the sawmill office in a new light after working in Corrigan's yard. She had not realised how untidy and drab it had become, as bad as when she had inherited it. She reminded herself that this was the headquarters of two thriving little enterprises and should look the part. She resolved, 'I'll turn it out and do it up properly when I get back. A good clean, paint and paper.' The shipyard annual holidays were approaching and she could give up a few days to work on the office. And she could take pleasure in a job like that.

Addy was almost as excited as Laura about the trip. 'It should be lovely!' And she offered, 'I'll look after Tommy, bless him. You don't need to let worry about him stand in your way. Why don't you tell him about the holiday?' She, Joe and Laura planned to spend a week in a seaside boarding-house with the children. They thought they were lucky and it was only possible because the boarding-house at Whitley Bay was owned by Joe's cousin. Most of the shipyard workers would stay at home, only able to afford to spend their holidays at Roker or Seaburn. Fine though those local beaches were, there was an extra excitement about going away.

So on the night before she left, Laura sat down with her boy on her knee, hugged him and told him, 'I'm going away for a week but Aunt Addy will look after you. And I'm going to make some money so we can go to Whitley Bay for a holiday.'

Tommy tensed in her arms: 'You're coming back, then?'

She promised, 'Of course I am.' And added, 'You'll be able to make sandcastles, go plodging in the sea with Aunt

Addy and the girls.' She knew he loved paddling, had taken him in herself several times.

He asked, 'Will there be ice cream?'

'Every day.' Laura felt him relax. Over the past months he had gradually gained some confidence, accepted that she was there and going to be there.

He returned her hug. 'That's all right, then.'

Laura held him close and thought he was a huge responsibility but a source of joy.

She was at the Central station ten minutes before the train was due to leave but Makepeace, in wire-rimmed glasses, navy blue suit and bowler hat, complained, 'Leaving it to the last minute! You should always try to be ready in plenty of time.' Fred 'Tich' Tallentyre, the draughtsman, short, placid and pipe-smoking, winked at Laura. Makepeace added Laura's luggage to the pile on the porter's barrow, her typewriter perched on top. 'Right, let's go down to the platform. Mr Corrigan is travelling by a later train and will join us aboard ship.' He followed on the heels of the porter as he pulled the barrow away to the lift. Laura grinned to herself and followed.

She smiled and stayed relaxed on the long rail journey south while Fred puffed at his pipe and Makepeace checked times of arrival at each station against a timetable he produced from his pocket, worrying that they might miss the connection to their ship. He worried as they transferred from King's Cross and right through to their arrival – very early – on board the cross-Channel packet. There he saw the baggage stowed and then mopped his brow and suggested, 'Shall we go on deck to watch for Mr Corrigan?'

Tich agreed. 'Aye, might as well.' Laura went along, too, not to humour Makepeace but because she wanted to see the white cliffs as they sailed. She and the clerk climbed the ladder side by side with Tich at their heels. The ship was rock-steady, still secured to the quay and not due to sail for another hour. But Makepeace slipped and fell.

He brushed against her, falling behind her, instinctively clutching at her for support. He found none and only succeeded in shoving her off her feet so she also tumbled down the stairs. But while Laura soon stopped, he went on. His yell came echoing up the companion and Laura saw him rolling on down in a tangle of arms and legs, bowler hat bouncing after. He crashed into Tich and the pair of them rolled on together. Laura laughed where she sat on the stairs, could not help it because they looked like a scene in a Charlie Chaplin film. Then her laughter stopped when she realised the matter was serious.

She got her legs under her and ran down to see if either was hurt. Makepeace was white-faced with shock and pain, his glasses awry. He moaned, 'Me leg! Oh, lass, me leg!' It was doubled under him. But he lay on top of Tich whose eyes were closed, his pipe lying beside him.

Two sailors came running and shoved Laura aside: 'Right, miss, let us see to them. Here y'are, sir. We'll soon have you on your feet.' They hauled Makepeace upright and he howled in agony.

Laura exploded, 'You damn fools! The man has a broken leg! Treat him gently or I'll have you up before the captain! Now do as I say!'

Startled, they answered, 'Aye, ma'am.'

'Lay him down, but *gently!*' They tried but still dragged a moan of pain out of Makepeace but at least he was clear of Tich. Now Laura could see the leg below Makepeace's knee was at an angle. Tich Tallentyre was unconscious with a bad graze on the side of his head. Laura made sure he hadn't swallowed his tongue and was breathing, turned him gently on to his side. 'They need to go to hospital but that leg has to be splinted before we move him.' She remembered the first-aid handbook had said to use a rifle, but she wouldn't find one on this peacetime ship. Instead: 'Find me two pieces of wood – a mop handle or a boathook, something like that. And some bandages or rope.'

One sailor said to the other, 'Righto, Jim, I'll fetch it.' He dashed off.

Laura told the other, 'See if you can keep people away but ask if anyone is a doctor.'

He began to order, 'Move along there, ladies and gents, please. Is there a doctor here?' They edged past, staring, heads shaking.

Laura knelt by Makepeace again. 'I'm sorry, but I'm going to have to hurt you again. I have to straighten this leg.'

He swallowed, 'Aye, I'm ready.' He clenched his jaw and his fists.

Laura straightened the leg, biting her lip as a sob was torn out of the clerk. Then the sailor she had sent for splints came with two lengths of wood: 'How about these, ma'am? Mop handle I broke in half and a length o' line. And I told the bo'sun and he's coming with a couple o' stretchers.'

'Fine,' said Laura. She lashed the splints to the leg using the line, rope a half-inch thick. Then she was glad to sit back on her heels and try to cheer Makepeace. 'You'll be more comfortable now.'

The stretchers arrived then, with the bo'sun and four more big and burly sailors. The two injured were lifted on to them and Makepeace reached out to touch Laura's hand. 'Thank you for looking out for me.'

Laura squeezed his shaking fingers. 'I'm glad I was able to help.'

The sailors were spreading blankets over the men. Laura plugged Tich Tallentyre's pipe with a scrap of newspaper stuffed into the bowl and stowed it in his pocket. He woke then, to Laura's relief, and tried to struggle to his feet but she held him down. 'You've had a nasty bump to your head and you'll have to see a doctor. Just lie still.'

He relaxed and lay back, but then remembered, groping: 'Me pipe!'

'It's in your pocket, Fred,' Laura reassured him.

There was a swirl in the little crowd that had formed, despite the sailor's efforts to disperse them, and suddenly Nick was standing beside her, demanding, 'What's happened?'

'Mr Makepeace fell and broke his leg and Mr Tallentyre was knocked unconscious. They're going ashore to the hospital.'

'Damn!' Nick stooped over the stretchers. 'I'm sorry, Mr Makepeace – Tich. Nasty thing to happen.'

Makepeace said, 'I'm sorry, too, Mr Corrigan. But Miss Stanfield fixed me up very canny.'

Tich added, 'Aye.'

Nick patted their shoulders as they were carried away, then turned to Laura. 'Are you all right?'

'Yes.' That was when she realised that in the fall she had lost her hat and her hair was in a mess, her dress was grubby and her stockings laddered. This man always caught her at her worst! And what was he saying? 'I beg your pardon?' She could see Makepeace being carried down the gangway.

Nick said deliberately, 'I said, Mr Corrigan – my father – has gone down with a fever, running a temperature, and he isn't coming.'

'Oh!' And thinking quickly: 'I must reclaim our baggage. The ship will be sailing.'

'Don't worry about that,' said Nick irritably. 'If we failed to keep an appointment with the Desoutters they'd doubt if we could deliver a ship on time. It'll be a hell of a job now there's only the two of us but we're going on.'

Chapter Nineteen

SUMMER 1919. LE HAVRE, FRANCE.

'That's enough for tonight.' Nick's words echoed in Laura's brain as she pulled off her clothes and fell into bed. And the rest of it: 'We'll make an early start before breakfast tomorrow and check it over.' That had been the pattern of their lives over the past week. Their days were spent in conference with the three Desoutter partners, then a leisurely dinner with one or other of them in the evening. But when they left the Desoutters' house, Nick and Laura would return to the hotel to work on into the night.

They were booked into adjoining rooms but Nick had spoken to the manager and he had also provided them with a sitting-room and a maid who brought them fresh coffee every hour. Nick sat with shirt collar undone and sleeves rolled up to show muscular forearms, sketching, scribbling and absorbed in abstruse calculations. Laura pounded at her typewriter transcribing the shorthand notes she had made through the day, and typing out the schedules and tables roughly prepared by Nick. She even set up a rudimentary filing system and Nick said, 'That's very good, Miss Stanfield.' He sometimes found it hard to concentrate, conscious of her within arm's reach.

They were formally polite, as they had been since they set out. Laura would have been taken aback if she had learned that Nick was to accompany his father; she was shocked to find that he and she were to go on alone. Putting up with Makepeace would have been bad enough, but she and Nick Corrigan had always been at odds, would always be. This showed in her face when Nick told her and he read the hostility there. He controlled his anger enough to say only, as the ship sailed, 'We have to make the best of some unpleasant situations in this life.'

Laura replied, 'I have been reminded of that frequently, Mr Corrigan. I hope your father recovers soon. I *was* looking forward to this trip.'

They had both behaved correctly. He had bought first-class tickets on the train for both of them, so that she should not travel alone in the lower class. As they settled in he said, 'I hope you find this comfortable.'

'I expect I will,' replied Laura coolly. 'I once travelled in a horse box with thirty-odd soldiers.' That had been in Flanders.

Nick saw the shock and disapproval on the faces of the

elderly Englishwomen sharing the carriage and swore under his breath.

He opened doors for her and handed her down from the carriage when they disembarked from the train. His manners reminded her of Ralph, an unpleasant memory, and she said icily, 'I can manage, thank you.'

They travelled via Paris, breaking their journey there and sleeping in separate, distant rooms of the hotel. They went on to Le Havre the next day.

On their first night with the Desoutters, Nick warned, awkwardly but seeing no help for it, 'This dinner will be a rather formal affair. Have you a dress you think suitable?'

Laura gave him a wide, cold smile and tart reply: 'Unless you are an expert on ladies' fashion I think you can leave that to me, Mr Corrigan.'

He explained with obvious weary patience, 'I didn't want you to be embarrassed. If you were worried I was ready to buy you a dress.'

Laura was ashamed then. She apologised. 'I'm sorry.' But he was already walking away. At dinner she wore a plain and simple cotton dress with a high collar. Nick nodded approvingly and she said meekly, but tongue in cheek, 'I thought it looked formal and businesslike.' He suspected she was laughing at him but let it go; the dress was good enough.

On the first morning at the Desoutter offices they were introduced to a crowd of department heads. Laura saw one oily-haired man glance from Nick to her, then mutter some comment in French to his neighbour that she did not hear, let alone understand. But Nick did and snapped a harsh reply, echoed a second later by one of the Desoutters. The man who had spoken turned brick red and backed away, never to be seen again. Laura guessed that the remark had suggested a relationship between her and Nick. She was reminded of the only 'fly in the ointment' she had found, bent her head over her notepad to hide her blushes and was angry because she had to.

So it had gone on. But despite her apprehension, Laura found she was enjoying herself. The sheer volume of the work – she had inherited all of Makepeace's tasks as well as her own – was a challenge and she rose to it. There was the one 'fly in the ointment' but she held her tongue about that. She wanted this job to go well for Dan Corrigan's sake.

Now she slept but Nick still lay awake, his mind running on. He thought they had done well, as well as anyone could, despite being short-handed. And that Stanfield girl was quick-tempered, prickly and, he was sure, hated him, but she had pulled her weight and more. If they did not secure the contract to build this ship the fault would not lie at her door.

They met before breakfast and went over the formal bid once again. Nick said at the end, 'It looks very good.' He grinned and patted her back. 'You've done magnificently.' He stood beside her where she sat at the typewriter, his hands covering her shoulders. Laura felt the weight of them through the thin stuff of her blouse. She smiled, oddly pleased by his praise, and aware that he had never touched her before.

'Now we can relax and celebrate after our labours,' said Michel Desoutter, the senior partner, after lunch that day when he had awarded them the contract.

'We can,' agreed a grinning Nick. 'And this time we will dine in a restaurant and Corrigan's will be the host.' He turned to Laura: 'I have some details to discuss with these gentlemen. Would you like to go back to the hotel and rest?'

Laura would. But first she went shopping.

The restaurant that evening was spacious. They were a party of a dozen, the Desoutters and a manager or two and their wives, with Nick and Laura facing each other across the big round table. Laura had worn a shawl around her shoulders but when they were seated she shrugged this off to reveal her purchase of that afternoon, a dress of figure-hugging blue silk with a daringly low-cut neckline. She saw the glances she got from the other men. And she saw Nick take in those glances and grin at her.

There was a small band and they danced, she with a succession of the men, Nick with any of the ladies left unescorted. Laura was ready to enjoy herself after the past week and danced very well. It was not until the end of the evening that Nick stooped over her where she was seated: 'May I?' He followed her out on to the floor and put his arm around her. It was only the second time he had laid hands on her; she could feel the pressure of him through the silk and she shivered. He looked down at her. 'Cold?'

She avoided his gaze. 'No.'

They moved into the dance but now she was tensed and awkward, out of rhythm. She was aware of him – too aware – breathless. At the end he asked, 'Are you all right?'

'I'm tired,' she lied.

'We're finishing now, anyway. They've invited us to go sailing tomorrow. We can't refuse; just have to catch a later train.'

They bade farewell to the Desoutters and returned to their hotel. Laura was angry at herself for being affected by him, angry at him for affecting her and at the ridiculous idea that she should ever want this man she had fought so long.

At the door to her room he said, 'You've done a grand job. Worked like a Trojan, taken everything that came and never complained.'

'Thank you.' But now she realised, with shock, that she had striven to please not Dan Corrigan but this man, and it had all been wasted effort. Because if he realised it he would only think she was angling for him – like a fancy woman. Incensed by this, and because the job was over now she decided she was free to bring up the 'fly in the ointment': 'I do have one complaint. It was thoughtless to book us into rooms side by side, when it was obvious what people would think.' What the oily-haired man had thought before he was dispatched. Laura recalled him and was angered again. 'I suppose you thought I wouldn't care because of the label you tied on me.'

Nick reacted angrily. What was the matter with the girl now? 'Will you listen?'

'Listen? I never get a chance to speak. You didn't ask if I liked the room!'

'You were supposed to stay in a *pension* with Makepeace but I didn't want you staying there on your own. The hotel was full and these were the only rooms left. You had to put up with it because I did. Now I'll wish you goodnight. I hope you feel better in the morning.'

'I'll feel better when I'm on that train. I've had enough of this place—' Her door slammed on the rest of her speech.

Nick winced and supplied the end of it: And of you, Nick Corrigan. He thought, The feeling is mutual.

Neither of them slept very well.

They spent the next morning, and ate a lavish picnic lunch, aboard the Desoutters' yacht, and returned to their hotel in the early afternoon.

'*Pour mademoiselle.*' The page in his buttoned uniform held out the tray with its yellow envelope.

Laura took it and smiled. 'Thank you.' The boy smiled back, smitten, then retreated. Laura thumbed open the envelope, wondering worriedly who had sent her a telegram and what it contained. She had an awful suspicion. She glanced across the foyer where she sat and saw Nick emerge from the lift. He had discarded a formal suit for a well-cut old sports coat for travelling. Laura wore a hip-length, cream wool jacket and a mid-calf, striped wool skirt, comfortable but shapely. The porter followed Nick out of the lift, pushing their baggage on his barrow. Both were laughing at some joke but Nick sobered when he saw her. Laura had broken her fast in her room that morning. She had remembered – admitted – that she could have been breakfasting in a *pension* and gave him credit for that but was still mutinous. He nodded to her now. They had hardly spoken all morning.

Laura spread out the flimsy sheet and read: COME HOME SOON TOMMY ILL ADELINE. That awful suspicion was confirmed. She put a hand to her head. Tommy! What was wrong? How ill was he? It had to be serious to warrant Addy spending money on a telegram. She crumpled it into a ball, miserably. She had thought she was unhappy before, but this! The only good thing was that she was already on her way home. Laura could not get there quick enough. She walked to the desk and said, 'I want to send a telegram, please.' She wrote on the form she was given: RETURNING NOW. LOVE TO TOMMY. And paid the charge.

As she turned back from the desk, Nick stood before her. 'The taxi is here.'

Laura could see it through the glass of the revolving doors. 'I'm ready.'

She said nothing to Nick of the telegram. They talked little as the train carried them to Paris, where they changed. Nearing Calais in the dusk, come early under low clouds and weeping rain, it braked with a shriek of locked wheels. Laura looked up from the book she was trying to read, startled. A moment later their carriage turned on its side and came to a skidding halt. In the cheaper coaches the passengers were flung into a heap. In the first-class compartment Nick and Laura had to themselves, they crashed together and fell apart. The lights had gone out and in the pitch blackness, bruised and shaken, shocked and disorientated, Laura cried out, 'Nick!'

He was already seeking her, fearful, but found her now with a soaring lift of the heart. He held her for a shuddering moment. Everything changed for Nick then. But their situation was frightening and he said, 'We have to get out. Hang on to me.' He stood – on the side of the carriage that was now their floor – and found he could slide open the door to the corridor. He climbed out and hauled up Laura, her long legs kicking to find a hold, to join him. From there they crawled along the corridor on its side to the next compartment. Their eyes were becoming accustomed to the gloom and they found a middle-aged French couple in there, dazed and groaning. Nick called to them, persuaded them to stand and hold up their hands. Then he and Laura dragged them up and out.

'This way!' Laura called. There was a door close by, now horizontal like a trap door, its weight having to be lifted to open it. She tried and failed but Nick succeeded, lying beneath it and thrusting it up and open. They helped the couple out into the night and the rain but thankfully clear of the wreckage.

Laura looked about her, at the train lying on its side, the embankment falling away to a road below. People were climbing slowly, disoriented, out of the wreck and staggering down the embankment to the road. It reminded Laura of when the donkey and its Serbian owner, the women and children, fell off the track in the mountains. Instead of snow there was long grass slippery with rain and mud, soaking her shoes, stockings and halfway up her skirt so it clung to her legs. She said, 'There must be more.' And she and Nick crawled in again.

They painstakingly and painfully cleared that carriage of its occupants, towards the end being joined by a young Frenchman who added his strength. Then they moved on to the rest of the train, Laura now putting her first-aid training to use and Nick assisting her. Most of the other passengers on the train were of little help. They got themselves out but then only wandered dazedly.

They found that the train had been the victim of a landslip, the earth under the track having been washed away, but the driver had been warned by an emergency signal. He had been able to slow the train though not stop it and the damage was much less than it might have been.

There came a time when a uniformed official told Nick and Laura that the train had been cleared. There were scores slightly injured and shocked but no fatalities. Nick translated all this as the man hurried away. By now rescuers and rescued swarmed around the train in the light of lanterns, the rain dripping silver through the lights. Ambulances and cars were lined along the road that ran parallel to the railway track. He added, 'He says they're going to move people by car and then bus. You can go.'

Laura remembered Tommy: 'Please.' She added defensively, 'I had a telegram this morning. My little boy is ill. I want to get to him as soon as I can.'

'Of course. I'm sorry.' He did not ask why she had not told him about the telegram, knew she would ask no favours of him for herself. He would have to change that now — somehow. 'You've done all you can here.' He gestured with one big, grimy hand, indicating the numbers of doctors and nurses working around the train, many of them nuns. 'I'll stay and bring on the baggage when we can get to it.' The baggage car lay on its side with its door hidden. He added, 'That'll be tomorrow at the earliest. It will take a crane to lift it.'

Nick delved into his jacket pocket. 'There are your tickets and some cash to cover expenses.' He turned to a fresh page in his notebook, scribbled rapidly with a pencil then tore out the note and handed it to Laura. 'Give that to my father, please.' He looked down at her.

Laura was aware that her hands and face were dirty, her skirt and the woollen jacket muddied and bedraggled and her hair in a mess. The silk stockings had shredded. She didn't care, was ready to go. Tommy . . .

Nick said, 'He's calling you.' The official was waving his arms. 'A lot of people have reason to be grateful to you tonight. You've done far more than anyone could expect of you.'

Laura explained simply, 'I've done it before.' Then she was picking her way down the embankment to the road, climbing into one of the waiting cars with their carbide headlamps blazing, to disappear into the night.

Nick thought that he had seen yet another side to this girl. He started to walk along the train, seeking work for his hands, then stopped. When the train crashed and the lights went out she had cried out his name in the darkness. He wondered why?

So did Laura, holding on to a strap in the car as it lurched and bounced over the pavé.

That part of her journey was slow but then the car set her down at a crossroads where a bus was about to pull away. Laura's driver bawled and shook his fist at his countryman at the wheel of the bus and it waited for Laura to climb aboard. In Calais she found the cross-Channel packet ready to sail and when she landed at Dover a train waited again. It was not until she came to King's Cross that she found there was a wait of several hours for the next train north.

It was three in the morning, Sunday, and the station was an almost empty, echoing cavern. Laura faced a wait in the cold, and loneliness. She had cleaned her clothes as best she could on the ship, and taken a bath. She knew she still looked shabby but for once she did not care about that. She was afraid for Tommy.

She took a cab to Chelsea and Berkeley Mansions and after some minutes — and a twitch of the lace curtains — Venetia Ingleby opened to her. She was dressed in a frilled pink dressing-gown, peered out of washed-out blue eyes and squeaked, 'Oh, my dear! What are you doing out at this time of the morning?'

Laura let the tears fall. 'I'm waiting to catch a train

from King's Cross and I thought about you. Can I talk to you for a while?'

'Come in! Come in!' Venetia held the door wide.

The taxi still *chug-chugged* at the kerb. Laura paid the cabbie but asked, 'Will you come back for me at eight?' Then she followed Venetia into the remembered fragrance of rose water.

The old woman stirred up the embers in the grate with a poker, put on more coal and made tea. Then she settled into her chair, put on her gold-wire-framed spectacles and looked across at Laura. 'Now then, what's wrong?'

Laura was now dry-eyed but with a damp handkerchief. 'I have a little boy, not mine, but . . .' She explained how she had 'inherited' Tommy, digressed to relate how she had gone to France, told of the long hours of work, the telegram and the train crash. 'And I don't know how he is now, poor little bairn.'

Venetia took her hand. 'I'm sure he's all right. Bairns have these little fevers. And I think you're over-tired and been under some strain for a while. Sally looked in a few months back. There'd been a young man, Vince Tully, asking after her, but I couldn't tell him anything because I'd promised you two not to let on. She told me a bit of what you'd done but that's all I know — except what was in your letters. So tell me what you've been doing with yourself.'

Laura managed a smile. 'There weren't many of those, I know. Well, I think I told you about joining Mrs Beare's ambulance column . . .' She told now of Serbia and the

IRENE CARR

retreat through the mountains, the desert and Flanders. Then finally, reluctantly and painfully, of Ralph's betrayal.

Venetia said softly, 'You've had a hard time. He spoiled the best years of your life. Don't let him spoil the rest.' And when Laura stared she went on to warn: 'Don't regard all men as like Ralph. I've known a few but only one like him. Has there been another man?'

Laura replied, 'No.'

'That's odd for a young woman like you. No man at all in your life?' Laura shook her head and Venetia asked, 'Have you seen anything of that Lieutenant Corrigan?'

Laura had not mentioned Nick and was taken by surprise. 'Why – yes. Too much of him.' She recounted her clashes with him while Venetia punctuated the tale with here a sharp intake of breath, there a click of the tongue, now and again an 'Oh, dear!'

At the end she said nothing for a while, staring solemnly at Laura. Then she summed up. 'It seems to me that he was a bit stiff-necked but always trying to help and you wouldn't let him.'

Laura was again taken aback, had expected sympathy and agreement. Now she recalled that Venetia had always had a soft spot for Nick. But she would not argue with the old woman.

Venetia saw that and grinned. 'We'll agree to differ.' Laura's eyes were closing. Venetia fetched a rug and tucked it around her: 'There now. You sleep. I'll call you when it's time.' Laura slept and Venetia woke her at eight. 'I think that's your cab.'

336

It was and Laura made her farewells. Venetia saw her off with the words, 'Remember what I said about the rest of your life.'

Laura was more cheerful now, comforted and reassured by the woman who had once nursed and supported her through the loss of her child. She boarded her train at King's Cross and dozed again on the journey north.

She wondered why Venetia had asked about Nick?

That Sunday evening Walter Skidmore wriggled his skinny body through the crowd in the pub to stand at the bar and order, 'Give us a pint, then.' He paid with a half-crown and scooped up his change, drank deeply then stood with hands in pockets, confident and superior. He was in the sitting-room, where women were allowed, and there was a scattering of them, mostly wives with their husbands. His neighbours glanced at him, dismissed him as a nobody, but then one woman took a second look and asked, 'Here, aren't you the new feller at the Finley timber yard?'

Walter eyed her, took in the greasy dress and the hat at a drunken angle. He rocked back and forth on his heels, sucked his teeth then answered, 'That's right. I run the place.'

Doris Grimshaw said, 'Well, fancy that.' She had seen him working about the yard when she was watching from her hide in the empty shop. 'You're the foreman, then.' Walter puffed out his narrow chest and Doris asked, 'How are you getting on?'

Walter boasted, 'Got it just how I want it.'

'I meant how are you getting on with *her*?'

'How d'ye think? I'm the boss.'

Doris said, 'You don't mean . . .' She gestured obscenely, thinking, That would be a juicy bit o' scandal.

But Walter admitted, 'Naw. Not yet. But I'm happy wi' the job.' He rubbed finger and thumb together: 'The money is far better than in the shipyards.'

Doris said, 'Have another.' She shouted, 'Give us a pint and a drop o' gin along here!' And slapped Walter on the back.

Later she told Seth: 'He fancies himself but he's got a good idea of what's going on in the Finley's yard. *And* he thinks he has a chance with her. Now if we could prove something like that . . . ?'

Seth scowled. 'Keep in with him but don't say owt about me. And pump him! I want to know all I can about that bitch. With her out o' the way I could make a fortune.'

Doris saw her opportunity: 'It's going to cost me a bit because he likes his beer.'

Seth gave her two shillings but warned, 'Don't booze the lot yourself.'

Major Jack Daubney returned the salute of the sentry on the gate as he was driven out of the barracks in Cologne. Two other officers were crossing the parade-ground and one asked, 'Isn't that Black Jack?'

He received a curt nod. 'On his way home; they're getting rid of him.'

'That's no surprise. It was a bad business with that German girl.'

'He was damned lucky she died from that abortion. If she'd lived to give evidence he'd have gone to jail – should have done. The man's a bounder.'

Daubney took from his pocket a letter which read:

Dear Sir,

I am pleased to be able to tell you I have located the party you sought and details are on the attached card. Also enclosed is an account of my fee and an itemised statement of expenses. I would be grateful for a cheque at your earliest convenience.

He read the name and address on the card and smiled. Laura's former bedsit landlady had yielded to bribery.

Chapter Twenty

'I'll be damned if I'm not impressed!' Dan Corrigan looked up from the mud-stained note to the girl who had brought it. 'He says you were an enormous help to him.' He leaned forward to run a finger over the note spread on his desk, found the passage he wanted and quoted, ' "Without her aid the bid for the contract might well have foundered." ' He sat back in his chair. 'Both of you must have worked very hard.' He thought, And you look worn out, my girl. 'You travelled straight through, I believe?'

'I didn't want to delay. After the crash on Saturday night a car took me on to a bus and then I caught the boat to Dover. I got home at midday yesterday – Sunday.' She hesitated, then explained, 'I care for a little boy.'

Dan interrupted, 'Yes, I know.' And when she stared. 'My son told me.'

341

'I see.' Laura wondered what else Nick had told his father, and if it was damaging to her. She would talk to him, but now she went on, 'I had a telegram to say Tommy was poorly so I came straight home.'

Dan nodded. 'How is he?'

'Much better. I sent a telegram from Le Havre to say I was on my way home. Adeline – the girl who was looking after him while I was away – she said he picked up as soon as he heard that.'

Addy had also said, 'Don't blame yourself! He was quite happy about you being away. It was when he went down with this fever that he started to fret for you. There's no reason why you shouldn't go off again if you have to.' That had relieved Laura of her feelings of guilt.

'He's still not well and has a temperature, but I thought it would be all right to leave him for an hour or so this morning to bring you this note.' She paused then, wondering how to put her request.

Dan forestalled her. 'This yard closes down for the summer holiday in a week's time. I think you may as well start now and have this week as an extra. You've earned it.'

'Thank you, Mr Corrigan.' Laura rose to leave, surprised how easily she had gained the time off she needed.

Dan added, 'I visited both Makepeace and Tallentyre. They had nothing but praise for the way you looked after them.'

'Thank you. I hope they are recovering.'

'Makepeace is getting better and Tallentyre is already back at work – thanks to you.' Dan added drily, 'I gather that if they'd been left to the tender mercies of the seamen who picked them up they might have died.'

Laura laughed. 'I doubt it, but they did suffer some rough handling.'

She went on her way, smiling.

Back in the timber yard Laura winced as she took in the shabby office, and told herself again: something has to be done. She walked up the yard to the sawmill where the doors were set wide. Frank was feeding timber through the circular saw with a high-pitched, buzzing whine. Walter was hauling lengths of it out of the open pit, its own short and thick baulks of timber — the flooring which covered it most of the time — set aside. Frank stopped his sawing when he realised she was there, and Walter said, 'Aye, ma'am?'

'You remember I said I was going to Whitley Bay for a week with Tommy next Friday afternoon?' Joe Gibson had taken advantage of his good standing with the head draughtsman at Buchanan's, where he worked, to wangle Saturday morning off. So he, Adeline and the children could travel on Friday evening and avoid crowded trains. The two men nodded and Laura went on, 'Well, I've had second thoughts. While this place is shut down I'm going to smarten up the office a bit. It'll take me a few days but I'll go off after that, probably Wednesday, and be with Tommy for the last few days.'

Frank asked, 'W-what about me finishing early on Friday? I asked you— '

Laura's nod stopped him: 'I know you're wanting to

catch a train.' He and his wife were going to spend the holiday week with her sister at Harrogate. 'That will be all right. I'll be here when you finish and I'll make a start then for as long as it's light.' She would not stay after dark. 'I'm just telling the pair of you so you know I'll be here and I'll lock up.'

'Ah! Thanks,' said Frank.

Walter agreed. 'Righto.'

But then Frank added, 'There's a brick or two coming loose here.' He moved to the far end of the pit and pointed. 'They're safe enough, the timbers won't fall through, but they want cementing in again some time.' Laura could see where the mortar had fallen out from around two of the topmost bricks lining the interior of the pit but she went no closer. From where she stood she could also see, faintly now with the passage of time but still there, the marks torn in the green slime and moss coating the sides of the trench. They had been made by the clawing fingers of George Finley as he fought for his life. Laura could see mental pictures of that every time she saw the open pit. When she was a child the sawmill had been a playground of exciting gloom, hidey-holes and secret nooks. Now it was a place of death and lurking horror. She stuck it for Tommy's sake; it was the nearest he had to a birthright.

Now she tried to wipe the pictures from her mind and shied away from the pit – and the subject: 'I'll get something done about that – but not now. I might have it filled in.'

Walter sucked his teeth then warned, 'We need it for seasoning timber.'

'I know that, but we'll have to get it done some other way.' Laura was becoming annoyed by Walter taking too much on himself. 'Take out what timber is left in there before you shut it up again. Then cover it over with sacking or something.' She did not want to see it.

Walter shrugged, sucked his teeth but smirked, 'If you say so, ma'am.'

'I do say so, and do it *now!*' Laura turned her back on him and the pit and walked away.

Walter's simper became a scowl but he started to fish the timber out of the pit.

Laura walked back across the yard. As she did so she noticed that one particular kind of hardwood seemed to be in short supply, only two or three lengths stacked in the open shed. She wondered if more had been ordered and turned towards the office.

The open motor car was a Standard coupé with its soft top folded down. It swung in between the open gates, ran straight at her then halted with a screech of brakes — but Laura had to jump aside to save herself. Now the driver stood up behind the wheel to glare at her over the windscreen. He had told Melissa only a half-hour ago, 'That lass takes more and more of my trade! I'll make her listen to sense or else!' Now he shouted above the noise of the revving engine, 'I want to talk to you!'

Laura replied angrily, shaken, 'You fool! You might have killed me.'

'No such luck,' jeered Seth. 'I'm here to make you a final offer.'

'I don't care what it is! You could offer me ten thousand pounds and I'd throw it in your face. I will never sell to you, never!'

'Ten thou—' For a moment Seth was speechless. He remembered George Finley saying he would not take a million for the yard – before Seth let him drown. Guilt inflamed rage and he mouthed an obscenity then shouted, 'I know where to find you and yours! One way or another, I'll make you suffer for this! Next time you won't get away!' Then he banged down into the driver's seat, the car skidded around on the cobbles and shot out of the yard.

Laura took a breath and realised her hands were shaking. She remembered she had been about to check on the supply of some timber. But now, after Seth's mad driving and his threats, she decided she had had enough and she had been away from Tommy too long for this first day back at home. She could look in at the office in the morning. Now she would have lunch and read him a story. After the hard work and disasters of the last week that appealed to her as a lovely way to spend an afternoon.

Late that evening she answered a knock at her door and found a cab standing at the kerb, its horse with head turned to look at her in her lit doorway, the cabbie before her and holding her suitcase. 'A Mr Corrigan said to give you this, miss.'

'Thank you.' Laura took it from him. 'Where was this?'

'Central station. He'd just come in on the London

train. Got into another cab with his baggage and asked me to give you the case.'

So Nick was back and had brought all their luggage. The case seemed unharmed, despite being trapped in the capsized baggage car all night. Laura said, 'I'll get my purse.'

'No need, miss. It's all been paid for. Goodnight.'

Laura stood, lost in thought, as he drove away.

Nick stayed up late that night talking to his father, recounting all the arguments he had used to secure the contract to build the next ship for the Desoutters. They pored over it together. Finally Dan sat back in his chair and said, 'So you'll be ready for Scotland next week.' They had planned a walking tour together during the closure of the yard for the holiday. 'You may as well take this week off, as well.' He grinned. 'That's what I told your assistant.'

'Miss Stanfield? She's deserved it.' Nick hesitated, then: 'I've been thinking for some time that we may have made a mistake about that girl.'

'I must admit I've had to change my mind about her,' Dan conceded. 'I still think she has a lot to answer for, but to speak as you find – yes, I agree. I was mistaken to some extent.'

Nick said, 'I think now that there may have been a lot of mistakes.'

*　　*　　*

Tuesday.

He did go to the shipyard the next day, albeit late in the morning, because there were some matters he had to attend to. He was walking through the yard in the afternoon and passed close to the ship being built at that time. It stood on the stocks and towered above the men working below, steel-walled inside its nest of staging. The thundering of the riveters' pneumatic hammers on the empty hull echoed like a giant beating on a great drum. As he moved on and left the worst of the din behind him, one of the men, in dirty overalls and old cap on the side of his head, said, 'That was a nasty accident with that train, Mr Corrigan.'

'Yes, but it could have been worse; nobody was killed.' Nick searched his memory, as good as his father's, and put the name to the face: 'Peter Young, isn't it?'

'Aye, that's right; the lads all call me young Peter. And I hear that typing lass – Tich Tallentyre, the draughtsman, came in and told us – she looked after him and Alf Makepeace when they got hurt.'

Nick nodded. 'She was very good when the train crashed, too.'

'Aye? Well, it doesn't surprise me. She did me and a friend o' mine a good turn down in London.'

'Oh?' Nick waited, curious.

'We'd been on leave and were going back to France – this was just before the last big push – and we all met up in this pub in the Strand. Our sergeant, Billy Gatenby, went missing, but this lass saw him, knew him from afore the war, y'knaw, and she took him home with her. If the Military Police had got him, drunk like he was, he'd ha' got busted back to private. And if he hadn't caught the train they'd ha' posted him as a deserter and could ha' shot him. He was killed afore the war finished but so were a lot more. A shell got him, but afore he died he told me how she looked after him, sobered him up and brought him along to the station. She did the best she could for him and saved him from a firing squad.'

'I didn't know that. Thank you for telling me.' Nick went on his way, thinking hard.

Back in his office he called in Ganny Bates from the typists' room and dictated some letters. It was done with only a part of his mind, from notes he had made earlier. By the time he had finished he had come to a decision: 'I won't be in again this week. I'm off to London tomorrow. Leave the letters with my father and he will sign them. I'll be writing up a lot of notes before I go and I'll leave them on my desk. I'd like you to have them typed up for me for when I get back after the holiday.'

'Aye, Mr Corrigan.' Ganny closed her pad. 'Are you going to see the sights?'

'No, I'm going to seek someone I should have looked for a long time ago.'

Ganny said vaguely, 'Oh?' She was not sure what he meant. 'Well, mind you take care of yourself down there,' she warned him, peering over her glasses.

Nick grinned at her fondly. 'I will, Ganny.'

Then, left alone, he settled down to writing up his notes on the French contract.

Laura returned to her office that morning only to glance through any mail, but then she remembered to check that the hardwood had been ordered. She found it had, but . . . Laura slowly sat down at the desk and began to go through all the paperwork of the past month. At noon she locked it away in her desk. She ate little of her lunch, for which she had no appetite, and read another story to Tommy. Then she said to Addy, 'Will it be all right if I'm a bit late tonight?'

Addy laughed. 'Course it will. Nobody can say you're not a worker. But you told me this was an extra week's holiday you'd been given.'

Laura smiled but it was an effort. 'Thanks, Addy. It's just that something's come up.'

She worked in the office all afternoon, bade Walter and Frank goodnight, then worked on until she had to light the gas lamp, her intention to leave forgotten.

When she finally finished she laid her head on her folded arms on the desk. She could have wept. Was she always to be betrayed?

Laura heard the sounds of movement outside, a measured tread on the cobbles of the yard. She lifted her head wearily to see who was calling at this late hour and a tall, black shadow crossed the window. She thought, Nick? And then wondered why his name came first to mind. She started to rise then the door was thrust open and Black Jack Daubney stood on the threshold, smiling. 'I've waited a long time.'

Laura froze in shock, half standing, her hands on the desk. For a moment her wits deserted her, then she stammered, 'W-what are you doing here?' And then thought that was a stupid remark because she knew only too well why he was there. 'Leave me alone.'

'I can't.' Daubney stepped inside and closed the door behind him. 'I've desired you ever since I met you and your useless husband. A lot of women would love to hear me say that.'

'Not this one. Get out.'

He said again, 'I can't.' Then he took a pace closer and she stepped back. 'And I don't want to. I've tried to take you before and you got away. I don't mind; that's part of the excitement of the chase. I like the women who are tempted or set out to tempt me, but that's too easy. I prefer those taken against their will. That's what excites me most.'

Laura took another backward step and said, lips trembling, 'If you don't leave I'll scream.'

'Who's to hear you?'

Who indeed? She tried to take yet one more step, flinching away from him as he loomed over her, but could not. Her back was against the wall. He laughed and seized her. Laura tried to fight but was overborne by the power of him. He pinioned her arms and legs with his, pressed his mouth on hers, stifling.

Laura bit him. His mouth was on hers and she sank her teeth into it. He let out a sob of pain and pulled back from her, let go of her then struck her. The blow knocked her sideways to sprawl on the floor and left her deafened with a ringing in her ears. Through her tears she saw him set a hand to his mouth. He looked at it, dripping red, and then at her. His eyes were blazing and she thought, He will kill me now. But his head was turned on one side as if listening, then he mouthed something she could not hear through the ringing and strode to the door. He threw it open, passed through and it closed behind him.

Laura wondered why he had gone, was sure he would return and she started to struggle to her feet as the door opened. She thought that she should have kept the gun, but there was a poker by the stove and she staggered towards it.

Nick Corrigan entered and said, 'I've just seen a chap out there . . .' His voice trailed away as he took in the weal on Laura's face, left by Daubney's fingers, and that she was holding her torn clothing together. 'Good God! What's happened to you?' He took a long pace towards her then: 'Hell!' He turned and dashed out into the yard and down to the gate. Through the open door Laura saw him halt there, head turning. His motor car, the Arrol-Johnston, was in the yard and Laura realised Daubney had heard its engine when she had been deafened.

He came back to the office and found her sitting in her chair. She had found a safety pin and fastened her clothes decently with shaking fingers. He said quietly, a tight rein on his anger and outrage, 'I got out of the car and this chap went past me. He said, "Goodnight," and I assumed he was a customer. But he did this to you?' And when Laura nodded, he asked, 'Who is he?'

Laura did not want to tell him; it would shame her. She felt unclean now. She shook her head.

Nick urged, 'You must report him to the police.'

'No.' To face him in court? To hear the gossip: 'She must have given him encouragement.' To be cross-examined on her past life by a probing, suggestive lawyer. 'No. *No!*'

Nick persisted, 'I think he only ran because he heard me arrive. What if I hadn't? He could have killed you.'

Laura knew that, knew she would live in fear from now on. She would have to defend herself . . .

Nick probed. 'You've seen him before?'

'Leave me alone!' She remembered she had pleaded with those words to another man this night.

'He's followed you.'

Laura guessed at what he was thinking, that Daubney was from some disreputable affair in her past. 'I don't have to answer your questions. I've always taken care of myself and I will now. From now on I'll leave here when the men do and I'll keep the door locked. But no police. Why can't you mind your own business?'

'Because . . .' But he did not go on. He was angered by her obstinacy but saw there would be no moving her, suspected that if he pressed her she would defy him. As she had always. He said, 'That's a promise?'

She was sorry she had spoken so curtly – rudely – but she was still shaking. She answered, low-voiced, 'Yes.'

He told himself to be satisfied with that.

Now Laura asked wearily, slumped in her chair, 'Why did you come here, anyway?'

'I was going to call at your house.' When she looked up sharply he said, 'Don't worry. I intended to leave the car at the end of the street.' She relaxed and he went on, 'I've been hearing praise of you from my father, Makepeace and Tallentyre. I wanted to add my twopennorth: I think you've done very well all through. I came tonight because I'm off to London tomorrow.'

'Thank you,' said Laura listlessly. Because it did not matter now. She was finished with Corrigan's yard.

'I'll take you home now.' Nick saw her stiffen again and he went on, 'It's dark, no one will see me with you and I won't let you walk alone after this night's attack.'

Laura thought of that walk and said, 'Very well.' She said nothing more until he braked the Arrol-Johnston and set her down at her door. Then she wished him goodnight. He echoed that and drove off.

Laura wondered why he was going to London and assumed it was for business reasons. She winced, recalling how she had spoken to him. And at one point he had started: 'Because . . .' Then he had changed his mind. What had he been about to say? Laura decided that however bad it had been she would have deserved it.

Nick drove home, thinking that if he had spoken the truth and said, 'Because I care about you', she would have suspected his motives. He was quite sure how she regarded him. She had made that plain in the past and he was going to do something about it. But now he slowed the Arrol-Johnston and parked it at the kerb. For a moment he stared, then got down and walked.

Melissa stretched catlike then moaned, but now not out of pleasure. 'It's time I was away. I must be back at the house for bloody dinner.'

They had met in the office of Seth's biggest timber yard, deserted at that time in the evening, save for him. As always he had been waiting for her, seized her as she entered and ignored her sniggering cry of: 'Shut the door!'

He had replied, 'They've all gone home.'

Now his passion was spent and his thoughts already elsewhere.

Melissa began to dress but complained, 'I wish I didn't have to sneak in here for an hour or so then show up at the Corrigans, all prim and proper. They bore me stiff. I wish we could be together all the time.'

'The neighbours would talk and I don't want gossip harming my business. It's bad enough already.' Seth scowled up at the ceiling.

Melissa wanted him to marry her. She stayed at the Corrigan house because it did not cost her a penny; in fact Dan made her a small allowance, but she had given up any hope of an inheritance. She now saw Seth as the better opportunity but he refused to wed.

Now he said, 'We'll be together next week.' He had arranged a holiday for them, a week in Holland, far from prying neighbours. Their berths were booked on a ship sailing from the Wear on Friday.

Melissa sighed and made the best of it: 'Aye.'

Seth grumbled, 'That bloody Stanfield lass is undercutting me all the time and taking trade away from me. If I tried to compete with her, I'd go broke.' That was because he had made his money in the war when there was plenty of demand and little competition, and not reviewed his practices since. His workers were as inefficient as he. He muttered, 'I wish she was going with us.'

Melissa paused, taken aback and balancing, pulling a stocking up one leg. 'What?'

'I'd tie her in a sack and toss her over the side when we were halfway over.'

Melissa began to laugh, then stopped as she looked into his face. Seth was deadly serious.

She left the office, crossed the yard then walked along the street. Her pace slowed when she saw Nick seated at the wheel of his car and her thoughts raced, hunting frantically for an excuse for her presence there. As she came up to the car she said brightly, 'This is a surprise, Nick. I've just been taking a walk.'

'A walk in the yard?' His face was expressionless.

'Well . . .' She sought a reason, any reason.

He said, 'I followed you.' He had, as she crossed the yard and entered the office, had stopped behind the half-open door but not for long. He had been waiting in the car for nearly an hour. 'I saw the pair of you.' Melissa stared as it sank in. He said flatly, 'I think we would all be grateful if you'd leave.'

Melissa was furious at being caught and spat at him: 'I'm leaving now, glad to get out of that miserable bloody hole! To hell with the lot of you!'

She turned and flounced back into the yard. Seth was closing the office and asked, 'What are you doing here? Forgotten something?'

Melissa raged, 'That Nick Corrigan followed me and saw us in here! I'll be sleeping in your bed from now on.'

Seth blinked, adjusting to this and what it meant. 'You mean you've left everything you've got up there?' He saw from her face that she had, and ordered, 'You get yourself up to the house tomorrow and fetch the lot. It's no more than you're entitled to.'

Nick drove home, delivered a curt account of his discovery to a startled Dan and shocked Jessica, then packed for his trip to London.

In the past he had tried to regard Laura Stanfield as just one more person in his life, to be liked, disliked or tolerated. Now he knew that wasn't so, had not been so for some time. He had realised it in France when he feared for her life. He believed he had wronged her but he was going to try to put that right. He had to.

Black Jack Daubney bathed his cut and bruised lip in the basin. He stood in his hotel bedroom in Newcastle, peered into the mirror and cursed. He decided he would have to keep to his room for some days. The hellcat! But now a lust for vengeance was added to desire. He would savour that.

Chapter Twenty-One

The fears were crowding in on Laura now. Addy, concerned, said, 'You're looking peaky. And what's happened to your *face*?' She stared, lip caught in teeth, appalled at the bruise left by Black Jack Daubney. 'It looks as if somebody punched you!'

Laura lied, 'I walked into the office door.'

'You'll have to be more careful,' Addy lectured her. 'That's awful.'

Laura had just brought in Tommy in his blue jersey to stay with Addy for the day and her mirror had already told her she was pale, with eyes dark smudges in her face. She had slept badly, haunted by Seth's mad rage and Daubney's attack of the previous evening. She was also worrying about the interview to come. But she would not tell Addy about any of those and now lied again, 'I'm fine.' She

359

smiled but hugged Tommy for longer than usual before she went off to the timber yard.

Once there she sat down at her desk, unlocked the drawer and got out her papers. She checked them through once more and there was no mistake. She took a deep breath and grasped the nettle. Crossing the yard to the sawmill she saw Walter working on the lathe, called him and returned to the office. He followed her in, smirked down at her where she sat in her chair and asked, 'Aye, ma'am?'

Laura tapped the papers. 'There's a saying: "What can't speak can't lie." These have been telling me a tale about timber bought and paid for but not used or sold, and you've been doing it. You've been taking a bit here and a bit there. I don't know what price you sold it for but I know what it cost *me* because the paid bills are all here! You've been robbing me for months!'

'Here! Hold on!' Walter's smirk had gone and now there was a look of wounded innocence. 'I've stolen nothing! I don't know owt about it! If owt's missing it wasn't me that took it. More likely it was that Frank.'

'No, it wasn't. Some of the bills were doctored. Frank can use tools but if he picks up a pen it dances all over the paper. You've thieved from me and don't try to shuffle it off on an innocent man.'

Walter had turned sulky: 'You can't prove anything. If you go around talking like this I could have you for slander.'

Laura had begun the interview with distaste and

revulsion at his betrayal of her trust. His attempt to blame Frank had disgusted her and now this threat outraged her. ' "Slander" is a nasty word. I know some more, like "arrest" and "prison". I can prove you are guilty and have you sent down.'

Walter saw his bluff had been called and now he believed her. His mouth worked and he begged, 'No, don't do that. I've got a wife. She'd be left alone.'

Laura knew that was true, knew she could not make the woman suffer for Walter's crime. She said, 'Get out. Before I change my mind. Get out and don't come back.'

He shrank away from her icy glare, shuffled across the yard and out between the gates. Laura thought he was passing out of her life but that brought no joy. She wept, not for the money she had lost but for the trust betrayed. Walter had defrauded her as Seth defrauded George Finley. This was not as bad as the hurt done her by Ralph, but it was a painful reminder. She recalled Venetia's words: 'Don't think all men are like Ralph.' But Laura thought it would be a long time before she trusted anyone again.

She heard the sound of an engine in the yard, straightened her back and stood up. She had to put this latest trouble behind her and get on. She opened the door and walked out into the yard. The lorry standing on the cobbles was a three-ton Bedford loaded with timber. The engine had been switched off now and two men got down from the cab. She took the invoice from the driver, whom she knew, but his partner was a stranger. Laura asked, 'I don't remember you. Are you new?'

'Aye, that's right, bonny lass. I just started this week. Davey Milburn.' He grinned at her fetchingly, a jaunty young man with red hair and freckles.

Laura, amused, thought, One for the girls. She grinned back at him, 'Never mind the "bonny lass". If you two unload it I'll show you where it all needs to go.'

Davey laughed. 'Right y'are — ma'am.'

The timber was lashed down on the Bedford and he started to loosen it with quick fingers. He finished on his side of the Bedford while the older man was still struggling with one of the ropes on the other side. He finally gave up and called, 'Davey! Come here wi' that knife o' yours and cut this rope.'

Davey went round to him, fished a clasp-knife from his pocket, opened it and cut the lashing. Then he set the knife aside while he pulled the severed rope clear.

Laura stared at the wicked blade, the carved handle. 'Where did you get that?'

Davey turned his head on his shoulder, saw the direction of her gaze and blushed to match his hair. 'Sorry. It's a bit naughty.' He tried to put the knife away, to hide the handle with its carving of the naked girl.

Laura said, 'Never mind that.' And repeated, 'Where did you get it?'

'I found it, not long after the start of the war. I had it all through Gallipoli, Mesopotamia, Palestine; it's seen some service, that knife has.'

'*Where?*' Laura demanded, frustrated.

'Where? Oh!' Davey looked uneasy.

Laura pressed him. 'I'm not going to make trouble for you. I just want to know where you found it.'

'To tell the truth,' Davey admitted, voice low so his mate would not hear, 'it was in the grounds of old Corrigan's house, the feller that owns the shipyard, y'know? It was in among some bushes and trees. I'd sneaked in there, climbed over the wall. I wasn't thieving or poaching, y'understand. But there was a young lady I was seeing.'

Laura picked up the knife and studied it. Davey watched, uncomfortable at her looking at the carved nude, but then his mate called, 'Let's get on with it, then. We haven't got all day.' Davey started to help unload the timber while Laura stared at the knife. Seth had climbed the wall, or how had it got to where Davey found it? Why had he climbed it? Not poaching because he was no countryman – and was there any game to poach at the Corrigan house? Lots of valuables worth stealing, no doubt, but game? One thing she was sure of, Seth had been up to no good. She asked, 'How much do you want for it?'

Davey paused, a length of timber on his broad shoulder. Incredulous, he said, 'You want to buy it?' He did not ask why she wanted a knife with a slightly salaciously carved handle, but the question was in his eyes.

Laura said, 'Never mind why I want it. Just say how much.'

Davey said hesitantly, 'I don't know – haven't thought – I wasn't going to sell—'

'I'll give you a pound for it.'

A pound! Davey knew he could take a girl out every night in the week with a pound, and not necessarily the same girl. 'Done.'

Laura paid him from her purse and locked the knife in the drawer of her desk.

Davey Milburn climbed the wall of the Corrigan estate again that night and the girl was waiting for him. She was not the girl to whom he had made love before going off to the war; that one had married another man to give her child a name and was now living in Gateshead. There had been other girls in between, but Davey had a special fondness for housemaids and particularly those he found among the Corrigan staff.

This one was plump and giggly and snuggled into his arms. After a time he said, 'I never told you what happened today.'

'You've been too busy,' Lizzie giggled.

'Now then, behave yourself. I've half a mind not to tell you.'

'Oh, go on!'

'Well, you know that knife o' mine.'

'I do. It's indecent.'

'No more than you without your clothes.' He didn't blush with Lizzie as he had with Laura.

'Oh, get away!' She slapped him playfully. 'What about it?'

'I sold it. To a woman an' all! For a pound.'

'A pound! And a *woman!*' Her wages were a pound a month. 'Who was that?'

'The one that runs what used to be Finley's sawmill. A right bonny lass called Laura Stanfield. I heard talk that she ran off with some rich feller before the war, took him away from his wife.'

'Ooh!'

'She saw me using it and wanted to know where I got it, and when.'

'What would she want with a knife like that?'

Davey shrugged. 'Blowed if I know. Anyway, next time you have a half-day we'll go to a show at the Empire, up in the gods.' Those were the twopenny seats at the back of the gallery.

Lizzie showered kisses on him then and ran back to the house before she was missed.

She was bursting with her news and could hardly wait to tell Margaret, another parlourmaid who was her friend. She met her in the hall of the house, apparently deserted save for the two of them, and started, 'You want to hear what my Davey says . . .' She recounted his words and in the bygoing explained, 'He found this knife in the grounds here just after the war started. Its handle is carved like the body of a lass stark naked!' Then at the end she added darkly, 'I reckon this Stanfield woman wants it to do in some feller or his lass: a crime o' passion.'

IRENE CARR

Melissa had obeyed Seth and come for her belongings. Now, standing around the bend of the stairs, out of sight but not out of hearing, she took in every word.

When she returned to Seth in the handsome house he rented, she crowed, 'One o' the maids let me in. I got the lot and never saw any of the family.' Then she repeated the story she had overheard. 'That sounds like your knife that you lost.'

Seth gaped at her, then ground out, 'I'm bloody sure it is! There wouldn't be two like it. And he found it where I lost it. Now that Stanfield bitch has it and she knows it's mine. It won't take her long to work out that I was up to something in Corrigan's wood. Then if she goes to him . . . !'

'We'll have to get it off her,' said Melissa.

'Easier said than done.' Seth glared at her. 'She's dead set against me! I've been trying to buy that yard off her for six months and she won't budge. She'd die before she gave that knife to me.' He peered about as if in search of inspiration and it was then that the big brass knocker banged on his front door. 'Who the hell is that?' He opened it and found Doris Grimshaw and a sulky stranger standing outside. 'What d'ye want?'

Doris smiled to show long, yellow teeth. 'This is Walter Skidmore. Do you remember, I told you about him? Foreman at Finley's yard.'

'Aye.' Seth also remembered he had told her: 'Don't tell him about me.' He scowled. 'So?'

'He's been given the sack by that Stanfield lass.'

'Aye?' Seth switched his scowl to Walter: 'What for?'

'She said I'd been robbing her,' Walter complained. 'She was telling a pack o' lies and I wasn't going to put up wi' that. I told her what to do with her job and walked out.' He added hopefully, 'Doris said you might be wanting a man.'

Seth thought, Not to dip his thieving fingers in my till. He said, 'How is she getting on? Is she still making money?'

'Oh, aye. She could be making more but what can you expect of a lass like her? She would never listen to me. She gets plenty of orders, though. Makes enough to send that boy of hers – Tommy Taylor, she dotes on him – away for the holidays. He's off to Whitley Bay wi' some friends of hers.'

'Him?' Doris had told Seth about Tommy. He didn't give a damn for the boy. 'What about her?'

'She's staying, wants to do up the office, make it more businesslike, she said. So she's starting on the Friday. Frank Pearson will be finishing early . . .' He reeled off all Laura's plans and Seth listened. Until Walter finished, 'So I told her we used the pit for seasoning timber but she wouldn't listen, just said, "Take the timber out and cover it up – *now!*" I reckon she's nervous about it but she's too bloody sure of herself.' He stopped for breath.

Seth had a lot to think about. The Stanfield lass was doing well, had plenty of orders and was making money. He was not going to get her yard through her going broke. She could afford to send the boy away and later follow on herself . . .

The idea came to him then, slowly at first but as he thought the other pieces of the plan fell into place. Doris and Walter waited as he glared off into the distance, and they began to shift their feet uneasily as the time went on. Walter said, 'Aw, to hell with it. If you haven't got a job for me I'll go back to Hartlepool.'

Seth came back to them and told Walter: 'I haven't got the sort o' job you want but tell me what I want to know and I'll send you back with enough to set you up in a pub. Now listen, the pair o' you: this lad – Tommy Taylor – what's he like?'

It was as if they were waiting for me, Nick thought later of his quest in London. Because of a breakdown his train arrived late on Wednesday but early next morning he rang the doorbell in Berkeley Mansions. He saw the lace curtains twitch in the bay window, knew he was being examined and caught a glimpse of a bespectacled Miss Ingleby before the curtain hid her again. He waited patiently and eventually Venetia, frail and garish in her frilled, pink dressing-gown, opened to him. 'My, you are early. It's Lieutenant Corrigan, isn't it?' She peered up at him, coyly, out of watery blue eyes. Nick guessed that her spectacles were dispensed with once her examination of him was done.

He said, 'That's right, but it's "Mister" now. You're looking well, Miss Ingleby. I've called because I thought you might be able to help me, regarding a lady.'

Venetia's lips parted to form a delighted O and her eyelids fluttered: 'I wouldn't have thought you needed any help with that, Mr Corrigan.'

'Call me Nick.'

'Well, you'd better come in, Nick.'

He followed her and the remembered faint aroma of rose water. They sat on straight-backed chairs in the window of Venetia's parlour, where they had a good view of the square and of anyone who called at Berkeley Mansions. Nick felt like a bull in a china shop, surrounded by spindle-legged tables laden with photographs of stern-faced men, many carrying top hats as they stared into the camera.

Venetia explained: 'Some of the gentlemen who escorted me during my theatrical career. There's one of me.' She pointed a thin finger, the skin on her hand like paper. 'Only one because I think it's bad form to flaunt oneself.'

Nick blinked at the photograph of Venetia as a young woman, draped on a couch, and decided she was flaunting enough to be going on with. 'Very nice.'

Venetia giggled girlishly. 'A lot of men say that. I was rather naughty, really.' Then she came to business: 'Now, who is this young lady? Would it be Laura – Mrs Hillier, as she called herself? I recall you came to visit her on two occasions.'

'Your memory is very good. Yes, I'm seeking information regarding Laura.'

Venetia asked baldly, 'Why?'

'I've known her – or thought I knew her – for five

years. We started off fighting and never stopped. Now I realise I didn't know anything about her except what I'd been told — and that came from a wronged wife. I'd like to hear from you.'

She asked again, 'Why?'

Nick told her.

Venetia was silent for a time, watching him with a half smile. Then she nodded and said, 'Very well. Right from the start I guessed she wasn't married to that Ralph. Laura was sweet but he was a bad lot. I had a fair idea what he was up to but I couldn't tell her without being sure and he was a good-looking young man with money. She'd probably never met anyone like him before and had no means of judging him. She was so young, so young.' Venetia sighed. 'I know. Believe me, dear, I know.'

She eyed Nick shrewdly. 'I think you came ready to meet a temptress in Laura. You were wrong there. I'm not condoning what she did but the real villain was that Ralph. He treated her very badly. She ended up working to keep him while he spent his money in the Duke or on the horses. There was a little gang of them used to meet in that pub. They were clerks and trainee solicitors, that sort running a bit wild. One of them who came through the war was called Vince Tully. He came back in January but I haven't seen him around since. He might have gone away. Anyway, Ralph was one of them but he used to boast about having independent means and not having to work, posing as the gentleman. I heard him at it when I was sitting in the Snug. And he had an affair with the barmaid n there. Then when he died the shock nearly killed Laura. She gave birth – prematurely – and the little lass only lived a few hours.'

The watery blue eyes were damper now and Venetia used a wisp of a handkerchief to dab at tears. 'I nursed her through that – me and a lass called Sally Barnes. Laura had found her wandering the streets, come down from up north with hardly a penny to her name. Sally lived with Laura until they moved out and then they went together. I didn't see her again after that. I'm not surprised she didn't come back here because this place could only have unhappy memories for her. She wrote now and again but then that stopped. Until a few days ago when she walked in at three or four in the morning. She said she was on her way back from working in France and she told me about you.'

'Oh?' Nick wondered what Laura had said.

Venetia did not tell him. 'I told her not to judge all you men by Ralph. I think you've both been very silly, but then, young people are. I was.'

Nick said, 'I'll plead guilty.'

She was silent for a while then, peering vaguely out of the window and busy with her own memories. Finally she stirred and smiled at him. 'I think I've told you all I know about Laura.'

Nick stood up. 'Thank you for talking to me. This Sally Barnes, do you know where I can find her?'

'Ah! I think I can. She came to see me and left her address. She's training to be a nurse at some hospital . . .'

Venetia sifted through the contents of a drawer and brought out a scrap of paper: 'Here you are.'

Nick noted the address. 'Thank you.'

As Venetia let him out she suggested, 'You can try at the Duke but I doubt if you'll find any of the old crowd there.'

Nick took up that suggestion. The publican serving behind the bar was a smart young man with the look of the ex-soldier about him. 'Good morning, sir. What would you like?'

'I'm looking for anyone who might remember Ralph Hillier from before the war.'

That brought a shake of the head. 'Not me, sir, only took over here a month back. But I'll ask.' He raised his voice: 'Do any of you chaps remember a Ralph Hillier?' That brought silence and more head shaking. The publican said, 'Sorry, sir.' He had thrown out the various messages he had found and which meant nothing to him.

But then a young man rose from where he sat in a corner on one of the leather benches. He was stocky and broad, with hair neatly combed. A glass holding a finger of whisky stood on the polished table before him. 'Who wants to know?'

Nick crossed to him, gave his name and said: 'I'm seeking information about Ralph and Laura Hillier. And you?'

'Vince Tully.'

They shook hands and Nick said, 'I've been talking to

Miss Ingleby. She said she hadn't seen you since last
January and thought you'd gone away.'

'I did,' Vince said shortly. 'I only got back last night.'
He had found the ghosts followed him, could not be left
behind. He was more comfortable with them here. 'Are
you a detective? Why are you asking about him and
Laura?'

'I'm not a detective, but I'm – concerned – for the
lady.'

'Laura was that, all right.' Vince nodded firmly. 'Ralph
was a different type altogether. She was too good for him
by a long way. He was a charmer, hail-fellow-well-met
with the chaps but he was carrying on with other women
behind her back. He had the morals of a tomcat. I won't
go on about it because he saved my life at the cost of his
own, but it doesn't alter the fact that he played her some
very dirty tricks. By the time I found this out for sure – I
suspected it before – we were on our way to Flanders. And
then, well, when you're in a trench and depending on each
other for your lives, you overlook that sort of thing.'

Vince shook his head, as if to cast off the memory. 'I
never told her. The last time I saw her it was after he was
dead and she still believed in him. For all I know she still
does and that's probably all he left her. The only good
thing he did for her was dying. If he'd lived he would have
broken her heart. He bloody near did, anyway.'

He looked at Nick. 'I hope she's all right.'

'She is.'

'Good. She deserves the best.'

'You sound – fond of her.'

'I am, but that's all.' Vince drank from his glass, then admitted, 'There was another girl, but when I came back she'd gone.' He finished that abruptly, just another ghost, and asked, 'Is that the sort of thing you wanted to know?'

'Yes. Thank you.' Nick pointed to Vince's empty glass, 'Will you have one on me?'

That drew a shake of the head. 'I was training to be an accountant before the war and I'm going back to it. I have an appointment with a firm who are going to give me articles. I just nipped in here for a quick one to steady my nerves.' He grinned wryly. 'When we went over the top they used to give us rum.'

Nick made a note of Vince's address, they shook hands and parted outside the Duke.

The matron at the hospital in Sussex wore a cap and apron starched as stiffly as the gaze she turned on Nick: 'You cannot possibly see her at the moment. Nurse Barnes is on shift and has patients to care for. Now, if you had written and made an appointment . . .' She let that reproof fade away, excusing his ignorance. 'I suggest you walk down into the town and take some tea. If you return in an hour I will ensure Nurse Barnes has been informed that you wish to see her.'

Nick had once served under a captain like the matron. He had been known among his crew as 'Ramrod'. So he said humbly, 'Thank you. I will do that.'

When he returned Sally Barnes awaited him in a room off the matron's office. Its door stood open and stayed open. Nick was conscious of the matron, out of hearing but sitting just outside.

Sally was a petite young woman with soft brown hair tucked under the nurse's cap. When Nick convinced her he meant no harm to Laura, Sally said, 'I was an orphan. I ran away from my uncle; he never touched me but he looked . . .' She stopped there, pink-cheeked, looking down at her hands folded in her lap.

Nick said quickly, 'I understand you came to London.'

A nod. 'I just wanted you to know how bad it was. I only had a few coppers. Laura saved me from starving — and, I think, from the streets — I was hungry and homeless when she found me.' She told him about the birth of Laura's child and her grief at losing her daughter. But Sally never mentioned Vince Tully, kept that sadness for herself.

'She saved me again in Serbia . . .'

As Nick listened he learned how Laura had come by the gun now locked in his father's cupboard, of the awful winter retreat across the mountains. When Sally paused, he asked, 'And Billy Gatenby? He was a sergeant. I called at the flat the pair of you were sharing and a woman there told me a tale, but the other day I met his corporal and he gave a very different version.'

'You can believe me!' The gentle girl snapped at him. 'Billy was drunk and wandering about in London. Laura brought him home before the Military Police caught him.

She looked after him, gave him her bed and slept in an armchair herself. I was there. That woman downstairs was evil, and a liar if she said any other. And I'll tell you something else: that time you came to the flat and Laura opened up to you — when she was just wearing a greatcoat, remember?'

Nick did and would not forget. He nodded.

Sally said, 'She was having a bath and thought she was letting me in.'

Nick sat in silence for a minute, taking in all he had learned. He was content. 'Thank you for talking to me.' He realised the shadows of the trees outside were lengthening, and that the matron next door had coughed resoundingly for the third time. He made his farewells to her and Sally, then returned to his London hotel. He had a good deal to think about but had already come to his conclusion. He would act on it on the morrow.

So on Friday he caught the ten a.m. out of King's Cross.

At that time a cab delivered Melissa to Seth's house and he greeted her curtly. 'Did you buy those bairns' clothes I told you about?'

'I've got them here.' She gave him a brown paper bag. Seth emptied it on the table and pawed over the children's clothes. 'They look right,' he muttered.

Melissa nodded firmly. 'Just what Doris said the bairn had been wearing. I made sure.'

'Right. Now I'll wipe the smile off the face of that Stanfield lass.' Seth cackled unpleasantly.

Walter Skidmore was on a train but not to Hartlepool. He was bound for London to enjoy himself with the money Seth had given him to buy a public house. Instead he would be broke in a month and jailed for embezzlement before the year was out.

And in his hotel room in Newcastle, Jack Daubney inspected his mouth in the mirror and saw the swelling had gone down. The bruising still showed as a dark blue stain but he felt he could show his face again. Now he would settle with that girl, take his vengeance and his pleasure. He picked up his walking-cane, flexed it and smiled. Then he set out.

Chapter Twenty-Two

FRIDAY. SUMMER 1919. MONKWEARMOUTH.

'Good morning, Frank. It's a lovely day.' Laura was happier, had determinedly put aside her cares. She stood in the doorway of the sawmill, the bright morning sun behind her, peering into its comparative gloom where Frank was working at a bench. She saw the pit was covered with an old cotton sheet to hide it. The folds of the cloth were already rumpled and grubby.

'Aye, it is.' He grinned at her. 'Your little lad will be excited now.'

'Tommy can't keep still.' Laura laughed. 'They're setting off for Whitley Bay tonight.'

Frank said, serious now, 'I'm sorry I got you to take on Walter. I didn't know—'

Laura held up a hand to stay him: 'It wasn't your fault. He fooled the pair of us but now we're rid of him.' Frank was relieved and she went on, 'I have to go down to Corrigan's but I'll be back later.'

'Right y'are.' And Frank set the circular saw to spinning with an ear-splitting whine.

Laura walked to Corrigan's yard, enjoying the sunshine and the clear blue sky. There was a stiff breeze blowing in from the sea but it only served to prevent the heat from being overpowering. The chimneys of the yard gave out only thin tendrils of grey smoke that morning and there were just wisps of it from the funnels of the ships lying in the river. The wind carried all the smoke away and played with Laura's gleaming chestnut hair. As she entered the yard she could see past the hull of the vessel building on the stocks to where a tugboat bustled upstream, siren blaring busily. She smiled back at the men who grinned at her. This was where Nick Corrigan spent a lot of his life, and where she had worked for a time. She was going to miss it but it was better for her to go now.

Laura went to the office and drew the pay that was due to her. She also handed in her letter of resignation to the chief clerk. Cheyney looked at it then said, 'I think Mr Corrigan will want to see you.'

He did. Dan Corrigan rose to greet Laura, her letter in one of his big hands, gesturing her to a chair with the other. He smiled, but only briefly; this was not a smiling matter. 'So you want to leave us.' He glanced at the letter: 'Because you have to look after this business of yours.'

And other reasons. 'It will take up all my time.'

'It seems to be going well.'

'Yes. Thank you. It was you giving me that first order that got the business going.'

Dan grimaced. 'Don't thank me.' He looked her straight in the eye and admitted, 'To tell the truth, I was dead against you. It was Nick who persuaded me to give you that order; I was going to put it elsewhere. And while I'm owning up I may as well tell you that I didn't want to take you on here. Again, it was Nick who pleaded your case. I'm glad he did.' He added sheepishly, 'I thought you were applying for the job just to bait me.'

Red-faced, Laura confessed, 'I was. I'm sorry.'

For a second he stared, then guffawed. After a moment, Laura joined in.

Cheyney knocked at the door, then put his head around it and apologised, 'Sorry to interrupt, Mr Corrigan, but you have an appointment now and the gentleman is waiting.'

Dan got to his feet again and smiled down at Laura. 'If you ever want your job back, just ask.'

Laura left the office smiling but then became serious. She had learned a lot. Nick might well have saved her from ruin when she was trying to start the business up again. That first order had been crucial and it had led to others; just the mention of Corrigan's as a customer had brought them. And she had him to thank for the job at Corrigan's. It was becoming hard to think about him but she would have to. First she must thank him and that would not be easy after all their rows.

Ganny Bates came out of the typists' room, a sheaf of

papers in her hand, a pencil stuck in her silver-grey bun. 'Ooh! Laura! Canny bairn! When are you coming back to work?'

Laura explained that she was leaving Corrigan's and Ganny wailed, 'Ah! What a shame! We'll miss you.'

They talked for a minute and then Laura warned, 'I don't want you getting into trouble. Is anyone waiting for those letters?'

'No! They're not letters, just some notes young Mr Corrigan asked me to type up and be ready for him to come back to after the holiday. He went off to London. He said a funny thing, that he was going to seek somebody he should have looked for a long time ago. I think he might have been talking about the girl he was courting in London before the war. Quite serious, it was. He used to go down there nearly every weekend.'

That gossip was only partly true; there had been a girl but the affair had ended amicably.

Laura went on her way. Now she knew why Nick had gone to London; because of a girl out of his past. Maybe they had had a row and broken up all those years ago and now he wanted to make it up. Well, that was his affair.

Laura walked back to the sawmill, not noticing the sunshine and the ships in the river now.

The post had arrived and there was a lot but Laura left it, told Frank she would be back after lunch and went to Addy's. They all ate together then Laura helped Addy to clear up and pack. Addy and the children would be setting off when Joe finished work. She had prepared a mountain of sandwiches, 'So nobody will starve on the train!'

When all was done Laura hugged Tommy, neat in blue jersey and new shorts, bought in Blacketts for nine shillings and sixpence. 'Now you have a good time on the beach and I'll be there on Wednesday. You've got your spade?'

He squirmed excitedly in her arms. 'Aunty Addy packed it for me. Uncle Joe says we'll be on two trains, one to Newcastle and another down to Whitley Bay.'

'Aye. Isn't that grand?'

Laura walked back to the yard, her thoughts far away once more. She was glad she had arranged not to go with them; she wanted some time on her own.

Frank was still there, finishing up sweeping out the sawmill, and Laura told him, 'That's enough. It's time you were away. I'll lock up.'

'Aye. Thanks, boss.' He stood his broom up against the wall. Laura noted that he did not shake so often or so badly as he had done at first, and was glad. He pulled on his jacket. 'So I'll see you a week M-Monday. Enjoy yourself.' He looked across at the office and grinned. 'When you get away.'

Laura laughed. 'I'll be away on Wednesday, don't you worry.'

He strode out of the gate and Laura went into the office. There was the whitewash for the ceiling, and the wallpaper, all bought in the past week, so she was ready to start. She changed into the old overall she had used before and hung up her dress. The post still awaited her on the desk but she left it there, sat down and thought about Nick Corrigan. She had always known he was a real man. It was no surprise that there was a lass . . .

He had arrived in Newcastle an hour earlier and was thinking of Laura as he crossed the footbridge from the main line to the local platforms. A porter followed, carrying his suitcase. As he reached the summit of the bridge, Nick saw the figure striding in confident and leisurely fashion, swinging a walking-cane, towards the waiting Sunderland train. He only caught a glimpse of the man but it was enough. He took in the face dark with incipient stubble, the thick, black moustache, the figure and the carriage. Nick knew him for the man who had assaulted Laura, who had passed him in the gloom of the yard but at only arm's length.

Nick ran, raging, after this monster who had tried to violate Laura. He ignored the surprised yell of the porter: 'Here! Where the 'ell are you off to — sir?' He swerved through the crowds of hurrying passengers, was halted briefly by a trolley loaded with churns of milk as it was dragged across his path, but sprinted again. He shoved through the ticket barrier, elbowing aside the inspector, leaving him bawling, 'Come back here, you!'

Black Jack Daubney was only yards ahead now and he turned at that bellow. His recognition of Nick was also immediate. Nick panted, 'Got you!'

'Not yet,' replied Daubney, and slashed the cane across Nick's face. It left a red weal, stunned him for a second but as the cane was raised again Nick tore it from him and threw it aside. They fought then, punching, wrestling, while the passengers on the train hung out of the windows, staring. The guard stood ready, flag in hand and whistle in mouth, transfixed. Then he remembered his duty, looked at his watch, waved his flag and blew his whistle. The train shunted then began to pull away.

Daubney cursed, for once fighting a man stronger than himself. But then a policeman came running to shove between them. At that, Daubney turned and ran. Nick was briefly halted by the policeman, shook him off but thought he was too late because his quarry was leaping for the train. But it was Daubney who was too late. The train was moving too fast. He got a foot on the step but his clawing fingers closed on air. He swung, off-balance, and fell between the coaches.

He was still alive. Nick was one of the first to reach him when the train had gone, though it halted again only a few yards further on. He jumped down on to the track with the policeman, breathlessly explaining to the astonished constable. Daubney would not recover, that was horribly obvious, but he was conscious and knew Nick. As he and the policeman tried uselessly to stop the bleeding, Daubney gasped, 'Damn you! Fetch a doctor — an ambulance.' He could not see the policeman, Nick blocking his view, and raged on, 'One day I'll settle with you — and the Stanfield girl. I'll dance on your grave and her I'll—' He gasped an obscenity, glaring at Nick, then his eyes widened as the pain came, but, mercifully, not for long.

The policeman said, 'He's gone.'

'Aye.' Nick climbed to his feet. Black Jack Daubney was dead.

But Nick shook his head when asked, 'What's his name, sir?' Nick had not known. As the constable searched the pockets of the body, Nick told him what he knew. The policeman found a wallet and a card case. 'Major Daubney.' He was impressed. 'Are you sure about this – gentleman – attacking a lady, sir?'

'Yes,' Nick answered curtly.

His questioner was still doubtful. Nick had to accompany him to an office and there repeat his story to an inspector. At one point the porter turned up with Nick's suitcase and was rewarded for his trouble. By the time the police had accepted that he was probably guilty of nothing but causing an affray, it was late afternoon. He returned to the platform, now functioning normally, and this time presented his ticket. The man at the gate sniffed, remembering him, but cautiously held his tongue and punched the pasteboard.

Nick sank into a corner seat and stared unseeing out of the window. He had to talk to Laura.

Laura had tried to forget him. She had taken up the post and decided to clear it before starting work on the decorating. The light from the low afternoon sun streamed in through the window, but the wind, for once blowing down the yard to the gate, blew the papers from the desk so she shut the door. Then it was quiet and still in the office. She worked steadily but with a part of her mind elsewhere, until she was almost done. She looked up at the clock then and saw it was six in the evening, remembered Black Jack Daubney and that she must be gone from the yard before dark. She needed an invoice from the desk so unlocked the drawer, opened it – and saw the knife.

Laura took it out and laid it on the desk. Seth's knife had been found in the grounds of the Corrigan house. Why would he be there? And at that time? Now she recalled Cath, in her letter, saying Seth seemed to have come into money. And then there was Nick, confronting her and Ralph in the flat in Berkeley Mansions, telling them of the burglary. *Seth had stolen the jewellery!* Laura was certain of that. But now she remembered how Nick had looked down at her, coldly disapproving. He had made her unhappy then, and not for the last time – while she had brutally rejected him again and again. Now her head admitted what her heart had told her in France. She had left Corrigan's yard because she could foresee trouble. No matter how much she changed her opinion of him – *wanted* him – he would always see her as the fancy woman. She whispered, 'Oh, Nick.'

And then, defiant, she determined to fight to win him back.

The knife's razor-sharp blade was folded into the carved handle but it still bore a message of evil to Laura. She stared at it, recalling Seth's last threat: 'I know where to find you and yours! One way or another I'll make you suffer!' *One way or another . . . You and yours!* He was talking of Tommy. Laura shivered and huddled inside herself, suddenly cold. What was Seth planning?

He stood across the road from the gates of the yard, flanked by Melissa and Doris. He was dressed in an old navy blue boiler suit, Melissa in skirt and blouse and without a hat. Doris wore the same greasy, old black dress. Seth carried a bulging sack swinging from one hand. All three of them were hidden in the shop, closed and shuttered, as were the other premises around the sawmill, empty and deserted with the day's work done. Seth asked, 'Is she in there?'

Doris had been there all morning, watching: 'She is now. She went back and forth a couple of times but she's been in the office for the past hour. Frank went off a while back.'

'Right, then.' He led them out of the back of the shop, round to the front and over the road. They passed through the open gates and then across the yard. They all wore 'sandshoes', the local name for the cheap, rubber-soled plimsolls, and made no sound on the cobbles. They knew the office window and door did not look out on the yard, so Laura would not see them. The doors of the sawmill were closed but Seth opened one of them, making a gap a man could walk through. Then they were in. After the bright sunshine outside it took them a few seconds for their eyes to adjust to the comparative gloom, but then they set to work.

Nick paid off his cab on the road outside the gate. He had left his suitcase at the station to be picked up when it was convenient, and walked up the yard empty-handed. He saw one door of the sawmill was ajar and assumed Frank Pearson was still working. The door to the office was closed and he knocked.

Laura started as if it had been a gunshot, her thoughts still on Seth, and she seized the knife. Now her heart lurched as she recalled Daubney's attack, but then the knock was followed by a voice: 'Nick Corrigan. May I come in?'

Nick! 'Yes!' She answered quickly and shoved the knife into the pocket of her overall. She smiled at him, blinking as she took in his suit, grimy and stained with a rent in one knee.

He saw that look and explained, 'I had a fight.' He told her, tersely, the bare facts, finishing, 'We tried to stop the bleeding, did what we could for him, but it was hopeless.'

Laura closed her eyes, trying to black out the picture of Daubney's dying. One question came to her, though: 'Did you say he was catching the Sunderland train?'

'He was just about to.'

Laura said nothing to that, though she knew where Daubney had been heading. He was one of those who had threatened her. She would have to forget him but knew it would not be easy. Then there was Seth but she shied away from that now.

'I didn't expect you back so soon – Nick.'

He noted she had used his first name but he made no comment. He thought that he would have to tell her what he had learned about Melissa but that could wait. What was all-important: 'I found what I went for.' He stood close to the desk so she had to crane to look up at him.

'Oh?'

'I told Ganny Bates I was going to seek someone I should have looked for a long time ago.'

Laura knew that and answered stiff-lipped, 'And you found her?'

'Yes.' He was smiling so Laura kept hers in place. He went on, 'Though she wasn't there.'

Laura's smile slipped lopsided with suspicion. 'Is this a riddle?'

He walked round the desk to stand over her. 'I went looking for you.'

'*Me?*' Laura stared, lips parted.

'The first time I saw you I'd already made up my mind about you – judged you. That was my mistake but you didn't help. We always seemed to see the worst side of each other. I gradually came to think that you were the victim, but I knew if I asked you I'd get a dusty answer. So

I talked to some other people: Venetia Ingleby, Vince Tully and Sally Barnes.'

'You talked to them in London?' Laura stared in disbelief. Then the old anger surfaced once more and the veteran of Serbia and Flanders spoke: 'You have a *bloody* nerve!'

Nick was unmoved and said drily, 'That's the kind of reaction I've been used to. I was determined to prove you innocent, whether you liked it or not.' He ploughed on, 'I know all about Ralph now, what a charming, amoral scoundrel he was. About your child and how you cared for Sally, and about Serbia. I wish I'd known earlier. I think we've both made mistakes, wasted years and it's time we stopped.'

Laura thought he was being generous. He reached out for her: 'But what I'm really saying, what's driven me all along, is that I want you.'

She rose up from the chair to meet him.

Melissa threw the door open and stood holding on to it for support. Her dress was dishevelled and her eyes wild. She held one hand to her breast as she panted, 'Oh, God! Seth's got your little lad!'

'Tommy? Where?' Laura recalled Seth's threat. She slipped past Nick, was round the desk in an instant and seized Melissa by the shoulders: '*Where is he?*'

Melissa wailed, 'He's gone too far! I can't let him do this!'

Laura shook her so her head rolled and demanded again, '*Tell me where he is!*'

'In the sawmill! I'm frightened what he might do! He's in such a mood . . .' But then she stopped because Laura was already racing across the cobbles of the yard, Nick close on her heels, their eyes narrowed against the low evening sun.

The big door stood partly open, leaving a gap a yard wide so they were able to run in without checking their pace. For a second they were blinded by the sudden transition from bright sunlight to the comparative gloom of the sawmill. There was no light in there save for the glow from an electric torch. Seth held it about two feet below his grinning face, which showed like that of a gargoyle as he directed the beam upwards. It also lit the boy, held supine, his face pressed against Seth's chest.

Laura shrieked, '*Tommy!*' Seth laughed and she hurled herself at him. She was only yards away when her flying feet took her on to the sheet covering the pit – and it gave under her. In an instant of horrified perception she realised the timber baulks over the pit had been taken away. Then she was falling into blackness. The glow from the torch showed, just, the flapping sheet letting her through. She glimpsed the oily surface of the dark water in the pit and then she plunged into it. A split second later she was followed by Nick and his weight, twice hers, drove her deeper. They touched bottom tangled together in the sheet, pushed up and broke surface again. Laura made out Nick's face, a pale blur in the darkness and saw it was level with her own. She realised he was standing with his feet planted on the bottom of the pit and his head above water, while she paddled, out of her depth. She could feel the folds of the sheet, trampled under her but still clinging softly to her feet.

There was a banging like a trip hammer above her head: *Slam! Slam! Slam!* She realised what little light there was in the pit was being blotted out as the covering baulks of timber were rapidly thumped down into place. Nick jumped, trying to dislodge the one now immediately above his head. He banged it with the heel of his hand but with no sound footing under him could not shift it and sank down again. They heard the sound of Seth's laughter and Melissa giggling and now and again there was a breathless cackle. Then their faces showed as they knelt above the last space that waited for a baulk. Seth crowed, 'In an hour or so I'll be on board a ship lying off the ferry steps and bound for Holland. I won't be back for a week, and that's the soonest they'll find you!' His face disappeared but Melissa remained, gloating.

Another took Seth's place and Laura realised the source of the cackling. Doris screeched, hysterical with hatred, 'I knew I'd see my day wi' you! Now you'll rot in here!'

Then she moved away as Seth snarled, 'Get out of the road!'

Melissa stayed, but only to jeer: 'Here's your little lad!' She threw something and it flapped lightly into Laura's face. She clutched it for a moment and realised it was nothing but a cloth dummy in a blue pullover and shorts like Tommy's. But it had been enough like him in the gloom of the sawmill. In her anger and fear she had believed what she thought she saw, and what Melissa had told her she would see. Melissa hissed, 'You took away my man, you harlot, but now I'll bury you!' She giggled shrilly then Seth appeared behind her, shouldered her aside and dropped the last baulk into place. They were imprisoned and the darkness was total.

Seth's voice came faintly to them: 'Give me a hand to lay this across.' Seconds later something was dragged grating, across the baulks now covering the pit. They shook as a heavy weight crashed down on them, then there was silence.

They were sealed in a tomb.

Chapter Twenty-Three

'That was Nick Corrigan!' Melissa panted as she and Seth closed the big doors of the sawmill. 'I didn't know he was here. I nearly died when I saw him in the office.'

'It's him that'll do the dying.' Seth led the way across to the office.

Melissa asked, uneasy now, giving thought to the deed now the tension and excitement were over, 'He's a big chap. D'you think he might get out?'

Doris laughed. 'I don't care who he is. You saw what we piled on top. Samson couldn't lift that lot off.'

Seth agreed. 'He might not have to swim like she will but he can't stand up for ever, and when he falls asleep he'll drown.' They were in the office now and he peered about him. 'We'll see if we can find that knife.' Ten minutes later they stood in the chaos of the office they had pulled apart, the desk emptied, the contents of the cupboard scattered. He cursed and complained, 'The bitch must have taken it home. Never mind, they won't be able to tie me in to this or the jewel business, not without her. We'll get away now, shut the gates behind us and go back to the house for our luggage. Then it's off to Holland.'

Melissa said, 'We'll want a cab.'

'We won't!' Seth glared. 'We'll go separately and we'll walk. I'm not having any cabbie remembering picking me up. Have you got that hat?'

Melissa still carried the sack, almost empty now. She delved into it and brought out two hats, one of which she perched on her head. It had a veil and she pulled this down. Doris copied her with the other hat, putting it on at her usual drunken angle, but Seth nodded approvingly, 'Hides your faces nicely. Nobody's going to recognise you when you're leaving here – not that it's likely anyone will see us.' He dug in his pocket and pulled out a sheaf of banknotes. He handed them to Doris with a warning, 'Keep your mouth shut.'

'Oh, aye.' She snatched them greedily.

They crossed the yard to the gates and closed them but the small door in one of them was still open. Seth paused then: 'Listen.' They stood silent. The clamour of the shipyards had ceased for the day, in fact for a week and in the hush they could hear a bird sing.

Melissa whispered, 'What is it?'

Seth sniggered, 'Nothing.' He pointed at the sawmill, its doors closed. 'See? They'll be screaming their heads off out it's quiet as the grave.' He slammed the door shut and they went away.

They were not screaming, though Laura felt like it. She was stunned by this trap, set and sprung out of the blue, the blue sky and blazing sun of summer, locking Nick and her in this dark, dank prison. Nick! She gasped, 'I'm sorry. They intended this just for me. I thought Seth had somehow got hold of Tommy but it was only that doll.'

Nick said, 'They fooled us, knew we would come running. It looked to me as if he was holding a child.'

Their voices echoed coldly off the walls, slimy under their fingers. Laura brushed against him as she paddled. Nick said, 'Hold on to me and try to save your energy.'

Laura put out a hand and touched his back, ran her fingers up, feeling the lumpy muscle, and rested her hand on his shoulder. 'Thank you.' She went on, 'They didn't know you would be here.'

'It makes no difference. They caught the two of us.'

It made a difference to Laura that he was there. If she had been alone, blind and trapped . . . She bitterly regretted that she had brought him to this but was glad he was beside her. She hoped: 'Does anyone know you've come here?'

'No.' He saw the point of her question and went on, 'Nobody knows I'm in the town. I didn't write or send a telegram. My family will think I'm still in London. The police at Newcastle know I came north but I think it may be some days before they try to contact me. Will anyone come here?'

'Not for a week.'

'We'd better start trying to get out because we won't be able to last long in here,' Nick finished grimly.

Laura silently agreed, knew that the cold would sap their strength. She might survive longer now, being able to hold on to Nick instead of swimming. They might last long hours but ultimately they would collapse, drown and die. Seth had the right of it: no one would come to the sawmill for the next week – unless Addy raised the alarm when Laura did not turn up in Whitley Bay on Wednesday. But that made no difference; they would be dead long before that. Imprisoned as they were, with the pit sealed and the sawmill closed, they could shout for ever and no one would hear them.

She grieved for Tommy, who needed her so desperately, who would weep for her.

Oh, God! How she *hated* Seth! And – she asked, 'Why was that woman, Ralph's wife, with them?'

Nick told her about Seth and Melissa, finishing: 'But who was that mad old woman?'

'She was my stepmother.' Laura gave him a brief history of Doris.

Nick breathed, 'What an unholy crowd.' And all the time he was reaching up to probe at the timbers with questing fingers, hoping to find one weak or dislodged, while Laura tried to think of a way out, though her mind was filled with pictures of a jeering Seth. She could clearly recall the first time he had frightened her, when she was only a young girl and he had flourished that knife of his and— She cried, 'I have his knife! I think!'

Nick questioned, 'What knife?'

Laura explained in a few words whose knife it was, how she came by it and her suspicions, as she fumbled in the pocket of the overall. 'I have it. Here! It's a clasp-knife.' She held it out now, pressing it against his shoulder or chest – in the darkness she could not tell which.

His hand closed around hers and took the knife from her. 'Now let's see,' he said.

'Can you reach?'

'Yes.'

Laura could feel, through her hand on his shoulder, the jerking of his body as he dug at the baulk above his head. She could hear the soft thud of the knife and listened to it, waited for what she thought was several minutes, then asked, 'How are you getting on?'

He said, not despairing but flatly stating a fact, 'This timber is hard as iron.'

'It's about three inches thick,' Laura remembered. She shivered, held on to his shoulder as he went on stabbing and digging at the wood. When she had remembered the knife she had thought she had found their salvation, but with every dragging minute she knew she had not. 'Can I see – feel?' she corrected.

'Here.' He gripped her hand as she extended it, groping, and he led it to the timber above his head. She pushed up with the hand still on his shoulder, stretching to reach the baulk, and found the place where he had been digging. It felt no more than a greater roughness on the surface of the wood.

Laura took her hand away, subsided and said only, 'I see.' She knew this was not going to work.

And then she pictured Frank with her mind's eye, seemed to hear him say, 'They're safe enough, the timbers won't fall through, but they want cementing in again some time.'

Laura shook Nick's shoulder: 'Some of the bricks are loose!'

The digging stopped. 'What?'

'Frank showed me! The cement has crumbled. The bricks are still in place but they want cementing in again.'

'Where?'

'Other end.'

He moved, wading slowly with the water washing up to his chin. Laura paddled alongside, one hand still on his shoulder, the other stretched up to trail her fingers along the wall. She heard him cough and spit and knew the water had slopped into his mouth. She said, 'Wait.' He paused and she felt at the slime-covered brickwork: 'Here.'

His hand found hers, took its place as she withdrew it. He was silent a moment and there was just the sound of their breathing and the soft lap of the water that held them in its cold embrace. He was probing with his fingers: 'There's one brick loose but not loose enough. One next door to it that might . . . Let's see.' Again Laura felt the muscles in his wide shoulders working as he dug at the cement. But this time, after a few minutes, that stopped. Instead a scraping and a grunt from Nick then triumphantly, 'Got it! Give me your hand and you can hold on to the hole where it was, while I put it down where I can find it again.'

Laura obeyed and he set her hand in the gap in the brickwork. She held to it as he sucked in air then his shoulder sank as he stooped to set down the brick. Laura could feel the grittiness of loose cement under her fingers, and the brick next along shifted slightly as she pushed at it. At the top of the gap was the thickness of the cement floor, solid, but right at the bottom – Nick straightened beside her, gasped and sucked in air. Laura said, 'There feels to be cement behind where the brick was but below that its different.'

Nick breathed beside her: 'Right. Probably soil, hard-packed but a lot easier to dig out than concrete.' He worked on.

They dug out another brick, then a third, so the gap was three times the width of a brick. Then he dug out the soil behind the gap and down behind those still in place below it. Until he paused and said, 'I'm going to give it a try. I can get both hands in behind the wall now, where I've dug. I might be able to pull out the section just below.'

Laura felt the muscles bunch as he strained, his feet now braced against the bottom of the wall, the top of which he was trying to pull down. The bunches relaxed under her hand and she felt his breath on her face as he panted, 'No good. I think I'll have to dig out the cement between the bricks.'

'Wait. Rest a moment.' Laura ran her fingers down his arm until she found the gap and his hands, hooked over the top of the brickwork below it. 'I'll get between your arms and we can try together.' She ducked under the water and came up with her back to his chest. Then she pulled her knees up almost to her chin, so now her feet were set against the wall just below their hands, her body like a coiled spring. She breathed deeply and asked, 'Ready?'

'Aye.' His voice in her ear, his face beside hers.

Laura breathed a prayer and sobbed: 'Now!'

They tugged together, Nick straining back and the spring that was Laura striving to uncoil. She heard his curse of fury, was herself incensed at Seth Bullock who had brought her to this. They both gained a berserk strength that was far beyond normal. Then she was falling backwards, going under, while a whole section of the wall fell to the bottom of the pit.

They were again entangled but this time Nick was underneath. Laura pushed herself off him and clear, surfaced and coughed, gasped as she paddled, called, 'Nick!' She realised there was now the faintest of light but it only showed her the water churning, bubbling. Then he shoved up, his head standing out of it, spluttering. Laura reached out to him. 'Nick!'

Hand sought hand, clutched as if to a lifeline and in a way it was. Nick said, 'Now let's see what we've got.'

They had a hole in the side of the pit a foot wide and

some two feet deep. The baulk of timber above this had now sagged at that end, into the hole, because the bricks it was meant to rest on now lay on the bottom of the pit. The light came from there, the hole they had made, filtering around the baulk. Nick was able to work it down to fall into the water and float there. So he had a hole above him that was roughly the size of the baulk he had displaced, about four feet by one. It should have been their way out, but now they could see the 'lock' that Seth had put on the door of the pit. A massive timber had been laid across the length of it, securing in place the baulks that covered the pit. It cut their 'escape hatch' into two. One was a little over a foot square, the other was less.

Nick reached up and could set his hands on the timber but not move it. He made a platform from the bricks lying on the bottom of the pit and tried again, without success. He rested, breathing hard with effort, and said thickly, 'He's dumped something heavy on each end of that timber.'

Laura swallowed a sob. After all their efforts, were they to lose and die in this hole? 'Let's try together. It worked before.' She climbed up him to sit on his shoulders, the skirt of her overall bunched up around her waist and her feet crossed on his chest. Her head was close under the baulk denying them, her hands set on it beside his. 'Now!'

They exerted every ounce of strength they had but Laura's position was awkward. She could push with her hands but this time could not brace her legs. The timber stayed as if rooted in stone. Laura panted, 'I'm going to try to get out.'

'Do you think you can?' Nick asked. Laura did not answer because she did not think she could, was attempting it out of desperation. She put up both arms through the hole, fought to follow with her body but was jammed. She wriggled desperately but got no further. She dragged back through the hole, sobbed again but this time made no attempt to hide it. 'Damn him! *Damn* him!'

Laura dropped down from Nick's shoulders to float beside him. He put one arm around her, soothing, 'All right. We'll try again in a minute. Take a rest.'

She wasn't listening and instead demanded, 'Help me out of these!' Laura tore at the neck of the overall one-handed, holding on to his shoulder with the other. Together they dragged it off her and cast it away. The rest of her clothes followed until she was near-naked. Then she climbed on Nick's shoulders again, but easily now without the clinging skirts, her body smooth and pale in the gloom.

This time Laura put one arm through the hole, followed it with her head then tried to wriggle the other arm through. Her shoulder stuck. 'Push!' She called down to Nick, '*Push!*' His hands gripped her under the thighs and thrust her upwards. Laura did not cry out but shut her eyes in pain as her flesh was torn. Now both arms were through, and she could use them to lift herself, bruisingly, tearingly out of the hole to flop forward on to the rough, cold concrete floor. But she was out of the pit.

She lay for only a few seconds, then turned on her knees to bend into the hole. Nick's face stared up at her and she reached down to seize his head between her hands and kiss him full on the mouth. He responded hungrily, reaching up to hold her, until she tore herself away. Then he disappeared in a huge splash. Laura called, startled, 'Nick!' He reappeared coughing, spluttering and lower in the water. 'What happened?' asked Laura.

'I slipped off those bloody bricks I was balancing on,' he replied disgustedly.

Laura giggled, then wondered if that was hysteria. She had kissed Nick Corrigan passionately, could not believe she had done it, wondered if that was hysteria, too?

She knew it was not.

Laura called, 'It's just as you thought. There's one big timber on top of the floor timbers, and others stacked on both ends to make sure the pit was shut fast and nobody could get out.' She set to work, at first throwing aside the less heavy timbers from where they were piled. Then, once they were clear of the main, big timber that ran the length of the pit, she seized that by one end and, with huge effort, dragged it clear of the hole where she had got out. Nick was then able to push out another two of the baulks covering the pit and haul himself out of it.

Laura stood back from him as he dripped water but then saw his stare and remembered her nudity. She could think of nowhere to hide but in his arms.

He held her, could feel her shaking, and she clung to him, drew strength from him. But only for seconds, then she pushed away, anger overriding love for now: 'He mustn't get away!' She wanted Seth to pay for what he had done to her, had almost done to Tommy. 'I won't let him get away!'

They came out of the shed. Nick sprinted long-legged for the gate but Laura ran barefoot across the yard to the office: 'Wait for me!' He raised a hand to show he had heard as he opened the little door in the gate. Laura plunged into the shed and found her dress had been snatched from its hanger and tossed aside. She pulled it on over her head and tweaked it down as it dragged on her damp body. She discovered one of her good shoes easily, the other by searching furiously through the piles of paper littering the floor. She cast a swift glance at the clock on the wall, the only item in the office not disturbed, and saw it was past seven. An hour had passed since they had fallen into the pit. Were they too late? Then she was out in the yard and running to the gate.

She stepped into the road and sobbed with surprise and relief. She had rarely seen a cab pass the yard but Nick had one waiting now, a motor taxi, engine chattering as it stood by the kerb. He handed her in and jumped in after her. He shouted to the cabbie, 'Fast as you can!' And then, explaining, 'Bit of luck. He was just coming back from delivering a fare and taking a short cut.'

The cabbie had seen no reason to mention that the fare had been to carry two people to the ferry steps. They had changed, were smartly dressed now, he in a suit and she in a figure-hugging costume. As the taxi had turned on to the long slope down to the river and the ferry, Seth had said, 'You can put us down here.'

Melissa had asked no questions then, but as the cab drove away: 'Why aren't we going to the ferry?'

'That can wait a few minutes. There's plenty of time.' Seth nodded at the public house across the street. 'We'll have a drink in there and then cross the river. Come on.'

Laura cried softly, 'We may be too late!' She realised she held Nick's hand and clung tighter.

He said grimly, 'We'll see. Wherever he goes we'll find him.'

The cabbie had put his foot down and the taxi was bouncing and swaying over the cobbles. There was a smell of petrol and leather. Laura was briefly reminded of her ride after the train crash in France. And of the week she had spent there with Nick. They had wasted a lot of time . . .

Almost there, but in Williamson Street the Salvation Army was holding a service with band and colours, hymns and tambourines. The taxi screeched to a halt and Nick swore, then: 'We'll have to run for it!' He dropped a fistful of coins into the cabbie's hand, shoved open the door and then they were running. They rounded a corner and left the blaring of the band behind. Now they could see the river and the waiting ferry at the foot of the long slope. Smoke was drifting from the little steamer's funnel and the *clang-clang* of her bell sounded the signal for her sailing. Halfway down the slope, a man and a woman walked towards the ferry. They were unmistakably Seth and Melissa and he carried two suitcases.

Laura gasped, 'There they are!'

At that moment Melissa turned and saw them. They heard her shriek and Seth's head twisted to stare back at them. For a second he hung there, gaping, incredulous at sight of his victims he had left to perish in the pit. Then he was running, the cases discarded. Melissa set off after him but awkwardly, teetering on the high heels and no athlete. Laura and Nick, racing side by side, rapidly overhauled her but Seth was their prime quarry and he seemed set to escape them.

Then they saw the deckhand had cast off the moorings and the ferry was moving, at first going astern to clear the quay. Seth was labouring now, rocking from side to side but still running hard over the last few yards. Nick panted, 'She's pulling away!' A gap was opening between ferry and quay. The steamer checked an instant, water boiling under its stern as the screw churned, then butted forward, bows easing away from the quay, the gap widening.

Laura screamed, 'No!' She remembered leaping for the ferry on the day she had met Ralph, and Addy's frightened cry, 'The propellers will get you!' She was too late and Seth was not listening, would not have listened.

He jumped but could not reach the deck, only landed with his feet on the wide bulwark running round the ship. He teetered on the edge, arms windmilling as he fought to throw himself inboard, but then fell back into the river under the churning screws.

There was wailing aboard the ferry and a horrified yell from the deckhand: 'For God's sake! Stop the engines!' They stopped, but too late. Melissa stood stunned and frightened, foreseeing her own fate in the ensuing silence, like that after the closing of a cell door. And in a Dock Street pub, Doris Grimshaw bawled for another bottle of stout, unaware that Melissa's testimony would imprison her for life.

Laura turned away and hid herself and her face in Nick's arms. Then they walked away, his arm about her and their backs to the river. After a while he said, 'It's time we made a fresh start.'

A woman living close by, her window open in this summer warmth, had wound up her gramophone and set it to play. The squeaky words came down to Laura: 'After the Ball'. She remembered the little girl pirouetting in the kitchen, in a grubby white pinny and with a hole in her stocking, recalled the years between. A fancy woman? That was in the past and the words did not hurt her now.

Laura answered, 'Yes.'

They married before the summer was out. Venetia Ingleby wore an outrageously large hat and flirted just as outrageously. Vince Tully and Sally Barnes came, neither expecting to meet the other. She blushed and he was tongue-tied but not for long.

IRENE CARR

EMILY

'Irene Carr knows the world she recreates in her tales and it shows in the detail . . . Lovers of North East sagas won't be disappointed'
Newcastle Evening Chronicle

Found abandoned on the quayside, the young waif is taken in by the Jacksons whose own daughter was lost in a tragic accident. They never know her true identity.

Emily grows up in the gatekeeper's lodge on Nathaniel Franklin's estate until Franklin's cousin, the evil would-be heir, conspires to discredit her family and turns them out.

Determined to help save her family from destitution, Emily takes up the offer of service recommended by Franklin's cousin. Only to find his accomplice is hell-bent on seducing her. Emily finds work where she can, but her ambition is to run a fleet of ships. An impossible dream according to handsome Captain David Walsh — at least for a girl.

Battling through heartbreak and terrifying threats, Emily determines to succeed in a man's world and to make her dreams come true.

This is a compelling and gritty tale of a young girl growing up in the harsh environment of Victorian and Edwardian Wearside.

HODDER AND STOUGHTON PAPERBACKS